MW01491677

Hornet's Nest

A Launch Point Press Trade Paperback Original

Hornet's Nest is a work of fiction. Names, characters, places, and incidents are either the product of the author's imagination or are used in a fictitious manner. Any resemblance to actual persons living or dead, business establishments, events, or locales is entirely coincidental. Internet references contained in this work are current at the time of publication, but Launch Point Press cannot guarantee that a specific reference will continue or be maintained in any respect.

All rights reserved. Launch Point Press supports copyright which enables creativity, free speech, and fairness. Thank you for buying the authorized version of this book and for following copyright laws by not using or reproducing any part of this book in any manner whatsoever, including Internet usage, without written permission from Launch Point Press, except in the form of brief quotations embodied in critical reviews and articles. Your cooperation and respect support authors and allows Launch Point Press to continue to publish the books you want to read.

Copyright © 2025 Lee Sato

ISBN: 978-1-63304-073-1
Ebook: 978-1-63304-074-8

First Printing: 2025

Editing: Cielo Lee, Anne Battis
Formatting: Anne Battis
Cover Design: Roderick Brydon

LAUNCHPOINT
PRESS

Portland, Oregon

Hornet's Nest

Book One
The Jara Quinn Series

Lee Sato

LAUNCH**POINT**
PRESS

www.launchpointpress.com

Acknowledgments

I would like to express my heartfelt gratitude to Krista Hill, editor from Linda Talbot, LLC, for transforming a chaotic story into something readable and coherent. Your expertise and dedication were invaluable. I am also deeply appreciative of the many pharmacists and cardiologists who helped me get the medications in my book accurate and authentic.

A special thank you to the numerous FBI and law enforcement personnel with whom I've had the privilege of working over the years—your insights and guidance have been instrumental. I am also grateful to author Stephanie Cowell, whose understanding and support helped me make sense of my writing process.

Above all, my deepest thanks go to my partner, Mary, my nephew Nick, my sister-in-law Jennifer, and all my friends who have consistently encouraged and supported me throughout this journey. Your belief in me has been a driving force in fulfilling my dream of becoming an author.

I would also like to extend my deepest gratitude to my publisher, Launch Point Press, for taking a chance on this new author and their belief in this project. Their expertise, guidance, and commitment to excellence have played an integral role in bringing this work to life.

I am also incredibly thankful to my publishing editor, Cielo Lee, whose insightful feedback, attention to detail, and dedication have significantly enhanced the quality of this book.

Both of you have been instrumental in this journey, and I am profoundly grateful for your contributions.

Dedication

To my partner, Mary
My supporter, my critic, and my love. Without you, this dream
would not have been possible.

"A hornet's nest is a dangerous thing to disturb, yet there is something wild and beautiful about the sting it carries."
— *Henry David Thoreau*

Chapter One

I've done my share of killing in my life. I'm not bragging mind you; I only did what I felt I needed to do. In my eyes, everything I killed deserved it. So why was I so conflicted? I had been watching them for days, all their comings and goings, scouting out the perfect place. Why then, out of all the balconies overlooking the harbor, did the hornets choose mine to build their nest?

My tiny, two-story house was perched atop a gentle slope, offering a picturesque view of the water and the bustling harbor below. Its weathered exterior, painted a soothing shade of blue-gray, blended seamlessly with the natural beauty of the coastal landscape. Compared to the view, my balcony was nothing special. It was small, with a little table and two chairs, multiple barely living plants, a balcony rail with peeling white paint, and some twinkling lights to add flair. But was the overhang the perfect place for a hornet's home? I didn't think the busy insects cared about the view.

I needed to think long and hard about whether my place was going to be big enough for both me and the bees. I knew building a nest was in their nature, but did it have to be here? I must admit watching this hive materialize had mesmerized me, but I was finding it very tough to focus on anything this morning for longer than a few minutes. My ideas were hornets entering and leaving my head. Quieting my thoughts had been an impossible task, and the unrelenting buzz wasn't helping.

I returned to my kitchen for a couple of aspirins and the paper. I loved my kitchen, and although small, it was the heart of my home. Its modest dimensions offset an abundance of character. A slender island occupied the center of the room, its surface cluttered with the detritus of daily life: keys, mail, dirty coffee cups, and yesterday's newspapers. A few stray dishes languished in the sink, remnants of the meal I enjoyed the day before. Open-air shelves lined one wall, holding an assortment of dishes, glasses, and a smattering of pots and pans. A small pantry tucked away in the corner provided storage for canned goods and pasta boxes, its shelves meticulously organized amidst the chaos of the kitchen.

I grabbed the aspirin bottle from the pantry, popped a few in my mouth and downed them with the last few sips of coffee. After pulling back my long brown hair, I refilled my coffee cup and returned to my balcony. Once I rubbed the sleep from my eyes, I looked down at the morning paper, the bold letters scrawled across the top catching my eye. Through the steam from my coffee, I read, *CT Senator Charles Lansing Announces his Run for Presidency.* I wasn't surprised, as he had been working his way to this moment all his life. After making it as a partner in a small law firm, he ran for state representative on a family and morality platform and won. Later, he won his governor's bid on his first try. After eight years as governor, Lansing ran for US Senate and won in a landslide. He had been in that position for almost eighteen years now. The article read like it was a sure thing that the senator's all-American family would soon be the first family of the United States.

I read the article again, a little closer this time. Although it portrayed the Lansings as the all-American family, little was mentioned about his wife, Victoria, or their children, Katerina, Charles Jr., and Chase. Katerina was coming to my place for both the Newport Jazz Festival and the Newport Folk Festival, but since I didn't want to wait to ask her about the article, I called her to confirm she was still coming and to congratulate her on her father's campaign announcement.

"Hey! Congrats on your dad running for President. That's huge news!"

"Yeah, uh...thanks."

I couldn't place the tone in her voice. Was she mad at me? What was going on? I decided to push a bit further.

"I can't believe it. Your dad's campaign is going to be something. I'm sure you must be thrilled."

"Yep, it's going to be something, all right."

I could hear yelling in the background. I recognized one voice as Charles, but it seemed as if more than one person was chiming in.

"Is your dad there now? What is all that yelling I hear? You okay?"

"Listen, Jara. I'll explain everything when I get to your place for the festival."

"Oh, okay. If there is anything I can do..."

"I know. I'll talk to you later."

Katerina abruptly hung up. Now the hive wasn't the only thing buzzing.

I looked forward to Katerina's visit. I last saw her close to a year ago. We had both been busy, me with my latest investigation and her with a large court case in Boston. I missed her terribly. We spoke on the phone at least once a week, but it still wasn't the same as seeing her. Heck, I hadn't even visited her family home in quite a while. I placed my phone down on the table, took another drink of coffee, and let the hornets' buzzing lull me into thinking back on how Katerina and I met.

In the winter of my sophomore year at Notre Dame, both my parents passed away in a car accident. I had been home for Christmas, a hundred miles or so from South Bend, visiting friends for New Year's Eve. My parents had also met up with friends to play cards. They weren't drinkers, so they decided to head home after the New Year started. It had been snowing most of the day, but in northern Indiana most people were impervious to a little snow.

They were a couple of miles from home when a drunk driver swerved over the line of the two-lane highway and hit them head-on. From what I was told, they died on impact. Of course, the other driver was minimally hurt, but a teenage passenger in his car was also killed. My parents' funeral arrangements and estate dealings were up to me, their only child.

I went on autopilot of sorts during the initial court hearings for the driver, Mark Davidson, who was twenty-five, and the following negotiations for a plea agreement. The prosecutor did all he could do to give the driver the longest sentence possible, but there was a snag on the investigation side. Since Mr. Davidson wasn't given a breathalyzer or blood test in a timely manner, a court case with a jury was out of the question. Mr. Davidson already had three DUIs on his record, so that helped the prosecution somewhat with their negotiations. He received a level four felony and negotiated three sentences of ten years with no chance of parole, each to run concurrently, with a ten thousand dollar fine. I was livid he only received ten years for taking three lives. He would be out by the time he was thirty-five. I was told to take him to court for wrongful death in a civil trial, but I didn't have the energy. Money wasn't going to change anything, even if he had the money to pay.

Between the funerals and working with the prosecutor, I had no time to grieve or even think about what my future was going to look like. I wasn't sure if I would return for my junior year, let alone complete my sophomore year, but my anger took over and I decided to return to school as soon as possible. I spent the rest of the semester cleaning out the attic, the garage, the house...memories. I sold the house and returned to school since I had nowhere else to go. I rented a small place off campus and enrolled in summer classes to try and make up enough hours to start the fall semester as a junior. The first thing I did during enrollment was change my major to criminal justice. I wanted to do what I could to not allow mistakes to be made in future cases, including letting criminals off with light sentences.

One hot, sticky summer morning, as I sat in a boring lecture on Statistics of Recidivism, the classroom door creaked behind me. In the doorway stood a lioness, her fiery red mane cascading around her like a blazing waterfall. As she walked in, I noticed her body exuded strength and grace with each step. The professor stopped his lecture and glared at her as the other students in class turned their heads toward the object of his gaze. She waved a hand, mouthed an "I'm sorry," and made her way in my direction, seemingly nonplussed that she had interrupted his lecture.

I was breathless and struggled to answer as she asked if she could take the seat beside me, where my backpack sat. I nodded, not taking my eyes off her, and moved my pack to my other side. As she sat, I noticed the freckles on her sun-kissed skin, adding a playful charm to her stunning features. But it was her eyes, her piercing eyes, that captivated me, as if they were daring me to look away. After a moment of awkward staring, I finally gathered my composure and introduced myself. She smiled and whispered her name: "Katerina." At that moment I knew I had fallen in love.

I admit I half-listened to the rest of the lecture, instead daydreaming about how I could learn more about this woman. As class ended, it took me a few moments to load my backpack and, to my dismay, I couldn't find my favorite pen, the one my parents gave me at my high school graduation. As I began looking for it on the floor, I felt a tap on my shoulder.

"Are you looking for this?"

She was holding my pen in her outstretched hand. I reached out to take it, my eyes climbing up to Katerina's face.

"Yes, actually, I am." I peered into those shimmering eyes. My hand lingered on my pen and the hand that held it. "Thank you, this is my favorite one," I said, as I fumbled for intelligible words.

Her eyes sparkled with amusement and a sweet laugh escaped from her lips. "I'm glad I could be of help, this being your favorite and all." She winked. "I think you owe me."

"Actually, I think we're even since I gave you my backpack's seat."

We laughed until I looked down and realized I was still holding her hand. Time seemed to stand still in the awkwardness. My cheeks flushed as I quickly pulled the pen from her hand, turned, and reached for my pack. I thought she might have used that opportunity to leave.

"So how about lunch? After that lecture, I need a pick-me-up. Then we can discuss who owes whom."

She said it so softly and sweetly, I was immediately put at ease. We decided to go to a nearby campus café because it was too hot to walk extremely far, but by the time we reached the café door, both of us were sweating profusely, our shirts sticking to our bodies. We ordered and found a booth near an air conditioner vent. In no time we were talking like old friends. She told me she was pre-law and taking summer classes to lessen the credit hour load each semester.

I told her about my parents and my decision to return to school. We discussed my change in majors, learned we both loved Irish football, the ocean, and afternoon naps. We both dreamed of changing the world. Time had flown by and before we knew it, we had missed our afternoon classes. We decided to meet back at her place. After a quick shower and a change of clothes, I showed up at Katerina's small apartment, where we spent the whole night giggling and chatting like teenagers.

Soon our friends met each other and before long, we were one big happy tribe, with study groups and sleepovers. At the end of summer before our junior year, a few of us who didn't want to live in the dorms decided to rent an old house a few blocks from campus. Katerina and I took the upstairs rooms and the other three took the downstairs. We shut our area off from our roommates. We called our area the "Penthouse" and decorated it with everything we felt was good with the world. It was our oasis, our safe zone, our sanctuary. Soon, she and I were inseparable. In the first few months we found ourselves sharing the same bed more often than sleeping alone. Initially it was cuddling and back rubs, but soon it progressed to kisses and eventually making love. Finally, we pushed our beds together and never slept apart. We never put a label on what we were doing, nor did we discuss what the future may entail. I knew I was in love with her, but never once did those words cross my lips.

During the spring break of our junior year, I went home with Katerina and met her family, the Lansings. After that I spent all my vacations and holidays with them. Since I had no family, they took me in as one of their own. After graduating, Katerina, who earned *magna cum laude*, and I—well, I graduated, both had big plans. Katerina was going to attend Yale Law School in the fall, and I was accepted to the FBI Academy at Quantico. We spent the summer at her family's home in Greenwich, CT, located by the ocean between two harbors. Needless to say, we spent most of our time on the water, sailing and soaking up the sun. When our blissful summer ended, we readied ourselves to go our separate ways.

I felt melancholy, remembering those last days before entering the academy. My phone's loud ring jerked me back to reality.

"Hey, it's me again. Sorry I was so short with you. Can I come to your place early? I need to get away from here."

"Of course. You know you don't have to ask to show up here."

Katerina let out a long sigh. "Thank you. I'll be leaving here soon. I can't wait to see you, but please don't tell anyone."

She hung up abruptly again. I looked up at the noisy nest on my balcony. "You guys hear that? Keep it quiet!"

Chapter Two

I hurriedly got ready for Katerina's arrival. I jumped in the shower, washed up, and toweled myself off. As I looked in the full-length mirror on the back of my bathroom door, my eyes searched my face and body, wondering how I was able to be the person I was today. Evident were the small lines on my face, light scars on my skin etched by some of my losses and experiences. Wounds still on my heart and soul, I carefully kept hidden. A small, satisfied smile crossed my face. I pulled back my hair into a sleek ponytail and noticed my hazel eyes had changed color again. They were now more of a cool brown than hazel with its flecks of gold. When this happened during interviews, it often unnerved the perpetrator, allowing me to get the upper hand. I prided myself on relating to whomever I was talking to, putting them at ease and showing empathy but not weakness. I looked again in the mirror and saw I had put on a few pounds but still had a physically fit body. In my line of work, you needed to be fit, both in body and mind.

I finished getting ready, threw on my favorite jeans and a T-shirt, and walked out to my small living room, furnished with an oversized couch, a coffee table, and a TV. I turned on a light and noticed a huge smear down my front window. Katerina pulled up as I was trying to wash the seagull poop off my window. I thought it was the least I could do for an old friend.

I put down my window rag to greet her and help with the luggage. Katerina looked stunning as she stepped out of the car. Dark sunglasses hid her green eyes, but her long red mane caught rays of sunlight that highlighted its copper and gold hues. A warm breeze blew, tousling her hair from her face, making it look wild and untamed. Of course she was impeccably dressed, wearing white linen pants and a flowing multicolored shirt. Her verdigris-colored strappy heels pulled out the hints of green in her shirt. She gave me a bright smile, but she was clearly a bit tired and distracted. We gave each other a long hug: she held on tightly, seeming reluctant to let me go. When we parted, I grabbed her luggage, looking at the driver. "What? Only two bags?" The driver just shrugged. I turned to Katerina to tease her and said, "Only two bags! Something is definitely wrong."

She gave me an unamused look as we made our way inside. She immediately took off her heels and sunglasses, leaving her bags in the living room. Her eyes, still beautiful, had a sadness to them. I decided not to address what I saw and put the luggage in my room. When I returned, I offered some water, soda, or wine.

"No," she said unequivocally, "Today is a beer and tequila day."

I laughed as I went into the kitchen to retrieve our beverages and glasses. I hadn't noticed that she had followed me until her arms were around me and her body was pressed against my back.

"I'm so glad I'm finally here. I needed to be with you," she whispered.

I sat the glasses on the island and turned around to face her. I brushed away a strand of hair from her face and gazed into the depths of her eyes. "I'm happy too. I've really missed you."

She turned her head slightly to avoid my stare, tucked her chin into my hand, and kissed it. I felt a tear touch my hand and I pulled her close. "We can talk about it when you're ready," I said. "You know I'm here for you."

We held each other for a few minutes, until she let go and stepped back. She took a deep breath, exhaling slowly as she wiped away the few lingering tears. "Okay," she said, straightening her shirt, "I think I'm ready for those drinks."

We made our way to the balcony with cold beer, two shot glasses, and a bottle of tequila. We settled in at the small table, both of us putting our feet up against the railing. Katerina looked up at the nest in the corner, her mouth gaped open as she leapt from her chair.

I calmly took a drink of beer and said, "I hope you don't mind hornets."

Katerina backed herself to the balcony door, pointed at the nest, and said, "But they're dangerous."

"Dangerous only if messed with." Then I explained my reasoning for not getting rid of them.

She slowly walked back to her chair and smiled. "You're right, they are only doing what's in their nature to do. And they haven't been an issue?"

I shook my head. "Nope, not yet. The hive is far enough away that they rarely swoop down here. Other than the constant buzzing and busyness, I hardly notice them." I gave her a wry smile and asked, "So, you ready to be part of the first family?"

Katerina shot me a look, sending a clear message that it was too early to tease about the campaign. She threw back a shot of tequila, took a sip of beer, and blurted out, "I hate my family sometimes."

I took some sips of my beer and let her continue.

"My brothers have been good for nothing. CJ, Mr. Uber-Responsible, working on the magazine nonstop, and Chase, well who the hell knows what Chase is doing? I can't even believe they're brothers. Mom is exhausted, spending more time in Bridgeport at the Foundation than at home, Granny May isn't acting like herself, then Dad goes and announces his bid for President without even consulting the family. We only learned his intentions when the paper came out." Katerina took another shot. "I have a huge trial I'm preparing for. I don't have time to run around and be the perfect angel supporting my dad's campaign. And Granny, well she's beside herself. She told Dad, 'Don't expect me and my money to support you. I know what skeletons you have in your closet, and I'm tempted to let the people of America know what they are.' Then Dad started yelling and threatening her. It was worse than Jerry Springer!"

I always knew Granny May more than disliked Charles, but to threaten him..." Do you know what Granny was talking about?" I asked.

"No clue, and if Mom knows, she's not saying. Chase was at the house and thought the fight was funny since Granny was pointing her cane and all. So immature. Before things simmered down, I had to leave for court. I called Mom after court and all she said was 'Well, you know how your dad and Granny are. It will all blow over.' She didn't sound convincing though. So now I'm here and ready to drink with the hornets." She took another shot and stared off toward the harbor.

"Wow, okay." I said quietly and took a shot myself.

We sat on the balcony for a few hours, drinking and catching up, before ordering some Thai delivery and then heading off to bed. I hoped tomorrow would be a better day and Katerina would start to relax a bit. It was nice to have her in my bed again, curled up in my arms.

The next morning was a beautiful sunny July day in Newport. The temperature was only going to hit a high of 78 degrees, and the sky was a beautiful blue. We both looked forward to the festivals, which we had made a yearly tradition even before I moved here. We spent the day readying ourselves for the weekend, and packed our picnic baskets, suntan lotion, blankets, hats, and sunglasses. To say we were excited was an understatement. We couldn't wait to see what artists would be in the lineup, and to make it a surprise, we had stopped looking at the updates prior to going. Both festivals through the years had attracted talented artists such as Norah Jones, Ella Fitzgerald, Louis Armstrong, Nina Simone, The Indigo Girls, Joan Baez, Bob Dylan, Peter, Paul and Mary, Johnny and June Cash, Bonnie Raitt, and James Taylor. So we knew whatever the lineup was, we wouldn't be disappointed. The folk festival was first, followed by the jazz festival the next weekend. We made sure we got a prime spot each weekend, near the stage but also close enough to the water in case we wanted to dip our toes in.

The festivals were magical, but the days between them weren't too shabby either. We took this time to reconnect, refuel, and recreate our penthouse days. We reminisced, laughed freely, caught up on jobs, and held each other at night. I didn't realize how much I missed being with Katerina every day and feeling her next to me every night. When the car service came to pick her up, I felt the same way as I did when I left for the academy, lost and heartbroken. I wasn't ready for her to leave, knowing it would be another year until I saw her again. I hugged her tightly, both of us promising to stay in touch and see each other more often.

Still in my arms, Katerina suddenly burst into tears. "Why can't we go back to the times of the Penthouse? I've never felt so safe as I did then."

I also teared up and gave her a kiss on the cheek. "You know I'm always here for you, always."

We hugged again as the driver loaded her bags. As she wiped the tears from her eyes, she said, "Guess it's time to go back to reality," and put on her sunglasses.

"Yeah, I guess so," I said as I opened the car door and helped her in. I stepped back off the curb and yelled as the car pulled away, "Don't let the bastards get you down. Including family."

Chapter Three

The next week I drank a lot of beer, felt sorry for myself, and missed Katerina even more. I tried hard to put her out of my mind by trying to finish up the last bits of my case documentation. It didn't work. So I took the weekend to allow myself to wallow. I played our favorite songs, looked at photos, and drank even more. I finally passed out on the living room floor, surrounded by empty tequila bottles, clutching the pillow she slept on.

Early Monday morning, I was jarred awake by my phone.

"Jara, it's Charles. I want to ask you a favor." Senator Lansing's voice boomed in my ear. I sat up and tried to clear my head.

"Okay, sir, if I can." I wondered if he knew his daughter had just been here.

"I would like to ask for your help on my upcoming campaign. You did such a good job when you interned for me, I wondered if you could help me again."

I worked for the senator the summer after my junior year at college. I spent long hours researching pending legislation and the people who may have wanted to oppose such bills. I had a talent for knowing how to work a person in opposition into seeing things the way the senator needed them to. I never crossed the ethical line, but I know I teetered on it a few times.

The senator continued. "I need someone with your insight and talents to help me figure out the best course of action against my opponents."

I heard rustling papers and footsteps. I figured I was on speakerphone, and he was multitasking as usual.

"Sir, I would be happy to do what I can, but I've never worked on a campaign before. What exactly do you need me to do? You know I can't use my job to help."

"Oh, no, no. I would never ask you to do that. I am proud, though, of how far you've gone in your career. I am so glad I was able to pull some strings for you."

I cut him off before he continued down this path. "Yes, sir, I appreciate all you did for me," I said as sincerely as I could. He always wanted a pat on the back for giving me a referral to the FBI Academy.

"Jara, you know people and how they work. I need help on being one step ahead and warding off any type of attacks on my campaign."

"Sir, like I said, I would be happy to help if I can. I'm in between assignments right now, so I'm thinking about taking some time off from my job. I'll have to ask my boss if it's okay to work on a political campaign. I can let you know after I talk with him." My head was buzzing. "I need to think about this. I might be able to help some."

"Sounds great! I look forward to having you on my team. You'll be a tremendous help. By the way, congratulations on your case. That was one hell of a bust. I'm sure the agency can make some time for you to help me. I can make a few calls."

Charles hung up before I could respond. I sat there with the phone in my hand, wondering how he knew about my case and what I had just agreed to. I met Charles Lansing in his first term as senator, and I was immediately impressed. Standing over six feet tall, broad-shouldered, with thick black hair and dark, determined eyes, he was larger than life. Katerina told me he came from a long line of Maine fishermen; his parents owned a small fishing boat that his father and brother worked on. Unlike everyone else who came from a generational lobster fishing family, Charles refused to follow in his father's footsteps and made it his goal to attend college and later law school. Charles often told people he had no family and was raised in an orphanage, thus separating him from what he thought was beneath him. He often bragged about overcoming the adversity of being an orphan and making it on his own. A news article later came out during his campaign for state representative, alleging his parents and brother had been killed on the fishing boat they owned. Charles would have been nineteen when they died. But since this was before social media and a major network didn't pick up the story, it seemed all was forgotten.

I thought about calling Travis O'Ryan, my liaison at Homeland Security and my former FBI partner. If anyone could help me shed light on this situation, it would be him. I had worked with him for years, and not only was he a colleague, but also a friend. I met Travis at Quantico. He was a year ahead of me at the academy, but we still had a few classes together. After an unusually hard work out for an upcoming physical fitness test, we met up for a few drinks to commiserate about how unfit we were. After that we were inseparable and most thought we were dating. We let them believe what they wanted to believe.

Close to a year ago, Travis called me to help with a joint task force between DHS (Department of Homeland Security) and the FBI. Travis had ended up in the Center for Countering Human Trafficking division of DHS and, due to my experience with crimes against children, he felt I could be helpful. I was familiar with the people and the organization DHS was targeting, so I was more than happy to help. The trafficking ring was based northwest of Atlantic City and used boats to run the women up and down the coast so as to not keep them in one place for very long. I had been working on the investigation of two child protection workers in Philadelphia on the traffickers' payroll. They referred single women with a drug history and young children to the men who ran this ring, all under the guise of getting work to prove stability to the Pennsylvania Department of Human Services. We learned the ring not only trafficked the women and used the children as leverage, but they also groomed the children to enter the sex trade. I was able to flip one of the caseworkers and learned where they were holding the children and where the women were heading to next. After a lot of hard work and multi-agency cooperation, we were able to bring down this ring and arrest most of its leaders. Travis and I became even closer during all of this, understanding most of the population didn't know this dark side of humanity.

So before I realized it, I dialed his number, getting him on the first ring. I explained the situation to him.

"Are you sure you want to do this? Get involved in politics?"

"Politics, no, but yes, I think I want to do this. It will help shake this last case from my head. Besides, I've always wanted to travel the country and meet new people, just not criminals."

I knew he was shaking his head. "You travel all the time. Okay, what's the real reason?"

"Travis, I have this weird gut feeling about this campaign that I just can't shake. I feel I owe the family for all they've done for me, and I want to try and protect them. From what and who, I don't know. I feel I must though."

Travis let out a big sigh. "Well, that gut of yours hasn't steered you wrong yet. Heck, it solved a few problems we never would have figured out. Just be careful."

Travis reminded me I needed to finish filing my reports and organize my paperwork in case our most recent investigation went to court. At this point, most of the persons caught had taken plea deals. I was so wrapped up in trying to figure out why this campaign bugged me that the thought of needing to go to court slipped my mind. I needed to officially request a leave of absence for the time I would be working on this.

Before we hung up, Travis wished me well. He jokingly said, "You know you can call me anytime if you need help—well, hypothetically that is."

"Thanks, I may need that. I'll be in uncharted waters here. I'll need all the help I can get, real or hypothetical," I said as my head started to buzz again.

Travis became more serious, his voice low as he stressed, "Oh, and I'm serious, be careful."

We hung up and I stared through the sliding glass door at the hornet's nest, its frenzied denizens hovering around the gray, leafy, papier-mâché-looking egg, like planets around the sun. I felt like I was about to enter a hive of a different kind, one just as frenzied and unpredictable.

A few days later, I caught myself talking to the hornets about what could be eating at me. They weren't much help with advice, but their concentration on detail was inspiring.

I finished the paperwork from my case and decided to meet a few friends for drinks and dinner instead of continually talking to my hornets. We met at a small pub near the water and sat at a dimly lit table on the patio, where we could hear the water hit the rocks below. I swirled the amber liquid in my glass, my mind more on missing Katerina than the conversation. I felt a sharp elbow in my ribs. Someone had caught my far-off stare.

"So where are you, Jara Quinn? You sure aren't sitting here at the table with us." My friend Sophie was staring at me, demanding an answer.

By now the other two were staring at me, all their glasses on the table.

"Well?" Sophie asked. "I think we deserve an answer. You've nursed that beer all night and have barely said five words to us. Bad enough we haven't seen you in the last three weeks."

Sheepishly I replied, "I've been busy, y'know, work and stuff."

"Stuff all right. Katerina came for the festivals, didn't she?" Liv asked from across the table.

"Yes, she did. Why? What's the big deal?"

"The big deal," Liv answered, "is she's in your head again. Every time you see her, you get all distant with us and melancholy. What happened this time?"

"Nothing happened, at least not really. It was like we hadn't spent any time apart. It was intense and exciting, like no time had passed. She had a lot on her mind, though, with her father running for President and all."

A collective groan rose from the table. All of my friends shook their heads. Mae got up from the table. "I'm going to get us another round." She nodded her head in my direction. "You all try and figure this out. Matters of the heart bore me."

"Good to know, Mae." I laughed. "I'll let your next hook up know that." I took the last drink of my beer and watched Mae walk to the bar. "I probably should be more like her, I don't think I'll ever have a relationship, especially with Katerina."

Sophie laughed. "Well, girl, she is a bit out of your league. Raised with the social elite and all, fed with a silver spoon. Everything seems to come easy for her and her kind. I'm not saying she doesn't care, but what are you to her, a rebellion of some kind?"

"I know she looks like she's had everything handed to her, but she's got her own struggles. Her family expects a lot and she expects a lot from herself. And her family, well, they're like my second family, but without the history and triggers. I'm not a rebellion."

"But where do you fit in? Does she even know how you are when she leaves?" Sophie asked.

I bent my head and held it with my thumb and index finger. "You don't get it. I know she cares. When we're together, it's like the rest of the world isn't there. It's just us. Acting like we did when we were in college."

"I get that," Sophie raised her voice, "but does she know you are an emotional mess every time she leaves? Does she even get that? Is she that shallow and uncaring? We pick up the pieces of your heart every time she goes. Has she even called you since she left?"

My face turned red and I grabbed my empty glass. I wanted to slam it on the table, yell and defend Katerina. But instead I let go of the glass, as tears welled in my eyes and I stared down at the table. "No," I said quietly.

Exasperated Sophie said, "Then what? I mean I know she is gorgeous, like unfairly so. But what is it that has you so hooked on her? I know it can't just be that."

Liv nudged Sophie. "Go easy on her, hon. Not everyone can have what we have." Liv took Sophie's hand. "Jara, if you love Katerina, you might want to tell her and let the cards fall where they may."

"Are you talking about me?" Mae had returned with another pitcher of beer. "I would definitely go after Katerina, that long, fiery hair and body...who wouldn't want to hit that?"

I gave Mae an incredulous look. "Remind me to keep her far away from Mae if she ever comes back."

"About that," Mae said as she sat down the pitcher and pulled a chair around by me. "Why haven't you ever brought her around us? Does she not want to slum it with us lowly people?"

"She's not like that, Mae! She gets along with everybody. I'm selfish. I want her all to myself when she's here. It's just...well, complicated."

"Then un-complicate it." Mae grabbed me by the shoulders, shook me, and yelled, "Tell her, damn it, tell her how you feel. If she doesn't feel the same way, then let her go. It's not worth the heartbreak. One day you will start feeling bitter and resentful toward her, and it won't even be her fault. You, the big, bad federal agent, able to face the toughest criminals, can't even tell the one person you've loved for years how you feel. Hell, wear your gun if that makes you feel safe. But, damn, this mopey lovesickness isn't a good look on you, so stop it."

The table was silent, along with a few tables around us. Mae scraped the chair back, grabbed her drink, and stood up. "I have a woman at the bar I'm going to fall in love with for the night, so good luck with all this." Mae excused herself and went back up to the bar.

We sat in silence, and I poured myself another beer. Sophie leaned over to me and whispered, "She isn't wrong, you know."

I knocked back the whole glass and poured another. Somberly I looked at Sophie. "I know, Sophie, I know."

I excused myself to the bathroom. I was tempted to call Katerina but thought better of it. I didn't want to verbally vomit a whole bunch of emotions before I could figure out what I really felt and wanted. I walked back to the table, hugged Sophie, and Liv and said my goodbyes. I went to the bar and ordered a six-pack to go. Mae walked up behind me and wrapped her arms around my waist. "Sorry if I was out of line back there," she whispered in my ear. "I'm not real good with matters of the heart."

"No, Mae, you were right on the money. Thank you."

Mae kissed my cheek. "Well, if either of you let each other go, let me know. Could be fun!"

I shook my head and laughed. "You'll be my first call."

I left the bar and took a walk through Newport. I made my way down to the water and found my favorite rock to sit on. I listened to the waves crashing against the shore and watched the sailboats bobbing on the water in the harbor while I contemplated everything my friends said tonight. I could have sat there all night, but I ran out of beer. I made my way home and wondered if I should even work on this campaign or call Katerina and tell her how I felt. My hand was on my phone to call her when it rang, Katerina's name appearing on the screen.

"Are you seriously going to work on my father's campaign?"

I was still foggy from the drinks and surprised she had called me, so I didn't answer.

She continued. "He is the last person who should be President, and you're going to support him?"

"Listen, I haven't actually agreed to it yet but, yes, I think I want to help because, well, I'm not sure why. You were so upset about him running. I, well," I kept stammering, "I wanted to protect you. I mean your family."

"Protect me? Protect us from what, my father?" she asked. "What do you know?"

"Nothing, I promise, nothing. I thought, well, I could maybe pay back your family for being so kind to me all these years and help him out. I'm not supporting the party and don't even care if he wins."

Katerina calmed down. "I still don't get it. I'm going to the house this weekend. Can you come and discuss it further with Granny, Mom, and me?"

I breathed a sigh of relief, glad she didn't push me any further on my reasoning, or lack thereof. "Of course I can."

We made plans for the upcoming weekend. I hadn't visited the Lansing home for a while.

"I'll see you soon," I said and disconnected the call. I held the phone in my hands, staring at it. What was my reason?

\

Chapter Four

I drove up the long, winding driveway with its neatly trimmed hedges and colorful flower beds to the circa 1930s mansion. Granny May once told me that her parents built the main part of the house in 1939, after they fled their native Poland during WWII. Additional sections were added later to help shelter other refugees from the war. No matter how many times I came here, I always marveled at the house's grandeur and its seamless construction.

The house sat majestically atop a gentle rise, surrounded by lush greenery and mature trees that provided a sense of privacy and tranquility. The mansion itself exuded timeless elegance with its sturdy white brick exterior, accented by intricate architectural details that harkened back to a bygone era. A sweeping front porch, adorned with classic columns and tasteful balustrades, stretched across the front of the house, offering a welcoming entrance. Large windows punctuated the façade, allowing natural light to fill the interior. Attached to the grandeur of the main house was the greenhouse, a sanctuary of botanical tranquility seamlessly blending the indoors with the outdoors.

I parked my Land Rover Defender on the edge of the horseshoe drive, out of the way in case other cars arrived, grabbed my bag, and made my way to the front door. As soon as I opened the large door, happy memories flooded my mind.

As large as the house was, whenever I walked through the door, I always felt greeted by a sense of warmth and sophistication. The foyer was spacious and inviting with polished black and white marble floors, ornate moldings, and a graceful staircase that ascended in an arc to the upper levels of the house.

Today was no different. When I came in, I immediately felt embraced by love. I sat my bag by the staircase. After driving in the August heat, I let myself linger awhile in the coolness of the foyer. Aromas wafted from the kitchen; they captivated my senses, tantalizing me with the scent of something delicious. I recognized the symphony of spices that were garlic, rosemary, and thyme but couldn't place the other savory notes that beckoned me further inside. I followed my nose and navigated through the familiar layout of the house, guided by the irresistible scent that lead me, like a compass needle pointing north. With each step, the aroma grew stronger, igniting my hunger.

I walked into the kitchen, expecting the usual gleaming countertops and shiny appliances that contrasted with the rustic charm of exposed wooden beams overhead. My eyes widened with delight at the sight before me: the countertops were cluttered with bowls and utensils, and fresh herbs and vegetables sat in colorful piles, waiting to be chopped and added to the pot. The sound of a knife rhythmically chopping echoed through the room.

I watched as Victoria, Katerina's mother, moved with the skill and ease of a five-star chef around the stove, engrossed in her culinary masterpiece. Victoria was an auburn-haired beauty who looked as if she stepped off the cover of *Vogue*. Little did I know when I first met her that she fit more on the cover of *Forbes*. She must have sensed me watching, because she turned around and looked at me with a smile, her eyes twinkling with pride at the feast she was preparing.

"I knew it was you, making this *pièces de résistance*," I said in my best French accent.

Victoria's smile broadened, as she ran over and hugged me. "You'll excuse the messy apron, I hope."

"Mess and all, you are as beautiful as ever and, anyway, this smells delicious. If it's half as good as it smells, I'll be satisfied."

I smiled as I sat at the island counter. I poured myself a glass of wine and refilled Victoria's glass. She told me Katerina should be arriving shortly and that Granny was still up in her room. I decided to broach the subject of the campaign before Katerina arrived.

"Victoria, I've something I would like to discuss with you. I'm sure Katerina told you the senator asked me if I would be interested in helping him with his campaign. He said the job would involve investigative work, putting out public relations fires like I did when I was an intern, and overall being a jack of all trades. I'm not sure exactly what he meant, but I'm intrigued."

Victoria listened intently as she sipped her wine and kept one eye on the stove.

"After the internship I knew I didn't want a career in politics," I went on. "But I want to do what I can to repay the senator for his help and to protect the family during this time in the spotlight."

She stood silent for a moment and then leaned over the island and put her hand on mine. "For one, you don't owe the senator or this family anything. Just please be careful is all I ask."

I wanted to ask what she meant, but she returned to the stove. I refilled my glass and topped off hers.

A moment later, a voice boomed behind me. "Girl, why are you wasting your time with wine? You need a real drink. Pour me a bourbon with an ice cube and fix yourself one."

I turned and threw my arms around Granny May. Now in her 80s, she still had an air of dignity and vitality despite a slight limp that required the support of a cane. Her once vibrant red hair had softened into a dignified gray, but the fire of her personality hadn't dimmed with age. Her face was lined with years of hard work and resilience, and her eyes remained sharp and alert. Her voice commanded attention, whether she was offering advice or expressing an opinion. Hardworking and unwavering, she remained a force of nature, never afraid to speak her mind. Her strong will had earned others' respect and admiration over the years.

"I was serious," she said. "Fix me a drink."

"Yes, ma'am," I said as I did a sloppy salute.

I went to the wet bar just off the kitchen and found the best open bourbon they had. I dropped an ice cube into a rocks glass, poured Weller's over it slowly, and sat it down next to me.

"Pull up a chair, lady, and take a load off," I said with a smile.

Granny hung her cane over the back of the chair and sat down. "So I hear you are going to help my good-for-nothing son-in-law with his grasp for glory?"

"I never heard it put that way before but, yes, I agreed to help him on the campaign. Least I can do."

Granny was unamused. "Hmmpf, well good luck and protect yourself. You never really know what that man is up to."

I knew Granny never approved of Charles marrying Victoria; she'd said repeatedly that she never trusted him. Even after Charles became governor, then senator, Granny never felt he was good enough for Victoria. I heard her say once, "The only good thing that man did was give me grandchildren."

The sound of the front door creaking open got our attention. "That must be my favorite granddaughter arriving," Granny exclaimed as Katerina burst into the kitchen.

"*Babcia!*" Katerina exclaimed, as she gave Granny a big hug. "I'm so glad to see you here."

Granny reached for her drink and took a long swig. With a loud, purposeful thunk, she sat the glass on the counter, her arthritic fingers still around it, swirling the ice cube. "Where the hell else would I be? Galivanting around the world? I need to be here and keep an eye on things."

"*Matka*," Victoria said, shaking her head.

We all laughed, but deep down I knew it was true.

After some small talk and catching up, Victoria announced that dinner was ready and asked where we would like to eat. We elected to remain in the kitchen around the island. Victoria had prepared a cream of wild mushroom soup, goat cheese with truffle oil and thyme next to a basket of fresh baked bread, and roast pork cutlets with a side of Brussel sprouts with a Polonaise sauce. For dessert a variety of sweet pierogi filled with fresh berries and cream sat on a large plate at the end of the counter.

Granny's eyes opened wide when she saw all the food. "Is this a holiday or something? You never cook like this when it is just us."

At that moment, a dark-haired woman with a serious expression walked into the kitchen.

"Jara," Granny May said, waving her glass at the woman, "I would like for you to meet my jailer, Sarah."

"Now, Mrs. Robinson," Sarah said, "I'm only doing what I've been hired to do." She turned to me: "Hi, Jara. I'm Sarah Miles, Mrs. Robinson's nurse." She turned back to Granny with a stern look. "Mrs. Robinson, you haven't taken your evening meds with your protein shake."

"Does it look like I need protein, young lady?" Granny May asked defiantly. "I'm eating with my family. Victoria has finally cooked something decent for a change."

Sarah huffed and handed Granny her meds, which she begrudgingly took.

"I'll let you get by without the shake tonight, but we're not making this a habit. Tomorrow, you have physical therapy with Brian, and you'll need all your strength." With that, Sarah turned and left.

I looked around. "Is she always so congenial?"

Victoria snorted. "She does her job, which is all I expect."

Granny May mumbled about being kept in jail, but we ignored her. During dinner, she announced to Victoria that she was accompanying her to the Foundation tomorrow.

"Oh you are, are you? Why's that?" Victoria inquired.

21

"I received a notice from the bank about some oddities in the books. I need to check those out."

Victoria frowned. "You never told me you received such a letter. Where is it? I want to see what you're talking about."

Katerina and I excused ourselves and allowed Victoria and Granny to have their financial discussion alone. We took our drinks and walked through the large French doors that opened onto a massive back porch loaded with lounge chairs. Off to the side was a meticulously manicured flower garden, and the scent of late summer flowers filled the air. In the distance, sailboats bobbed in the harbor as the rising moon reflected off the water. We found a couple of comfy chairs and sat our drinks on a small, weathered table between us.

I looked around and realized just how much I missed this place. Every time I visited, I found something new to love about it. I gazed around at the grounds that seemed to stretch for miles. The graduated deck had multiple levels that beckoned with the promise of relaxation. Each level was outfitted with comfortable furniture, cozy fire pits, and heaters to ward off the evening chill.

The skeleton crew kept the gardens and porches in top-notch condition. Tonight they had arranged on the uppermost porch around a crackling fire pit plush sofas and lounge chairs. Their soft cushions invited guests to sink into their embrace and enjoy the panoramic views of the surrounding landscape. They had set up a dining table for *alfresco* meals nearby, draped with crisp linens and sparkling tableware in case we decided to eat outside this evening. Each deck offered its own unique vantage point from which to enjoy the beauty of the estate.

At ground level, nestled within the expansive grounds, was a luxurious pool and pool house. The pool, a shimmering oasis of azure, was framed by elegant stone decking and lush landscaping. Surrounding the pool were more comfortable lounge chairs and plush daybeds to relax in the sun or seek shade beneath the canopy of a nearby pergola. Opposite the pool was the pool house with its large French doors, adorned with ivy-covered trellises and climbing vines.

The last deck opened onto a sprawling lawn that led down to the water's edge, where a covered dock awaited the arrival of boats and watercraft. A thirty-foot sailboat named *Ex navicula navis*, the motto of the Polish city of Lodz, was moored, its sleek lines cutting a graceful silhouette against the backdrop of the shimmering waters.

Katerina caught me in my daydream. "Thank you for coming here this weekend. Our time in Newport went by so quickly."

"I always love coming here. You know that. It feels like home to me."

Victoria came out and joined us. She pulled up a chair. "*Matka* has gone up to bed. She pretends she's younger than she is, but she tires easily. She's dead set on going to the Foundation tomorrow. This should be interesting."

Although Victoria was trying to shrug off the bank notice, her face told a different story. Her brow was furrowed, and her eyes stared off to nowhere in particular.

Katerina had told me about how important the Foundation was to her mother and grandmother. After Granny May became a widow in the late 1960s, she and seven-year-old Victoria moved back to Connecticut and into the family home. Being a young widow of a successful man and having come from wealth, Granny May thought it a sign of weakness to depend on someone else for money. She always wanted to give back to the community that had welcomed her and her family so warmly, so she researched how she could help others and set out to become one of the first family foundations run by a woman: the Majewski Foundation, named after her parents. The Foundation was a nonprofit organization, run by an all-female board, focusing on grants and loans that furthered education, culture, religious studies, support for women's rights, and the overall well-being of humankind.

Victoria became involved in her mother's foundation when she was just a teenager. She learned that by helping others get a step-up in life, they could help themselves and in turn pay it forward. Granny May did not believe in hand-outs but in offering a hand-up. Although one might assume Victoria to be spoiled and snobbish since she was an only child, she was as far from that as Pluto's distance from the sun. Victoria was strong, independent, and intelligent. She was quick to laugh, quick with support, and always quick with a kind word. Granny May raised Victoria to value education and the people around her. She always reminded her, "It's not money that makes you rich and successful. It's intelligence, sincerity, and character."

"Is there anything I can do, Mom?" Katerina asked.

"Thanks, honey, but no. I'll find out tomorrow what this is all about, and I'll let you know if you can help." Victoria stood from her chair, barely having left a dent in the cushion. "Sorry, girls, we'll spend more time together tomorrow. I can't seem to sit still.

23

And with that, I'm also heading to bed. I feel tomorrow is going to be a long one."

We all said our goodnights. Katerina and I remained on the porch. The moon was low in the sky, making the tops of the small waves look like glittery jewels. I got up, grabbed a couple of blankets, and returned to my chair. I looked over at Katerina, who had a distant but serious look on her face.

"Are you okay with me helping your dad?" I asked.

Katerina looked down for a moment, sighed, and looked at me directly with those emerald eyes of hers.

"I can't stop you. I know that. But I don't want you to get mixed up in whatever Dad's plan is. I know he's always wanted to be President, but I can't help but feel he's up to something. It was unlike him to keep this from us."

"I promise, I won't do anything stupid or illegal. Now I can't promise that for your father," I said jokingly.

Katerina looked unamused, so I didn't push it. I reached over and took her hand.

"I assure you, I will try to help your father and do my best to protect your family. In the meantime, maybe you and I can spend some more time together."

I let go of her hand, and she snatched mine back, squeezing it tightly. "Nothing can happen to you. I couldn't bear that."

Katerina was close to tears. I hadn't seen her this emotional since I went to the academy. I got up and pulled her into a hug. I'm not sure how long I held her, but I didn't want to let go.

\

Chapter Five

The next morning, I awoke with the August sun beaming through the window. I didn't remember coming to bed, nor did I remember Katerina joining me. I saw my bag on the chair by the fireplace, so I got up, took a shower, and got dressed. Katerina was still sleeping soundly with her flowing red hair strewn over the pillow. I quietly went down to the kitchen to grab some coffee. Victoria was already up, coffee in hand, glasses on, reading over the letter Granny received. When I put my hand on her shoulder to say good morning, she jumped.

"Oh, hi. Good morning. I didn't hear you come in. I hope you slept well. Help yourself to breakfast."

I looked over at the kitchen island, resplendent with an assortment of bagels and schmears, along with capers, fruit, and freshly squeezed orange juice. I grabbed a plate and took a bit of everything. I heard rustling in the den. A moment later, Granny May appeared.

"I snuck down the back way, so my jailer didn't see me," she said. "Victoria, we need to get on our way before Brian gets here. He'll exhaust me."

"*Matka*, why do you say such negative things about Brian and Sarah? You know you like them. Plus, they're only trying to help."

Brian and Sarah were, according to what Katerina had told me the night before, hired to care for Granny May after she fell and hurt her already bad hip. The doctor said she was lucky she didn't break it, but he still felt it was best she had a round-the-clock nurse and a physical therapist. The doctor suspected she may have been growing weaker than she'd let on or wasn't taking her medications correctly. Either way, Brian and Sarah were hired to help the situation.

Victoria shoved her paperwork in her laptop bag, grabbed a coffee to go, and helped her mother out to the car.

A brief time later, Sarah entered the room. "Have you seen Mrs. Robinson?"

I had a mouth full of bagel and shrugged. Sarah sighed loudly. "That woman will be the death of me. To be as old as she is, yet I can hardly keep up at times."

I laughed and swallowed my bite of bagel. "She and Victoria went to the Foundation. Not sure when they'll be back."

"That woman!" Sarah huffed. "I'll call Brian and tell him not to come. I'll be in my room if anyone needs me." She stormed out of the kitchen just as Katerina entered. Katerina turned to watch Sarah run up the stairs and looked back at me.

"What's wrong with her?" she asked.

We paused and looked at each other. In unison, we said, "Granny!"

Katerina and I stayed at the house all day, walking the grounds and checking out the family sailboat. I always called her the Polish Princess because I couldn't pronounce the name. We climbed on board and sat at the bow, looking out onto the open water. I instinctively put my arm around Katerina's waist but quickly pulled back. Katerina giggled and took my hand. We watched the other sailboats coming in and out of the harbor. The water taxis scurrying along to pick up or drop off sailors. We reluctantly disembarked from the boat and headed to the side of the house to look for anything new sprouting in the garden. We walked hand in hand, laughing and reminiscing about sneaking out to the garden to make out so no one in the house would know.

When we walked through the back door, we heard a man and a woman talking in hushed tones. We rounded the corner into the den where Senator Lansing was standing, red-faced, pointing his finger at Sarah. She looked like she was going to start crying at any moment. Katerina cleared her throat, and her father dropped his hand and quickly turned around.

"Darling! Jara! Hello! I was, uh, just talking to Sarah here about the importance of keeping Mrs. Robinson on a schedule and giving her meds on time."

A trembling Sarah remained silent.

"Dad, you know Granny does what Granny wants to do, especially if her mind is set on something, and what do you care anyway?"

Senator Lansing frowned. "Sarah, Ms. Miles told me Victoria and Mrs. Robinson went to the Foundation today. Do you know why?"

Katerina shot me a look, hesitating, but then said, "Even if we did, what business is it of yours? You have nothing to do with the Foundation."

Before her father could answer, Victoria and Granny May walked into the den.

"She's right, Charles," Granny May said with a growl. "What business is it of yours?"

Victoria took her mother's coat and laid it on the couch. Granny May looked at Sarah and smirked. "C'mon, jail keep. Help me upstairs. I've somehow lost my appetite."

Sarah, with a look of relief, rushed to Granny May's side. She reached for the folder in the old woman's hand.

"I can carry this myself," Granny May said as she snatched the folder away. "Grab me some tea. I'll meet you upstairs."

Sarah huffed but did as the woman asked.

Victoria narrowed her eyes and asked, "Charles, I wasn't expecting you home this weekend. What's the occasion?"

"Occasion?" Charles huffed and asked, "When do I need an occasion to be in my own home?"

Victoria waved him off and took a seat on an overstuffed divan. "Charles, let it rest. Why are you home tonight? Is something wrong?"

I grabbed a beer from the small fridge in the corner.

"No," he replied with deliberate casualness. "I had heard Jara was here, and I thought we could discuss her role in my campaign as a family."

I was glad I hadn't taken a sip, or I would have spat it across the room.

Katerina rolled her eyes and asked sarcastically, "As a family, Dad? Seriously? You made the decision to run all on your own, and now you want to discuss things as a *family?*"

Charles picked up his briefcase from a nearby desk. "Well, if I'm going to be attacked and made to feel unwelcome in my own home, I'll just head back to Washington." He grabbed his coat from the leather chair near the window and turned to me. "If you could, I would like to meet with you in the next couple of days to discuss this further. I'll be in touch." He stormed past us and out of the house.

After we heard Charles' car leave the driveway, Victoria asked us to join her, but to bring her some wine first. Grabbing two bottles of wine and three glasses, I returned to the den and placed the glassware on the coffee table before opening one of the bottles. Victoria laughed when she saw I had brought in two instead of one. "Did you get ESP training when you' were at the academy?"

The wine cork popped, and I started to pour the golden liquid into the glasses. "No, I replied, but I wish they had. This was just a gut instinct on how to shake off the aura of Charles."

Victoria raised her glass. "I'll drink to that!"

After our toast, I sat in the oversized chair across from Victoria and Katerina and relaxed against the coolness of the leather. After a few large sips of wine, Victoria refilled her glass. With a heavy sigh, she said, "*Matka* was right, as usual. There are some discrepancies in our books."

Katerina gasped and set down her glass. "Oh my god, Mom, no. How bad is it?"

"Quite significant I'm afraid. We went through all of the old accounts, both open and closed, by hand. I have no idea how it was done, but some of the accounts that should have been closed, aren't. Money is disappearing." Victoria took another drink as our attention remained focused on her. "I don't know how much or if it's continuing, but I do know it's from accounts we had before computers came along."

Thoughts were swirling in my head on how I could help, and as if Katerina could read my mind, she spoke up and asked, "Jara, is there anything you can do?"

"I can try. The FBI has an internet crime unit. I could ask if someone can look into this for you."

Victoria smiled and replied, "Thank you, because I don't know how much more Polish cursing I can handle from *Matka*."

The next day, I packed up my things and loaded them in my Defender. Katerina laughed as she followed me outside. "I can't believe you still have that old thing."

"Old thing? She has been totally restored, top to bottom, front to back, and even has some surprises built into her."

Katerina made a mock bow to my SUV. "Well, excuse me, then, Ms. Defender, for calling you old."

I bought the used Defender Puma 110 after my parents passed away and drove her while I was at college. It still had good bones and the safety items Land Rovers were known for, so I decided to have her restored to an elite off-road condition. I switched out the engine to a turbo V8, added high performance all-terrain tires, repainted the car to its original color, a deep Aintree green, then added a winch, roll bar, and lights to the top of the vehicle. Since college, I had reupholstered the inside to a classy tan leather with black trim, added a state-of-the-art stereo system, and had two custom fabricated compartments built into the back. These compartments were for a gun safe and evidence safe. Since I was working for the FBI, I felt these were essential.

We walked back into the house so I could say goodbye to Victoria and Granny May. Katerina wasn't leaving for Boston until Tuesday. We found Victoria in the den, looking over a stack of papers.

She looked up and said to us, "*Matka* was right. This could be catastrophic for the Foundation if we can't recover the money that is being siphoned off. Looks like a lot of meetings for me in the next few weeks."

"If there is anything I can do to help," I said, "please feel free to call. I'll do what I can, although math and finances are not my strong suit."

"Thank you, I appreciate that," Victoria said as she put her reading glasses on top of her head.

Katerina looked around. "Where's Granny?" she asked.

Victoria nodded her head toward the window and answered, "Out with Brian, doing her laps." She chuckled.

Katerina and I walked toward the garden where Granny May was talking nonstop to a totally ripped African American man.

"Mrs. Robinson," he said, his tone one of polite amusement, "if you walked half as much as you talked, we'd be done by now." Katerina and I burst into laughter.

"Oh, you two hush!" Granny snapped. "He should feel lucky to get my words of wisdom."

Katerina introduced me. "Brian, this is Jara Quinn, one of the family."

As Brian reached out to shake my hand, Granny May said, "This is the only good thing Charles has done for me in a while, hired me some eye candy to jumpstart an old woman's—"

"*Babcia!*" Katerina tried to stop her.

"I'm just saying," Granny said with a wicked smile.

Brian smiled and ignored Granny's comments. "Nice to meet you, Ms. Quinn," he said. "Now c'mon, Mrs. Robinson, two more laps of the garden."

Granny May reached up and hugged me goodbye. Was it my imagination, or did she hold on a little longer than usual?

"Be good, Granny," I said as I turned to leave.

"You first!" she replied.

Chapter Six

I went back home to Newport and my hornets. The nest was still buzzing, but the hornets were moving slower. I found a few of the small worker bees dead on my balcony. I knew they had worked up until their death to prepare their queen for her winter slumber. I contemplated the fact that these bees only worked for the life of the queen. Death was only a part of the cycle.

I cleaned the house and watered my plants, while wondering if working with the senator was the right thing to do. He said he would be in touch with me in a few days. Nearly a week had gone by and I still hadn't heard from him. I had prepared a list of questions for him in anticipation. I was on the balcony, wondering if I should call him, when my phone rang. I didn't recognize the number but answered anyway.

"She's dead, Jara! She's dead!" Katerina shrieked. "Granny is dead! Just like that, she's dead!"

"What happened?" I said as I rushed to find my overnight bag. "What do you need? I'll be right there."

"I don't know, I don't know. I just need you here. We're at Memorial Hospital. Please hurry." Katerina said as she sobbed.

I drove like a madwoman, my mind reeling in a state of shock. I was just there. Granny May was fine.

When I arrived at the hospital, Katerina was standing rigid in the doorway of her grandmother's hospital room, as if she were on guard. The stringent antiseptic smell hit my nose as I approached, and I noticed how Katerina had braced herself, her knuckles white as she clutched the doorframe. She had refused to let them send Granny May to the morgue until I got there. The nurses had already finished removing any equipment, washed Granny's body, and let the family have time with her. I didn't see Victoria, so I assumed she had left.

Katerina threw her arms around me. "Someone had to have done this! I just know it. You saw her. She wasn't sick."

She explained that, after I left on Sunday, Granny May had said she was feeling "odd" but couldn't really describe it. "I'm just not myself" were her words. She refused dinner and went to bed early. Sarah had administered her bedtime meds, given her the protein shake, and tucked her in.

Katerina said, "Granny stayed in bed the next two days, but then she started feeling better. I stopped by yesterday to see her, and she was walking around the yard with Brian. I met them on the back patio for tea. Granny seemed great, joking and laughing with Brian. He told me he would be back but would leave us alone for a bit. He reminded Granny she still had one more lap of the garden to go and needed to finish her protein shake. She had given him a thumbs up and he'd left. She seemed in good spirits, not like a person who was going to die in twelve hours."

"How did she get to the hospital?" I asked.

"Oh, I demanded that the ambulance bring her here," Katerina said, exasperated. "I wanted to know what happened as soon as possible!"

A doctor suddenly walked up and apologized to Katerina. He told her an autopsy wouldn't be completed. "I've been informed by hospital admin that it won't be necessary," he said as he gave me a curious glance and went on. "Senator Lansing and his wife feel an autopsy would be disrespectful to Mrs. Robinson at this time."

Katerina fumed and her eyes flared. She pulled up to her full height and forcefully said, "If I have to get a court order for an autopsy, then I will!" She stormed off.

The doctor looked at me and said, "We'll hold the body for a maximum of ninety-six hours."

I ran to catch up with Katerina and found her down the hall, collapsed against the wall, crying. The harsh overhead lighting washed out the already pale green walls. I had never seen Katerina look so small and defeated before.

"This is wrong, all wrong." She sobbed. "Granny May wasn't supposed to die."

I reached down, pulled her into a hug, and let her cry. She was right. Granny May wasn't supposed to die. My gut started tensing...something wasn't right.

We sat on the hospital floor for what seemed like hours until finally Katerina looked up at me and said, "I need to go home."

The summer sun had finally set, and a few stars started appearing as I drove Katerina home. I held out my hand as I drove and she rested her face on it, wetting it with her tears. When we got to the house, Katerina headed straight to her mother. I was fast on her heels.

"Why did you tell the doctor not to perform an autopsy on Granny?" Katerina shrieked as she entered her mother's sitting room, sobbing.

Victoria sat in an overstuffed armchair, upholstered in a fabric covered in bold, pink hydrangeas. She was clenching a wad of tissues in her right hand. "I said nothing of the kind!" she said through her tears. "I want to know what happened just as much as you do."

"But the doctor said you and Dad said not to do it, that there wasn't a reason for it."

Her mother blinked and said, "Well, I never said that—actually we never even discussed it."

"Where is Dad, by the way?" Katerina asked. "He left the hospital before the doctor even saw Granny."

Victoria shrugged. "We drove separately, I didn't even see him at the hospital."

Katerina pulled out her cell phone, set it on speaker, and called her father. Charles didn't even get to "Hello" before she screamed into the phone, "Why did you refuse an autopsy? You had no right! I need to know what happened."

"What? I didn't—"

"Don't deny it, Dad. You told them not to do it. You, the all-powerful senator. You had no right." she screamed. "Well, I'm getting an autopsy even if I have to get a court order to do it."

Before he had a chance to answer, Katerina hung up. Victoria got up and put her arms around her. "Mom," Katerina sobbed into her mother's cashmere sweater, "what are we going to do without Granny?"

I made my way upstairs with my bags, allowing Victoria and Katerina to spend some time alone. I changed into a T-shirt and sweats and climbed into bed. I was exhausted, but my mind was racing, not letting me sleep. I heard a light knock on my door before Katerina entered and slid in beside me. "Can I sleep in here with you?" she asked. "I don't want to be alone."

"Of course." I said as she put her head on my shoulder and cried. I held her in my arms, not saying a word, until we both fell asleep.

The next morning, the house was eerily quiet as Katerina and I walked down to the kitchen. "This place isn't going to be the same without Granny," Katerina said. A fresh pot of coffee sat on the warmer in the coffeemaker, and some bagels and muffins were left on the counter.

Neither of us had an appetite, so we took our coffee into the den. I sat by as Katerina pulled out her laptop and cell phone and began to pull every legal string she had to obtain a court order or the consent of a medical examiner to have the autopsy completed. Finally, after a lot of runaround, she reached the Chief Medical Examiner of Connecticut, Dr. Michael James. She told him of her suspicions and with the consent of Victoria, Dr. James ordered the local medical examiner, Dr. Stanley Rice, to complete the autopsy. When she spoke to Dr. Rice by phone, he said he would complete the autopsy, but it would be at least a week or two before he started since other criminal cases took precedence. Katerina argued that she suspicioned her grandmother's death was also criminal, but it fell on deaf ears.

The doctor compromised and said he would go ahead and draw blood for the toxicology report and take samples of organs, skin, and nails to send to the lab. "Mind you," he told her, "the toxicology results will not be back for possibly three to four weeks after I get started."

Katerina tried to argue, but she knew it was to no avail. After hanging up, Katerina put her head in her hands and quietly cried.

I walked up behind her and put my arms around her trembling shoulders. "Honey, be glad they're even doing this," I said, trying to comfort her. "You'll get your answers."

"I know," she said gruffly through her tears, "but I want the answers now."

"These things take time. You can't rush a blood test or a toxicology report," I said as I tried to be rational. "You just need to be patient."

Abruptly, Katerina shrugged out of my embrace and twisted away from me. "Patient?" she yelled, her eyes sending darts through me. "How can you ask me to be patient? This is Granny! I need to know now!"

I stepped away from her, but didn't leave or answer back. I knew this was her own inner conflict and this process would take time. It was not for me to argue rationalities.

Katerina continued to let out primal screams and shoved all the papers off the desk. She picked up her laptop, and lifted it above her head to throw, her knuckles turning white from her grasp. As she searched the room for a place to throw it, her eyes met mine again. I stood calmly, my eyes without judgement. She froze mid-motion, and in a whisper said, "What the hell am I doing?" The tension in her body began to release. She gently set the computer back on the desk. Her body slumped, and she slowly melted to the floor. Her hands moved to her temples, pressing them, as if trying to rid something from her mind, her eyes squeezed shut while tears escaped from them.

I knelt beside her, gently reaching my hand to her shoulder. She grabbed my hand like a lifeline and collapsed into me.

Over and over, she mumbled, "I have to know. I have to know." I leaned against the desk, pulling Katerina to me and stroking her hair until Victoria entered the room.

"Oh my," Victoria exclaimed. "Is everyone okay?"

"Sorry, Mom, I'll clean up the mess," Katerina said as she started to stand. Her hands and legs were still shaking, as she braced herself with the desk. I stood up behind her, holding her waist in case she fell.

"Oh honey, I don't care about a bunch of papers around the room. I'm more worried about you." Victoria walked slowly toward us and put her hand on Katerina's. "Did you speak with the medical examiner?" Katerina took her mother's hand and told her what the doctor had said. "Good," Victoria said with determination. "That's a start. Soon we'll get the answers we need.

Katerina used her sleeve to wipe the tears from her eyes. She held on to her mother's hand even tighter. "How can you be so calm about all of this?" Katerina asked as she searched Victoria's face for answers.

"Because, dear, I know getting upset is not going to speed up the process." Victoria let out a small laugh. "I know from experience. But I will admit, yelling does feel good sometimes."

With that we all laughed, and the tension left the room.

I let go of Katerina as Victoria guided her to the plush olive-colored couch. Katerina grabbed a feathery pillow and put it on her lap. Her hands kneaded the pillow like a cat. The sun had disappeared from the den windows, replaced by an afternoon moon. I turned on the desk lamp and started picking up the papers that had been strewn throughout the room.

"Leave that," Katerina said as she patted the cushion next to her. "Please sit with us."

I put the papers on the desk and sat beside Katerina. An awkwardness came over me, so I leaned toward the arm of the couch and kept my hands in my lap. I listened intently to Katerina and Victoria talk.

"I'm going to go to the Foundation tomorrow and see what still needs to be done," Victoria said. I have a couple of meetings lined up with the accountants and want to be prepared."

Katerina offered to help, but she added she had to return to Boston soon to do final prep for her trial.

Victoria stood and turned to me. "I was wondering if maybe you could stay for a few days and help me go through Granny's things here at the house since Katerina has to leave. I'm feeling so overwhelmed with the Foundation that I don't think I can do both justice."

"Of course I can help. I'm taking a leave of absence to help Charles, and since I haven't started that yet, I have plenty of time."

"Wonderful! Then it's settled," Victoria said. "We can start tomorrow. Thank you!"

Sarah appeared in the doorway of the den. "Mrs. Lansing, I have all my things packed and I'm going, unless there is something else you need me for."

"Thank you, Sarah. Please leave me your forwarding information if you would."

Sarah handed Victoria a card with her name and number on it. "Call me anytime," she said with a polite smile before walked out.

"Victoria, do you think we should have asked Sarah to help with Granny's things?" I asked.

Victoria sniffed. "I think she's done enough already."

Katerina shot me a look. "Mom?"

"Nothing, darling, I'm going to start dinner." Without any further explanation, Victoria left the room.

"What the hell was that about?" Katerina asked.

I shook my head. "You're asking me?"

I headed to my place the next day to get some more clothes and check on things. I also thought it would be a suitable time to call Katerina's middle brother in Washington DC and ask him if I could stay with him when I met with the senator. Charles Jr., or "CJ" as he liked to be called, lived in the Georgetown area with his wife, Julia, and their son, Calvin. Although he was very smart and charismatic, CJ did not want to follow in his father's political footsteps. Instead, the talented journalist took a job at *The*

Atlantic after interning at *The Boston Globe*. He said he enjoyed going in depth on stories and finding the truth.

"Hey, CJ," I said when his voice came on the line. "I was wondering if I could stay at your place for a few days when I'm in DC?"

"Well of course! Why are you coming to Washington?"

I was surprised he wasn't aware of my decision to help his father with his campaign, so I told him.

"What the hell? You're going to help my father? Why on earth for? You know he's going to take advantage of you. Why would you want to do this?"

When he caught his breath, I broke in, "Because being a part of his campaign could help me figure out what's really going on. And protect your family." I couldn't believe I had said it out loud.

"Going on?"

"Yes," I replied, electing to bite the proverbial bullet. "Something isn't right with his bid for President announcement and not talking to your family first. Then Granny May died suspiciously, and he went on like it was any normal day."

"What? Granny's death was suspicious?"

"Well, Katerina seems to think so, and I trust her opinions."

CJ gave a nervous laugh. "Well, if it's anything controversial, please let me know so I can write a story about it. My family sure knows how to make the news."

I didn't appreciate his being so glib, but I ignored it and told him I would see him in a couple of weeks.

I grabbed a beer and went out onto my balcony. The hornets were still busy flying in and out of the hive. A pun entered my mind, and I laughed to myself: do hornets building a hive have a 'house-swarming' party?

I called Katerina to see how she was doing. She seemed rushed. "I have this weird immigration trial prep going on and have no idea how to argue it. Buses of immigrants were driven here and to New York City. I think even DC. The problem is they were sent from another state by its governor. We have nowhere to put these people and no idea if this is a criminal or civil case. Plus, who do we actually charge?"

"So this is what our country is becoming?" I responded. "No longer welcoming the masses into the 'Melting Pot.' What does your father think of this?"

"Hell if I know. We haven't spoken since I confronted him about the autopsy."

I caught her up on going to Washington to meet with her father and also staying with her brother. She mentioned she might be in the area and would love to see her young nephew.

"Give him a call. I'm sure they would love to see you."

"Sounds good. I'll give him a call later. I miss you."

"I miss you too," I replied and hung up.

I texted Victoria that I would be back at the estate in a couple of days.

Chapter Seven

I arrived back at the Lansing house on an unusually humid, mid-September afternoon. Victoria was home alone. She had a couple of dozen oysters on ice on the island and was busy butter-poaching lobsters as she sipped a glass of chilled Sauvignon Blanc. She offered me a bottle of crisp cider, which I gladly accepted, as I was parched from my trip. I gave her a hug and she grabbed my arms, starting to cry. "I'm so glad you're here. I have some things to talk with you about, things I just don't understand."

I gazed into her puffy, swollen eyes with concern. "You know I'm here for you and your family, always."

She wiped her tears and plated the lobster with a mouthwatering grilled Caesar salad and brioche rolls.

"I'm going to have to come to this restaurant more often," I said teasingly. "I may even leave a tip."

Victoria smiled and said, "I miss cooking for people but don't get used to it."

We took our food and drinks to a small table on the dock to watch the sailboats come in for the evening. We ate quietly, drinking in the atmosphere and savoring the delicious food.

"Jara, there are some things I want you to read, if you would."

"Sure, I'll do what I can."

We lingered over our meal for a while longer and then made our way back to the house. After we took our dishes to the kitchen, Victoria produced a handful of papers with Granny's handwriting.

"Please read these and tell me what you think. They are some of the papers I found after you left."

I read them while Victoria took care of the dishes and refreshed our drinks.

The first one read, "I can't believe him. I knew he wasn't right for my Victoria. I should have stopped it before it started. I knew he would hurt her."

The second one appeared to be in Granny's native language, Polish. "*Próbuje mnie oszukać. Muszę go powstrzymać. On nie skrzywdzi mojej rodziny.*" Victoria had written the translation "He is trying to trick me. I have to stop him. He will not hurt my family."

The next paper appeared to be a page from a bank journal listing at least eighteen payouts and one large deposit to a trust dating back to the mid-1980s. It had no names listed as to whom the money was going to or why.

"What do you think?" Victoria asked.

"Are you sure this trust isn't for Katerina? It started around the time she was born. I can see Granny May setting something up just for her."

Victoria nodded. "Katerina already has her trust and has never touched it. This must be for someone else. I don't understand the eighteen payouts, though, and they come from a bank I'm not familiar with."

I suggested we go to this bank and flat-out ask. "Let's go this Monday."

That night I sat in the den and continued to look over the papers. They contained basically the same information. Was this Charles she was talking about, or someone else? Also, why a different bank? Granny May always used Liberty Bank since the time her parents moved here, but this bank was in Rhode Island. I researched online and learned that in the 1990s, the bank changed its name and in 2004, a large international bank bought it. That was from where the last two payments were made.

I emailed Travis, reminding him he told me I could ask him for help. I asked him, hypothetically, how Victoria and I could get access to this bank account. He was so much more knowledgeable about the legality of things than I was. I closed my laptop and went up to my room. It was eerily quiet. I missed Katerina sharing my bed.

The next morning, I stumbled downstairs to load up on caffeine. I didn't sleep well, tossing and turning, my mind racing over the mysterious trust and Granny May's cryptic notes. I had just filled my cup when the doorbell rang. I shuffled to the door, balancing my cup of steaming coffee and trying to take a sip with each step. When I opened it, there stood Sarah.

"What are you doing here?" I asked, a bit more accusatory than I had intended.

"Oh, hi, actually, I was summoned if you must know. Mrs. Lansing asked me to come over."

"Victoria called you?" I asked, surprised. "That's odd."

"Why is that odd? She said she wanted to talk about Mrs. Robinson."

"Really?" I opened the door wider and moved to the side. "Well, come in then, I guess."

"Is everything okay? You seem surprised to see me."

"It's just, well, things have been a bit stressful lately. Granny May's death, you know. And, well, there have been some questions about it, is all."

Sarah stiffened, raising a laminated brow. "Questions? What do you mean by questions? I assure you, I did everything I could to help Granny May. I cared about her deeply."

"I'm sorry, Sarah," I said, my tone softening. "I didn't mean anything by that. Like I said, it's been stressful lately, and this is my first cup of coffee."

Sarah huffed. "Fine. I understand it's a difficult time for everyone, but can you tell me where Mrs. Lansing is?"

"Yeah, sure. Follow me. She's in the den."

I walked a few steps ahead of Sarah, feeling daggers in my back. Seems like I struck a nerve.

Victoria was sitting at the desk in the den. She looked up as I entered. When she saw Sarah behind me, she stood up, set aside her reading glasses, and walked around to greet her.

"Sarah, hello, thank you for coming," she said, smiling and extending her hand. "I hope this wasn't an inconvenience."

"Not at all, Mrs. Lansing. Jara said you had some questions about your mother's death?"

Victoria tossed me a sideways look.

"I-I'm sorry, Victoria. I mentioned to Sarah there were questions about Granny May's death. Sorry if I spoke out of turn. And Sarah, I'm sorry if I seemed rude. I promise I wasn't accusing you of anything, lack of caffeine." I excused myself and went upstairs to get dressed.

So this is what a size nine foot tasted like?

I got dressed and came back downstairs for another cup of coffee. I saw Sarah and Victoria through the mullion French doors, talking at one of the tables. Victoria motioned for me to join them. I noticed each had a cup in front of them, so I brought the coffeepot for refills.

"Thank you," Victoria said as she looked up at me and smiled.

Sarah passed on the refill. I noticed her face appeared softer and her eyes had unshed tears in them. I sat the pot on the table and gave Victoria a quizzical look.

41

"Please, have a seat. After you went to bed last night, I looked over more of *Matka*'s papers and found a few pertaining to Sarah, at least I think they were. So I called her last night and asked if she could come over to read them. I'm sorry, Jara. I didn't have a chance to tell you."

"No worries. But I don't understand. Granny wrote stuff about Sarah?"

"Yes," Victoria replied, nodding her head. She reached over and touched Sarah's knee. "Can you please read out loud the note you have?"

Sarah wiped her eyes with her sleeve and nodded. Her voice caught when she tried to read, so she handed me the note.

I took the paper from her and read it out loud. "Sarah has grown up into such a lovely woman and has done well in school despite her circumstances." I looked up at Victoria with a confused expression. Granny treated Sarah like a jailor, so why the change of heart?

Sarah said, "I talked with Mrs. Robinson many times about how I grew up without a father and had an angry alcoholic mother. I told her about my mother passing away when I was sixteen and that I had to stay with an aunt for a couple of years. My aunt was nice enough, but I wanted to get far away from my family and memories. As soon as I graduated, I moved to North Carolina and enrolled in nursing school. I had read somewhere that Duke had one of the best nursing programs in the country."

My face grew warm with embarrassment and sympathy. "I'm terribly sorry about that, Sarah. My parents died when I was young also. I know how hard that must have been for you. And wow, Duke, that's a good school." I was still confused over why Granny May would write that down though.

Sarah clutched some other papers in her hand. "Do you want to read more?"

"No, not unless you want me to." I could tell she had only asked me because Victoria was sitting there. I had a feeling she wanted to keep the other writings private.

Victoria looked at me. "I've asked Sarah if she would be available from time to time to go through the rest of *Matka*'s papers. I'm sure she knows more about *Matka*'s last days than we do." She smiled at Sarah. "It will be good to get to know you better."

Why has Victoria changed her mind and asked Sarah to help us? "If you think this is best," I said after some obvious hesitation. "The extra help could be useful, in fact, since I'm bringing more of Granny's boxes up from the basement. Victoria, let me know if you need more help in Granny's room."

My head started buzzing like my faraway hornets. There must be a method to her madness. I never really got to know Sarah. She always disappeared when I was around. But I trusted Victoria and I knew Granny May had liked her, so who was I to question?

I poured myself another cup of coffee and excused myself. I went to the den and opened my laptop to see if Travis had responded. When I saw there was no message, I sent him another email asking another favor. "Could you do a background check on Sarah Miles, age between thirty-two and thirty-six, from Connecticut or maybe Rhode Island? Thanks in advance. I owe you."

I heard the front door close. A short time later, Victoria stood in the doorway.

"I hope you didn't mind that I asked Sarah over. I found these other notes in *Matka*'s room. I have no idea when they were written," she waved them in the air, "and was curious what she would say about them. Plus, I want to get to know her better. Something's odd about her."

She has some sort of plan. "I actually think it's a good idea, Victoria," I said matter-of-factly. I shared with her what I learned about the bank but didn't tell her what I had asked Travis to do. "I think," I said finally, "what we need to do is relax some, meaning I want to go out on the boat and have a picnic."

"Oh, wow," Victoria exclaimed. "We haven't done that in years."

Katerina and I often took the boat out when I visited, so I'd learned how to sail with the best of them. It was a perfect day for sailing, a bright sky with wispy clouds floating in a gentle breeze. Yesterday's humidity had vanished. We had precious few of these days left before the harsh, northeast winter set in.

We gathered our picnic items, some warm clothes, and blankets to insulate us from the cooler wind on the water. We detached the dinghy, checked the lines, sails, and motor—all were shipshape. We filled the motor with gas in case we got caught with no wind, loaded our supplies, and cast off around noon, headed for open water.

I never tired of the breathtaking views of rugged cliffs, rocky beaches, and quaint coastal towns nestled along the shore as we made our way up the coastline. Seabirds dove overhead, their cries mingling with the sound of the waves lapping against the hull. Salty ocean water sprayed the air as the breeze picked up, giving us a taste of the ocean. I guided the boat into a sunny cove that was a family favorite, dropped anchor, and rolled in the sails.

"This is so relaxing," Victoria said as she sighed. "Katerina taught you well. You sail like a pro."

I smiled, happy that she noticed. "Yes, I owe her a lot. I love this boat. So many great memories."

We sat on the bow and soaked up some early afternoon sun. We must have drifted off, as the next thing I knew, it was after three.

I went to the cabin and pulled out our picnic basket, cooler, and blankets. Victoria was still asleep on the bow. I didn't have the heart to wake her. She looked so peaceful for the first time in weeks. I set out our food and cracked open a beer.

Victoria woke, yawned, and smiled. "That was the nicest nap I've had in years."

"I one hundred percent agree. Now, let's eat. I'm starving."

We dined on lobster rolls made from yesterday's leftovers, fruit and cheeses, blue cheese-stuffed olives, and some fresh kettle chips with sea salt.

"I found so many more papers last night," Victoria said as we were eating. "I have no idea what they mean. There are also some about you."

I almost dropped my sandwich in shock. "Me? I'm no mystery. What are those about?"

Victoria smiled sweetly and said, "*Matka* really loved you. She felt you were a perfect fit in our family. So do I."

I blushed when she said this. "Thank you. I feel right at home with all of you."

"Remember last year when I asked you about the Foundation board? Guess *Matka* had the same thoughts. There is a written request, in her handwriting, to put you on the board *in absentia*. I guess you were deep in an investigation, and she didn't want to bother or pressure you to sit actively on the board. But you're on there."

"Seriously? I can't believe...wow," I said as I stumbled over my words. "I guess I can't turn Granny May down now."

We talked some more about memories, family, and future plans. I commented that mine were still up in the air. "But first we're going to find out about these notes and what Charles is up to."

Victoria nodded and said, "I still want to go to the bank where the trust originated."

"Sounds like a road trip is in our future."

We packed things up, hoisted up the anchor, unfurled the sails, and headed back to the house. As we sailed along on the water's glass-like surface, I wondered again if I had a reply from Travis.

It was dusk when we reached the dock and secured the boat. We grabbed our stuff and headed to the house. Katerina was sitting on the portico, drinking a glass of wine.

"I thought you were working," I said, happy to see her.

Victoria hugged her daughter and gave her a kiss. "I'm so glad to see you. How long can you stay?"

Stepping back Katerina laughed and asked, "Is this an interrogation? Yes, I can stay a few days. I need to clear my head from the trial prep. I don't work *all* the time."

Victoria and I both stifled a laugh. Victoria sat down while I put away the food and blankets and grabbed a beer, a bottle of wine, and a glass. I poured Victoria a glass of wine and refilled Katerina's. Victoria was telling Katerina about her meeting with Sarah.

"...and yes, I asked Sarah to help us go through *Matka's* things. I'm even thinking about having her move back in."

Katerina looked at me, then back to her mother. She took a gulp of wine. "You sure about this? What has changed your mind about her? I'm still not sure about her involvement in Granny's death."

Victoria almost choked on her drink. "*What?* You think she killed *Matka*? Jara, is this what you were trying to get at this morning? You both think she had something to do with it?"

I shrugged my shoulders as Katerina answered, "I don't know. I mean, you don't have suspicions, Mom? I'm still waiting on the tox results, but she was the one who spent the most time with Granny."

"Gosh, I don't know," Victoria replied. "I mean, I thought so at first, but then I figured I just wanted someone to blame. But now..."

"It seems Granny has left us a lot of mysteries to solve," Katerina said.

Victoria raised her glass. "A toast. To *Matka* and her mysteries!"

I excused myself and went to the den to check my email. Still nothing. It was getting chilly, so I started a fire in the fireplace and stretched out on the couch. Victoria and Katerina needed some time to talk. I drifted off until Katerina entered and asked if I was going to sleep there or upstairs. I got up, put my laptop away, and screened in the fireplace. I turned around to find Katerina standing right in front of me.

"Where's my hug?" she asked.

I embraced her, and she led me upstairs to my room. She had already lit the fireplace; and she'd spread a blanket with towels and massage oils on the floor. "What is this?" I asked.

"I thought I'd treat you since you've treated my mother so wonderfully this weekend. I figured you'd be a bit sore from the sailing you did today."

I smiled. "Well, we anchored, slept, and ate. It was just a sail to the cove and back."

Katerina stroked my face. "So you don't want a massage?"

I leaned into her touch. "Who am I to turn down a massage?"

I changed into pajama pants and got comfortable on the blanket and pillows by the fire. "I should be giving you a massage, as hard as you're working," I commented. "This trial prep sounds tough."

"Shhh. No talking about work, but I will get that massage. The night is young."

I felt her warm, oiled hands on my back. The tension in my shoulders started to melt away with each firm, deliberate stroke. I was more tense than I'd thought.

"That's better," Katerina whispered softly. "You need to relax and let the oil do its thing."

Easier said than done. Memories of our bodies together raced to the forefront of my mind. I felt a knot of emotion surface, but I pushed it back to where I kept it hidden. I closed my eyes and relaxed in her warm hands. When I woke up, Katerina was next to me, her bare breasts pressed into my side, her head on my shoulder. How did I sleep through this? I had one arm under her, with my hand on her back and her leg draped over me. I turned and pulled her on top of me, feeling her breasts against mine.

Katerina smiled mischievously. "Oh, now she's awake," she teased. "Guess I'm not getting my massage. But I like this so much better."

She bent her head down and gave me a light kiss. Soon her lips were pressed firmly against mine in heated passion. I put one hand in her hair and the other caressed her back.

"I've been wanting—no—*needing* this since I was at your house in Newport," she whispered.

"I know. I have too," I replied. "I've missed this."

We continued to kiss and rub our bodies against one another. Katerina started moving up and down on my body. Soon she was breathing hard and moving faster. I kissed her neck and shoulders in between thrusts until her body shook, and she buried her head in the crook of my neck and shoulder, her red hair falling around me. She bit down to muffle her moans. I rolled her over and continued to make love to her.

"Oh my god!" she moaned. "I've missed you so much."

I whispered how beautiful and sexy she was and how I had always wanted her. Katerina's nails dug into my back. I leaned down and kissed her deeply, wanting this to last forever. Katerina's body tensed and shook again, pulling me hard into her. She held me for a few minutes until her body started to relax.

Breathless, she said, "Wow that was so much better than a massage—not that I won't take a raincheck."

We stayed on the floor for a bit, wrapped in the blankets, kissing and enjoying each other's bodies. In time we got up, put the oil on the desk, and threw the blankets on the chair.

I turned to put on my shirt, and Katerina grabbed me. "Oh no, I get you like this for the night."

"Who am I to argue with a lawyer?" I turned on my side, and Katerina moved right into my body. We kissed again and then she turned over with me wrapped around her. I whispered to her that I was leaving in the morning with Victoria to visit a bank, but we should be back by evening. I asked if she was staying, hoping that she was.

"Of course I'm staying. You two go figure out your mystery, and I'll have dinner for you when you return. I have some things to do too."

We cuddled closer. "I've missed you so much," Katerina whispered. "I love you."

I was now wide awake.

Chapter Eight

After a night of tossing and turning, I woke up early to Katerina breathing softly next to me. I quietly got up and stepped into the shower. I was just finishing when she stepped into the bathroom.

"I thought we'd have a little more time together, you know, to reminisce," she teased as she pushed me back into the shower.

"As much as I want to 'reminisce' this morning," I pulled her close and kissed her, "I have a date today with your mother."

"Oh really, already dating other people? And my mother even! Should I be worried?" Katerina teased as she tried to push me back.

"You know you're the only Lansing woman I want, although your mom does look good for her age."

Katerina playfully smacked me, then kissed me long and hard. "Okay, but I'll be here when you get back."

I laughed as I slipped out of the shower and started getting dressed.

Katerina called out from the bathroom, "You don't know what you're missing."

Yes, actually I do.

I went down to the kitchen—Victoria was making breakfast.

She turned and smiled. "You girls sleep okay?"

"Yes, ma'am, yes, we did," I replied with a smile sweeping my face ear to ear.

I put my laptop on the counter and booted up my email. I had a response from Travis.

> Jara, what have you gotten yourself involved in this time? The trust you're asking about, is it a living trust and if so, is it an irrevocable or revocable trust?
>
> Also, who is the trust creator? Sometimes the family of the creator can get all this information from where the trust was created. If it's Granny May's trust, Victoria might be able to get this information or, since her mother has passed, the beneficiary might already have the funds, depending on the terms.
>
> About the background check, is there something I need to open? Call me! T

I related Travis's message to Victoria about the trust.

"Well, what do we have to lose? Road trip to Rhode Island it is," she said.

I excused myself and called Travis.

"What in the hell are you doing, Jara? You know I can't do a deep dive background check on someone unless I have a reason."

"Who asked you to do that? I just asked for a background check on Sarah, not a deep dive. This is for the senator's family!"

"Fine, fine." There was a pause. "She doesn't exist."

"What? What do you mean?"

"I mean she doesn't exist, at least not that I could find in Rhode Island, Connecticut, or anywhere in the New England area."

I felt as if I had been punched in the gut. "Can you email me what you searched?"

"Since it is for a sitting senator and a presidential candidate, I guess so, but don't stick your neck out too far."

"Thanks, Travis. I definitely owe you, and yes, before you say it, I will be careful."

I remained on the porch, trying to evaluate what I had just been told. Should I tell Katerina and Victoria right now? If not, how long should I wait? I walked back into the kitchen. Katerina and her mother were eating breakfast.

"You better get in here and eat," Katerina admonished me. "You'll be needing that energy."

I nodded and smiled faintly.

Her eyes narrowed. "Okay, what's wrong? You look like you got some bad news."

"Did Travis finally get you fired?" Victoria asked teasingly, a twinkle in her eye.

"Sometimes I wish," I said, laughing, "but no. I will need to do some work later tonight and tomorrow."

Katerina rolled her eyes. "No rest for the wicked, I guess."

"Guess not," I said as I sat down and ate a bite of omelet.

When I went upstairs to get my jacket and laptop case, Katerina followed me.

"What's wrong with you? You really need to work? Travis couldn't let you have a little time off? I thought your case was over."

"It's not Travis' fault," I said, as I walked into the bedroom. "I asked him for a favor, and now I have to follow up on it."

"What?"

"I promise, I will tell you everything once I know what's going on."

Katerina studied my face and knew I was serious. I wasn't going to tell her anything. "You know," she warned, "I have ways of getting information out of people. So you better keep your promise." She turned and went back downstairs.

Victoria and I loaded up in my Defender and headed to Providence. The weather was holding its own, seventy degrees and clear, sunny skies, not bad for September. We were on the road for about fifteen minutes when she asked, "What were you and Travis yelling about?"

I shot her a glance. "You heard?"

"Yes, I heard. What is going on?"

"You told me to be careful regarding Charles and his campaign, so that's what I'm doing. I don't want to say anything until I get more information, then I will tell you and your inquisitive daughter what I know. You'll just have to trust me."

"Fine, I won't pester you, but I can't speak for my daughter," Victoria said, as she winked at me and laughed.

For the rest of the trip, we chatted about Granny May and what this trust might be about, knowing her frugality and stubbornness. We made up theories on what was behind the trust and why it was so secretive. Nothing made sense.

We arrived in Providence. Victoria had called ahead and asked for a meeting with the manager, but we had time for a bite to eat and a bathroom break. We stopped at a small restaurant on Main Street and enjoyed bowls of clam chowder and shared lunch entrees of fish tacos and mushroom grilled cheese. Once we finished eating, Victoria went to the restroom to freshen up, and I met her at the car.

"You ready for this?" I asked.

"No," she said, "but I have to be."

We drove a few miles to the bank, parked, and went inside. The building was unremarkable, compared to the "Superman Building," also known as the Industrial National Bank. This bank was only three stories high, built with stone. I opened the metal-framed glass door for Victoria, and we entered a small marble lobby. If Victoria was nervous, she sure didn't look it.

The manager greeted us and appeared to be bothered by our presence. He ushered us to a small conference room, pulled out a chair, and hurriedly said, "Mrs. Lansing, I'm Paul Sullivan, manager of the bank. I understand Ekaterina Majewski-Robinson was your mother, correct? Please sit."

He looked at me, but before I could speak, Victoria said, "This is Jara Quinn, FBI and my assistant."

I nodded and sat down next to Victoria. I was instantly awed by how she took command. I could see where Katerina gets it.

"Mr. Sullivan," Victoria went on, "as you may know, my husband has decided to run for President. Upon my mother's death, we were informed she had taken out a trust here in Rhode Island. I wanted to meet with you in person, so you knew I wanted discretion. I want to know what my mother's trust was established for and who the beneficiary is."

Mr. Sullivan squirmed in his seat. I didn't think he was used to being told what to do. After a hard swallow, he reached for his laptop and began typing. "Mrs. Lansing, this was a living irrevocable trust. It is not in the public record."

"Mr. Sullivan," Victoria said a bit louder, "I am *not* the public. I'm the daughter of this trusts's creator and a senator's wife. I have a right to know about this trust. I do not want any money, but I do want to fulfill my mother's wishes."

Mr. Sullivan poured himself a glass of water from the insulated pitcher sitting in the middle of the table and took a large gulp.

"If I need to go to the board of directors," Victoria added, "or have Ms. Quinn here open an FBI investigation, it won't be pretty."

I poured myself a glass of water, trying not to show my surprise at her empty threat.

"Mrs. Lansing, none of that will be necessary. Your mother opened the record before she passed because she didn't want it in the will. She has terms here that upon her death, you could be informed of the beneficiary and to give you this key." Mr. Sullivan handed Victoria a small envelope. Inside was a small key, possibly to a safe deposit box.

"What does this key open, Mr. Sullivan?" Victoria inquired.

"I know it is for a box at a bank somewhere in Maryland or Washington DC, but that is all I know."

"And the name, Mr. Sullivan?" Victoria demanded.

"Uh, dependent Elizabeth S. Shaw, mother, Susan Shaw. An undisclosed deposit was made with payouts to be paid until Elizabeth was eighteen. Any remainder monies have been transferred out of this bank and to an offshore account which I have no access to."

"Is there an address for either of these women?" Victoria asked.

Sullivan shook his head. "No, ma'am. The rest of the information has been redacted."

Victoria stood up quickly and gave me a look that said we were done. I hurried to my feet and opened the conference door. She put the key in her purse and glared at the bank manager. "If I need more information, I'll be sure to contact you."

Mr. Sullivan followed us out the door.

When we reached the Defender, I opened Victoria's door. "Damn!" I said. "Look who's the scary, badass lawyer of the family."

Victoria flashed a devilish grin. "I *am* a badass, and yes I can be scary when it comes to my family."

I had just climbed into the driver's seat when Mr. Sullivan came running across the parking lot. "Mrs. Lansing! I need to give you this also." He handed me a sealed, worn manila envelope. "This is all I have. I swear." he said as he wiped perspiration from his forehead.

"Thank you," I said as I handed the envelope to Victoria and shut the driver's side door.

"Let's wait until we get home to open this," she said. "That way I won't have the urge to interrogate that poor man any further."

He did not know how lucky he was.

We drove back in silence. Victoria looked exhausted. When we pulled into the driveway, she spied the senator's Mercedes. "Oh my god! Charles is home. I hope he and Katerina didn't fight."

We were headed for the front door when Charles suddenly emerged. He looked at us and screamed, "I'm not sure what you all are up to, but if you ruin my bid for President, I'll—"

Victoria lunged toward her husband. "You'll do what, Charles? Don't threaten me. I've had about as much of your threats and accusations as I can handle. I should be accusing you of things. I know you are up to something, and I *will* figure it out. So don't fuck with me."

Charles stormed toward his car. "I'm going back to DC." He slammed his car door shut and sped off.

I helped Victoria inside and headed toward the den. Fires were lit there and on the portico. I put my laptop and the envelope down on the desk, got Victoria a glass of wine, and went out to the portico. Katerina was sitting there, rocks glass in hand, a bottle of tequila on the glass top coffee table.

Her eyes were a furious, wild green.

"Bad day?" I asked as I approached her cautiously.

"I'm so glad you're home." She jumped up, her eyes softening to jade pools, and hugged me. "He makes me so mad. Is he gone?"

"Yes, he was leaving when we arrived. Your mom is in the den, resting. She was a badass today."

Katerina's eyes widened and a crooked smile came over her face. "Oh, the manager got that Victoria, huh?"

"Yes, and your dad too." I shook my head and laughed. "Remind me never to get on your mom's bad side." I took a sip of Katerina's tequila and asked if there was anything I needed to do for dinner.

"Nope," she said. "It's all ready. Just resting in the oven."

Victoria walked out onto the porch. "Do we share first or eat?"

"Eat," we said in unison.

Katerina pulled out a succulent roast from the oven, with new potatoes, carrots, onions, and mushrooms. It looked and smelled heavenly. I couldn't get over the fact Katerina had actually cooked. I pulled down some plates as Victoria retrieved the silverware. I grabbed a beer, and we all sat at the island.

Katerina must have caught my disbelief, "Quit looking so surprised. I can cook when I want to. Internet recipes are an amazing thing."

Victoria took a couple bites and sighed. "I may be too tired to eat right now, but it tastes divine."

We all sat and picked at our food. Exhaustion hit me and I yawned.

"See if I cook anything for you two again," Katerina teased.

Victoria and I stumbled over excuses while Katerina put away the food.

"I don't have much of an appetite either since Dad stopped by," she said. "I don't even know what he wanted. It seemed like he knew I was here and stopped by to pick a fight. He's so frustrating."

We all grabbed our drinks and went out to the porch. The moon was stunning as it glistened off the water. I brought out two more glasses for tequila. Victoria passed, but I refilled Katerina and poured some for myself over ice.

"So is it time to share? Who goes first?" Katerina asked.

I shrugged. "I don't know any more on my mystery. I was too busy being driver and assistant for your mom."

Victoria said, laughing, "I wasn't that bad, was I?"

"Like I told Katerina when we got home," I said, "I never want to be on your bad side."

Victoria chuckled to herself and sat down. "I'll go first then," she said. "We got a name, or should I say names, for the beneficiary for the trust, Elizabeth S. Shaw and Susan Shaw. No address. I also got a key for a safe deposit box in DC or Maryland and a fancy envelope."

Katerina scrunched her face and frowned as she pulled a crumpled piece of paper from her pocket. "Well, I got the preliminary tox reports on Granny. There was a high amount of potassium in her system, but the coroner couldn't rule it as a homicide. He said when a person passes sometimes their potassium levels go exceedingly high, plus Granny was on potassium chloride for her heart. He also said he will start the autopsy tomorrow and contact me when all the tests are back." She looked at her mother. "He'll release the body at the end of the week."

Victoria nodded, took a deep breath, and let it out slowly. She closed her eyes, as she sat her glass of wine on the side table. Her face took on a sad, sullen look. As she opened her eyes. she gave us a small smile and asked, "Do you mind if I wait to share the envelope tomorrow? I think I need to read it by myself first."

"Victoria," I said, "this seems like a personal letter from Granny May to you. I'd be honored if you shared it tomorrow, but that will be all up to you...and Katerina of course."

Katerina said, "Take all the time you need. We'll be here."

Victoria teared up, stood, hugged us both, and wished us good night. "You two better not still be out here with an empty tequila bottle in the morning," she scolded as she took her glass and the envelope and headed upstairs.

"What do you think it says?" Katerina asked when her mother was out of earshot.

"I don't know, but I have a funny feeling your mom does." I took a long sip of tequila.

Katerina moved over to my lounge chair and leaned back against me. "God, I wish Granny was here. I miss her so much. All this mystery, she could have just told us."

"Maybe it wasn't her secret to share."

"Well, she made it her secret when she made that trust!"

I knew not to argue about this.

We finished our drinks and headed upstairs. Katerina came to my room and locked the door.

"Does your family know that every time I'm here, you sleep in my bed?"

"You complaining?" Katerina said as she took off her clothes.

"Uh no, just wondered what the family thinks. That's all."

"Mom doesn't care. She wants me to be happy, and she knows you make me happy. Dad only cares about himself and his position. And CJ and Chase, I don't think they even notice. You're part of the family. Now, have I answered all your questions?" She motioned for me to come closer. I let her slip off my shirt as she kissed me. I took off my pants and got into bed.

"I have to admit, I'm spoiled right now, coming home to you. I'd hate to see it end."

"Maybe it doesn't have to," she whispered.

We kissed for a while before we realized we were both too tired to do anything else. Katerina fell asleep quickly, so when I heard her soft, even breathing, I got out of bed, put on a shirt, and pants, and headed downstairs. I went to the den, turned on the desk lamp, and opened my laptop. I pulled up my secure government site and went to background checks to start a query on both Elizabeth S. Shaw and Sarah Miles, age thirty to thirty-eight, and an open-ended one for Susan Shaw. I watched for a while, but since it was a national search, it was going to take some time. I closed my laptop, turned off the light, and went back upstairs.

When I reached the top of the stairs, I heard Victoria's voice. "Oh, *Matka*, you didn't have to. I didn't need protection. *Matka*, I miss you so much."

I guessed she had read the letter. I opened my door to see Katerina sitting up in bed, the light from the fireplace shimmering off her face and breasts. I froze.

"I got cold, and you weren't here. I wasn't about to look for you, so I lit the fire, hoping I'd warm up." She glared. "What are you up to?"

I closed the door, took off my shirt, and climbed into bed.

"Excuse me, I asked you a question," Katerina said.

"Damn, I told you I had some work to do tonight. I remembered it after we went to bed. I'm sorry. You can be as mad at me as you want."

Katerina's eyes softened. "I'm sorry. I remember now. Are you sure you can't tell me anything?" She raised an eyebrow. "I have my ways of interrogation." She jumped on me and began kissing me.

"Do you do this with all your clients?" I asked. "No wonder you have such a win record."

We laughed and cuddled up under the covers. "Now, don't move out of this bed until I wake up," Katerina playfully threatened.

"Yes, ma'am!"

The next morning, I woke up with a weird feeling. Katerina was draped across me, sleeping soundly. I started to kiss her head, but something caught my eye, and I looked up: Victoria was sitting in the chair by the fireplace.

"Victoria!" I said, nearly jumping out of my skin. I nudged Katerina to try and wake her, while trying to nonchalantly pull up the covers. I looked down at Katerina, "Victoria, I'm...uh...I'm so sorry."

"Honey, it's okay. I miss being held," she said sweetly. Victoria's eyes were red and puffy. "I always told my daughter to fight for happiness," she went on, looking at me, "and I know she's happy with you. That makes me happy."

Katerina stirred and, still with her eyes shut, asked me, "Who are you talking to?" I nudged her again and she opened her eyes. "Mom?" she muttered sleepily, then sat straight up. "Mom! What are you doing in here? I, uh, we fell asleep talking and I..." She reached for my shirt and pulled it over her head.

"Oh honey, don't worry. I've known you were sleeping in here every time Jara came to visit, and sometimes after she left. Anyway, the door was unlocked," Victoria said. "I peeked in to see if anyone was awake. The fire was so inviting that I sat down and waited until you both woke up."

I pulled the covers tighter around me and sat up. I wasn't sure what to say.

Victoria went on. "I read the letter last night. *Matka* wrote it about a year after Katerina was born." She looked at her daughter lovingly. "She was so happy I had named you after her. But she felt she had to protect me, my feelings mostly, from

Charles. She wrote that she did some things to make sure I wasn't bothered or hurt by anything that Charles did or would do."

Katerina and I looked at each other, our eyes full of questions, but we stayed quiet and let her go on.

Victoria continued. "She wrote she was not letting anything happen to her *wnuczka* either, meaning you, Katerina. She had high hopes for you, and you didn't let her down. *Matka* didn't go into much detail. She wrote about the key, and said it was a bank she and my father used when they lived in Maryland. She never gave a name. I was hoping, Jara, that you could find what bank it was?"

"I'll do my best," I replied.

"Good! I'll let you girls go back to sleep, or whatever." She smiled. "I have some work to attend to myself." Victoria came over, kissed Katerina, and patted my hand. "I love you both so much."

"Love you, Mom," Katerina replied as she snuggled into me.

I sat there, dumbstruck, thinking about what was in the letter, my background search, and the fact that Victoria had just caught me in bed with her daughter. I had only been awake for half an hour, and already my head was buzzing with activity.

\

Chapter Nine

We both dozed off again for a couple hours and woke up around 9 a.m. The fall sun streamed through the room, its rays shimmering as they caught the drifting specks of dust. I reluctantly got out of bed and got dressed. Katerina was still sitting under the covers.

"Do you think you should go check on your mom?" I asked.

Katerina got up and pulled on a pair of my sweatpants. "Yeah, good idea. What are you going to do?"

I told her I was going to check my laptop and either start breakfast or run into town for some bagels and pastries.

"I'll look in on Mom and tell her about going into town, see if she needs anything. I'll meet you downstairs in a bit."

I kissed her on the cheek and headed downstairs. I made coffee first, then went into the den. I opened my laptop: seventy percent complete. Wow, it's going faster than I thought. Maybe I'd have some information by the afternoon. I heard footsteps on the stairs and Katerina appeared in the doorway. She came around behind me and hugged me around my neck. I had already closed the website window.

"How's your mom?"

Katerina kissed me on the head and sat on the couch. "I can't tell if she's happy or sad, tired or not feeling well. She asked for fresh fish and fruit from the market, I'm not sure what she's planning. We can take our coffee to go."

I filled two travel mugs for us and we headed to the car. We arrived at the local fish market just after it opened. Katerina ordered everything from salmon, halibut, and haddock to jumbo crab claws, shrimp, and oysters. Even threw in some calamari salad, sauces, and seasoning. She told them we would stop back to pick it up. We paid the bill and took off for a farmer's market. We found one outside of town and bought fruit, corn, red potatoes, and a few beautiful fall bouquets. On our way back to the fish market, we bought coffee refills and a huge box of bagels and pastries.

"Who all are we feeding?" I asked. "The whole town?"

Katerina laughed. "You know I like variety. I want what I want when I want it!"

I rolled my eyes and loaded the Defender. We stopped back by the fish market and loaded all the wrapped seafood. We had enough to feed us for at least a week. When we arrived back at the house, Victoria was in the kitchen, drinking coffee and reading the paper.

"I'm just checking to see if there are any more news stories about our family," she said.

"Is there one about a man scared shitless in Rhode Island?" I asked.

Victoria put down the paper as she chuckled. "Funny, very funny. I wasn't that mean."

We went outside and brought a few more armfuls of groceries in. Victoria's eyes grew as big as saucers as she watched us unload all the sacks. "I asked for fish and fruit, not the ocean and the orchard," Victoria said.

"I want us to be prepared for anything," Katerina retorted. "I guess no one appreciates my shopping methods."

I rolled my eyes again. "All we need now is the cow, the pig, and the chicken."

Katerina huffed and said, "Oh, I hit up the butcher yesterday."

We laughed as we finished putting away the food. Victoria took the flowers and arranged them in multiple vases, placing them all over the house.

I went into the den with a bagel, cinnamon sugar cream cheese, and my coffee. I logged into the laptop and saw the search was complete. Wow! They must have updated the system recently. *Now to start some cross referencing.* I inputted the parameters, "Elizabeth S. Shaw" and "Susan Shaw" being at the same location, and locations of "Sarah Miles," plus all known aliases. Katerina and Victoria walked into the den and sat on the couch.

"Any luck?" Katerina asked.

"Actually, yes, but I'm not ready to say anything yet."

"I wasn't talking about that exactly," Katerina teased and pointed to my shirt. "Any luck getting any food in your mouth?"

I looked down at the large lump of cream cheese and a coffee stain. "Very funny, I was actually saving this for later."

I started to get up to change when Victoria cleared her throat. "I've been wanting to speak with you both about something. I'm thinking about selling this house."

Katerina sat up. "What? Mom, no. This is our home. Where would you go? I don't want you to be alone, and I know you mentioned having Sarah move back in, but I'm not sure having her here is the right thing either. We don't really know much about her."

"Well, wouldn't you be more worried about me alone in this house? Your father is never home, and you two have your lives to live. You shouldn't have to babysit me. Although I do love having you both here. It makes it feel like a home again."

I spoke up. "I could stay longer, help Charles from here and help with the Foundation. I still have to go to DC for a bit to see how he wants to do this, that is, if he even still wants me to help."

"Don't forget," Victoria reminded me, "I need to know *Matka*'s DC or Maryland bank."

I pulled out my phone and texted Travis about getting this information.

***Do I have to do all your work for you? LOL*,** he texted back.

Unless you want me to get into trouble, yes, I do. :)

I walked up to my room to change when a notification popped up on my phone. I read the text. ***J–.Herbert and Burke Bank, Alexandria VA box 139. You really owe me now.–T***

I grabbed a notepad and pen from my laptop case.

"Victoria," I called out, writing down the address and heading for the stairs. I found her and Katerina in the kitchen. "I have the bank for you. Well, actually Travis got the bank for you. It wasn't in DC or Maryland. It's in Virginia." I gave Victoria the slip of paper.

"Wow, *Matka* really traveled around for her banking. Good to know. Thanks, Jara. And thank Travis for me also. When do you think I should go down there, and would either of you girls go with me?"

"Sure, I would. What are assistants for but to assist?" I teased.

We sat in the den and discussed all that still needed to get done. It was a long list. Victoria needed to go to DC to speak with Charles. "We have some things we need to discuss. I'm going to go upstairs and make some calls now. I'll be down for dinner."

Katerina was eerily quiet. "You okay?" I asked.

She nodded. "Yeah, just worried about Mom. I'm still not comfortable with her selling the house or Sarah moving in, but if that's what she wants…"

I thought about the information I had that said "Sarah Miles" didn't exist. Katerina would kill me if anything happened to her mother, and I hadn't told her everything I knew. My laptop dinged, notifying me that the cross-reference was complete. I logged into the site and scanned the results. Just like Travis had said, no Sarah Miles in that age range existed anywhere in the Midwest, East, or New England areas. But there was an "Elizabeth S. Shaw" and "Susan Shaw" who had lived in the DC area for sixteen years. After that, Elizabeth S. Shaw moved to Middletown, Connecticut. Now, this is getting interesting.

"Katerina, I need to tell you some things, but I'm not wanting to say anything to your mom yet."

"Now you have me worried."

I explained to her what Travis had found out about Sarah and what I had confirmed.

"I knew it. I knew there was something not right about her," she exclaimed. "What do we do now? She can't move in here."

I thought about it for a moment. "I suggest we tell Victoria tomorrow and let her decide. Maybe we let her move in and learn more about her."

Katerina's green eyes sparkled with tears. "Nothing can happen to my mom. She's been through so much."

I pulled her in my arms and let her cry. "Nothing will," I promised her.

We warmed up leftovers for dinner and dined *alfresco* on the veranda. It was hard not to discuss Sarah with Victoria. I could see Katerina was on edge, feeling that we should tell her. I made eye contact with her. What difference was a day?

"Victoria," I said, setting down my beer, "Katerina and I have something to discuss with you."

Katerina closed her eyes and let out a sigh of relief. "Mom," Katerina jumped in, wiping her mouth on a cocktail napkin, "we learned some things about Sarah."

Katerina explained what Travis and I researched. "She doesn't exist, Mom.'

Victoria indulged us for a while, not acting surprised or worried. When we finished, she said, "There has to be a reasonable explanation for this. If Sarah moves in, I'll ask her."

Katerina looked incredulous. "You are still thinking of letting her move back in here? Did you not hear what we just told you?"

"Yes, but I just have this feeling that this is the right thing to do," Victoria replied. "I can't explain it. Thank you, ladies, for a wonderful dinner. I'm going to finish up some Foundation work and head to bed." She hugged us both and went upstairs.

Katerina huffed. "What the hell is wrong with her? Is she losing her mind? Now we *will* have to move in here."

I slowly sipped my beer and let Katerina finish venting. "We have to trust Victoria and her decisions. She's a smart, tough woman. You know that. She's made her decision. Now we have to support her somehow." I got up and grabbed two glasses and a bottle of wine. "You coming?"

Katerina stared at me in disbelief. "How can you be so calm?"

"Because this is what I do, Katerina. I investigate and get the facts. If I'm not satisfied, I dig more until I get the truth. I have no control over where the investigation will take me. So whatever the outcome is, worrying about it gets me nowhere. I must have faith that I will make the right decisions when the time comes. And I drink." I paused. "So, you coming?"

Katerina narrowed her gaze. "How long have you been working on that speech? Damn!" She grabbed a glass and the bottle from my hand and headed toward the lower deck, where there was a nice outdoor sofa and a fire pit.

"So what else are you not telling me?" she asked after we sat down. The moon was low in the darkening sky.

"Not much, really. I'm doing searches and cross referencing on the names Mr. Sullivan gave us for the trust."

"And anything?"

I hesitated. "I found Elizabeth and Susan Shaw in the DC area for about sixteen years before Elizabeth moved to Connecticut for two years. I lost track of her after that. I'm going to dig some more tomorrow."

We sat quietly for a while, sipping our wine and watching the moonbeams dance across the water. "Did you ever want to run away and start over?" Katerina asked.

I thought for a moment. "And take Stats 102 again?"

"No, smartass! Make different decisions and be happy. Pretend there's nothing out there that can hurt us."

I put my glass down on the weathered plank table in front of us. "As long as you're in it with me, I'll run as far away as you want me to."

I woke up to a slight chill and bright light. We had fallen asleep under the stars. Someone had covered us up with a blanket. A big orange ball was rising over the water. For a moment I pretended Katerina and I were on the boat, sailing away from all this and heading into the sun. I kissed her on the head, and she stirred.

"Oh wow. I forgot how beautiful the sunrise is," she said. "What were you thinking about just now?"

I told her my boat thought.

She laughed and shook her head. "We both have a lot of avoidance fantasies."

We talked about what the rest of the week was going to look like. Katerina said she had to get back to Boston on Monday, then head down to DC to interview some of the immigrants who had showed up. We decided to coordinate our time and invite Victoria to go to the bank in Virginia. By then, Sarah may have moved in and hopefully, I would know what Charles actually wanted with me on his campaign. Perhaps I would have more information on the Shaws as well.

We got up, and I folded the blanket while Katerina collected our glasses.

"Whoops, no wonder we slept so well," she said, showing me a couple of empty bottles.

We laughed like schoolgirls who had gotten something over on our parents. We went to the kitchen, still laughing. Victoria was seated at the kitchen island.

She looked at us, her eyes twinkling. "Oh, to be young again."

"I'm not feeling so young right now," I said as the first twinges of a red wine hangover hit me.

"It's okay. Why don't you girls go back to sleep or whatever while I look over more of these papers from the Foundation," Victoria asked. "Then I can tell you what my plans are for the rest of the week."

We all made our way upstairs, Victoria heading to her room and Katerina and I to mine.

Victoria paused in the hallway, grinning. "Oh, and by the way, girls, no need to lock the door. All is good."

Katerina and I slept until noon. I awoke to her kiss. "I'm going to make a few calls for work," she said as she got up and threw on her sweats.

She slipped out and I stayed in bed. I could get used to this. I got out my phone and called Travis.

"You sound happy," he said. "What are you getting yourself into now?"

I told him about Katerina and the info I found on the Shaws. "I'm going to do a deeper dive," I said. "I'm going to run obituaries, school records, and maybe hop on a genealogy site or two." I told him that we had informed Victoria about Sarah, but she was still considering moving her in.

I could hear the concern in his voice as he said, "It's like the old saying, 'Keep your friends close, but your enemies closer.'"

After I hung up, I got out of bed, showered, and changed clothes. Katerina was in the den, interrogating someone over the phone while typing emails and drinking coffee. Talk about multitasking. I headed into the kitchen and rummaged around until I found what I wanted. I pulled out a griddle and made bacon, basil, and tomato sandwiches with a slice of fresh mozzarella, sea salt, and aged balsamic vinegar on the side.

Victoria walked into the kitchen. "I see we have a new chef in the house."

I had always loved to cook but rarely had time, and cooking for one was no fun. Victoria called out for Katerina to join us.

"Ooh, one of my favorites," Katerina said as she walked up and kissed me on the cheek.

As we sat down to eat, Victoria announced, "I'm going to postpone the move-in date for Sarah."

Katerina and I looked at each other as Victoria went on, "Beginning of next week, I'm going to do some tidying up at the Foundation, then head down to DC and have dinner with Charles. I called him last night and told him we needed a strategy if he's serious about this election. Maybe I'll learn of his true intentions." She took another bite of her lunch. "I still plan to have Sarah move here, but I don't want her to have to be in this big old house alone right after moving in. I'll let you know what Charles intends."

We told her we also were going to DC the following weekend and after her meeting with Charles, she should come to CJ's.

"That's a splendid idea," Victoria said. "I'll call CJ and let him know. It'll be nice to see his family again."

"Sounds like a plan, Mom," Katerina said. "Jara and I will be there on Saturday. If Dad behaves himself, maybe he could come to dinner on Sunday. CJ is going to *love* this."

We all laughed, thinking of CJ trying to host all of us.

"I'll warn him of our arrival," Victoria said, still chuckling. Her phone rang, and she left the room as she answered it. Minutes later, she reappeared with a concerned look.

"They're releasing *Matka*'s body today. I want to have a memorial service for the public, but something small just for the family," Victoria said. "I'm going to the funeral home now to make the arrangements. I also called our family lawyer, William Maxwell, who is the executor of the will. He said he's filed the will with the court and will have everything sorted out by spring. I guess there were a lot of things to settle with the estate. I told him about the trust and the safe deposit box. He said *Matka* had some things in her will that she requested be given to us in person, so we'll be having a meeting with him in a couple of weeks. He also said Charles and another lawyer called him about his portion of the inheritance and asked if Charles could take an advance on his. He warned me Charles is terribly angry because, as far as Mr. Maxwell can tell, there is no inheritance for him. *Matka* cut him out completely."

"Wow, that's why he was so mad the other day," Katerina said. "It makes sense now."

"Charles may contest the will," Victoria said, "but Mr. Maxwell isn't sure. If he does, I'll be notified."

"Mom, do you want me to go with you to the funeral home?"

"No, sweetheart, I'll be fine. I think I need to do this alone." Victoria headed upstairs.

Chapter Ten

The family planned a memorial service for Granny May for mid-October, and we postponed the DC trip. The memorial was held at the family estate on the grounds by the garden, overlooking the water. Granny had loved October; the trees were turning, a briskness was in the air, and according to her, it was 'sweater weather,' which made everyone look good. Of course, I followed Granny's wisdom and wore a sweater and black slacks. Katerina, on the other hand, wore a mid-length black velvet dress, with long sleeves, a cinched waist, and pearls. Granny would have been pleased.

One by one, the family trickled in, their footsteps echoing through the halls as they made their way to their respective rooms. First to arrive was CJ, his wife Julia, and their child, Calvin. They entered with tired smiles, their journey from DC having taken its toll. With practiced efficiency, they unpacked their bags and settled in. CJ retreated to the den after unpacking, opened his laptop, and began working.

Shortly after, Chase arrived with a new girlfriend, Abby, their laughter echoing through the foyer as they made their way upstairs. Katerina rolled her eyes at the fact Chase had brought yet another girlfriend home. Chase and Abby disappeared into their rooms without a word, leaving a trail of scattered belongings in their wake. Chase was what people called a "professional student." At nearly thirty, he had yet to earn a degree at NYU, though he had many majors. Nothing seemed to keep his interest for long, including girlfriends.

Chase made his way back downstairs and straight to the kitchen. His eyes lit up at the sight of the spread on the kitchen island and table. Without a second thought, he reached for a handful of food and a bottle of wine meant for the upcoming memorial, removing the cork with a satisfying *pop* before taking a long swig straight from the bottle.

Katerina and I had just entered the kitchen, and her expression darkened at the sight of her brother's self-indulgence. "Chase, what do you think you're doing?" she scolded, her voice sharp with disapproval. "That's meant for the memorial. Have some respect."

Chase shrugged, his carefree demeanor unchanged. "Relax, Kat," he replied. "Hey Jara," he said casually before taking another sip from the bottle.

Katerina's eyes flared with anger, and I backed away.

"You're acting like a pig," she snapped, her frustration bubbling to the surface. "When are you going to grow up and start taking things seriously? We need help setting up the memorial."

"You mean like, how much CJ is helping out? Mr. Serious in there can't step away from his precious laptop to help, so why are you bitching at just me?" Chase replied sarcastically.

As Katerina's frustration reached its boiling point, her voice cracked. "Can't you see?" she cried, her words echoing through the room. "We're supposed to be here for each other, helping each other, not acting as if this is just another party."

CJ emerged from the den, his brow furrowed. "I'm sorry," he murmured, his voice soft with regret. "I was just trying to get some work done before a deadline. *Some* people have jobs and responsibilities." He glared at Chase.

"Hey, I have responsibilities," Chase said, as he put down the wine bottle.

CJ rolled his eyes and huffed.

Katerina, her eyes brimming with tears, shook her head. "Stop it, both of you. It's not about work, CJ. It's about being present, about being here for each other when it matters most."

I took Katerina's hand and coaxed her out of the kitchen. The last thing their mother needed at this time was to hear her children fighting. We walked around the grounds, checking the tents that had been set up for the memorial, and made our way to the garden. We found a recently painted wrought iron bench in the shade. Its stark white color contrasted against the colorful blooms and green ivy.

"Kat, let's sit for a bit, away from the chaos," I urged, walking toward the bench. "It's already been a long day, and it's just getting started." I leaned back, the surprising coolness of the metal feeling good against my back.

Katerina rubbed her eyes again and sat beside me. "I'm so angry right now. Can't my brothers think of anyone but themselves? CJ, uber-responsible, and Chase, the total opposite, they drive me nuts."

"Kat, everyone deals with grief differently. Maybe this is how they handle it. Give them a break."

Katerina yanked her hand from mine and turned to me with her piercing green eyes. "Whose side are you on?"

I put up my hands in protest. "Kat, please, I'm not on anyone's side. This isn't a battle. Be glad your brothers are here, even if they only show up for the memorial."

Katerina heaved a long sigh. "I didn't think losing Granny would be this hard. My nerves are shot, and I'm exhausted. Maybe I'm letting them get to me a bit too much." She retook my hand and squeezed it. "At least you're here."

I brought her hand to my lips and kissed it softly. We sat quietly until we heard more people arriving. "I guess we better get back," I said, starting to stand. Katerina pulled me back down.

"No," she whispered, "let's stay a little longer." Her eyes welled with tears. "You know I was named after Granny May."

I remembered Victoria mentioning this recently.

"Granny's full name was Ekaterina Anastasia Majewski-Robinson. Mom has the middle name Anastasia, but I got the first." She smiled, and her eyes sparkled. "It wasn't until I was older that I dropped the E, but Granny was okay with that. She told me, 'You need to be your own person but still have the best of me.' I'm going to miss her so much." We sat for a little while longer until Katerina wiped her eyes, stood up, and straightened out her dress. "Okay, I'm ready."

We walked back to the house and went through the French doors to the kitchen. Victoria and the boys were standing by the island. Victoria was crying, and CJ had his arm around her.

"What happened?" Katerina asked, looking from one then to another.

Chase answered first. "Sorry, sis. Ya know, about before."

Katerina nodded and looked at her mother. "Fine, but what's this?"

"Oh, it's Dad being an ass," Chase replied. "He came in and, instead of being supportive, the first thing out of his mouth was about the will. What a callous piece of—"

"Chase," Victoria scolded. "He's your father."

"But he is, Mom," CJ shot back. "He has always treated us like crap, like we were beneath him, and you know it. The only person he seemed to tolerate was Kat."

"Oh, please," Katerina hissed.

"ENOUGH!" Victoria yelled. "We're not letting your father or anyone else ruin this memorial for *Matka*. Got it?" She pulled away from CJ, blotted her eyes with a crumpled tissue, and stood up straight. "We have guests, and we need to act accordingly."

We all stood in silence, letting Victoria's words sink in. Granny would have been the first person to agree, even though she thought Charles was an ass too.

A massive turnout of people came to pay their condolences. Granny May was much loved by her community, family, and friends. A picture of her and the family was placed on a long table on the back portico. Granny's favorite music played softly, and even though it was October, the garden was overflowing with fresh blooms, as if it were paying its respects too. Granny would have loved it.

"*Matka* always loved sitting out here," Victoria said in her eulogy, "watching the sailboats come into the harbor. It was one of her favorite places. Her parents made sure that when they built this house, at almost every angle, you could see the water. And the garden," Victoria wiped a tear, "*Matka* said she helped work in the garden for as long as she remembered. Initially it was for food, which was hard to come by during WWII, but her family made it work. Now it's a picturesque flower garden, with species from all around the world. She wanted to remember where her family came from and all the other families they helped."

Victoria told more stories and asked the people present for their participation. More than twenty people stood and said something. Some of it was sad, but for the most part they were funny. The overall feeling was how giving and warmhearted she was. The rest of the family also told a story or two about Granny. When they finished, I didn't think there was one dry eye, except maybe for Charles, who of course didn't speak.

After the ceremony, Katerina walked up and gave me a hug. "I can't believe so many people came today."

"How is Victoria doing? I've hardly seen her in this crowd."

Katerina sighed and said her mother was holding up very well, considering. "I haven't spoken to Dad since we received the order for the autopsy. I'm not sure why he was so against it."

Her father had been cold and stoic throughout the memorial-planning process. He kept saying it was a waste of time and money. I wasn't sure why he even bothered to come. During the memorial, I noticed the senator seemed preoccupied, talking to a group of gentlemen who no one else seemed to know. One man in particular had a high and tight haircut and carried himself like a military man. At one point both this man and Charles' voice became loud, with both men wildly gesturing. I was going to go break it up, but Charles shouted for him to get out. As he was leaving, he pointed at Brian and mouthed something unintelligible. I was on my way to see if Charles was all right when Katerina took my arm and walked me over to Victoria. She was standing with Sarah and Brian. Was he saying something to Brian or Victoria?

I stood by Brian and tried to gauge his reaction to the scene. He stood stoic and unemotional. Had he also been in the military? "Brian," I said, interrupting Victoria, "did you know that man who was yelling with Charles?"

Brian sniffed, twisted his head then stood up straight. "No, ma'am, can't say as I do. Why do you ask?"

"He seemed very angry with the senator, then pointed at you. I was just curious as to why."

"I wouldn't know, ma'am. I don't know the senator and anyway, he and I don't run with the same people."

I started to ask some more questions when Victoria interrupted, shooting me with a sharp look. "Jara, everything is fine. Charles has a lot of people mad at him right now, myself included. Please don't pay it much mind."

"Yes, ma'am." I nodded and stepped back to watch the senator some more.

Victoria continued speaking with Brian and Sarah. "I wanted to thank you both for all that you did for *Matka*. She liked you both very much, even if she didn't show it all the time."

"If you need anything, Mrs. Lansing, I'll be happy to help," Sarah offered.

Victoria thanked her and gave her a hug. "You'll both receive six months' severance pay and recommendations," she assured them.

They thanked her and turned to leave. Brian pulled Katerina aside. "I know this may seem insensitive, but Mrs. Robinson had said she may leave me something in her will. Do you have any idea when that may be available?"

Katerina's mouth was agape as her eyes darkened to mossy green. I stepped in front of her and faced Brian. "Uh, Brian, I don't think this is the time or the place to be asking about that. Granny May just passed. When the family knows something, and the lawyers figure everything out, people will be notified if they are in the will."

He shrugged nonchalantly. "I was only wondering."

He walked off toward the refreshment table. Sarah broke off and went over to Charles, gave him a brief hug, and returned to Brian's side.

Katerina snorted. "I didn't think she even liked Dad. Things keep getting stranger and stranger."

"Yes they do. Did you hear Brian say he didn't know your father?"

"Yes, why?"

"Wasn't it the senator that hired him for Granny?"

Katerina got a puzzled look on her face. "You know, you're right," she said, nodding her head. "He was Granny's eye candy, as she called it."

I looked back at the senator and noticed he was glaring at me. Something was not right.

Katerina knocked me out of my daze and asked, "You're staying at the house with us, aren't you?"

"Sure," I said. "I wouldn't be anywhere else."

By late afternoon, the crowd was thinning, and the catering staff was cleaning up. Katerina and I picked up memorials and flowers placed by Granny's picture. Charles was talking with CJ and Chase over by the pool. CJ appeared to be paying more attention to his son, Calvin, who was running around the pool, searching for tree frogs, than to what Charles was talking about. Chase had an obvious look of disgust on his face.

Victoria, Katerina, and I sat on the veranda as the catering crew finished. Charles and the boys came and joined us.

"Sorry, Mom," CJ said, "but we're going to head back home to DC. I need to be in the office early in the morning."

Chase also said he had to get back to school. The boys hugged Victoria and said their goodbyes to me and Katerina. Both again told Katerina they were sorry.

"No worries, guys." She smiled. "I may have overreacted a little. Love you."

Charles shifted from one foot to the other. "I can stay if you want me to, I guess."

Victoria waved him off. "Don't stay on my account, Charles. I'll be fine. The girls are staying with me."

The senator glanced over at me. "Fine, fine, then. I'll head back to DC too. Have meetings this week and such...and Jara, I haven't forgotten. We still need to talk."

"Yes, sir, we do. Do you happen to have a quick moment now?"

"Uhh, yes, sure, I have a moment." He leaned over and tried to give Victoria a kiss on the cheek, but she pulled away. "Okay, then," he said, clearing his throat. "I'll be in touch."

I followed him through the kitchen and into the foyer. "Sir," I said, raising my voice, "I need to ask you a couple of things if you don't mind."

"Fine, what is it? I need to get back to DC." He put on his coat and headed toward the door.

"Sir, that man who was here, may I ask who he was?"

"You may ask, but really it isn't any of your business now, is it?" he asked gruffly.

"Well yes, sir, it is. Especially if you still want my help with your campaign. If not..." I turned and started to walk away when he grabbed my arm. I flipped around on him and yanked my arm loose. "Senator," I said.

"I'm sorry, I'm sorry." He pulled his hand back and changed his composure like a chameleon. In a sickly-sweet tone, he said, "You have to understand I'm under a lot of pressure right now and I..."

He never finished his sentence, so I repeated myself. "Sir, who was that man?"

The senator hemmed and hawed at first. "He's an ex-military officer. He blames me for being kicked out of the service. That's why he was so angry."

I listened to what he said, but since I knew that couldn't be all there was to it, I pushed on.

"Sir, why did he come here of all places. Why not speak with you at your office?"

"I don't know," he shouted. "Why do crazy people do anything they do?"

"How long ago was he discharged?"

"Quinn, leave it be. It's not a big deal. Are we done here?"

He had never called me by my last name before. "Well, sir, are we?"

"About this we are. Like I said, leave it alone," he said sternly. "I'll call you about the campaign next week." He pushed past me and out the door. I didn't follow.

I walked back into the kitchen and composed myself. When someone yelled at me to leave something alone, that was usually the last thing I did. I wanted to go to my laptop and start digging, but I heard laughter coming from the porch. I grabbed a bottle of chardonnay for Victoria and Katerina and a beer for myself. We sat quietly as dusk rolled in until we could no longer see the boats on the water.

Out of the blue, Victoria started laughing.

"Mom?" Katerina said, looking at her mother with bewilderment.

Victoria was laughing so hard she was crying. "I'm sorry, girls. I was thinking of *Matka*, always pointing and shaking her cane at Charles. There were a few times I thought she was going to hit him with it."

Victoria looked over at Katerina. "Did I ever tell you about my wedding day?" Both of us shook our heads. "Well, *Matka* always had a dislike for Charles, as you know. She said he had a handshake like a limp fish, and you couldn't trust a man who couldn't shake hands. So at the wedding, *Matka* sat in the front row with her cane. Even then she had one. I think she used it more as a scepter though than a cane. She sat and glared at him. During the vows, you could hear her cane tapping on the floor of the church. We made a deal that the vow to honor and obey was left out because I knew *Matka* would blow her top. When the priest started that vow by mistake, *Matka*'s cane hit the floor so hard everyone jumped, including Charles. Needless to say the priest backtracked quickly and moved on. I, though, made the smart move of removing the question, 'Should anyone present know of any reason that this couple should not be joined...' After the wedding, I saw she had Charles cornered. His face had a look of utter terror, and she kept poking him in the chest with that cane. Luckily, the priest broke that up."

Katerina and I were laughing, picturing a petrified Charles being held by a little lady over a foot shorter than him.

I spoke up. "I remember the first time I met Granny. I came to the house on spring break with Katerina. We had just pulled up when I saw this small woman with a cane—you're right about the scepter by the way—staring at us. Katerina jumped out of the car and hugged her, while I got out slowly and grabbed our bags."

"As I was almost to the front door, this larger-than-life voice came out of that little body." I pulled out my best Granny impression. 'You her servant?'

"'No ma'am.

"'Then quit acting like one. My grandchildren can get their own bags.'

"I dropped the bags and stood dumbfounded, not knowing what to do. She raised her cane and guided me to the garden, where she took my arm and showed me her budding flowers. I remember I addressed her as Mrs. Robinson, and she let out a huge laugh.

"'Girl, Mrs. Robinson is in the movies. I'm real life. Call me Granny, that is if you plan on being around my granddaughter.'

"I was shocked but answered, 'Okay Granny.'

"She then began pelting me with questions about my family, school, you," I said, taking Katerina's hand, "and without saying it, let me know I would be in big trouble if I ever hurt you. She also told me if I was to fit into this family, I would need to honor mine and become the best person I could be." Tears were rolling down my face by now, my voice choking up. "I hope I made her proud."

Katerina squeezed my hand. "I never knew she did that. I wondered where you were when I came back to the car."

"*Matka*, always protecting the ones she loved." Victoria raised her glass again. "To *Matka*, the protector of the flock." We all took a drink and sat in silence for a while.

Victoria finally said, "Well, it looks like I'll be running the Foundation now, at least temporarily. There is a lot of paperwork to get done, plus those financials to check over."

"I'll pull more boxes out and try to separate things for you."

"Thanks, dear. It's been a long day and overall, I think *Matka* would have liked it," Victoria said with a bittersweet smile. "I need to get some rest. As *Matka* always said, 'There's still work left to be done.' I wonder if I should start carrying her cane?" We all laughed as Victoria excused herself and left the porch.

Katerina and I were both fighting off yawns, so we decided to turn in also. After we went upstairs, I slipped out and texted Travis about the day's events. I could hear Victoria sobbing in her room. She was finally allowing herself to grieve. I had a hard time falling asleep, still having a gut feeling something wasn't right.

Katerina tossed and turned before she sat up straight in bed and looked at me. "I can't believe my dad. Greedy bastard! All he cares about is money and popularity. He should have known

Granny wasn't going to put him in the will...but to cut him off completely, wow, that's bold."

I reached up to touch her back, but she pulled away. "This family frustrates the hell out of me," she said, fuming. "My dad is an asshole, and my brothers act as if they can't be bothered to help with Granny's stuff. Then there's Granny and all her secrets she left us. I just want to give up." She started to cry again. "What did my dad say to you?"

I decided to keep this one to myself until I learned more. "We talked about the campaign. He's going to call me next week."

Katerina flopped back down on the bed and curled into me. "Lucky you."

Chapter Eleven

Monday came early; I was exhausted from Granny's memorial but couldn't let my interaction with Charles leave my mind. What bugged me about the military man Charles was arguing with? Why be so angry and secretive about it? I decided to spend some time on the boat. In the past I'd done some of my best thinking there. Katerina was back at the desk in the den, working diligently. I walked behind her, putting my hands on her shoulders, and gave her a kiss on the head.

"I'm going out to the boat to do some thinking."

Katerina looked up at me and smiled. "Okay. I may come out in a little bit if you don't mind. I think I need some fresh air."

I kissed her again and made my way to the boat, grabbing a bottle of water on the way. I climbed aboard and sat on the bow, watching the sailboats go in and out of the harbor. *What's really going on? Granny May was mad enough at Charles to leave him nothing, but she created a trust for someone no one in the family knows about.*

"Granny, what are you up to?" I said out loud.

I stood up and started checking all the sails and riggings, making sure I had put them away correctly. I thought about my hornets, kind of missing them. It's only in their nature to do what they were doing, building a hive and encroaching on my world. *Does everything have to have a reason or purpose behind it? Do we really have a choice in our actions?* My thoughts were racing when my phone rang.

"This is Jara Quinn."

A familiar voice with a thick accent said, "Jara? This is Bella from Senator Lansing's office. He wanted me to call and confirm you will be at his office a week from Monday."

"Hi, Bella. Yes, I plan on being there. I wasn't sure if the senator still wanted me to help. I was going to call later to confirm."

"Of course he does! He was very adamant that I call you to get your confirmation. Why would you think he wouldn't?"

"Oh, it's nothing," I lied. "I haven't talked with him for a while, so I didn't know."

"Don't be silly. I have you down for Monday, then. Looking forward to seeing you, Jara."

I hung up. So, Charles was "adamant" about me coming there?

Katerina appeared on the dock. She boarded the boat and handed me a beer. "Mom left, said she would probably be late tonight and not to wait on dinner."

I nodded, took a sip of beer, and said, "Guess who just called me? Your father, well actually, it was Bella. She was making sure I was going to meet him in DC."

"Speak of the devil, huh?" Katerina replied. We sat on the boat for a while, drinking and telling more stories about Granny May.

"Well, the boat looks good, ready anytime we want to sail away," I announced.

"The captain has declared her seaworthy," Katerina said, as she motioned for me to join her. "C'mon, captain, let's finish going through Granny's boxes." We laughed and held hands as we walked back to the house. This to me was heaven. Beautiful day, beautiful scenery, and the most beautiful woman holding my hand. We walked slowly, giggling and kissing along the way, savoring every moment of this alone time.

We walked into the kitchen and Katerina's phone rang. She looked at the screen. "It's the medical examiner." She stepped out of the room and took the call. A few minutes later, she found me in the den, poring over more papers. "He said it could be up to twelve weeks before he gets all the tests back. They need to run some in-depth tests that take a while." Frustration exuded from her. "I'm glad they are finally taking this seriously, but it's going to be a long winter."

I took her hand. "What if I stayed here this winter? It only makes sense. I can keep an eye on your mom and deal with your dad at the same time."

Katerina squeezed my hand. "Really? Mom would love that! I'm not sure where I'll be and how long this case is going to last, if it ever starts, but that would be great. I'm so glad you brought this up." She beamed. "I wanted to talk to you about all that, winter plans and all."

"Sure, let's finish up here and go relax."

While I went to the kitchen, Katerina went to the wine cellar and returned with a couple cases. "There, that should do it," she said, setting the cases on the counter. She grabbed a bottle of wine and a beer for me, and we went out to the veranda.

"This is one of my favorite spots," I said. "I'm just missing my hornets."

"Hey now, you still have me, and I don't sting much," she said as she giggled. "What are you complaining about?"

"Most definitely not complaining, feeling very lucky actually."

Katerina poked me in my ribs. "You better! That's something I wanted to ask you about." She looked at me earnestly. "Is what we have right now a situation of convenience, or something we should cultivate?"

I opened my mouth to respond, but she interrupted me.

"I've never felt as happy, safe, and comfortable as I do now. Like at the Penthouse. It was so hard to leave there. I don't want this to end and move on like we did after college. But I have no idea what that even looks like." She took a sip of wine and continued. "You haven't even been to my place in Boston. Where would we live? What—"

I set aside my beer and kissed her deeply. When our lips parted, I said, "I don't want this to end either. We don't have to make a concrete plan. I'm in love with you. I have been ever since college, and now we've come back together. I'm not letting you go easily. I'll go wherever you are." I kissed her again.

"I'm in love with you too. I wasn't sure how you felt...I said I love you the other night and you didn't respond. I figured maybe you were here just helping a friend."

I looked deep in her sparkling eyes. "I wanted to say something, but I didn't want it to sound like an auto response. I do love you with every ounce of my being, but I was scared too. I wanted you to be sure this is what you want."

A tear escaped Katerina's eyes. "I'm sure. I never thought I could be this happy. It was horrible in grad school. I was heartsick, so I busied myself as much as I could and started my career. I feel so complete with us together." Full tears fell, as she grabbed me and put her head on my shoulder.

"Well, if we're at the crying-about-it stage, it better be love."

"Smart ass," she said as she cuddled into me.

The evening began with the promise of a sumptuous dinner and lively conversation. Katerina and I were still cuddled on the outdoor couch when the sound of pots and pans banging around in the kitchen caught our attention.

We both jumped up and ran in to see what was happening. As we entered the kitchen, our eyes fell upon Victoria, standing at the stove with a pot in her hand, her shoulders slumped in defeat. She startled at our presence, her eyes rimmed in red and swollen from tears.

"Mom, are you okay?" Katerina asked.

Victoria looked up, her face flushed. "No, I'm not okay," she replied, her voice trembling with emotion. "I just received a letter from the bank. Charles is trying to take out a loan against the house to fund his campaign. I called him to ask what this was about, and he had the audacity to tell me that he felt he was owed something from the family. As if he has any right to jeopardize our home for his own selfish gain."

As Victoria's words echoed in my mind, puzzlement settled over me like a thick fog. Why would Charles, with his seemingly endless network of connections and contributors, resort to such drastic measures to fund his campaign? It didn't quite add up, and I couldn't shake the feeling that there was more to this situation than met the eye.

"Victoria," I said, "was he able to get the loan? Can he even do that?"

Victoria's gaze met mine, her expression a mix of frustration and resignation. "The house is technically in *Matka*'s name," she explained, her voice tinged with bitterness. "And since the will hasn't been finalized, it's only assumed that the property would go to me and my family. Charles sees it as his inheritance, and he's willing to do whatever it takes to get his hands on it."

As her words sank in, a sense of unease settled over me. Without the legal documentation to solidify Victoria's rightful ownership of the house, Charles may indeed have the authority to take out a loan against the property, regardless of the repercussions it would have on the rest of the family.

"Mom, he can't...he wouldn't..." Katerina took the pot from Victoria's hand and set it on the counter. "I can't believe he would purposely do anything to harm us."

Victoria's usually poised demeanor crumbled before our eyes as she pulled out a kitchen chair and sank into it. With a heavy sigh, she buried her face in her hands, her shoulders trembling with silent sobs.

The sight of Victoria in such distress was jarring. A sense of helplessness washed over me, compounded with my own feelings of confusion and frustration.

"I don't know," Victoria's voice was muffled by her hands, her words barely audible through her tears. "I don't think I know your father anymore. Something has changed in him." As she spoke, her words resonated with a profound sense of betrayal, as if the very foundation of her world had been shaken to its core.

"He's always been ambitious," she said, "but to be this ruthless and uncaring...I don't understand him anymore."

As Victoria sat, broken and vulnerable, I couldn't help but feel a surge of empathy. I had never seen her in such a state. It was clear that she was mourning the loss of the man she thought she knew.

The weight of her words settled over me. I knew that we were all grappling with the same harsh truth: sometimes, the people we love the most were the ones capable of causing us the greatest pain.

I found myself mechanically putting away the pots and pans in the kitchen. As I worked, my mind raced with a whirlwind of emotions, each one vying for my attention and threatening to overwhelm me. Anger, frustration, and sadness mingled together in a tangled web. I knew I couldn't change the circumstances that had brought us to this point, but I could do something to ease the burden of those around me, if only in a small way. With a newfound sense of purpose, I turned my attention to the task of preparing dinner. I knew, deep down, that none of us really had an appetite, but I felt an innate need to do something, anything.

Rummaging through the pantry and refrigerator, I gathered ingredients with urgency, my hands moving with a sense of purpose, as I set about preparing a meal. As the kitchen filled with tantalizing aromas, a small sense of satisfaction washed over me. I had found solace and purpose, a way to channel my energy into something constructive.

As the evening sun dipped below the horizon, I put the finishing touches on the dinner I had prepared and plated the final dish. Katerina and Victoria had quietly joined me in the task of setting the table.

We gathered our plates and made our way outside to the veranda, where the soft glow of candlelight danced across the glass dining table's surface. The air was cool and crisp, infused with the distinct scent of fall, as the last few leaves rustled in the gentle breeze.

As we settled into our chairs to eat, a comfortable silence enveloped us, broken only by the sound of our utensils clinking against our plates. And then, as if sensing the weight of unspoken thoughts, Victoria opened up.

"Thank you, girls, for being here," she said, her voice soft but filled with gratitude. "I know this hasn't been easy for any of us, but having you here with me means more to me than words can say."

Katerina and I exchanged glances, and she gave me a slight nod. I explained to Victoria my plan to close my place for the winter and stay here. "If you don't mind?"

Relief washed over her.

She sat up and took a deep breath. "I think I'll go to the bank tomorrow and get this straightened out about the property," she said. "And I informed Charles that I would be in DC on Thursday to talk this out."

"Sounds like a good plan, Mom," Katerina said, picking up her wine glass. "I'm going to Boston tomorrow. I have to work on more trial prep. Jara, you're going home to say goodbye to your hornets, right?"

Victoria had a quizzical look on her face. "Hornets?"

I laughed. "Yes, they decided to move in on me, building quite the nest. It looks like they are staying for a while. I hope they're enjoying it."

Victoria nodded, her eyes manifesting a faraway gaze. "Thinking about it, these past few months have been like living in a hornet's nest." Her eyes darkened with warning. "Just wait, Jara. The hornets may seem benevolent now, but they will sting you. It's in their nature."

Chapter Twelve

The next morning, we all went our separate ways: Victoria to the bank and Foundation, Katerina to Boston, and me to my place. It was sad to leave, but I had some work to do without distraction.

When I got home, I opened the windows to air out the house and went on my balcony. The bees were still there. I greeted them, telling them I would be gone for a while, but winter was coming so they probably needed somewhere warmer to stay. Where did bees go during wintertime anyway?

I grabbed my laptop and a beer and started a new search: "Sarah Miles, Duke University, Nursing School, class of 2006 to 2012." There were a few Sarahs, a few Miles, but no Sarah Miles. I widened the search from 2000 to 2015. No Sarah Miles, but there was a Sarah Shaw, class 2001 to 2005. I tried to pull up the yearbook, but it was unavailable. I made a note to contact the school and see if I could get a copy of the nursing graduation picture. That might tell me something.

The next search I did was dishonorable discharges from the past ten years. There were more than I could have imagined, so I decided to narrow the search to any involving Senator Charles Lansing. Eleven popped up, all from the same unit. Most of the information was redacted, but from what I could read, this unit completed an unauthorized mission and it involved civilian casualties. Charles was the head of a senate subcommittee that ordered their discharge. The leader of the unit was Navy SEAL Commander Marcus Montgomery. I searched for his name, and when the results appeared, I almost knocked over my beer. It was the same man that was arguing with Charles at the memorial. I searched for more information and only found watered down news stories.

I decided to do a deep dive on Marcus Montgomery. Granted, it was out of my purview with the FBI, but I did it anyway. As the results appeared, my phone buzzed notifying me I had a text message. It was a blocked number.

The text read, ***Stop your search. You have no jurisdiction here.***

At the same time a message popped up on my computer. ***WARNING UNAUTHORIZED SEARCH DETECTED. Access to this information is prohibited under Title 18***

US Code 1030. Your activity has been logged. Cease all further searches immediately. DO NOT attempt to bypass security protocols.

I immediately shut down my computer, but I decided to respond to the text. **Who is this?**

That doesn't matter. For your safety, leave this alone.

Why?

My text was undeliverable.

I sat in shock, staring at the phone in my hand. The buzzing in my mind was almost deafening. I definitely tapped the hornet's nest this time. I wondered what would happen if I hit the damn thing like a piñata...what would fall out?

The next few days I spent winterizing the house and doing more computer searches. I received a call from Victoria, who was concerned about more irregularities in the Foundation's banking.

"You're not going to go scare anyone again, are you?" I asked, trying to lighten the moment.

"If I have to, yes!"

"What can I do to help?"

"Nothing yet. I'm going to meet Charles tonight. Maybe he has some ideas."

"Couldn't hurt," I said. "See what his reaction is. Be safe traveling."

I went out on my balcony, knowing this would probably be the last time for a while. It was supposed to rain tomorrow, Friday, and I wanted an early start to CJ's on Saturday. I was watching the clouds slowly roll in off the water when one of the hornets swooped down and stung me on my left arm.

"Son of a bitch," I yelled. "What was that for?"

I thought back to what Victoria had said. *Just wait...they will sting you.* I knew she meant metaphorically, but damn that hurt.

Friday morning, I woke up to rain, finished packing, and cleaned out the fridge. My phone rang. It was CJ.

"Hey, if you don't have other plans, why don't you come on down tonight instead of tomorrow?"

I paused for a moment. "Why not. I'll leave in the next couple hours. Can I bring anything?"

"Nah. Julia has a great dinner planned. Plus, I want to talk with you a little bit alone."

"That sounds ominous," I replied.

"No worries. Just want to get caught up on some family stuff. I'm concerned about Mom, and Katerina won't give me a straight story."

"Well, I'll tell you what I can," I said. But what could I tell him, exactly?

It started raining harder as I loaded up the Defender. I went back in to lock up and say goodbye to the bees, who were paying me no mind. "Have a great winter." My left arm throbbed.

As I headed south the storm got worse. This was going to be a long drive. It rained most of the drive until I hit Baltimore. I was fortunate to have missed the beginning of rush hour and made good time. It was early evening as I navigated through the tree-lined streets of northwest Washington, DC. The familiar sights of the Georgetown district filled me with a sense of anticipation. This neighborhood, with its mix of historical charm and suburban tranquility, always felt like a retreat from the city's hustle and bustle. I slowed down as I approached CJ's home, taking in the picturesque surroundings.

CJ's house, a modest, Victorian beauty, stood proudly amid its well-kept neighbors. The two-story structure exuded a timeless elegance, its intricate woodwork and delicate trim a testament to the craftsmanship of a bygone era. The pale-yellow exterior, accented with white details, gave the house a cheerful yet classic appearance. The real gem, however, was the wraparound porch that hugged the front and side of the house.

Parking my car in the small driveway, I couldn't help but feel a pang of envy. In a city where parking was a luxury, CJ was fortunate to have a one-car garage. The driveway, though short, provided a convenient spot for visitors like me. I stepped out of my car and immediately felt the welcoming embrace of the porch.

The porch was a cozy haven, furnished with an assortment of rocking chairs and outdoor loveseats that beckoned visitors to sit and stay awhile. Two mature trees framed the front yard, their branches spreading out like protective arms over the house. They provided ample shade during the summer, but now their leaves were sparse and cast dappled sunlight onto the porch and front lawn. The oaks and maples, likely as old as the house itself, added to the overall sense of history and permanence that pervaded the property.

The sound of my footsteps on the wooden planks of the front steps echoed softly. The front door swung open before I had a

chance to knock. CJ greeted me with a wide grin. "You made it!"
He wrapped me in a big hug that immediately melted away the
drive-induced stress. He took my bag from my shoulder, a
gesture that made me feel instantly at home. "Let me take this
upstairs for you," he said, as he headed toward the staircase with
my bag. "Make yourself at home. Dinner's almost ready."

I stepped inside the foyer and was immediately tantalized by a
blend of spices and herbs that made my mouth water. I hadn't
stopped to eat on my way down, and my stomach growled. As I
walked toward the kitchen, a small whirlwind of energy collided
with my legs.

"Auntie J!" four-year-old Calvin shouted with pure delight.
His bright blue eyes sparkled as he looked up at me.

"Hey there, buddy," I said, lifting him up and giving him a big
hug. Calvin giggled and wrapped his arms around my neck.

In the kitchen, Julia was busy preparing a feast. Pots and pans
bubbled on the stove, and a beautifully set table awaited us. The
kitchen, with its warm wooden cabinets and cheerful decor, was
the heart of the home. CJ returned from upstairs, looking
pleased as he saw Calvin and me together.

"I see Calvin found you," he said, laughing and shaking his
head. "Come on. Let's get our little sailor settled and then we can
sit down to eat."

Calvin had eaten earlier, so when our dinner was nearly ready,
he got ready for bed. I gave him a hug and kiss goodnight.

"Auntie J," he said, yawning and rubbing his eyes, "when can I
drive the boat?"

"Sweetheart," I said, "if it were up to me, you could sail it
anytime you like."

Ever since Granny's memorial, Calvin had been obsessed with
the sailboat. Giving him a break from the people at the memorial,
I had taken him down to the dock, let him climb on board, and
gave him a sailor's hat. He'd pretended he was the captain. We
fought off imaginary pirates, looked for buried treasure, and
sailed to faraway places.

Julia took Calvin up to bed. When she returned, Julia put an
old tablecloth and newspapers across the long table, then spread
piles of steaming blue crabs across it. Their shells were a deep
red-orange, dusted with Old Bay seasoning. The aroma of the
ocean, mingled with the spicy, smoky scent of paprika, celery
salt, and mustard seed, teased my nose as I cracked open the
shells. Each of us had a pot of melted butter, its golden surface

shimmering with flecks of garlic and lemon zest, releasing an irresistible fragrance. Alongside the crabs, a heaping platter of corn on the cob glistened with even more butter, the scent of sweet kernels mingling with a hint of char from the grill. To the side was a bowl of creamy coleslaw and a basket of hush puppies to round out the meal.

Little talking was done as I sat and stuffed myself to the point I wasn't sure if I could push myself away from the table. "Wow, Julia, that was magnificent," I said as I wiped my mouth on a napkin. I looked down and realized part of my meal was down my shirt. "Let me wash up, and I'll help you clean up. It's the least I can do." I started wiping the butter off my shirt and clearing the table. CJ disappeared to the backyard to close up the grill.

"No, no," she said, getting up from the table and grabbing the rest of our plates. "I got this. CJ wants to talk to you before Katerina comes."

I reached over and put my hand on Julia's shoulder. "I want to thank you for opening your home up to all of us. This family can be a handful."

Laughing while wiping her hands on her apron, she smiled and said, "Yes, they are! But aren't most families, especially when you are an in-law looking in from the outside? Ever since I met CJ, his family has treated me like one of their own. I guess that's what they mean by 'for better or worse.'"

I started laughing also. "You've definitely got a point. We girls need to do another girls' night soon. We can invite Abby this time, tell her all the family stories. We'll see what she's made of."

"Perfect idea! Let's plan it when all this is over, whenever that will be. But you need to get that shirt soaking before it stains. I see some things never change."

I went upstairs, washed my face, and changed shirts before I returned to the kitchen to try and help anyway. Julia already had most of it picked up and put away. I grabbed a beer out of the fridge that was covered top to bottom with Calvin's artwork. I marveled at it for a bit, then stepped out to the screened back porch where CJ was waiting. A small heater stole the chill from the fall air.

The space was an inviting retreat. The floorboards creaked slightly underfoot, a comforting sound that added to the rustic charm. Comfortable wicker furniture was thoughtfully arranged with cushioned armchairs and a large sofa, adorned with soft, colorful throw pillows. A couple of side tables held potted plants, their green leaves adding a touch of nature to the cozy enclosure. String lights hung from the ceiling, casting a warm, ambient glow that made the porch magical after sunset.

Floor-to-ceiling screens allowed the gentle evening breeze to flow through while keeping any mosquitos at bay. Through the screens, I could see the small backyard, where a few lanterns flickered softly in the garden. The sound of crickets chirping provided a peaceful soundtrack to the night.

CJ was sitting in one of the armchairs, a look of unease on his face. He looked up and forced a smile, holding up a wooden cigar box. "Want to join me for a smoke?" he asked.

I nodded, appreciating the gesture. "Thank you, but no. I never really liked smoking, but I do love the smell of a pipe or a good cigar. I will go for a glass of brandy if you don't mind."

"Make that two."

I walked over to the small bar cart in the corner, where a bottle of brandy and a couple of crystal glasses awaited. I poured two generous glasses, the rich amber liquid catching the light from the string lights above.

I handed one to CJ, who accepted it with a grateful nod. "Cheers," he said. We clinked our glasses together as I took a seat.

"So, CJ," I said, "what do you want to know?"

He chuckled. "I was hoping you would just volunteer information."

"You know I'm not like that. I answer what is asked…that is, if I can."

His expression darkened. "What's really going on?"

I shook my head. "CJ, you know you are going to have to be more specific than that."

He took a sip of brandy and said, "I know there are questions about Granny's death, maybe some foul play. Do you have any suspects?"

I formed my answer carefully. "Yes, we do, but until all the autopsy results come back, we won't be able to narrow it down. That's still a good month or so away. Until then, I can't even say it's a murder."

CJ nodded. "Are you really helping my dad on his campaign?"

"Honestly, I don't know. The last time he saw me, he was very angry. I have a meeting with him on Monday."

CJ's eyes looked about the room, as if he were uncertain of his next question.

"Just ask me what you want, CJ, and I'll try to answer you as honestly as I can."

He looked at me directly. "Is Mom keeping Sarah around? She's nice enough, but Mom isn't sick, is she? Plus wasn't she the last person to see Granny alive?"

"No, no. Your mom isn't sick. She just wants to get to know Sarah a little more, that's all."

CJ studied me. "She seemed really tired last weekend, You sure she's okay?"

"Yes," I said, patting his arm. "She's okay. Tired, but okay. She has had a lot to do for the Foundation after Granny's death, sorting through stuff, trying to figure out where everything is."

"Where everything is?"

"Yes. Granny has your mom going on a kind of treasure hunt. She and I are going to a bank in Alexandria on Tuesday. Supposedly there's a safe deposit box there." I paused. "Your mom really should be the one to tell you more."

CJ pulled his hand to his chest and feigned shock. "So I get nothing? No juicy gossip, no mystery?"

I shook my head and smiled. "I do have a question for you though, Mr. Newsman."

"I guess turnabout is fair play. Shoot."

I knew I had to word this carefully. I didn't want to put CJ in any danger. "Did you know all the people at Granny's memorial?"

"Most of them, but Granny had a lot of friends, here and all around the world. Why?"

"Just curious. I saw your father arguing with a man. I learned his name was Marcus Montgomery. Allegedly he feels your father is responsible for his dishonorable discharge."

CJ snorted and laughed as he said, "Dad? Responsible for another person's demise? Say it isn't so." CJ continued his sarcastic rant. "Dad would ruin anyone who got in the way of what he wanted. He doesn't care who he hurts."

"So you think this is just one more person your dad has pissed off in a long line of people?"

"Probably. You want me to look into it?" he asked.

"Nah, like I said I was just curious," I said, trying to brush it off. "Blame it on the investigator in me."

That seemed to appease him, and we sipped our cocktails, talked about Katerina and her trial, the house, my job, and his family. CJ had been like a brother to me in the years that I had known Katerina.

Julia came out and joined us. I thanked her again for dinner.

"Thanks." Julia blushed a little and hit CJ playfully. "It's nice hearing compliments about my cooking."

I caught myself yawning. "I'm so sorry," I said. "I'm tired after the drive."

"I hope it wasn't our boring company," CJ said, teasing me.

I excused myself and headed to bed. My bee sting still hurt, so I grabbed an ice pack, headed upstairs to their guest room, and changed into some shorts and a T-shirt. I hadn't been to CJ's house since he and Julia had gotten married.

The guest room was a perfect blend of old-world charm and modern comfort, updated to maintain its historical character while providing all the amenities one could wish for. At the center of the room was a large, inviting bed that promised restful nights. It featured a comfy feather bed topper with a blue duvet and an assortment of fluffy pillows.

The walls were adorned with a mix of family photos and Calvin's artwork. The neatly framed pictures showcased joyful moments. Calvin's vibrant and imaginative drawings added a touch of whimsy and warmth, reminding guests of a love-filled home.

I sank into bed and called Katerina, telling her that I couldn't wait to see her.

"Ditto," she said.

"What are you doing?"

"Oh, just finishing up a couple things. I love you." Then she hung up.

"Okay," I said to myself. "See you tomorrow."

I fell right to sleep. At some point in the early morning hours, vivid images of Katerina and me making love entered my dreams. Her strong hands were caressing me, moving up and down the length of my body, her hair tickling my skin as she kissed my breasts, sending goosebumps down my spine. I could almost feel the weight of her body pressed into me. My hands reached out to pull her even closer when my eyes flew open, finding Katerina on top of me, kissing my neck and shoulders. I pulled my head back to take in her Cheshire Cat grin.

"So I wasn't dreaming!"

"Maybe you are, and I'm a figment of your imagination," she whispered in my ear.

I pulled her close and kissed her. "Figment or not, I don't want this to stop. I'm so glad you're here."

"Well, I knew I couldn't do much more for the trial, and since I didn't want to sleep alone one more night, I drove down here."

"What time is it?" I asked, reaching for my phone. It was almost 7 a.m. Suddenly a pajama-clad Calvin, with his captain's hat on, burst into the room.

"Auntie Kat! Auntie J! Are we going sailing today?" He ran and jumped on the bed.

I covered up as Katerina clutched the blankets. I had forgotten how early kids woke up.

"No, Cal, we're just visiting for a while," Katerina said before she hollered out for CJ. A second later Julia appeared. She pulled Calvin off the bed and ushered him to the door.

"Sorry, guys, we had to take the locks off the doors," she said, gesturing down to Calvin. "He kept locking us out of his room. And Calvin, you need to learn how to knock," she said, as she ushered the boy out of the room and shut the door.

We flopped back against the pillows and started laughing.

"Might as well get up," I said, throwing the covers off and getting out of bed. "No alone time for us."

Katerina propped her head on her elbow, her hair flowing down her arm onto the pillow, playfully pouting. I leaned over and kissed her, as she tried to pull me back into bed.

I pulled back, laughed, and said, "With no locks on the doors, no way!"

After an exhausting but joy-filled day of make-believe, dinosaurs, Legos, and the like, we all gathered in the kitchen to help Julia make dinner. Well, we thought we were helping, but she ran us out quickly enough. With our left-over crab meat she made Maryland lump blue crab cakes with *quattro formaggi* and a terrific cherry pie for dessert.

Over dinner, CJ asked Katerina about her trial. She explained that her firm represented a group of about fifty immigrants who were transported to Martha's Vineyard by both Florida and Texas and left there. They had been told they would be provided with stable housing, work, education, and help with their immigration proceedings, but they were abandoned with nothing.

After dinner, Katerina and CJ took their heated discussion to the porch, as Julia and I sat around and shared recipes. They had allowed Calvin to stay up later than usual, and he was sitting on my lap, yawning. I looked out on the porch and saw Katerina doing the same thing. She was exhausted after having driven all night. We excused ourselves and turned in a little earlier than usual in anticipation of the four-year-old alarm clock.

Chapter Thirteen

The next morning, Katerina and I woke up around eleven without Calvin's exuberant summons. We went downstairs, lured by the aroma of coffee.

"Where's Calvin?" Katerina asked.

"Oh, he's with my mother. She takes him every now and then." Julia picked up Legos from the floor. "Gives me time to clean up before Victoria gets here."

We poured some coffee and helped Julia pick up the house. It was amazing where Legos and small dinosaurs could end up.

Victoria arrived around one that afternoon by car service. We went outside to greet her and unload her bags. Victoria sat slumped in the seat, looking weary and drained. Her eyes, once bright and full of life, were framed with dark circles. There was noticeable tension in her jaw. She slowly opened the car door.

Katerina went to the door to offer her a helping hand, but her mother refused it.

"I'm fine," she said unconvincingly.

"That bad?" Katerina asked.

"Your father! Sometimes I wonder why I even married him. My kids are the only good things that man has ever done for me."

I carried her bags as Katerina gingerly took her mother's arm and guided her inside.

"Just give me a few minutes to freshen up, and I'll be back down. I promise," Victoria said as she reached the stairway.

Katerina let go and stormed off to the backyard. "If he hurt my mother..." she said with a growl as I followed her.

About thirty minutes later, Victoria came down the stairs, looking like a new woman. She had changed clothes, pulled her hair up, and applied new makeup. Her face was radiant, and her eyes were bright, fierce, and full of determination.

Calvin burst through the front door. He clasped his little arms around Victoria's legs and yelled, "Granny V."

Victoria beamed as she hugged her grandson. "Your timing is perfect. I only just arrived."

Julia took Calvin to the backyard to play, giving us a chance to discuss Victoria's time with Charles.

"Before I get into this, I need a glass of wine and a comfy chair," Victoria said.

We went to the back porch so we could watch Calvin play as we talked. Victoria sat in one of the large, overstuffed porch chairs, and I volunteered to supply the beverages. I pulled a bottle of cold chardonnay out of the fridge for Victoria and Katerina and a couple of beers for CJ and me. I turned on the small heater and sat down beside Katerina. She was on the edge of her seat, tapping her fingers rhythmically on the armrest, her eyes fixed intently on her mother.

Victoria took a sip of wine and a deep breath. "I came down to DC on Thursday," she said, "thinking Charles and I could have some alone time to talk about things. Unbeknownst to me, he had committed us to a formal political dinner that night. It was horrible. You would think after all these years of him being in politics, I'd be used to these gatherings. I was so mad that he had sprung the affair on me, I went out and bought two expensive gowns and charged them to him."

Katerina and I chuckled.

Victoria gulped her wine and went on. "He then had the audacity to ask me for a donation to his campaign fund from the Foundation, but I refused. He knew better than to ask me. He knew I would need board approval to give him the funds. I gave him some money from my personal account, but that was all. He was gone all day on Friday and then on Saturday, he asked for more money! I couldn't believe it. He said he was 'entitled' to it." Victoria made air quotes with her index fingers. "He said he was leaving a legacy for the family. I told him to go to hell, and he left again. He hadn't returned by the time I left this morning." She looked at me. "Jara, I confirmed our appointment on Tuesday at the bank in Alexandria. I need to find some things out."

"Sounds good," I replied. "I'm to meet Charles at his office tomorrow morning. I wonder if he still wants me on the campaign?"

"He said nothing about it. Who knows what thoughts go through that man's head anyway?" Victoria shrugged and sighed. "I guess I let him get to me a little too much this time. It seems he cares more about the money and his campaign than his family."

CJ put down his beer. "Mom, he's always been like that, putting himself first. Jara and I discussed that Friday night, having a scene at the memorial, without a care."

I kicked CJ under the patio table. He got the hint to shut up.

"So, Mom, now what?" Katerina inquired. "How was it left with Dad?"

"Sweetheart, I have no idea. Like I said, last time I spoke to him was Saturday morning, and that didn't end well."

My mind wandered back to why Charles seemed so gung-ho about accumulating money. I figured the campaign had raised plenty by now with corporate sponsors and special interest groups banging down his door. Granted, he wanted his campaign to appear like money was coming in through grassroots organizations, but still. What in the hell was he doing?

We sat and talked for a while until it was time for dinner. Julia asked CJ to tend to Calvin and fixed another spectacular meal. I addressed Julia, seated across from Katerina and me. "I'm eating too well. I keep saying I could get used to this."

"Too bad Katerina can't cook," CJ teased. "Looks like you'll be ordering out a lot."

"A lot you know brother," Katerina said, taking a drink of wine and before she continued. "I have been cooking quite a bit lately and have heard no complaints." She squeezed my hand, daring me to disagree.

A soft laugh came from Victoria. "Now, now, she is right, CJ. Katerina has come a long way in the cooking department. She has really grown into her own." Victoria smiled proudly at her daughter.

Early Monday morning, Katerina and I were spooning in bed, her breasts pressed against my back and her arms around my body. This was what safe and secure meant.

My thoughts turned to the day ahead. I was to meet Charles that morning at his office in the Dirksen Building. I didn't know what to expect. *Does this campaign mean that much to him? Does the toll it's taking on his family matter? Do I really want to help him?* I had no answers.

I pulled Katerina's arm tighter around my body, feeling her warmth. I tried to relax and sleep, but soon the alarm sounded. Katerina set it to make sure she was on time for her interviews.

"I want to stay in bed with you the rest of the day," she moaned as she snuggled more into my back.

I turned over, put her head on my shoulder, and pulled her close. "I really wish we could," I whispered, "and ignore the world for today."

We stayed in bed for a few more minutes until she reluctantly got out. "I really want these interviews to go well today," she said, grabbing her bathrobe from the floor. "I'm nervous about how I'm going to react to all the depravity these people have endured. I wish we could do more for them." Katarina paused and looked at me. "Are you still meeting with Dad today?"

"Yes, at nine," I replied. "I don't have a good feeling about this. I want to know what he's up to, but at the same time I want to stay as far away as possible." My arm began to throb again.

Katerina bent down and kissed me. "Like you told me, 'Don't let the bastards get you down.' That includes family."

I laughed and tried to pull her back into bed, but she reluctantly resisted and went to the bathroom to shower. I got up, distracted by the weird sensation in my arm. Victoria's metaphor echoed in my head. I searched through my suitcase for appropriate attire, something comfortable but professional. Katarina emerged from the bathroom, dressed down to meet these people who had nothing, but she still looked stunning. She kissed me and said, "I'll see you later. Good luck!"

Katarina grabbed her tote from the chair and as she walked out, I yelled, "You too!"

I showered and dressed, still uncertain about Charles. Should I just blow off the meeting? I walked downstairs to grab some coffee before my drive to his office. CJ was sitting at the kitchen table.

"Good morning," he said over his coffee mug. "Good luck with my father. I can't wait to hear what happened when you get back."

I chuckled as I replied, "I'm going to need more than just luck." I took my to-go cup and walked out.

I had always hated DC traffic, so I left early and arrived about forty-five minutes before our appointment. I sat in my car outside the Dirksen Building, admiring the seven-story white marble architecture. I checked my email on my cell and was disappointed to find nothing from Travis. I drove over to Mass

Avenue and was lucky enough to find a free parking spot. I took another gulp of coffee, got out of the car, and put on my coat. I knew there was controversy about firearms on Capitol grounds, so I left my FBI service weapon locked in the safe in the back of my Defender. I hadn't worn it in so long, I stopped feeling naked without it. I made my way to the building, and up to the senator's office. Flanked by the American flag and the State of Connecticut flag, Bella was seated at her desk like a sentry.

Bella was a petite Hispanic woman, standing about five feet tall, with a presence that far exceeded her height. Her rich, tanned skin had a natural glow. She had a round face and a broad smile that brightened the room. Her eyes were large and expressive, a deep brown that sparkled with energy and intelligence. Her long, dark wavy hair was pulled back in a makeshift bun with a pencil through it.

"Jara!" she said in her thick, rhythmic accent as she rose from her chair. "It is so good to see you." She came over and hugged me. "Charles is in his office. You're welcome to go in."

I walked around her desk and, after a brief knock on the solid oak panel door, entered. Charles was just wrapping up a call.

"Hello, good to see you," he said, as he put his cell on his mahogany desk and extended his hand. "I wasn't sure if you were going to show. I'm glad you did."

I shook his hand. "Well, Charles, to be honest, I wasn't really sure if I was going to make this meeting or not. After our last encounter, I thought you were still mad at me, though for what I didn't know."

"No," he said as if our last discussion was nothing. He walked around his desk and sat back down in his weathered, brown leather chair and motioned for me to sit. "I wasn't mad at you, I was only frustrated. I'm really needing your help with the campaign."

"Okay," I replied tentatively. I sat in a high-back, executive chair, upholstered in sleek, dark fabric that complemented the richness of the leather. I looked at Charles over his massive antique desk and asked, "What might that be?"

"Well, for starters, I know you have connections through the FBI and are working with Homeland Security. I wondered if you could do some checking on some of my opponents. It would really get me ahead in the polls if I knew more about them, you know?"

I shook my head and glared. "You know I can't do that, I've told you this already. I would never do anything to compromise my job or the integrity of my office. I can't believe you have the gall to ask me! I told you when you initially asked me that I would never use my job for this campaign."

Charles scowled. "I know you've done checks on things that weren't open FBI investigations, so I don't see what the difference is."

I wasn't sure what he was getting at, but I answered him anyway. "There's a huge difference. What you're asking me to do is look up things that could affect the outcome of the presidency."

He leered at me. "Exactly! I'm the best man for the job. I just need to get into office."

"I'm sorry, Charles," I said as I stood. "This is not something I can do."

He huffed and slammed his hand on the desk. "Well, can you do at least *one* thing for me?"

I stared at him, waiting.

"I saw you and my daughter have been very open in your, shall we say, mutual affection. This cannot happen! Especially during my campaign, the party will not accept it."

"What in the hell are you talking about?"

"I saw that, during the memorial and around town, you and she were quite demonstrative in your fondness for each other in front of our family and friends. If this gets leaked to the press, it will not look good."

My fists balled up and my teeth clenched. I leaned over his desk, until my face was inches from his, and hissed, "If you're trying to tell me who I can and cannot love, then this is not a campaign that I'm interested in supporting in any manner. I love your daughter and nothing you or anyone else can do to stop that." He had rolled back from his desk, leaning away from me. I straightened, buttoned my coat, and turned to walk out of the office.

"Please stop. I'm sorry, I'm sorry. I shouldn't have said it that way."

"Then how should you have said it?" I asked as I faced him again. "I'm in a lesbian relationship with your daughter. Period. It's called love."

Charles was a seasoned politician. He knew how to manipulate people into seeing things his way. However, I could tell he was visibly agitated. His polished demeanor was slightly ruffled as he leaned back in his chair, fingers steepled beneath his chin. "You don't understand. I, well uh, I'm personally fine with whatever you two do," he replied, his voice measured but firm. "This, uh, relationship of yours with Katerina, it's a liability. It could harm everything I've worked for in this campaign."

I sat back down in the chair, the air tense with the weight of our disagreement. The adjacent room, typical of any congress office, was filled with the buzz of activity, the sound of ringing phones, and the occasional murmur of strategy discussions. Yet, amidst the organized chaos, Charles and I were locked in our own private battle.

I was undeterred by his stern tone and leaned forward, my hands gripping the edges of his antique desk. "I understand perfectly well, Charles. But I won't hide who I am, or who I love, just to fit into your campaign strategy."

Charles' frustration boiled over, his voice rising in a crescendo of anger. "You're being selfish, Jara. You don't see the bigger picture here. This isn't just about you and Katerina, it's about my entire campaign."

"I'm sorry, but I won't compromise who I am for your political ambitions. If you want my help with this campaign, it has to be on my terms."

For a moment, silence hung heavy in the air, the only sound the distant hum of activity outside the closed office door. Then Charles sighed heavily, his shoulders sagging in defeat. He knew he couldn't force me to bend to his will, no matter how dire the consequences might seem.

"Fine," Charles said. "You win, damn it. But I still need you on this campaign."

"I have no idea why. Remember, I won't be a part of anything illegal or anything that would jeopardize my job. Nor will I sacrifice my relationship with your daughter."

Shaking his head, he conceded. "I know, I know."

"And regarding Katerina and me, the 'party' will just have to get over it. Who knows? Maybe you can bring in a whole new group of voters because of us."

Charles' face lit up at the thought of new voters. "Wow, you may be right. How long are you going to be in town? The primaries will be starting in a few months, and I may need you to go on the road with me."

"I'm staying with CJ for a few days, but then I'll be going back to your home to help Victoria." I wasn't going to tell him Katerina and Victoria were at CJ's also, and I especially was not going to tell him about Victoria's and my bank trip tomorrow.

"Hmm, Victoria. She's pretty mad at me, isn't she?"

"That's between the two of you. I'm not going to be put in the middle."

"Well, if you see her, tell her I'm sorry," he said half-heartedly.

"Sir, I think it would be better coming from you."

"I suppose you're right. But if you can help in any way to get her to free up some Foundation money...I hear you're on the board now."

I was shocked that he knew. "Yes, I guess I am, but I don't think it's official yet. Anyway, I wouldn't have any access or influence over any of the Foundation money. Why are you needing donations from the Foundation? I would figure your campaign has raised enough."

"Oh, well, uh...yes it has. But it's always good to have more. And a donation from the Foundation would show I received support from my family."

I laughed and shook my head. "Money isn't always a show of support. You need to talk with them and ask them for support instead of demanding it."

His face turned red and his lips tightened as he drummed his fingers on the desk. "I know my family, Jara. You don't have to—"

"Charles," I said, as I stood up once more and headed for the door, "think about what you really need from me on this campaign and get back to me. I need to go."

He waved me out. Bella was not at her desk, so I walked straight out the door. By the time I made it outside, I was fuming and my arm felt like it was on fire. I walked a ways and let the brisk air cool me down. I stopped at the corner of First and C Streets, wondering if I needed to turn around and go back in to quit this campaign. In my peripheral vision, I caught some movement and looked down C Street. Was that Brian walking in the side door to the building?

"No way," I thought aloud. What reason would he have to be in DC? I stood dumbfounded. I walked back toward Dirksen's main entrance, and I saw Charles leave the building and walk toward the Capitol. I yelled his name, but he didn't turn around. I stood as if I were a lost tourist and stared. More often than not, politicians used the pedestrian tunnel to get to the Capitol, not the street. Where was he going? I followed him, but he had quite the lead on me. I lost sight of him when he went through the visitor's entrance to the Capitol Building. I shook my head, trying to understand why he would go through the visitor's entrance. This makes no sense. I contemplated this as I walked back to my car.

I drove slowly back to CJ's, trying to calm down and gather my thoughts. My head buzzed and my arm throbbed. I knew if I told Katerina what her father had said about our relationship, she would be over-the-top livid. It was in both of our best interests that I kept the conversation to myself, for now. I decided not to mention seeing Brian either.

Chapter Fourteen

I intended to pull into CJ's driveway, but since Katerina had taken the space, I parked at their curb. When I walked in the house, she and CJ were sitting at the kitchen table, discussing her immigrant case. I headed to the refrigerator and helped myself to a beer, popping it open and chugging it.

"That bad?" CJ asked.

I suppressed a belch. "Put it this way: Charles is rethinking my role in his campaign." I took another drink. "No disrespect to you two, but your father is a selfish, pompous ass."

Both burst into laughter. "Sorry," Katerina said, holding up her hand. "We aren't laughing at you. We've known that fact for quite some time." They motioned for me to join them, and I took a seat.

I told them about Charles' request to do research on his opponents and how I had refused. I didn't say anything about his other requests, but I had a feeling they both knew I was holding something back.

I waved my hand. "I don't want to talk about him. How did the interviews go?"

Katerina smiled. "I think they went very well. We're getting similar stories from most of them. Some have settled in nicely, while others are finding it hard to find jobs, housing, and even food. I think I have my brother here talked into doing a story on this."

CJ nodded. "Nothing brings about debate more than government, national or state, messing with people's lives."

I excused myself, grabbed another beer and a bottle of tequila, and went out to the screened porch. Victoria was working on her laptop.

"Oh, I'm sorry. I don't mean to disturb you," I said.

"No, no, no," Victoria said. "I'm only responding to some emails. The funeral home is finally setting up a small graveside service where my grandparents are buried. That's where my father was buried, and a plot is next to his for *Matka*. There was a mix up on where the plot actually was, but they have it straightened out now. I want to do it before it gets too cold. Please sit down, but before you do," she said, eyeing the bottle in my hand, "bring me out a glass, if you are willing to share." She grinned.

101

I went back inside and grabbed two glasses, limes, and ice. I poured some tequila over ice and added the lime on the side, handing one to Victoria.

"What are we toasting to?" I asked.

"Loyalty, love, and honesty," Victoria replied.

"I can drink to that."

We clinked glasses and downed some tequila. I sat quietly for a moment. "Did you tell Charles about me and Katerina?"

Victoria reared back in her chair. "Heavens no! Why would I do that? He acts like he doesn't even have a family, so why tell him about anything? Why are you asking?"

I told her what Charles had said about my relationship with Katerina and my response.

Victoria shook her head, disgusted. "That jackass. He doesn't even care about his own daughter's happiness. Does she know?"

"Not yet," I said, setting my glass aside. "I want her to be able to focus on her job right now instead of ripping her father a new one. I have a couple of things I want to talk to you about that aren't making sense."

"Go for it! I have a few things for you too."

"The other day," I began, "at the memorial, Brian came up to us and out of the blue asked about Granny May's will. We thought it strange, but since Granny was full of surprises, we let it pass. But today, Victoria, I could swear I saw him at Charles' office. What would he be doing there?"

Victoria took a drink and sighed. "Things are getting stranger and stranger by the day. I received an email today from Mr. Maxwell. Brian had a lawyer call him about when probate would be settled. Mr. Maxwell told them he didn't know, but if there was reason for him to notify Brian, he would."

"Yes, that is strange. Brian is popping up all over the place. Should I go back to Charles and ask him why Brian was there?"

Victoria shrugged and said, "What good would that do? He'd probably just lie."

I nodded and refilled my glass. Victoria handed me hers for a refill.

CJ and Katerina came out to the porch. "We weren't invited to the party?" CJ asked.

Katerina came around and sat on my lap. "Well, this won't be the first party I crashed," she said, and took a big gulp from my glass.

Victoria laughed. "Who said we're celebrating? Maybe this is just a normal afternoon."

CJ shook his head and said, "Since we're not celebrating, let's do the last grill of the season." We all cheered as he went outside to light the grill. Calvin came bounding down the stairs, quite refreshed after a short nap. "Auntie Kat! Auntie J! You're back. We can play now!"

"Oh, to have the energy of a child," Victoria commented. She shut her laptop and let Calvin drag her outside. The rest of us followed since it was a sunny but cool October afternoon.

Katerina suddenly grabbed my arm.

"Ow!" I said, flinching.

"What's wrong?" she asked.

"It's nothing," I replied. "While I was at home, I got stung by one of the hornets. It's no big deal."

"I want to see it," Katerina insisted.

I rolled up my sleeve gently. There, on my left forearm, was a fiery, red-hot bump.

Katerina gasped. "My god, no wonder you yelled."

"I didn't yell."

"Whatever. That doesn't look good." She went inside and returned with some vinegar, baking soda, ice, and an ace bandage.

I told her I had already cleaned it and applied antibiotic cream. She ignored me and attended to my wound. "We used to have hornets near the sheds at the house. Anytime any of us got stung, this is what Granny May and Mom did."

I sat and let her pamper me for a bit. After she finished, I asked, "Can I bother you for another beer and some ice for my drink? It really does help the pain." I smiled pathetically.

"Hmmpf, fine," she said. "But don't get used to this."

I saluted. "Yes, ma'am."

We joined the others. CJ observed my bandaged arm. "What the hell happened to you?"

Katerina explained about the hornet sting.

Victoria raised her glass with a wry smile. "Looks like you've been stung a couple of times these past few weeks."

"Yes ma'am, it seems that I have."

CJ and Katerina exchanged looks.

Julia brought out thick ribeye steaks, cubed potatoes with onions, butter, garlic, salt, and pepper all wrapped in foil, plus

103

some large portobellos for the grill. We let CJ, the grill master, do his thing and set the table on the porch.

Calvin ate his dinner first, after which he begged his grandmother for a story. He climbed into Victoria's lap. We all gathered round, except for CJ, who went off to tend the grill.

Victoria stroked Calvin's blonde hair as she began. "Once upon a time, there were three little children who loved to laugh and play all day outside. One day the oldest one, a girl, talked her two younger brothers into running down the street to the neighbor's farm to see their horses. When they got there, the farmer came out of his farmhouse and told the children to be careful and not to saddle the horses. 'But you can feed them some oats if you like,' he told them. A short time later, the farmer left in his truck to go into town and buy more grain for the horses."

"Did the children feed them *all* the oats?" Calvin asked.

"No, sweetie," Victoria replied. "Farmers have to stock up on food for their horses, just like your mommy buys groceries for you."

Calvin seemed satisfied with that answer, so Victoria went on. "After a while, the little girl wanted to get closer and pet the horses. Again, she talked her brothers into climbing over the fence. The three children approached the horses slowly and began to pet them. The little girl ran over to a rock by a tree and called out to her brothers, 'Bring a horse over here, and I'll get on it!'

"They coaxed a young chestnut quarter horse with some grain and led him over to where their sister stood atop the rock. She climbed on, grabbed the horse's flowing mane, and they took off, galloping down the fence line. Somehow, she managed to slow down the stallion and trot back to the rock. Her brothers were in awe. The youngest begged to ride the beast, but the other two told him he was too small. The girl teased the oldest brother and challenged him to get up and ride. Unlike his sister, the brother had never been on a horse, let alone had lessons like she had. He took her up on the challenge, stepped up on the rock, threw a leg over the horse, and grabbed the golden mane. He imitated cowboys he had seen in movies and kicked the horse in its sides, hollering, 'Yaw!' The stallion shot out like he was racing for the finish line. The boy held on to the mane as tightly as he could, but his legs weren't long enough for him to straddle the horse firmly. He bounced around like he was on a trampoline."

Katerina closed her eyes as if she were imagining the scene and chuckled.

"He kept bouncing up and down and side to side," Victoria went on, her arms and body bouncing as if she were the young boy. "He held on to that mane for dear life! The horse finally slowed down enough for the boy to embrace its neck and steady himself. When the animal finally came to a stop, the little boy slid to the ground and faced the quarter horse, who instantly head-butted the boy and knocked him to the ground before he trotted off across the green pasture.

"His sister and brother ran to him where he lay with blood dripping down his face. 'Don't you dare tell Mom!' the sister threatened. 'We'll all get in trouble.' The boy wiped his eye with his shirt, and they all went home. They sneaked into the house and the boy ran upstairs, where he washed his face and changed his shirt. At dinner that evening, their mother asked them about their day. The children looked at one another and the sister spoke up. 'We were playing by the boathouse.' They all went to bed that night, thinking their mother never knew what really happened. So, Calvin," Victoria tousled her grandson's hair, "if you see a man about your daddy's age with a scar over his right eye, ask him about his horse ride."

"Daddy has a scar over *his* eye," Calvin said excitedly. "I'll go ask him."

Calvin ran off as Katerina guffawed.

"You knew?" she asked her mother. "I thought we were being so slick."

"The farmer's wife called me and told me you were in the field with the horses. I ran down there in time to watch you skillfully ride that horse, with your red hair flowing behind you, and then I saw CJ get on and away he went. Although I was worried, I was laughing so hard while watching him bounce around, I couldn't get through the fence in time to help him. The horse taught him a lesson that I couldn't. But if you remember, Katerina, you told me the truth later. Said you couldn't sleep knowing you had lied. You never lied to me after that."

Katerina nodded. "No, I never have. You and Granny knew somehow before I could even get one out of my mouth."

CJ walked in with Calvin on his back. "What's this about a horse ride?"

Katerina waved him off. "Forget it, CJ. Mom always knew."

"Whew! One less thing to confess," he replied. "By the way, dinner is served."

Victoria took Calvin up to bed.

When Victoria came back downstairs and joined us, I asked her what time our bank appointment was.

"We need to be at the bank by nine in the morning. I don't want to be late for this one."

I nodded. "We'll make an early start of it to make sure traffic doesn't slow us down."

It was getting late by the time we stopped talking and got the kitchen and grill cleaned up. Once in our room, I started laughing, picturing Katerina talking her brothers into the horse ride and then galloping down the field. Katerina was in the attached bathroom.

"What are you laughing at?" she asked, pulling her toothbrush from her mouth.

"You," I said, "my little cowgirl. I can see you talking your brothers into most anything back then. But I never knew you could ride."

"I haven't ridden in a while. But I did love it growing up. I never knew Mom had seen us, glad I confessed. How's your arm?"

"I think it's better. Your pampering helped."

"Just wait until we get this trial, campaign, and Granny's business behind us. I plan on hiding away with you and pampering you day and night." We lay down on the bed and she kissed me.

"*That* I will definitely look forward to," I said as I kissed her on the neck and her mouth, pulling her close. "I love you, cowgirl."

Chapter Fifteen

I woke up intertwined with Katerina under the sheets. She was so alluring, her red hair splayed across the crisp, white pillowcase. I wondered if I should wake her, not knowing what her workday schedule was like. I kissed her and quietly untangled myself, heading for the bathroom.

The bandage on my arm had come off sometime during the night. The wound looked a lot better, less inflamed. I got in the shower and thought about what could be in that deposit box. I was hoping whatever the contents, it would bring Victoria some closure.

I was deep in thought when a gust of cold air hit me and hands grabbed my body. Katerina stepped into the shower, backing me up against the tile wall.

"I haven't had enough of you yet," she whispered as she kissed me and slid her hands down my back. "I thought I'd help you shower."

We kissed until we heard Victoria call out.

"Jara! Let me know when you're ready!"

Katerina and I covered our mouths to suppress our laughter. "I love family," she said, "but I can't wait until we're truly alone again."

"I wholeheartedly agree," I said, kissing her one more time before we stepped out of the shower. After I dried off and got dressed, I asked her what she was doing today.

"I'm not sure. I thought about going to see Dad, but I'm sure it'll just make me angry. I'll probably catch up on emails and things and take a blissfully long nap." She teasingly poked me in my good arm. "Actually, I'll probably work on putting the information from my interviews together and play with Calvin, see if some of his energy will rub off on me."

"My dear," I replied, "you have the perfect amount of energy." I kissed her and grabbed my jacket.

"You're really going to leave me like this?" Katerina looked at me, pouting as she fell back onto the bed, her naked body beckoning. I moved toward her, unable to resist.

A short time later I quietly left the room, shutting the door behind me. Calvin ran down the hall toward me. I scooped him up, carried him downstairs, and told him not to wake his Aunt Kat.

Victoria was waiting for me in the kitchen.

"You missed breakfast," CJ said with a smirk. "Here's a doughnut and coffee to go."

"Thanks," I said, taking the brown bag and to-go cup from him before heading out the door.

Victoria followed me, seeming a bit distant.

"I'm sorry if I'm running late," I said, looking over my shoulder at her as I led the way to the car.

"Don't worry about it," Victoria replied. "I'm a bit nervous about what we're going to find today. I feel a little on edge."

"Whatever it is, we'll deal with it."

She reached out and squeezed my hand. "I know. Thank you."

We drove to the bank and made it by nine. Victoria got out her key and ID.

"If you want me to wait in the car," I said, "I will."

Victoria shook her head. "No, I think I need you beside me."

We headed into the bank and were greeted by a man in a pricey gray suit and a purple tie. "Hello, Mrs. Lansing, I'm Reginald Bishop. I'd like to welcome you to our bank. Mrs. Majewski-Robinson was one of our favorite clients. You look a lot like her."

Victoria smiled as she shook his hand. "Thank you, Mr. Bishop. Can you explain what we need to do or what this is about?"

"Not a problem. Please follow me to my office."

We crossed the marble and brass lobby and entered his office. He pointed to a leather sofa to the right. "Make yourselves comfortable. Can I get either of you a coffee, soft drink, something to eat?" Victoria asked for coffee, and I asked for a Dr. Pepper. Mr. Bishop called out and soon a young man in another tailored suit came in and served us.

I whispered to Victoria, "No wonder Granny May liked this bank."

She laughed as she nodded her head slightly.

Mr. Bishop retrieved a stack of papers from his mahogany desk and walked over to us, taking a seat in a matching leather armchair.

"This is Jara Quinn," Victoria said, introducing me. "She's family."

I smiled at Mr. Bishop.

"Nice to meet you, Ms. Quinn. Mrs. Robinson spoke very highly of you also."

"She did?"

He smiled and said, "Mrs. Lansing, I've made all the arrangements for you two to have privacy for as long as you need it. There's a room off the vault. We'll bring you the boxes, and you can go through them at your leisure."

"Boxes, Mr. Bishop? As in plural?" she said, somewhat astonished.

"Yes, ma'am. Your mother and father had a total of three boxes. I know you have only one key, but you'll have access to all of them. I need for you to sign a few things, then we'll head to the vault."

After the paperwork was out of the way, Mr. Bishop took us to what appeared to be an older section of the building. We entered an ancient vault that looked like something from a James Cagney mobster movie. Mr. Bishop pointed at three large metal boxes stationed along the wall of the vault. "If you would insert your key in the hole on the right of this first box, Mrs. Lansing, we'll get started."

Victoria inserted her key and turned it. Mr. Bishop also inserted a key in the left keyhole and turned his. He pulled the first box out of the wall and sat it on a table in the middle of the vault. He asked Victoria to open it. She lifted the lid and found two more keys and handed them to Mr. Bishop.

"Mrs. Lansing," he said, putting one of the keys back in her hand, "if you will insert this one in the right side of this second box." Mr. Bishop took his key inserted his in the left side. They repeated this for the third box also. When all three boxes were on the table, he made a call on the wall phone. He motioned us to the hallway. "I'll bring all three boxes to the room next door."

Out of nowhere, two young men appeared. He showed them each a box, which they carried to the next room as Victoria and I followed. Mr. Bishop showed her another wall phone and gave her an extension to call if she needed anything or if she was finished. Then he and the two other men departed.

"Jara, where do we start?" Victoria asked, shaking her head. "I wasn't expecting this."

We went over to the first box and reopened it. On top was a picture of Granny May and her husband, holding Victoria. Below the picture was a letter addressed to Victoria. Victoria opened it gently. I just knew it was one of those, "If you are reading this..." letters. Victoria read the letter briefly before she motioned to

109

another box. "Please open that one, Jara, and start going through it. I have a feeling this is going to take a while."

Victoria continued reading, her face indecipherable. I opened the second box. It was filled with war bonds, certificates of deposit, and an old banker's journal with names and monetary units called Reichsmarks with US dollar amounts beside them. There were also names and addresses in France, Germany, and Poland. A small journal written in Polish was in the same bundle. I pulled all these out, sorting and separating them into stacks. I located the first deed to the land in Connecticut and drawings of the original house. All these documents fascinated me. Another deed, very old, appeared to be for property in Poland.

These all have to be from Granny's parents, I thought. I looked over at Victoria:. She was crying as she rummaged through the deep box.

"Victoria, are you okay?" I asked. "Do you need a break?"

"No, I have to keep going, but thanks."

She read a document and froze. I watched with curiosity as she quickly folded it and put it in her purse. I said nothing, returning to my box and finding more war bonds, deeds, and miscellaneous papers. I separated them the best I could. At the bottom of the box were five gold bars stamped with "1KG" and a German Eagle, its outstretched wings and sharp talons clutching a wreath containing the infamous swastika.

I sat them on the table with a thunk.

"What the hell are those?" Victoria asked.

"I think these are gold bars from wartime Germany."

"That's amazing. How—?" She noticed the swastika. "Ah."

I relayed what I had read in one of the banker's journals. "Some entries state 'gb' for papers and passage, with initials by each line and a date. The journals are full of them. Some list deeds, jewelry, and art, with descriptions of all of them."

Victoria sighed. "Let's take an inventory of it all and find something to carry the items we want to take with us now. I don't think all of this will fit in my purse."

I went upstairs to find Mr. Bishop. I didn't want anyone to come into the room and see the gold bars. Plus I needed to get some air. I found him in his office.

"Ms. Quinn, what can I help you with?"

"I'm in need of a pad of paper, folders, large manilla envelopes, and a couple of large bank bags with locks, if you have them. I'll pay for whatever."

"No need for that. We're here to serve you and your family. Just give me a few minutes to gather those things for you."

"Thank you, sir, you're very kind. If you don't mind, I'm going to step outside and make a call. I'll pick up the stuff when I return."

I walked outside and took a few breaths of fresh air as I walked over to the Defender. I opened the tailgate, sat down, and phoned Katerina.

"Are you on your way back to me?" she answered. "I was about to take a nap."

"Oh, I wish. There are a total of three boxes. We still have one large box yet to go through."

"Wow, okay. Actually, I was getting ready to go to the park with Calvin, but it sounds like there's some serious history in those things. Wish I was there," she replied.

"To say the least. How's your day?"

"Very productive, although not as productive as yours, it seems. I got all my information put together and have been playing with Calvin and talking to CJ. It's been very relaxing. I really enjoyed being around my brother this time. He actually stopped working for a bit. What time do you think you'll be done?"

"No idea, but I'll call you again when we're on our way."

I sat my phone down beside me and a wave of melancholy washed over me. A memory of going through my mother's desk played in my head. The smell of erasers and old coins wafting up as I opened the middle drawer. Finding notes and small objects she had tucked away. The never-ending supply of pens and pencils, paperclips and rubber bands. My father's pipe stand sat on the corner of the desk, the smell of pipe tobacco I loved so much still present. I wiped my eyes with my sleeve as I pushed the memory out of my head. I knew my heart ached for Victoria, but I hadn't realized until now how much my heart still ached for my parents.

I locked up the Defender and went back inside the bank. Mr. Bishop met me with a small cart loaded with all the things I had asked for. He showed me to the elevator and gave me directions on how to return to the room. I thanked him and rode down the slow, creaky elevator to the basement. I rolled the cart into the room, and Victoria looked up at me with a start.

"Sorry," I said. "I got the stuff we needed."

Victoria smiled. "I can't thank you enough for all your help. I don't think I would have made it through all this."

I grinned. "What's family for?"

She stood up, hugged me, and pointed to the third box. "Do we dare open that one?"

"Let's inventory everything in these two boxes, that is, if you are done, and consolidate them."

"Great idea," Victoria replied, nodding. "I'll finish up on this box and start the inventory."

She looked like she had been crying. I hadn't noticed before because I'd been so focused on my inventory. I put my hand on her shoulder. She looked at me and said, "I'll be fine. Open up the third box."

I moved over to it and opened the lid. Another picture of Granny, her husband Edward, and Victoria, who looked to be around five or six years old. Under that were pictures of Granny's wedding day, possible honeymoon, Victoria, their house in Maryland, a picture of Edward in front of a new Navair building, and Edward's death certificate. Underneath was a folder stamped in red with "Confidential" and "Top Secret." I opened it anyway and glanced through. A lot was redacted, but I could make out this was an incident report on the "accident" that took Mr. Robinson's life. This must have been Mr. Robinson's deposit box. At the very bottom was another folder marked "Top Secret." In it was a patent and multiple diagrams of a machine part. The initials "VFX" were stamped on it and a diagram of a fighter jet. Of course, it was far from my understanding, but the patent was still current with another stamp stating, "Property of the Navy." I inventoried all of this and sat my pen and pad down. Victoria was finishing up, looking emotionally exhausted. She put almost everything in folders and locked them in a large bank bag. She stood up and walked over to my stacks and lists.

"You've been busy," she said. "This is great."

"I had an easier job than you did," I replied.

She nodded and quickly went through all the stacks, putting things in the first box and marking "Removed" on the things she packed in a bank bag. By the time she was done, everything was able to fit in one large box. What was left was neatly packed in five large, locked bank bags and placed in the cart. Victoria picked up the phone and contacted Mr. Bishop to come down. He arrived quickly, eyeing the cart and the two empty boxes.

Victoria explained to him we no longer needed the empty boxes, then looked at me and asked, "Unless you and Katerina want one?" I wasn't sure what to say, so I asked Mr. Bishop if he could keep one for us until I asked Katerina about it.

Mr. Bishop helped us outside and handed me the bags to load into the Defender.

Victoria looked at her watch. "I'm so sorry, Mr. Bishop, We've been here all afternoon. I bet you're ready to end your day."

The man smiled solicitously. "I didn't do the hard emotional work that you did."

I loaded all the bank bags in the two safe compartments and locked them up. Mr. Bishop took the cart, wishing us a good day and safe travels.

When I got in the car, I exclaimed, "That sure was different than our last bank experience."

"Thank god," Victoria said. "I don't think I could have handled rudeness today."

I asked if she wanted something to eat since we missed lunch. "No," she replied. "If you don't mind, I'd like to get back to CJ's."

I quickly texted Katerina.

On our way back. Your mom's exhausted. See you soon.

A moment later, I received a reply. **I'll have something ready to eat when you get here. Love you.**

I smiled while typing out, **Love you too.**

The nights came earlier now, and it was dark by the time I pulled into CJ's driveway. I looked over at Victoria. "Do you want me to leave these things locked in the car?"

She nodded. "I have the folder I want. That'll be all I'll need for a while. When you get back to the Connecticut house, we can lock the rest in the safe."

We got out of the car and went into the house. Julia and Katerina were in the kitchen. Katerina hugged her mother and asked if she needed anything. Victoria saw the broccoli cheddar soup on the stove and the fixings for sandwiches.

"May I have a soup and sandwich in my room?" she asked as she took a bottle of chardonnay from the refrigerator.

"Of course," said Julia. "I'll bring it up shortly."

"Jara, will you bring it to me?"

I nodded. "Definitely."

Victoria smiled and went upstairs. I filled an ice bucket half full, grabbed a small bottle of brandy, a glass, and a bed tray.

Julia placed the soup and sandwich on the tray as I kissed Katerina on the cheek and told her I'd be down shortly.

She smirked. "I think Mom likes you better than me now."

"No, my dear. I'm simply not as emotional as the rest of the family. She needs to deal with her own emotions right now, not worry about the rest of you."

"How'd you get so smart?" Katerina quipped as I walked out of the kitchen to go upstairs.

I balanced the tray and knocked on Victoria's door. After she answered, I opened the door and placed the tray on a desk near the window. Victoria asked me to stay for a minute and to shut the door.

"I brought you an ice bucket for your wine and a small bottle of brandy in case you needed something a bit stronger."

She smiled. "You're getting to know me too well. Please sit with me for a minute. I want to explain why I acted the way I did today at the bank."

"You have nothing to explain to me. I know how emotional all this can be."

"Nevertheless, I want to explain something, but I ask you not to share this with Katerina as of yet."

I promised and she handed me a document. It was a birth certificate for one "Elizabeth Shaw," daughter of "Susan Shaw." The document listed the father as "Charles Lansing." I gasped. "Victoria—"

"Yes, Charles had an affair and a child about the time I was pregnant with Katerina. I'm still wrapping my head around how this was put in the safety deposit box, but I'm figuring it out. Please don't tell Katerina yet. That is, unless you feel you have to."

"Do you think you'll confront Charles on this?"

"Not right now," she said. "I want to get all my information before I show my hand."

I gave her a hug and told her to let me know what I could do. She wept. "You're already doing it."

I left, my stomach sinking as I teared up. That son of a bitch. And he had the audacity to judge me and Katerina? The more I thought about it, the angrier I got. I considered how this had to be a gut punch to Victoria: Charles fathering another child while she was home pregnant. I sat down on the top step and tried to get myself under control. Calvin came out of his room and put his arms around my neck.

"You need a hug, Auntie J?"

"Thanks, buddy. Yes, I do."

He squeezed my neck and let go, gone as fast as he had shown up. Maybe I should call him a 'hug ninja.' Could sea captains also be ninjas? I walked downstairs and hugged her Katerina from behind. I wasn't as stealthy as Calvin.

"Is Mom coming back down tonight?"

"I doubt it. She's pretty tired."

Julia came in and said the soup and sandwiches were on the porch table. I thanked her, still holding on to Katerina.

Katerina turned around and asked if I was going to tell her what was going on.

"Your mom needs some time to think about what she found and how to handle it," I replied in earnest.

"And?"

"And that's all I know. She has a lot to digest. The third box was full of your grandfather's papers, a patent, and government stuff. Oh, and she offered us one of the boxes if we wanted. We have a few days to think about it before we have to call Mr. Bishop."

Katerina nodded. "That's a lot. I can't wait to see this stuff."

I finally let go of her and backed up. Katerina looked at me directly. "If there is something I need to know, or something you or Mom need, you'll tell me, right?"

"I promise," I said and kissed her. "Can I eat now? I'm starving."

"I'm going up and putting Calvin to bed," Julia said as she wiped the kitchen counter. "CJ will be home soon. He and I have to go to a dinner for the magazine. We won't be too late. Calvin should be fine."

"No problem," we said in unison. I grabbed a beer and headed out to the porch. Katerina followed with her wine.

We ate, and when we finished, I took our dishes into the kitchen and got another beer. I grabbed a bottle of wine for Kat.

"I forgot to tell you," I commented as I sat down once more, "your mother is arranging a graveside service for the family, either next weekend or the following week."

"That sounds nice. Just the family. Does Dad know?"

"I doubt it," I said. "She's still angry at him. When are you going back to Boston?"

"I've wrapped up all the interviews I think I can get here. I haven't heard back whether they want more follow-up or not.

Since you aren't doing anything with Dad's campaign for a while, we should leave early and go to Boston for a few days."

"Wow, that would be wonderful," I replied, "but I want to make one more trip to your dad's office, and I have to drop by the Connecticut house before I can drive to yours."

Katerina frowned. "Why do you need to see Dad again? And why go to Connecticut?"

"I have a few things I need to clear up with your father that I don't want to talk about over the phone, and I have the contents of the safety deposit boxes locked in my Defender that your mother wants in the safe at her home."

"Then you can drive to Boston?"

"Yes, definitely."

Katerina kissed me on the cheek. "I'll head back tomorrow, get some groceries, and clean up a bit."

"Sounds great. I'll go see Charles when you leave and head to your mom's after. Depending on my driving time, I'll be at your place either tomorrow night or Thursday morning."

Katerina smiled. "Now that sounds more like it. I don't want to spend too many days where you're not with me." We went inside and settled in on the couch, kissing and holding each other.

CJ and Julia came home, and we informed them that we were leaving the next morning. Katerina also reminded them about the graveside service coming up.

Katerina and I woke up with Calvin jumping on our bed.

"It's time to get up! It's time to get up!" he chanted.

Victoria peeked around the door frame. "You got the same alarm I got."

"Where's the snooze button?" Katerina yelled, grabbing Calvin and tickling him.

He cackled and hollered, "Granny V. Granny V, help me."

CJ's heavy footsteps pounded on the stairs before he appeared in the doorway. "What's all the noise up here? The chefs are cooking breakfast. You'll crack all the eggs."

"But Daddy, the eggs have to crack, don't they?"

We all laughed even harder, as Calvin leaped off the bed and ran downstairs. CJ followed him, and Victoria came and sat on the bed.

"I'm leaving today to head back home. I have lawyers to call and a lot to do before *Matka*'s service. I also need to make a trip to the Foundation. Jara, when do you think you'll be coming to the house?"

Katerina and I went over our plans with her.

Victoria sighed and said, "I'll be glad when life returns to normal."

Katerina scoffed and asked, "What's a Lansing normal, Mom?"

Victoria shrugged in defeat. "Hell if I know."

Katerina and I got dressed and brought our bags downstairs. CJ had already retrieved his mother's bags and loaded them into her car. I took ours out and packed them in our respective cars. When I returned to the house, the table was set with waffles, omelets, bacon, sausages, rolls, and fruit.

"I may need a nap after this meal," I said.

"No naps today," Katerina said. "Drive, drive, drive!"

"If only we could snap our fingers and be there," Victoria added wistfully.

We finished our meal and got up to help with the dishes.

"No," Julia said. "CJ and I can do these, you all get on the road. Miss some of the traffic."

We all hugged each other goodbye. Katerina told Victoria she would follow her to the exit for Boston. I told them both I would keep in touch. We thanked CJ and Julia for their hospitality and gave Calvin big hugs. Secretly I was looking forward to some alone time.

Chapter Sixteen

I embarked for Charles' office, surprised traffic was so heavy for a Wednesday. When I arrived unannounced, Bella hesitated for a moment, looking like she was going to put me off or lie by saying he wasn't in the office. If he was actually out, I was prepared to go to the Capitol to find him.

"L-let me tell him you're here," Bella stammered, as she rushed around her desk.

"Don't bother," I replied, heading for the door to his office.

"What the hell?!" Charles jumped up from his leather chair.

"Sit your ass back down, Charles. I won't be long."

"How dare you," he yelled.

"How dare I? Seriously? You asked me to work on your campaign just because I had the means to do things others can't, to do illegal things against your opponents. Then you had the audacity to yell at me for loving your daughter. You, sir, have caused your family a lot of heartache and pain, and I swear, if you hurt them anymore, I'll do everything in my power to ruin you."

"What are you talking about?" he asked, all bluster. "I've done no such thing. I thought we had an understanding."

"Understanding? Understanding of what? Of you not being honest? All you do is lie and hurt people, and it's going to stop."

Charles leaned way back in his chair, laughed, and rolled his eyes.

"We'll find what other lies you have concealed. And mark me, we will!"

Charles sneered. "Who's 'we'? Victoria? Katerina? Please don't say the boys because that would be a laugh. You can't do anything to me."

My anger got the better of me, and I leaned over his desk, staring into his steel-blue eyes. "Oh yes, I can, and Elizabeth Shaw might just be in a position to help me." I immediately regretted saying her name.

Charles' eyes widened like dinner plates, then narrowed. "I don't know who that is. Am I supposed to?"

"Live in denial, Charles, but the footsteps you hear behind you may just be all your ghosts, ready to haunt you."

I walked out before he could say anything further and slammed the office door. I called out over my shoulder as I walked out, "He may need a diaper change, Bella."

I had put my FBI temporary parking tag on my Defender and parked it as close to the Dirksen Building as I could. I had a clear view of the entrance Brian entered yesterday and fairly decent view of the main entrance. I knew if Brian showed up, it would be because Charles called him. I already had my camera with the telephoto lens prepared. I waited about thirty minutes and, sure enough, Brian appeared. I took a bunch of pictures of him entering the building, getting proof that he and Charles knew each other. I noted the time of my visit and the time of the photos. I immediately called Victoria. She answered on the second ring, on speaker.

"Victoria, first off, I want to apologize. I just left Charles' office, and I laid into him pretty good, threatening to ruin him. I made the mistake of confronting him with Elizabeth Shaw. I didn't tell him what we know though."

"Hold on. Let me find a place to pull over." A minute later, with a raised voice she said, "Jara, what did you do?"

"I wanted to see if I could get a reaction out of him, and I did. Within thirty minutes, Brian showed up. I have photos. Something more is going on, and I'm going to find out what it is. Charles may call you. Talk to him, don't talk to him, it's up to you. I wanted to give you a heads-up, though, if he does."

Victoria was quiet for a moment. "I really didn't want him to know that we knew that." She let out a heavy sigh.

"I am so sorry Victoria. I didn't think, I just blurted it out.

"Okay, fine. I guess we'll deal with it." Victoria was quiet again for what seemed like hours to me. "Are you okay?"

"Yes, I'm fine. A bit amped, but fine."

"I don't know what to say. I'll be ready for him if he calls. Are you telling Katerina?"

"No, not all the details, but she knew I was going to his office."

"How far are you from the house?"

"I'm leaving DC now. I have to stop first, but I should be there by six," I replied.

"Okay, but I'm going into Bridgeport this evening after I drop off some things at the house. I received a call from Mrs. Walsh, the CFO of the Foundation. She wants to meet with me immediately. Our lawyer is also going to be there."

"Do you need me or Katerina there?"

"No, I think I've got this. I'll let you two know what happens. Be safe."

"You too."

I texted Katerina and told her I would be at her place by 8 p.m.

Wonderful! Did everything go okay with Dad?"

Depends on your definition of 'okay,' but I think it went well.

After I sent the text, I realized Katerina was supposed to be following her mother and might have seen her pull over.

Are you still following your mom?

No, I lost her in New York traffic. We'd been making pretty good time.

Good to know, I texted. *I won't take long at the Connecticut house. Your mom is going into the Foundation tonight. I'll tell you all about it when I get to your place.*

Is everything all right? Do I need to be worried?

No, love. I'll explain everything when I get there.

Okay, love you. Be safe.

I will. Love you too.

I traveled the next few hours in silence, collecting my thoughts and figuring out my next move. The farther north I drove, the more the trees had turned color. I saw vivid reds, oranges, yellows, and deep purples all along my route, the sun hitting them just right to make a riot of color. I saw the exits for Philadelphia and wondered about my trafficking case. I felt guilty that I hadn't kept up to date on it. I made a mental note to call Travis soon. My phone rang, startling me back into reality. "Quinn," I answered.

"Hello, this is Victoria. I'm home and getting ready to head to the Foundation. I left instructions on the table for the safe. Just lock up and destroy the note, okay?"

"Sure thing," I said. "Anything else?"

"I'll be home Friday to do some last-minute things. We'll be having Matka's service on Wednesday. Then I may need to drive the few hours back to the Foundation and stay for a few days."

"Sounds good. I'll inform Katerina when I get there tonight unless you want to."

"No, Jara. I've thought about it, and I want you to tell her everything. Everything we've talked about and everything you think she can handle. I want the three of us to be standing strong together at the service, so that means no more secrets."

I let out a breath I didn't know I was holding. It was killing me keeping things from Katerina. "No problem. I'll tell her everything. Please call if you need anything else."

We hung up and I called Katerina. Her phone went to voicemail. "Katerina, I'll definitely be at your place by eight, maybe earlier. Please, if you would call in tomorrow or not tell them you're home, I'd appreciate it. I need to have your undivided attention to explain some things and, well, just to be with you. I love you. See you soon." I hung up, hoping beyond all hope she didn't freak out due to my cryptic message.

I made my extra stop and still made it to Victoria's house by 4 p.m. I unloaded the safe compartment in the Defender, making three trips to get everything inside. I followed the instructions Victoria left me and burned the note. I was back on the road by four-thirty. I wanted to take the coastal scenic route, but my need to see Katerina outweighed the need for scenery.

I hit Boston at about seven-thirty and it only took me fifteen minutes to find Katerina's place in the Northside, near Boston Harbor. The building's exterior was a mosaic of aged red bricks, each one bearing the scars of countless New England winters and summers. Ivy tendrils crept up its sides, lending an air of timeless charm to the structure. Windows with wooden shutters punctuated the brickwork, their frames weathered and worn from years of exposure to the elements.

I called again.

She picked up on the first ring, saying, "Where are you?"

"I'm outside your building, wondering where to park."

She gave me easy instructions. As I got out of my car to get my bag, the scent of aged wood and musty brick filled the air, mingling with the faint aroma of salt drifting in from the nearby harbor. The entrance, flanked by wrought iron lanterns, opened into a dimly lit foyer adorned with intricate moldings and ornate chandeliers. Years of foot traffic had worn smooth the floor with its black and white hexagonal tiles. Even though the building was old, I could tell the tenants had an appreciation for history. Most of the fixtures and possibly the floor seemed original to the building. Other than a few chips and cracks in the tile and the knocking of the exposed radiators, the building had a feeling of a much-loved home and not an apartment building.

Katerina met me in the foyer and hugged me as if we hadn't seen each other in weeks.

"Now that's what I call a greeting!"

"You ain't seen nothing yet," she said as she winked at me.

We made our way through the labyrinth of narrow hallways to her door. Her place had oversized windows that flooded the space with natural light, offering panoramic views of the historic neighborhood below. The walls were exposed brick, their mottled surfaces lending a rustic charm to the place. The air was filled with the scent of old books and polished wood. A candle glowed on the coffee table, emanating sage and sandalwood.

In one corner of the living area, a plush sofa and armchair beckoned, their cushions adorned with mismatched bohemian style throw pillows and soft blankets. A vintage rug, worn smooth by years of use, added a touch of warmth to the hardwood floors. Oversized floor lamps cast a soft, golden glow across the room, illuminating the built-in bookshelves that lined one wall. The shelves were filled to the brim with an eclectic assortment of books spanning genres from classic literature to romance novels and mystery thrillers. Leather-bound tomes sat alongside well-loved paperbacks, their spines worn from countless readings. A collection of law books also occupied a prominent place on one shelf.

Adjacent to the living area was a small, eat-in kitchen, its compact layout optimized for efficiency without sacrificing style. A sleek island served as both a workspace and a dining area, its surface adorned with more lawbooks and folders. A vintage-inspired stove and refrigerator added to the apartment's old-world charm.

Katerina started apologizing about how small it was, saying that she had roof access.

I took her in my arms and kissed her. "I don't care if you live in a cardboard box, as long as I'm here with you. This is gorgeous. I love it."

We lit more candles. Something smelled good in the oven. I had only brought in one bag, which she grabbed and tossed into her room.

"I decided to make lasagna," Katerina said. "Hope it turns out okay. Make yourself at home. We'll go up to the roof to eat."

"Sounds perfect." I took a seat at her island and watched her maneuver around the kitchen.

"You seem nervous," I said. "I hope it isn't because of me?"

122

"A little bit. This is the first time you've been here. You were at my other place a few years ago, but we weren't...well, you know."

I smiled. "Yes, I know. But there's no need to be nervous."

"I listened to your message. Everything okay? I was at the market down the street."

"Yes, everything's okay. Let's settle in, and I'll catch you up," I told her.

She handed me a beer, took my hand, and walked me to the couch. It felt so good to be out of the car and with her. I yawned.

"Oh no! You're not fading out on me yet."

I smiled and said, "No, just relaxing. Did you call in tomorrow?"

"They don't even know I'm here. They aren't expecting me until Monday at the earliest. You okay being stuck with me for that long? *Alone?*"

"You better believe it. No mothers, brothers, four-year-old alarm clocks. I'm so ready to be stuck with you."

The oven timer sounded. Katerina got up and put the lasagna on top of the stove. She returned, straddled me, kissed me, and asked, "Where were we?"

I held her tightly, kissing every spot I could put my lips on. We pulled off each other's shirts, giggling like two teenagers, kissing and exploring each other. We made our way into the bedroom and made love, loving each other past the brink of pleasure and back again. We finally collapsed, catching our breath and laughing.

"Guess dinner is cold now," Katerina said. "You hungry?"

"Starving!" I said, kissing her again.

We made love all night, only taking brief bathroom and drink breaks, until we both lay in each other's arms unable to move.

Katerina put her head on my shoulder. "You had some things you wanted to tell me?"

"Yes," I whispered, "but not right now. I only want to think about you."

Chapter Seventeen

The next day the smell of coffee woke me. Katerina had gotten up before me. She walked into the bedroom, carrying two cups and wearing only my button-down shirt, unbuttoned, and a smile. I sat up in bed, smiling. "Good morning."

"Good morning?" She laughed and placed my coffee on the nightstand. "It's two in the afternoon. I couldn't wake you for anything, and believe me, I tried."

I covered my face, embarrassed. "I'm so sorry. I guess I was more worn out than I thought. How is it you're awake?"

"Oh, I slept in some, but I still don't think I've shaken all the anticipation I had built up waiting for you to see my place for the first time," she said. "It gave me time to salvage the lasagna and clean up a bit. I hung up some of your clothes, and the others are in the middle drawer, over there." She nodded toward the dresser.

I gasped. "I already have a drawer?"

She playfully smacked me and set her cup next to mine. "So when do you want to talk? Is this about my mom? My dad?"

"Can I choose C, all the above? Let me wake up some more, get dressed, and I'll be ready to talk."

"Dressed how?"

I shrugged and asked, "How dressed do I have to be to go on the roof? I would love to see it."

"A bit more than we are right now," she said, as she laughed and left the room.

I took a quick shower and dressed comfortably. When I went into the kitchen, I found a note that told me to meet Katerina on the roof.

I found the roof access and headed upstairs. The view was like a postcard. I could see boats in the harbor, and on the other side I swore I could see the Old North Church. Katerina had set up a little oasis, filled with patio lights, a picnic area, some chairs, and a couple of cool, colorful rugs.

"I love this. It's adorable." I sat down on one of the fluffy rugs and leaned back against a chair. Katerina had put together a picnic of finger foods, fruit, and cheese. I took a drink of beer and ate a piece of cheese. "Do you want to eat first," I asked, wiping my mouth on a cocktail napkin, "or for me explain things while we eat?"

"Please explain now before my imagination runs off with me," she replied.

I told her about her mom's presence at the Foundation and the possibility of having even more irregularities with the books. "I can't tell you much more because we don't know. She may be calling us later with some info." I detailed everything that was in the second and third safe deposit boxes. Katerina had some questions, and I answered as much as I knew. I told her that Granny May had written Victoria another letter, explaining some of the items in the first box.

"It contained a birth certificate. We don't know how Granny had it, but it seems Charles had an affair with Susan Shaw and had a baby, Elizabeth Shaw, while your mother was pregnant with you. This was what Granny was trying to protect you and your mom from. She gave the Shaw family a lump sum trust and other payouts for Elizabeth every year for eighteen years. The lump sum money was transferred by someone out of the bank and is in an offshore account somewhere we can't find."

I could tell Katerina was grappling with this overwhelming information. Her brow was furrowed, and her face wore a mask of strain. Her shoulders slumped as if each bit of information was an invisible brick on her back.

"Do you want me to stop?" I asked.

"No, but my dad is a suck-pig, and I have a half-sister out there somewhere?"

"According to what we've learned, yes on both accounts."

Katerina shook her head and sighed. "Okay, go on."

I told her what her father had said about our relationship and his campaign.

Katerina sat with a blank look, her face growing redder by the minute until she finally exploded. "That short-sighted, mother-fucking son of a bitch. I'm going to call him and give him a piece of my mind."

I reached out and grabbed her hand. "I've already done that *and* threatened to ruin him." I then told her about Brian showing up at Charles' office twice.

"Are you sure it was Brian?"

"Yes, I have photos." I showed her.

"What the—?"

"We don't know," I said. "Your mother wants us all on the same page and strong at Granny's service, if Charles even shows up."

"I doubt he'll do anything if he shows up, but I dare him to try," Katerina said, tearing up. "He's not my father anymore! Is this what Granny was talking about when she threatened him?"

"We think so, yes."

"How much do CJ and Chase know?"

"Not a lot, but CJ is asking some questions. Victoria may tell him, but you're the one we thought should know. You are the one I'm concerned about."

I sensed everything was slamming together in Katerina's head. I moved closer and took her in my arms. She was trembling.

"I don't know whether to be pissed off, or cry, or both," she said. All at once she let out a blood-curdling scream, as if she were going to war and this was her battle cry. I didn't hear any sirens, so it was safe to say no one had called 911. Katerina apologized. "I had to let it out."

"No apologies to me, my love, no apologies to me."

We sat on the roof for a while longer, finishing our drinks as Katerina tried to wrap her head around everything. She looked at me sadly and asked, "How long have you and Mom known all this?"

"As fact or as theory?"

"Either, I guess."

"Your mom and I each had our own hunches, you might say. But until the last bank box, nothing was confirmed. Granny wanted to make sure Victoria wasn't hurt by a scandal or the knowledge of Charles cheating. Plus, she knew how much Victoria wanted you and a 'normal' family. Everything Granny did was for your protection. The letters were a way Granny could apologize to you and your mother if you ever found out about Charles."

"She didn't have to do that. She didn't have to do any of it," Katerina replied. "We would have managed. Now I have an older half-sister I don't even know."

My phone rang: Victoria.

"Have you told her yet?"

"Yes, we're still discussing it."

"Before I talk with Katerina, will you put me on speaker?"

I touched my screen. "You're on, Victoria."

"Hi, honey, before we talk, I need to tell you both something. The Foundation CFO and its lawyers believe we're missing even more money than we initially thought. They don't see where *Matka* allocated any funds to anyone from the Foundation before she died. I'm going to come home this weekend and get ready for *Matka*'s service, then return here to the Foundation."

"Mom," Katerina interrupted, "are you sure we should be having Granny's service now?"

"Sweetie, I know it's a lot, but I feel we need to have it soon. It's almost November, and it's not getting any warmer. *Matka* wasn't one to put off anything. I just got off the phone with CJ and tried to explain everything to him. For Chase, I left a message."

"Oh, Mom!" Katerina started crying again.

I clicked the phone off speaker and handed the phone to Katerina to talk with her mother privately.

I kissed her, picked up our picnic and drinks, and headed downstairs. After cleaning up the kitchen a bit, I grabbed another beer and opened my laptop. I sent an email to Travis, telling him about the financial irregularities at the Foundation. I asked him if he knew anyone who specialized in tracking financial trails that he trusted. I informed him about what I had said to Charles, about Brian showing up, and Elizabeth Shaw's birth certificate. I also asked about the trafficking case. *I bet I'll get an earful about threatening a senator.* I was finishing up when Katerina came downstairs.

"Mom wants to know when we're returning to the house."

"How about Monday evening?" I suggested.

After she hung up, I closed my laptop and put it on the floor. Katerina curled up on the couch with her head in my lap. I could feel her shaking between sobs as I ran my fingers through her hair. She looked up at me with tears in those deep green eyes, and it broke my heart.

"I'm not sure what I'm feeling I'm angry, sad, anxious, one feeling keeps replacing the other. At least we know some of Granny's hold over Dad and why she hated him so much."

"Actually, Katerina, I'm not sure how much your father knew. When I mentioned Elizabeth's name to him, he had a reaction, but I couldn't read him entirely."

"He probably has so many secrets he can't keep them all straight," Katerina replied.

Katerina and I didn't talk much for the rest of the night. I knew she had to process all of this in her own way. CJ called her and asked if she was okay. She rode her merry-go-round of emotions again but seemed to be calming down. I walked out to my Defender and grabbed another bag to bring in. She was still on the phone when I headed into the bedroom.

I had just set my bag down when I heard, "Dad, it's Katerina, you know, your *daughter*."

I ran into the living room and Katerina put her hand up for me to stop.

Katerina went on. "The family is having a brief graveside service on Wednesday afternoon for Granny. You need to be present, at least for the sake of appearances. It's not our fault we don't look like a family. You're the one who is never around. Yes, Dad, I'm fine. I have a lot going on right now. You'd know that if—okay, I'll stop saying it. Fine. See you on Wednesday." She hung up.

"What the hell was that all about?" I asked.

"If he's going to play games with me and my life, he's at least going to have to do it in person. I want to look him in the face and see if he has anything to say to me. I'm sick of all the lies and secrets in this family. I think Granny would appreciate a showdown at her funeral."

"As long as you don't start wielding a cane," I said and laughed. "I would hate to have to arrest you for assault."

Katerina burst into laughter. "You wouldn't dare! I'll claim temporary insanity."

"Girl, you would have to be crazy if you went after your dad with a cane."

"Well, I do take after Granny. And if she did it, so can I!"

We were laughing so hard by now we were crying. "Show me what Granny taught you, my love. Did she go after your father like she was entering a duel or did she only bang it around?"

Katerina got up and pulled an umbrella out of a stand, taking a fencing pose. She jumped around the room, jabbing the umbrella toward me, recounting the day Charles announced his presidential bid. What once was a day of anger and family fighting was now a wonderful memory of Granny's resilience.

Katerina and I spent the rest of the weekend enjoying the historical sights of Boston and walking around the harbor. It was turning colder, and the air was crisp and refreshing. We were lucky enough to catch the Boston College at Notre Dame football game on Saturday in a small sports bar near her apartment. We had to be careful, cheering for the Irish in "enemy territory." We got a few strange glances and dirty looks, but I don't know if that was because of our cheering or kissing on every good play. Probably a bit of both. Everyone ended up being good sports, especially when we bought a few rounds for the house.

On Sunday, we decided to stay in, watch NFL football, and not wear much more than a jersey. We ate leftover lasagna, toasted tequila on touchdowns, and made love throughout the afternoon. We kept our phones off and laptops shut. We were reliving the days in the Penthouse. The week ahead would be a rough one, so we decided to be selfish and enjoy each other without interruption. Katerina had texted Victoria that our phones would be off, so we weren't expecting any calls.

While waiting for the Sunday night game, a news show came on and neither of us had the energy to change the channel. A "what's on next week" segment stopped us dead. "Connecticut Senator Charles Lansing, champion of human rights and equality, will spend time talking with us next week on his plan to heal this country's division and keep family first." An old photo popped up of the family having a party in the backyard in Connecticut.

Katerina screamed at the TV, "You son of a bitch. What the hell does he think he's doing? Does he really think he'll get away with this?" She turned and looked at me. My expression was one of utter shock. "I need to call Mom," she said.

I nodded and tossed her phone to her. She had multiple missed calls. A couple from CJ and Chase, one from her mother, and even one from Charles himself. Katerina listened to the messages. CJ and Chase both asked if she had seen the broadcast, Victoria asked Katerina to call her back, and Charles' message she put on speaker. "You want to play games with me, little girl? Then fine, family it is. Be prepared."

"What the hell did that mean?" I asked.

"Beats me, but I think I should call Mom."

Katerina called Victoria and put her on speaker too. "Mom, what's going on? We saw this thing on TV about Dad, and he left me this bizarre message."

Victoria said she learned about it when a reporter came up to her outside the Foundation, asking questions and taking pictures. "I don't know what your father's doing, but if he starts getting nasty, I'll call his bluff and leak the birth certificate to the press. I would hate to do that. The girl is innocent in all this."

129

"Mom, we'll be okay. No secrets, remember? And we'll stand firm at the funeral. I love you. We'll see you tomorrow."

She hung up and I turned off the TV. Katerina flopped down on the floor. At first, I thought she was crying, but she began laughing hysterically.

"Champion of human rights. Equality. Family first. Seriously? Oh, this is going to be fun."

I started laughing at the absurdity of it all.

"Granny is going to go out with a *bang*," Katerina said, laughing even harder. She crawled over to where I was sitting, a mischievous glint in her eye, and sat on my lap, facing me. "You ready to be part of this family as my girlfriend? Let's see how he handles equality and family now."

She leaned in to kiss me, but I pulled back.

A look of shock crossed her face. "What's the matter?"

"I would most definitely, a hundred percent, want to be a part of the family as your girlfriend but because you want me to, not as a pawn to throw in your father's face."

"Why can't it be both?" she said. "You were the one who threatened to ruin him."

"I did, I agree, but not by using you or your family."

Katerina leaned back on her heels and sighed. "You're right. No lies, no secrets, no games with our feelings. Jara, will you stand with me at my grandmother's funeral as my partner?"

I pulled her close and kissed her. "Of course I will. I would be honored."

Chapter Eighteen

Monday morning, Katerina and I reluctantly packed up and headed to Connecticut. We wished we could hide a little longer from the world, but back to reality we went.

We reached the house in late afternoon. It was already dark, the days growing shorter and the air colder. Victoria was in the kitchen, cooking chili. The aroma of fresh baked bread filled the air. She seemed happy to see us, but a somber feeling filled in the house. Instead of feeling hugged as I always had in this safe space, I felt as if the house was guarded and preparing for battle. A fight for what and whom, I wasn't sure.

Katerina and I took our bags up to my room. Katerina said I had the better room, anyway, with a fireplace, balcony, and large attached bathroom. I took it that the room was ours now. We lit the fireplace to warm up the room while we ate downstairs. Both of us were tired. We changed into warm sweatpants and jackets and went back down to the kitchen.

Victoria chuckled. "I see you've both dressed in your finest for dinner."

I looked down at my outfit. "At least this one doesn't have any stains on it."

"The night is young, and you haven't eaten dinner yet," Katerina teased.

We ate in the kitchen. It felt homier. The rest of the house seemed so cold without family or laughter. We finished eating, making small talk and chatting about the weather. Victoria said it was at least supposed to be sunny on Wednesday, but cold. "As long as it isn't windy, I think we'll be fine."

After we cleaned up our dishes, we went upstairs. I flopped down on the bed, yawning.

Katerina giggled and pointed at my sweat jacket. "You can't make it through one meal, can you?"

I looked down to see right in the middle of my jacket was a chili stain.

"Saving it for later in case I need a snack." I laughed and pulled off my jacket, getting under the covers, sweats and all.

Katerina put her hands on her hips. "Oh, so we have already moved into the 'wear sweats to bed' part of our relationship, huh?"

"If you quit standing and get in bed to warm me up, maybe I won't keep them on."

"Give me a minute. I want to check in on Mom first." Katerina went down the hall to her mother's room. I fell asleep before she returned.

Katerina and I woke up to what sounded like a large group of people downstairs. It brought an immediate feeling of liveliness and warmth. I heard the low hum of conversation, the clink of dishes in the kitchen, and the occasional burst of laughter. The voices were familiar and loving. It was the kind of moment where I just wanted to linger in bed for a few more minutes, half-awake, listening to the sounds below, an atmosphere of comfort and connection. The floorboards of the staircase creaked as we heard small feet running up the stairs. Katerina and I braced ourselves, as Calvin bounded into the room and jumped on the bed.

"Auntie Kat! Auntie J! Are we sailing today?"

We heard more footsteps on the stairs, and in walked CJ and Julia.

"Party in our room," I yelled.

CJ, out of breath, said, "We're so sorry. We tried to catch him in time."

Julia took Calvin in her arms. "He's getting faster and slicker every day. At least it isn't early morning."

"What time is it?" Katerina asked.

"One in the afternoon, sleepy heads," CJ teased. "Time to get up and well...get up, I guess."

We promised we would dress and be downstairs in a bit. The others left our room, and I flopped my head back onto the pillow.

"Our nirvana bubble has been burst," Katerina said, laughing.

We soon made our way downstairs to the kitchen, where the island counter was full of food. We loaded up our plates, grabbed drinks, and headed into the living room. Chase was with Abby, and Calvin was running around the house as his parents chased him. The spirit of the house had lifted, feeling more like a home again.

After we finished eating, I stood up and announced there was a surprise for everyone in the theater room.

Victoria smiled at me and mouthed, "Thank you."

We made our way into the theater, finding seats and getting comfortable.

"Now that I have your attention," I said, "during the past month Victoria and I have gone on a bank tour of the Eastern seaboard, or at least it's felt that way. During this adventure, we learned many things, and lots of memories surfaced. With Victoria's permission, I've put together a memory reel of sorts in honor of Granny."

I lowered the lights, hit play on my laptop, and sat down beside Katerina.

Picture after picture of Granny May and the family flashed on the big screen, including an early photo of the Connecticut house, followed by pictures of the renovations. When a picture of Charles' and Victoria's wedding flashed on the screen, a hush came over the room. Then, out of the mouths of babes, Calvin asked, "Why is Granny May so mad?"

We stared at the photo. Granny May had the type of look you would have if you sucked on a lemon. Victoria burst into laughter. The elephant had left the room.

More photos of the Foundation, family, and friends popped up, including short videos of Katerina, CJ, and Chase in the hospital after being born; the kids playing in the yard; birthdays, graduations, dances, the first time they sailed; Granny sitting on the back porch, watching over the family as if it were her kingdom to protect. The video ended with Granny holding Calvin on her lap soon after his birth, a huge smile on her face.

Katerina looked at me with tears in her eyes. "You've been busy. No wonder you've been so tired. Thank you."

I pulled out the flash drive and gave it to Victoria. "If anything, Victoria, this is what you should leak to the press. You have a beautiful family."

We returned to the living room, everyone sharing stories and memories of Granny. I went to the kitchen, poured myself a beer and, as I listened to the animated voices in the other room, hoisted my drink in the air. "Here's to you, Granny May."

The next day, we made our way to the cemetery. Although rain was in the forecast, it was cold but sunny. The hearse was parked by a large tent, which covered fake grass and folding chairs. The picture of Granny we used at the memorial was set up on a tripod next to the casket. Roses, larkspur, lilies, and delicate white orchids, all of Granny May's favorites, were draped over the casket.

We formed a circle around the casket, leaving the chairs empty. The minister was just starting to speak when Charles emerged from a limo parked nearby and walked toward us. Katerina grabbed my hand. She was shaking. Chase and CJ moved to either side of Victoria. The proverbial wagons were circling.

Charles stood directly across from us, glaring at Katerina. The minister looked around before he resumed his sermon. When he finished the final prayer, Victoria placed a small bouquet of lisianthus on Granny's grave, representing a lifelong bond, love, and gratitude. Each grandchild placed a different colored lily on Granny's casket, representing devotion and love.

I chose a flower that reminded me of a walk I took with Granny in the garden. I had seen a row of double bloom peonies, which reminded me of my parents' backyard. Granny gave me a knowing look then took my arm and gave it a small squeeze. She walked me over to a large group of sunflowers and said, "These, my dear girl, symbolize strength, loyalty, happiness, and friendship. You should never run out of any of these qualities." I felt it was only appropriate to place a large sunflower on her casket for her. CJ, his arm around Victoria, walked her from the casket even as Charles moved up and took her arm. She flinched when a camera flashed. The press had shown up.

CJ pulled Victoria away from Charles, and Katerina grabbed my hand and walked up to her father. More cameras went off. CJ took Victoria to the car as Julia, Chase, and Abby followed. Katerina never moved as she glared at her father. Charles mustered a smile and reached out to her. She knocked his hand away and started to speak, but I tugged her arm gently and whispered, "Not here, he's not worth it."

She relaxed some but didn't move. She looked at me, then back to Charles. I leaned in and kissed her on the cheek. She softened.

"You're right. He isn't worth it," Katerina said, turning back to him, "and I'm *not* your little girl!"

She allowed me to walk her to the car. Cameras continued to go off. I wasn't sure if they were taking pictures of us or Charles, standing alone at the grave. I was sure we would know tomorrow when we read the papers.

Once we were all in the limousine, Victoria ordered us not to speak to the press. "No comment from now on. I will think of a statement if one is needed. We're not airing our dirty laundry in the press, even though Charles may deserve it."

We all agreed. I contacted some law enforcement personnel I was on close terms with and asked if they could block the road to the house. Since only one road ran in or out, it was easy to secure.

When we reached the house, some reporters were lurking about. How did they mobilize so fast? The government would be lucky to learn a trick or two from them. Everyone went inside. I changed into my FBI jacket and put on my gun and badge. Not that I had any authority, but sometimes looking official went a long way.

I went outside, greeted the press, and stated the family had no comment at this time and to please move off the property. A short time later, a few of my friends from the local law enforcement showed up and moved the press back. A few of my friends remained in cars along the road, out of courtesy, to secure the rest of the property.

We kept the TVs off and limited our access to phones and computers, knowing a story would come out about today's activities. Reading every little piece of news would only add fuel to the fire of our emotions.

Calvin came over to Victoria. "Granny V, can we watch the movie again?"

"Calvin," she said, bending over and kissing his head, "that sounds like an excellent idea."

The family joined them in the theater room to rewatch the memory reel. I stayed back, lit the fire on the porch, wrapped myself in a blanket, and sat in one of the cushioned chairs. How did the press know about the service? I was trying to wrap my head around it all when CJ came out to join me.

"Rough day, huh?"

I nodded. "I doubt this will be the only one."

CJ said he had recognized a few of the reporters and called some of his contacts.

"They all said they received an anonymous tip from a woman to show up at the service. Could Katerina have called them?" At that moment she appeared, eyes swollen and red, and sat down beside me. CJ told Katerina a woman had called the press.

"Well, it wasn't me, if that's what you are hinting at," Katerina replied. "Had it been, I would've given them an earful."

I wrapped my blanket around her, and she moved in closer. I wasn't sure if she was shaking because she was cold or angry.

The evening was a quiet one. No one knew what to say to one another. Victoria came out to the porch, where Katerina and I remained for most of the evening.

"Jara, I was wondering if you could stay for a while and help me with some things around the house and at the Foundation? I hate asking you this, but I need to know what's going on with the funds."

"I'd be happy to."

I looked at Katerina, who nodded. "I'd help too, Mom, but I have to return to Boston to finish prepping."

"Honey, I totally understand. With the people Jara has helping us track this, I think we'll have it covered. But anytime you can help, it would be appreciated."

"So Travis sent you some people?" I asked.

"Yes, he emailed me their names and credentials. I believe they started looking into it on Monday. I forgot to tell you with everything going on. Travis said it was easier to send me the info than to keep putting you in the middle. He's going to contact you later this week."

Katerina and I discussed what our next few weeks were going to look like, with her going back to Boston and Christmas creeping up on us. The family had been together so much the past few months, they had decided to forgo Thanksgiving. Katerina was to head back to Boston tomorrow and try to wrap up her work. I would stay at the house and help Victoria. CJ decided he and Calvin would stay until the weekend and help me winterize the boat. Chase and Abby needed to return to school.

The next day, Julia, Chase, and Abby headed back to their respective homes.

Katerina and I walked around the grounds, holding hands. "I'm going to miss you so much," Katerina said, "but thank you again for helping Mom. I'm not sure what the family would do without you. Heck, I'm not sure what I would do without you."

"Then I need to keep making myself useful, so you'll never have to know."

Chapter Nineteen

Katerina decided to drive one of the family cars back to Boston. I offered to take her, but she refused. We walked back to the car. I hugged her tightly and kissed her goodbye. Victoria, CJ, and Calvin came out to say farewell also. After all the hugs, I walked Katerina around to the driver's side and opened the door.

"Please be careful," I whispered. "I'm going to miss you." We both had tears in our eyes, as she got into the car.

"I love you," Katerina said.

I smiled. "I love you too. Call me when you get home."

Katerina waved to everyone and drove away.

I walked back into the house, feeling a bit lost. Time to get to know myself again. I grabbed a beer and headed into the den, where I sat down on the rug in front of the fire and leaned against a chair. I watched the flames dance, relaxing more with every minute.

CJ walked in. "Mind if I join you?"

I motioned for him to sit. He had brought his own drink. We sat in silence for a while and stared at the fire.

"Where's Calvin?"

"He's with Mom, watching the memory reel over and over. Thanks for doing that, by the way."

"My pleasure. Least I could do to celebrate Granny May."

"I got another call from one of my contacts," he said. "The woman who called had an accent, unless she was faking."

I thought about it for a second. "Bella!" I said out loud. "Your father's assistant, I bet it was her. That conniving ass, what was he up to?"

We sat by the fire, pondering the situation, until Katerina phoned me. She had made it home safe. "I think I'm going to have a glass of wine then and go to bed. I didn't realize how tired I was."

I told her what CJ had said and about my hunch that it was Bella.

Katerina agreed. "Dad is up to something."

The next day CJ, Calvin, and I went out to the dock to winterize the boat. It took longer than I anticipated. We spent Friday prepping and all of Saturday getting it done. Calvin was mesmerized. CJ explained to him the importance of taking care of things and the responsibilities of owning a boat. Calvin hung on his every word, asking questions well past his years. We drained the fuel and all the other fluids, and CJ refilled the compartments with antifreeze. We inspected the ropes, riggings, mast, and all the little mechanisms needed for the boat to sail properly and safely. Calvin helped me inspect all the sails before we pulled them down and wrapped them for the winter. CJ removed the battery, and we all grabbed leftover supplies and extraneous stuff that had been left on the boat throughout the season. CJ had called a couple of his friends who worked in the harbor to help us cover the boat and store it in the boathouse. With all the cleaning and prepping, we had worked up an appetite.

We reached the house, greasy, dirty, and tired. Victoria said nothing; her look said it all. She pointed toward the bathroom, telling us to clean up and get out of our clothes. She handed me a robe and told the boys to strip down to their underwear, putting the dirty clothes in a special hamper. CJ and I had done this many times after working on the boat and thought nothing of it. Calvin, though, thought it was great fun we were all in our underwear and started jumping up and down.

Victoria walked around the corner as Calvin made a break for it, grabbing my robe for a cape. CJ ran after him in his underwear, and I stood there in just a bra and panties. Victoria watched in disbelief as Calvin tore through the house covered in grease, CJ hot on his heels, trying to catch him before his greasy hands touched everything in the house.

I gave up on trying to cover myself and looked at Victoria. "You gotta admit, it's never boring around here."

Victoria laughed as CJ caught Calvin midair, jumping off a couch.

"Great catch," I called out as I went up to my room.

I took a hot shower to scrub the dirt off my face and hands and wondered how grease made it to areas that were covered up. The hot water felt good on my cold, aching body. I hadn't done that much physical work in quite a while.

I put on some comfy pajamas and lay down on the rug before the fire with a large pillow in my arms. I missed Katerina. She would have loved to have seen the underwear brigade. I smiled to myself and at that moment, she phoned.

"Hey, I was just thinking about you," I said. "How was your day?"

"Busy! There's so much information and governmental red tape. This is going to take forever. How was your day? Did you get the boat work finished?"

"Yes, thanks to a lot of help from Calvin." I went on to tell her about the underwear shenanigans. Katerina howled with laughter. We kept talking until Victoria called out for me to come down and eat.

"Your mother has summoned me," I said. "Better get downstairs before she sends out a search party."

Katerina sighed. "I miss you. I wish I was there."

"Me too," I said. "Soon though, very soon."

Sunday afternoon, CJ and Calvin packed up and headed home. I hoped Calvin could bottle up some of that energy and leave it for me. Victoria and I waved goodbye to them and returned to the house.

Victoria put her arm around my waist. "Thank you for being here. We have a lot of work to do. You ready for it?"

"I was never any good at math," I replied, "but I can pack a box and hunt down a good lead."

We spent the next few weeks going through what seemed like mountains of boxes in the basement, with Victoria going back and forth to the Foundation. We had a quiet Thanksgiving, ordering food instead of cooking. Katerina came home for it but headed back to Boston on Saturday. She said her boss needed to speak with her first thing on Monday morning, and she wanted to be prepared.

On Monday, Victoria and I headed to the Foundation in Bridgeport. We met with the Foundation attorney, the CFO, and three financial detectives in a large conference area. Papers, names, and strings were all over, connecting stacks of financial records to names on a big board. I'm not sure what I was expecting, but it looked more like a murder room than a financial investigation. Also on the board were the papers Granny May and Victoria uncovered before Granny passed.

Victoria and I were briefed on the progress made so far. Someone had hacked into an area of the Foundation finances that was rarely accessed. It was still "old school," as it was put, and should have been shut down years ago. When the firewall and security recognized the hack, it reached out to the administrator of the server to authenticate use of the area. Login and security questions were answered correctly, and after the hacker gained entry, they changed the login, password, and security questions for their own access. The hacker used this back door to establish an outgoing fund stream to a shell company.

One of the detectives spoke up. "We have where the funds are coming from and where they're going to, but we're unable to identify the fund stream's final destination. We don't want to do a force stop on the funds because it would dry up any leads as to where they're going."

"Mrs. Lansing," Mrs. Walsh, the CFO, asked, "is it okay to allow these funds to continue going out?"

"How much has been taken, Mrs. Walsh?"

"Approximately two hundred and sixty million dollars."

The blood drained from Victoria's face. "Seriously? And we never missed it?"

"It's been leaking out a little bit at a time," said Mrs. Walsh, "no huge withdrawals from the allegedly defunct fund."

"Mrs. Lansing, I'm Agent William Foster, a friend and colleague of Travis O'Ryan. I track these kinds of crimes whether it be money for drugs, weapons, or money laundering. My team and I have been working on this for only a week and have made this much progress. Please allow us some more time to find out where this is going to, plug it, and arrest the people who are doing it."

Victoria looked at me and I nodded. "Okay, Agent Foster," she said, "I'll allow it to continue, but if it starts to interfere in the other work this foundation does, I'll have to cut it off, and we'll need to find another way."

"Understood."

Victoria and I left the conference room and returned to her office. "I can't let this foundation go under. So many are counting on us. *Matka* would be so disappointed."

"Victoria," I said, taking a step closer to her, "you can't think that way. This team is one of the best. They'll find out what's going on and hold them accountable."

Agent Foster appeared in the doorway, and Victoria motioned him in.

"What can I do for you, Agent?"

"Mrs. Lansing, Agent Quinn, I have some questions I would like to ask you, if you don't mind."

"Of course, go ahead." Victoria pointed to a chair. "Please sit, Agent Foster."

"Mrs. Lansing, we've found the originating hack's IP address to be a computer from inside your home. It was only logged into once, but that's what started the ball rolling. Can you account for all the computers in your home?"

Victoria frowned. "Are you sure?"

"Positive."

"Well, I have a computer, my husband, my daughter and two sons when they're home, and Ms. Quinn here."

"We've checked all those addresses, and they're not a match. Does any of the help have a computer?"

"Most of the help are gone now since Mrs. Robinson has passed. I never saw anyone with one though."

"Agent Foster," I said, "can you tell me the IP address you're looking for? Also, when this login took place?"

"Oh, I'm sorry, I thought we told you that. It was in November of last year."

Sarah and Brian started then. I kept my thoughts to myself but told the agent I would do some checking on my own and get back to him. He rose from his chair, wrote the IP address on two of his cards, and gave us each one.

"Don't hesitate to call anytime if you find something, Agent Quinn."

After Agent Foster left, Victoria looked over at me. "Spill it," she said. "I know that look."

I bit my lower lip. "Okay, I didn't want to tell the agent, but I'm positive November of last year was when Sarah and Brian started. Did you see either of them with a laptop?"

"I didn't pay any attention," Victoria replied. "So much has gone on that I've had to ignore stuff like that. I know Sarah had a phone she often used, but honestly, I don't think I saw a laptop."

"How about Brian? Did he have one?"

"He might have had a tablet to record *Matka*'s exercises and progress. Same with Sarah, with all those medications to be accounted for," Victoria said.

I got up and walked to the door. "I'll head to the house and check it out. I'll call you if I learn anything."

On my way to the house, I called Sarah.

"Sarah, can I ask you a couple of questions? It's about your time with Granny May." I didn't wait for her to say no. "Can you tell me who hired you and when you started working?"

"Oh my! Is something wrong? Do I need to come there? I was just leaving, but—"

"No, no, no, but I need to ask you some questions to rule some things out. So do you remember?"

"Sure, it was a little over a year ago, right before Thanksgiving. I was contacted by an agency, I don't remember their name, but I may have the paperwork from them. Let me look. They wanted to hire me to be a home nurse for Granny. I don't do much home nursing, but I was between jobs and thought, 'What the hell.' I'm glad I jumped on it. She was rough on me at times, but overall she was such a wonderful woman."

"That she was," I agreed. "Do you know where this company is located? Or do you have a number for them?"

Sarah told me the name and number. "Is there a problem with them?" she asked.

"No, I'm looking for another home nurse for a friend of mine," I lied. "I figured I'd give them a shot."

"Oh, I think they went out of business. I tried to call them after Mrs. Robinson died to see if any more work was available, but no one ever called me back."

"Were you able to get your last check through them? Maybe there's an address on it."

"After the first check from the agency, VFX, Mrs. Robinson paid me personally from some bank out of Alexandria, Virginia."

Thoughts were bouncing around my head like pinballs. This made no sense.

"Sarah, one last question, then I'll let you go. Did you use a computer or tablet to document Granny May's medications and activities?"

"Yeah, sure. That was another reason I was trying to call the agency. I needed to return their tablet. I still have it if you want it. You can't get internet or anything on it. It's just for documentation."

Finally! Something was going my way. Sarah said it was in a box in Granny May's room.

"You're welcome to it, hope it helps."

"Thanks, Sarah!"

When I got to the house, I went to Granny's room and found the box Sarah mentioned. Inside was a small black tablet. I almost ran to my room to charge it but caught myself. I looked all over the tablet; it was nondescript. Black, no markings, no tags or serial numbers. I couldn't even tell what brand it was. I called Victoria and told her about my conversation with Sarah.

"That's strange," she said. "I never thought about Sarah coming from an agency. I thought the hospital referred her. She was with Granny at the hospital when she was discharged."

"Victoria, Sarah said the agency was VFX...that name sounds so familiar, but I can't place it. Also, Sarah told me Granny May paid her through a bank in Alexandria. Is that a coincidence?"

"I'll call the bank in the morning and ask them about this. Should I tell Agent Foster what you learned?"

"Yes, I'll send you pics of the tablet and, if it ever charges, pics of what comes up. Are you staying in Bridgeport tonight?"

"Yes, I'm too tired to drive home. Why don't you bring the tablet here in the morning? The team can go through it."

We hung up with more questions than we had answers. I called Katerina. "Do you have time to talk?"

"Sure, what's up?"

I told her in detail everything that happened today. She was as confused as I was.

"I wish I was there to help. They have me on limited duty because of the BS Dad pulled with the press and on TV. Most of them didn't know I was a senator's daughter since I was using Granny's last name and not Lansing, and I liked it that way. Now that everyone knows, I may take a leave of absence and come home."

"You put in all that hard work on this case, and they're cutting you out? That's bull!"

"Yeah. So, you said the team checked all of our IP addresses?"

"Yep, all that were in the house."

"Even Granny's?"

"Granny's? I never knew she had a computer. Did she even use it?"

"Sometimes. I showed her how to check the news and weather, plus she played some card games on it. I always laughed at her because she had a Post-it note stuck on it with all her passwords. I told her that defeated the purpose of keeping her things secure. She answered me by saying, 'Who wants to know my solitaire scores anyway?'"

I went silent. Granny May had a computer, and all the passwords were stuck on it.

"Jara, you there?"

"Yes, yes, where is this computer?"

"I don't know, probably packed in some of her stuff in the basement. Oh my god, you think that's the computer that was used!"

"Yes, I do, and I have to find it. I love you, gotta go."

I called Victoria right away and told her about Granny's computer.

"I'll tell Agent Foster. He'll drive me back in the morning, and we'll look for it."

I hung up and looked at the clock: 3 a.m. I needed to sleep, but I was too amped up. I went down to the basement and started looking through the boxes.

The following morning, Victoria and Agent Foster arrived at the house to look for the laptop. I had fallen asleep in the basement, not making much headway with my search. We continued searching for the laptop in the basement storage, pulling out box after box.

Victoria brushed back a loose lock of hair. "I don't ever remember seeing a laptop when we were going through her things. Did you, Jara?"

"No, I would have remembered that. Granny with electronics, just can't picture it."

My phone rang. It was Katerina. "Hey, gorgeous! How are you?"

"Good," she replied. "I'm coming home. There's nothing I can do anymore on this trial. With all the publicity from Granny's service, the powers that be felt I would be a liability now everyone knows I'm the senator's daughter. Dad made sure of that."

Knocking the dust off another box, I sneezed. "Excuse me. I'm sorry about the trial. I know how much heart and soul you put into it, but I can't say I'm sad that you are coming home. I'm up to my elbows in boxes, cobwebs, and dust."

"Sounds inviting, but that really isn't why I called. The medical examiner called and has the autopsy results ready to discuss. I know Christmas is coming up, but I scheduled a meeting so the family could be there. I want the answers as soon as possible. I'm going to call Chase and CJ and see if they want to attend."

"That's great news! We'll know once and for all how Granny May died. So when are you coming home?"

"Tomorrow, I think, going to wrap up some things here first then head home."

"Can't wait to see you. Talk with you tonight?"

"Yep. Love you."

"Love you too."

Victoria, Agent Foster, and I tore through the storage boxes like bloodhounds on a hunt. Finally, in the back corner, in a box marked "cards," they found it, a small laptop. Of course it was marked "cards." That's what she used it for. The computer needed to be charged, so Agent Foster gathered all the chargers and Sarah's tablet and headed back to the Foundation. Victoria decided to stay behind for the meeting over the toxicology results.

Chapter Twenty

We were going through the pantry when they heard a knock on the door. I opened it and there stood Sarah, holding two sacks of groceries. "Hello! Looks like I got here in the nick of time. I decided to go shopping for dinner, in case you haven't eaten. I hope I didn't assume wrong. I thought maybe you needed my help with the tablet, so I drove over and then saw all these cars. Has something happened? You've all been so busy lately. The least I can do is make you a meal."

"Thank you, Sarah, that's very considerate of you," Victoria said. "I'll help you put these away and see what we have." Victoria gave me a confused look and headed into the kitchen.

I watched as Sarah and Victoria started pulling the groceries out of the bags. Something was bothering me. Didn't Sarah just say she was leaving?

We started making dinner and my phone rang. "Quinn."

"Hello, Ms. Quinn, this is Detective Andrew Cooper from the Connecticut State Police. May I have a moment of your time?"

"Of course, what can I do for you?"

"I know you're a friend of the family and also with the FBI. We're working with local law enforcement on the murder of Ekaterina Majewski-Robinson. We were wondering if we could set up a meeting to talk with the family?"

I was quiet for moment, letting the word "murder" sink into my head. I knew Katerina suspected as much, but to actually hear the word come out of a detective's mouth was another thing.

"Ms. Quinn?"

"Yes, I'm here, Detective," I replied, pulling myself together. "Who would you like to meet with and when?"

"We'll need to speak with all persons who were in the house the week Mrs. Robinson died. Can you make a list for me?"

"Of course. I'll speak with Mrs. Lansing about it as soon as we hang up."

"We'd also like to come to the house and look at the scene. I know we won't find much since it's been so long, but we want to cover all our bases."

"I totally understand. You're free to come anytime."

"Wonderful. We'll be out shortly."

I went back into the kitchen and looked at Victoria and Sarah. "Uh...I just got off the phone with a Detective Cooper. Granny

May's death has been ruled a homicide. He and some other officers are coming out here tonight to search the house and ask us questions. We also need to make a list of who was in the house the week Granny passed."

Victoria was cutting vegetables and dropped the knife she had in her hand. Sarah went white as a ghost.

"Murder," Sarah exclaimed. "Why do they think it's murder? She died in her sleep."

"Sarah, I don't know all the details, but I do know the autopsy results are finally back. Something in them must have prompted the change for the cause of death."

Victoria was wringing her hands with the hand towel. She walked over to a chair and sat down. "They're coming tonight?"

I went over to her and put my arm around her shoulders. "The officers will just be doing their jobs. We need to answer honestly and start making the list for the detective. I'll call Katerina now. I know she was here the day before Granny May died."

I wanted to grab a beer but felt it wouldn't look the best, me drinking around a house full of cops. I called Katerina and told her what was going on.

"Oh my god! I was right. She was murdered!" Katerina cried. "I knew something was up when the medical examiner wouldn't tell me about the results over the phone. I'm going to pack a few things and head home now."

"Okay, I'll tell your mom. Please be careful."

Victoria and Sarah were making the list when the doorbell rang. Detective Cooper and his team entered, apologizing for the late evening intrusion. "Since we're already behind the eight ball on this," he said, "I wanted to talk with you all as soon as possible."

"Detective Cooper," Victoria said, offering her hand. "I'm Mrs. Lansing, Mrs. Robinson's daughter. May I ask how she died?"

"Hello, Mrs. Lansing. Thank you for allowing us to come to your home so late. I really don't want to discuss the details as of yet, but I do know you and your family have a meeting with the medical examiner coming up. I can say it was an intentional type of overdose."

"Overdose! *Matka* never took any street drugs or painkillers. She only took her heart medications and some supplements for her arthritis. How could she overdose?"

"Mrs. Lansing, there are all types of overdoses that are not caused by opioids or street drugs. I'll need a list of all medications and supplements she was on."

I looked at Sarah. "Detective Cooper, this is Sarah Miles. She was Mrs. Robinson's home nurse until she passed."

Detective Cooper raised his eyebrows. "Ms. Miles, could you make a list of medications Mrs. Robinson was on?"

Sarah nodded and looked at me. "I may need the tablet you have, though, for all the meds she was prescribed from the hospital upon her discharge."

"Yes, Ms. Miles, I'll need that also," said Detective Cooper. "That will be quite helpful."

I asked to speak with the detective alone, and we went into the den. "Sir, there's another investigation going on that you need to know about. We've handed over the medication tablet and Mrs. Robinson's computer to an agent from financial investigations." I explained to him the investigation involving the Foundation and gave him all their contact information.

Detective Cooper sent his team to Granny May's room and her area of the house. Not much had been done to it since she passed, other than boxing up papers and miscellaneous stuff. Victoria gave him the list of people and contact information for all who were at the house. Detective Cooper asked to speak to Sarah first. Victoria showed him to the library, away from where we were all gathered. He and another officer, a detective I presumed, took Sarah into the room and shut the door.

The crime scene personnel finished rather quickly in Granny May's room and asked to see the rest of her belongings.

Victoria spoke up. "This whole estate was *Matka*'s. You're welcome to look anywhere you like. Most of her paperwork and records are boxed up in the basement or at the Foundation in Bridgeport."

Victoria showed the officers to the basement storage and returned to the kitchen.

"She's been in there an awfully long time," Victoria said about Sarah's interview. "I wonder what that means."

At that moment Katerina burst through the front door and rushed over to her mother. "Mom, I'm so sorry this is happening," she said. "I just needed to know what happened to Granny."

Victoria hugged her daughter. "It's okay. This isn't your fault. We all need to know what happened and who's responsible for it."

Katerina came over and kissed me. "How are you doing? The police are still here?"

"I'm okay," I said, "and yes they're still here looking around and talking to Sarah."

"Do they have a search warrant?" Katerina asked.

"Honey, I gave them permission to search the whole house," Victoria said. "I signed the paperwork and everything. It's okay."

The library door swung open, and Sarah emerged, crying. She looked at Victoria and said, "I'm sorry, Victoria! I'm sorry!" and ran to her car.

We all looked at each other in shock.

Detective Cooper came out of the room and asked for Victoria, who squeezed Katerina's hand and went into the library.

"I'm going to check on Sarah," I said to Katerina.

I found her in her car, still crying. I tapped on her window and asked, "Sarah, are you okay?"

"They're implying I killed Mrs. Robinson. I didn't. At least, I don't think I did. I promise I gave her the amount of medication I always gave, what was prescribed." She sobbed. "I would never hurt her!"

"Sarah, could you have made a mistake or read a dosage wrong?"

"They asked me that. Without the tablet, I can't tell you what I gave her. I told them what I remembered were her medications and dosages. I always checked and rechecked that, right person, right med, right dose, right route, right time. I know that sounds stupid doing that for one person, but you never knew when a medication or a dose would change. It was ingrained in me. Do I need to get a lawyer?"

"Sarah, I can't answer that for you. You have to decide that one for yourself, but please don't drive if you are too upset."

"I'm fine. This all caught me off guard." Sarah wiped her tears. "And now the police are involved..." Sarah started to cry again.

I put my hand on her shoulder, hoping it would help in calming her down. "The police are only doing their jobs. No one is being accused yet. Your tablet will be very helpful. Thank you for that."

Sarah's phone rang and both of us jumped. She answered and immediately said, "I don't know. I'll have to call you—" She pulled the phone from her ear and said to the screen, "—later."

I could only see it was a Washington DC number, but not who was calling.

"Sorry about that," Sarah said. "I just need to go."

With that she put the car in gear and drove off. I barely had a chance to pull my arm out of the driver's window. I stood in the driveway for a minute until I heard Katerina calling me from the front door. I walked back, wondering who had called her.

"What's going on with Sarah?" Katerina ask.

"She feels they're accusing her of killing Granny May, even by accident. She didn't tell me what they asked her or how they implied it, but it definitely has to do with Granny May's meds."

Katerina frowned. "Do you think she did it?"

"I have no idea."

Victoria walked into the room. "Katerina, they'd like to talk with you now."

Katerina took a deep breath, swallowed, and went into the library.

Victoria sat on the couch. "I can't believe someone would hurt *Matka* intentionally, but then again, I don't think it could have been an accident."

"I don't understand. What did he say?"

"Something was given to *Matka* to cause a heart attack, and she had way too much of it in her system for it to have been an accident."

"Did he say what it was?" I asked.

"Potassium chloride, a medication *Matka* had been taking for her heart for years," she answered. "I guess we'll learn more from the medical examiner. Where's Sarah?"

"After her talk with the detective, she ran to her car and left."

It had been hours since Detective Cooper started the interviews and searched the house. I had only spoken to him briefly, due to not having been in the home the week of Granny's death. Finally his team left, and he entered the den where we were waiting.

"Mrs. Lansing, I'll coordinate with the financial investigators about the computers," Detective Cooper said. "They're in the best hands possible. Can we meet the week after Christmas to discuss the Foundation investigation in depth?"

"Of course, anything you need, Detective. I'll schedule a day out for you."

"One more thing, Mrs. Lansing. Am I able to see a copy of the will for my investigation?"

"Of course, Detective. I'll contact our probate lawyer and see what we can do about that."

"Thank you. Have a good holiday, Mrs. Lansing."

After the detective left, we all let out a collective exhale. None of us were hungry. We grabbed the tequila and headed to the back porch, where we flopped on the lounge chairs after lighting the fire.

Katerina spoke up. "She wasn't supposed to die."

We sat in silence, drinking and staring off toward the water. The moonlight made the tops of the rippling waves twinkle, and though beautiful, I don't think any of us appreciated it.

Victoria finished her drink. "I'll call CJ and Chase and let them know the detective may want to speak with them. I'll also call Mr. Maxwell. I don't think I have it in me, so could one of you call Charles? He needs to be told."

I nodded. "Sure, I'll do it first thing in the morning. That is, if he answers my call."

Victoria kissed us each on the head and went up to bed. Katerina and I remained on the porch drinking, not saying much, until we were too tired to drink anymore.

Chapter Twenty-One

I awoke before the sun rose the next morning, my head pounding. *Why is it such a good idea to drink at the time, but you pay for it dearly the next day?* Katerina was still sleeping soundly. She looked different this morning somehow. A bit more fragile, maybe. I kissed her, whispered, "I love you," and went downstairs to the den to start my calls. I called Travis, but it went to voicemail. I left a brief message about what was going on and if he was mad at me to get over it and call me. Light was coming through the windows, and I realized the sun was just now rising.

I went to the kitchen and had a few cups of coffee, hoping they would help my throbbing head before I needed to make the call to Charles. A whole different type of headache.

I called his personal cell phone, his personal phone line at the office, then the front desk. I was transferred to Bella. If she knew it was me, she didn't let on.

"Senator Charles Lansing's office, soon to be the next President. May I help you?"

"Bella, this is Jara. Don't hang up, please. I need to speak to Charles, uh, Senator Lansing, as soon as possible. It's quite important."

"Why should I transfer you to him after the scene you made in here?"

"Because, Bella, the police want to speak with him, and I thought it would be polite of me to give him a heads-up. That's why!"

She paused. "I'll transfer you."

Seconds later, Charles came on the line. "What do you want?"

"Listen, if I didn't have to call you, I wouldn't," I said. "I promised Victoria I would call you and inform you that Granny May's cause of death has been changed to homicide. The police would like to speak with you."

"Why do they want to speak with me? I didn't kill her. Are you trying to blame this on me? I'll have your job—"

My head throbbed harder. "Listen, no one is blaming you. They spoke with most of us and went through the residence. They're trying to touch base with everyone who was in the house that week."

152

"I had nothing to do with that vile woman. She hated me for no reason. I had nothing to do with her medicines or activities around the house."

"Medicines?" I asked. "Why would you say that?"

"Well, we would have known if she were shot or stabbed, so the only things left are poisoning or suffocation. So I guessed. I personally tried my damnedest to stay away from her."

"Okay, okay," I said. "I just wanted to give you the heads up. You can speak to them if you're coming up for Christmas. I'm sure your grandson would like to see you."

"Leave my grandson out of this! I'll let Victoria know what my plans are. Don't call me again!" *Click.*

That went well.

Victoria came into the den. "I gather that was Charles?"

"Smart guess."

Victoria shook her head. "That man."

I smiled.

Victoria said, "It looks like it's going to be an unusual Lansing Christmas this year. I called Mr. Maxwell and informed him of the death investigation. He stated most things have been sorted out with the will, the court has ruled on most of it, and no one has contested it as of yet. He would like to read what he can for the family, per *Matka*'s wishes."

"When is this going to be?"

"He said he could come in between Christmas and New Year's or wait until the first week of January. I know we're meeting with the medical examiner tomorrow, so I thought since everyone would hopefully still be here, we'd do it after Christmas."

"Does this mean I have to call Charles again?" I whined.

She laughed and shook her head no. "You're off the hook. Mr. Maxwell will call him. I called the boys last night, and they'll be here this afternoon."

I walked back upstairs to tell Katerina and found her still in bed, curled into a ball, crying. She raised her head as I entered and said, "I thought I wanted to know how Granny died. I don't think I do anymore. It' caused so many issues." I sat on the bed and took her hand as she moved to place her head in my lap. Between sobs I heard, "I only want Granny back! I thought if I knew..."

We stayed in our room the rest of the day and into the evening. Victoria knocked on the door and came in, asking if we were okay. She walked over to the bed and sat on the edge.

Katerina pulled her mother into a hug and started sobbing and apologizing.

"Now stop that," Victoria said sternly. "You have nothing to apologize for. We needed to know what happened, and you were the only one with enough courage to do what needed to be done. *Matka* would be very proud of you."

"But it doesn't bring her back," Katerina said, still crying.

"No, honey, it doesn't. But we can get her justice. I know that would be what she'd want." We sat quietly for a few minutes, then Victoria sighed and stood up. "I wanted you to know your brothers are here if you want to come down, but don't feel you have to."

Katerina wiped her face, and said, "No, Mom, I want to stay up here. I'll see them tomorrow. I don't want to deal with either of them today." She leaned back and looked at me. "You can go down if you want," she said.

"No, my love, my place is with you." I brushed the hair from her face, looked at her swollen, red eyes, and kissed her on her forehead. "Let me get you a cold cloth for your eyes."

Katerina nodded, took her mother's hand, and told her she loved her. I returned, wet cloth in hand, to see both Katerina and her mother, hugging and crying again. My heart broke, knowing the pain they were feeling, although no arms had held me or shared the weight of my grief when my parents died, only the crushing silence of being alone. A pang of envy hit me, and I lost myself in the wish that I could hug my mother again. I was startled when Victoria got up, wiped her eyes, and hugged me. I sat on the bed and gently placed the cloth across her eyes. Her shoulders relaxed, and soon her breathing became soft and steady. My love had fallen asleep.

We stayed in our room after waking the next morning, other than me slipping down for coffee. I retreated back to our room when I heard the others coming down the stairs. We took our time getting ready, lingering in the shower until the last minute. Before we got downstairs, we could hear arguing.

The family had gathered in the kitchen. "What a way to spend Christmas," Chase said. "I could be skiing."

"Shut up, Chase," yelled CJ. "We all need to be here and get this stuff figured out. Sorry Christmas and Granny dying interfered with your ski plans."

"I don't know why I have to be here," Chase complained. "I wasn't in the house that week, and you all can tell me what the ME says. I don't understand that stuff anyway."

CJ sneered. "So medicine and human compassion weren't covered in any of the hundreds of majors you've declared, huh?"

Victoria slammed her hand on the table. "Stop it. I'm sorry this is such an inconvenience to all of you. This is not how I wanted the holiday to go either. But it's something we must do, and we'll get through it. We're going to meet with the examiner today and Mr. Maxwell next week. So if you all could just play nice for one long weekend, maybe, just maybe, we can get this over with, and you can go your separate ways." By this time, Victoria was crying. "And to top it off, your father will arrive today for the meeting and stay for the weekend."

Moans and groans ensued.

"Like I said, play nice or go home," Victoria said. "I don't have the energy to babysit all of you."

The room fell silent when Katerina and I entered the kitchen. Then Chase spoke up. "Mom, I'm—"

"I don't want to hear it from you, nor any of you for that matter. I'm going to my room until it's time to leave." Victoria headed for the stairs.

Katerina glared at her brothers. "Way to go, guys. Just what Mom needs."

"Oh, stuff it, Sis," yelled Chase. "We're only in this mess because you demanded an autopsy."

"What? *My* fault? I demanded an autopsy because someone *killed* Granny. That is what we're here for, to find who did it and how." Katerina was nose to nose with her brother. "You got something to hide, Chase?"

"Back down, Kat. I'm not blaming you, and you better not be blaming me." Chase pushed her back.

I grabbed Katerina, and CJ grabbed Chase before it became a knock-down, drag-out fight.

"No one is blaming anyone," I yelled. "We've all been under a lot of stress, and we need to relax. We need to be here for your mother. She's been strong for this whole mess, supporting all of you. Victoria lost her mother, damn it, give the woman a break."

CJ pushed Chase out of the kitchen, and I guided Katerina upstairs to our room. Katerina threw herself on the bed and pounded her fists on the mattress. "I'm so damned mad!"

I placed my hand on her back, and after a few minutes, she turned over. "Will you hold me?"

I moved more fully onto the bed, and after she laid her head in my lap, she cried herself to sleep. I must have dozed off, too, because a knock on the door startled me. It was Julia.

"Hey, Jara," she whispered. "We'll be leaving in about thirty minutes. Wanted to give you a heads up."

"Okay. Thanks. We're going to drive separately, I think, but we'll be down shortly."

I reluctantly woke Katerina and told her we needed to get ready and leave. We freshened up and headed downstairs.

Everyone was in the foyer, much quieter this time. "Katerina and I are driving separately, so we'll meet you there," I said, as we walked out the door.

When we got to the car, Katerina slid into her seat and looked up at me. "Thank you. I don't think I could handle anyone else in the car with us right now."

"I figured as much," I said, and I closed her door.

We made it to the medical examiner's office with time to spare. We were escorted to a conference room and provided with bottled water and some packaged cookies. I grabbed a couple of bottles of water and handed one to Katerina, who had taken a seat. In my peripheral vision, I saw Charles enter.

"What are *you* doing here?" Katerina hissed.

"I was told the examiner was going to reveal the cause of death, so I felt I should be here for your mother," her father replied.

"For Mom? That's a laugh!" Katerina said just as Victoria entered the room.

"Katerina," she admonished, "I did ask him to come. We need to be a family for this, and he's family."

She's up to something again.

The rest of the family filed in and took seats. The medical examiner came in, followed by Detective Cooper. *Bingo! The detective is here to see our reactions, and Victoria wants him to see Charles.*

"Hello, I'm Dr. Stanley Rice, the medical examiner for this case." The doctor spoke matter-of-factly. "This is Detective Andrew Cooper from the Connecticut State Police. Some of you have already met him. I'm going to try and explain this as simply as possible. Ekaterina Anastasia Majewski-Robinson died of an overdose of potassium."

Everyone began to murmur, but the doctor went on. "It's highly unusual to accidentally overdose on potassium, although it is possible. In this case, though, Mrs. Robinson had extremely high levels of potassium in her bloodstream, along with an ACE inhibitor called Lisinopril. She also had a large amount of potassium at a very high dosage in her stomach, showing she ingested the drug orally and not long before she died. It would be hard for either of these medications to actually kill you, but together, they can be very lethal. It's rare both of these drugs would be prescribed at the same time except as a last resort, and then under very close supervision of a physician. I believe the Lisinopril had been ingested at the same time high levels of potassium were also given and over an extended period. Lisinopril then prevented the renal system from doing its job properly and the kidneys couldn't excrete the excess potassium, causing a buildup. This is called hyperkalemia.

With Mrs. Robinson's heart issues this was very dangerous. She probably had symptoms prior to her death, but they could've gone unnoticed. Due to the excess potassium, it caused a fatal heart attack sometime during the night. From what I've learned from my research and from the detective here, Mrs. Robinson was on potassium chloride for her heart but had no prescription for Lisinopril. The prescription she had for potassium was not nearly enough to harm her, let alone kill her. We found no other drugs found in her system. All her organs and body tissue were in good shape considering her age and heart issues. Any questions?"

Victoria spoke up. "Had she been given this combination for a long time, or in one dose?"

The doctor's tone was sympathetic. "Mrs. Lansing, it looks to me like she received increased doses of potassium for a while, and the Lisinopril was given in high doses possibly over the course of a couple of weeks to a month."

The detective broke in. "This death is currently under investigation, so many details can't be given out until they're followed up on by my office. If you have any other questions, please direct them to me, and I'll try and answer them the best I can. I see a few of you here I haven't met with yet, so if you could follow me over to the station, I can get your interviews knocked out as quickly as possible."

As we got up from our seats, Charles headed toward the door. "Senator, Senator Lansing!" The detective came up beside him with an outstretched hand. "Senator, hello, I'm Detective Cooper."

"I know who you are," Charles replied tersely.

"Well, Senator, we've been trying to reach you. You have one good secretary, there."

Charles gave a dismissive nod.

"Senator, I need to interview you today if you would, so I'm asking you to come to the station. You can either ride with me or follow, your choice."

"Seriously." Charles sneered. "I have a choice?"

"Please, sir, I would like to get your interview over with so you can enjoy the holiday weekend."

"Fine. I'll meet you there." Charles stormed out.

I looked over at Victoria and saw a faint grin. Never mess with a queen bee.

Chapter Twenty-Two

Most of the family followed Detective Cooper to the station for interviews. Victoria rode back to the house with us.

"I would love to be a fly on the wall," Katerina said as we drove, "when they talk to Dad. He's going to huff and puff, then do the political two-step with them. I hope they know what they're up against."

We all laughed, though nervously.

I spoke. "I wonder if they've interviewed Brian yet. Does anyone know where he is?"

"Sarah may," Victoria replied. "They were very close."

We ordered a large assortment of Chinese food on the way home.

Calvin greeted us at the door. "Is it Christmas yet, Granny V? Is Santa coming here?"

I grimaced. We had no presents, no decorations, not even a tree. The look on Katerina's face revealed we were thinking the same thing.

"Hey, Calvin, do you know what we need to help Santa find the right chimney?" I asked.

His eyes widened. "A tree," he yelled.

"You got it. Do you want to go with Aunt Kat and me to pick one out? Maybe while we're gone, Granny V and your mom can look for some decorations. I'm sure the rest of the family will be here soon to help."

Victoria sighed. "That sounds like a wonderful idea."

I grabbed a small container of house lo mein and a fork and headed to the door. Calvin was right on my heels, followed by Katerina. I checked the Defender for ropes and bungees and off we went.

Katerina remembered a tree farm not too far from the house. We soon located it, all lit up with Christmas lights, with lush trees for sale. We pulled into the lot and Katerina released Calvin from his car seat. He jumped out and headed toward a small shack that served as an office. A large, red-suited man with a white mustache and beard stepped out.

"Ho, ho, ho! Hey there, big fella! Are you ready for Christmas?"

"Santa!" Calvin cried. "We need a tree so you can find where I am this Christmas."

"Ho, ho, ho!" Santa bellowed. "Well, let's go find one, but I think you may need an elf hat. What do you think?" He placed a small green elf hat on Calvin's head and took his hand.

Calvin was over the moon excited, as we all walked over to a huge pine grove.

I looked around at all the shapes and sizes of trees. "How big do we want this tree? The house can accommodate any of these, but do you know where we'll put it?"

Katerina smiled. "I have an idea. Let's order a huge tree for the foyer, have it delivered and decorated, and we'll take the family out for brunch. Tonight, let's get a small one for the living room."

Katerina and I returned to the makeshift shed, which was painted to look like Santa's workshop, and spoke to a lady inside.

The lady, who was dressed like Mrs. Claus, smiled. "Of course! This will be wonderful."

We returned just as Calvin found the perfect tree.

"Santa," he said, "can you find us with this one?"

"I'll be on the lookout for it. You've been a good boy, right?"

"Oh, yes!" Calvin tugged on the man's sleeve to whisper to him. "Santa, my family's been sad this year. Can you bring things to make them happy?"

Santa glanced in our direction. "I think something can be done about that." He called over two of his helpers to cut the tree and load it on the Defender. Santa pulled me aside and asked what he could do to help. He was a local and had recognized Katerina. Jacob Snow, also known as Santa, knew the family and was very fond of Granny. He owned multiple stores and strip malls. He offered to open a few of them after hours so we could shop for Christmas.

We came home with the tree and set it up in the living room in the corner by the fireplace. Victoria and Abby had found some decorations and Chase and CJ were struggling to untangle lines and lines of lights. Katerina announced we were taking the family out for brunch tomorrow, no exceptions. I called Mr. Snow, making plans for a Sunday shopping trip. Katerina and I sat back, watching as the family decorated the tree, Calvin supervising in his elf hat. Katerina pulled her brothers away from the festivities and told them about the shopping trip.

"Thank goodness," a relieved CJ said. "We were in such a hurry to get here, we never thought to pack any of his presents."

Chase shook his head. "So what are we going to do?"

160

Katerina explained our plans regarding the large tree and Mr. Snow opening a few of his stores after hours.

"How are we going to keep this shopping trip a secret?" asked CJ.

We hadn't thought of that.

"Hey," I said, "I have a brilliant idea!"

I called Mr. Snow and asked if any of his stores had a website. When he confirmed, I asked, "Can we order things, have them wrapped, and if I can push it a bit, could you dress up like Santa and deliver them on Monday? I know you have your own family to be with, but we would greatly appreciate it."

"Ms. Quinn, I owe Mrs. Robinson my livelihood. When no one else believed in me, she did. She helped me start my first business and even supported me when I expanded. When we didn't have food, she had groceries delivered. My daughter even got a scholarship from the Foundation. I would be honored to help you out."

"Thank you so much, Mr. Snow." This would be a Christmas to remember.

I texted Mr. Snow when we were leaving for brunch, and the tree was ready to be delivered. We made our way into town and filled up the back room of a restaurant. Everyone was animated and having a good time. A hush came over the room when Charles walked in.

I stood up and said, "I hope you all don't mind. I invited Charles. After all, it *is* the Christmas season."

Charles was unusually quiet during the meal. He sat next to Victoria and Calvin, who was ecstatic to sit next to Grandpa. The senator seemed like he was having a good time. We had been at the restaurant for a couple of hours when my phone buzzed.

Ms. Quinn, this is Mr. Snow. Your package has been delivered and is ready for viewing.

I looked over at Katerina and grinned. A short time later, everyone prepared to leave. Victoria invited Charles back to the house to be with the family. Katerina and I drove ahead, trying to get there first.

When we pulled into the drive, we saw lights twinkling from the front windows.

When she arrived, Victoria gave us a look. "What are you girls up to?"

CJ and Chase joined us as Victoria and Calvin opened the front door.

"Santa was here. Santa was here." screamed Calvin.

Victoria put her hand over her mouth and started crying as Charles put his arm around her and helped her inside.

The tree was magnificent. It was at least eighteen feet tall, with a sparkling angel looking down from the top. The smell of fresh cut balsam fir filled the air. The tree was decorated with reds and golds, antique and shiny ornaments of all sizes, and old-fashioned lights, with a running Lionel 100th anniversary Gold 700 E Hudson train set winding through a Christmas snow village beneath. Presents were piled up all around the village. I felt like I was inside a snow globe or a Norman Rockwell painting. It was nice to see the family together again. I missed Granny May but knew in my heart she approved. I could almost see her, her eyes wide with excitement, inspecting the tree, checking every ornament, her cane tapping softly as she moved about. Granny putting her hand over her mouth as she whispered, "Oh my stars, look at that..." when she saw the angel on top of the tree. Victoria and Julia had found the tree topper that was used all the years Victoria was growing up. *Yes*, I thought, *Granny would approve.*

The next few days flew by with lots of decorating and cooking. Charles stayed at the house. He appeared a bit uncomfortable at first but settled in after a couple of bourbons. Christmas Day arrived with Calvin getting up way too early, announcing it was time to open the presents. All of the groggy adults got up, put on their robes and slippers, and went downstairs. The coffee maker came on, and Victoria set out the breakfast pastries. An empty glass and plate on the hearth served as proof that Santa had eaten his midnight snack. After breakfast we all got dressed and Calvin put on his elf hat to help pass out presents. Julia told him he had to wait, and he tensed up like a spring coil.

Suddenly, everyone's ears pricked up. "Do you hear that?" CJ said.

I ran to the window. "Sounds like sleigh bells," I yelled.

Calvin joined me at the window. "It's Santa! He's come back!"

Out on the front drive were Mr. and Mrs. Snow, dressed as Santa and Mrs. Claus, sitting in a sleigh pulled by a pair of tan, white-maned Clydesdales. We opened the big front double doors and gasped in awe. Santa helped Mrs. Claus out of the sleigh and grabbed a large, red velvet bag.

"I hope you've all been good boys and girls this year!"

Calvin squealed with glee. We invited them into the house and brought out two chairs.

"Who is Calvin?" Santa bellowed.

Calvin ran to him and jumped on his lap. Santa handed him a stuffed Mickey Mouse and an envelope for his parents: four tickets to Disney World, all expenses paid.

Next, Santa called Charles up. "Have you been a good boy?"

Charles shrugged his shoulders and laughed. "Some don't seem to think so," he said.

Charles took his gift and opened it: a family bible from his grandparents, the only thing he had saved from his childhood. I had never seen Charles cry before. "I thought I'd lost this."

"This is for your inauguration, for your swearing in," Santa said.

Victoria had found it when we were going through the storage boxes. I remember looking through it, thinking it was a peculiar thing Charles had saved, since he seemed to have no real attachment to his family. Inside the back cover were all the names of his family, with dates of birth and death, except for his parents, John and Maxine, and brother, William. A date was written in, but his brother's date of death was blacked out. The date of his parents' death was also written in but seemed to have been erased and another date added. I could understand not knowing death dates for older relatives, but I felt a son would at least know when his immediate family passed. There were also a couple of old photos of what I assumed was Charles' family on the lobster boat. I was still deep in thought when I heard another loud, "Ho, ho, ho!"

Santa was patting his belly and looked over his wire-rimmed glasses at Katerina.

"My dear, have you been a good girl?"

The room burst into laughter as Santa handed her a box. Katerina opened it and pulled out a bundle tied with a blue ribbon. It was thirty-four letters, one for each birthday, all written by Granny May. Katerina was speechless.

She walked over to me with tears in her eyes. "Did you know about these?"

I smiled sheepishly and said, "Like you said, I've been busy."

"Hmm..." Santa said, rummaging in his big red sack, "I don't have anything for Chase. Wait a minute, maybe it's farther down." Santa reached deep into the bag and pulled out a small box. "Sorry, Chase," he said, "this isn't for you, it's for Abby."

163

An astonished Abby glanced around the room as Chase took the box from Santa. He opened it, exposing a dazzling diamond ring, and got down on one knee. He gazed up at Abby. "If you would be my wife, it would be the greatest Christmas gift ever."

Abby covered her mouth in shock. A moment later, she cried, "Yes, yes, yes!"

Everyone embraced the couple, and the congratulations went on for several minutes.

Santa looked around, feigning confusion. "Is there a Jara here?"

"Don't ask me if I've been good," I commented wryly.

He handed me a small box that jingled.

"Is there an elf in here?" I asked as I opened my present. Inside were the keys and the title to the sailboat. I looked up, my mouth agape. "This isn't real."

Victoria came up beside me. "Yes, it's real. Granny and all of us know how much you love the sailboat, so now it's yours."

As Victoria stood with her arm around me, Santa reached out his hand to her. "I know you've been a very good but sad girl this year. Here is a special present for you." He handed her a small, weathered jewelry box. Victoria opened it and produced a gold oval locket, along with a letter. She read it aloud.

"My beautiful daughter, your father and I love you so much. This locket was my great grandmother's, and my mother brought it here from Poland, one of the few possessions she allowed herself to keep. It has held many pictures over the years of ones who were also loved very much. I give it to you now, hoping you know how much we love you and how proud we are of you. You will always be in our hearts."

Inside the locket were pictures of Victoria's parents and a picture of her as a child. A teary-eyed Victoria hugged me and whispered in my ear, "I know you had something to do with this." She looked around the room. "Thank you, everyone! This has been a fabulous Christmas. I love you all."

Santa and Mrs. Claus stood up and were saying their goodbyes when we heard a commotion outside. I rolled my eyes and glared at Charles. "Of course," I muttered under my breath, "the fucking press!"

Charles called out, "If everyone could come out and pose for one or two family photos, it would mean the world to me."

Victoria gave him a look of warning. "Okay, a few, but this better be the last of it. No self-promotion. Today is Christmas."

We all walked outside into the blowing snow. I held on to Katerina and we stood next to Mr. and Mrs. Claus. Calvin stood in front of us with a broad grin. Flashes went off everywhere.

Katerina turned to me. "Merry Christmas, my love!" she said before she planted a lip-lock on me.

"Ho, ho, ho!" Santa bellowed.

Victoria became the dutiful politician's wife and stood smiling next to her husband, the perfect family Christmas pose. Calvin was a ham for the cameras and showed off his presents to the reporters. Charles even let the press in the house to take photos of the tree in the foyer. I pulled Katerina into the kitchen. We grabbed some drinks and headed to the back porch.

"Thank you for saving me," she said. "I hate all this press stuff. I know Dad needs to do it, but damn!"

Chase came out to the porch and sat beside us on the rattan couch. "How did you two slip off?"

"We hid behind Santa and made a run for it," I said. We all burst into laughter.

Abby appeared, wearing her sparkling engagement ring. Katerina grabbed her hand. "Wow! Chase, we could have used this for a tree topper!"

"This Christmas has been perfect," Abby said as she sat down next to Chase and put her head on his shoulder. Everyone nodded, but I felt bittersweet about the whole thing.

Soon the press was gone, and everyone had moved into the living room by the small Christmas tree. Only Charles and Victoria were missing. A minute or two later, we heard a loud crash. We ran to the foyer and heard Charles and Victoria arguing. I could see reflections off of broken glass in the kitchen doorway.

"Get the hell out of my house." Victoria's voice echoed from the kitchen. "You have manipulated me for the last time. A perfect day, and you went and ruined it by calling the press. You can't stay out of the spotlight for one minute and enjoy your family. Damn you."

"Victoria, I had to. I need to show family support during this campaign. Today was perfect for that."

"Today was fucking Christmas. You couldn't have stopped and asked me if it was okay? Or any of us, for that matter? You just selfishly went ahead."

"I'm trying to benefit us all. Don't you want me to be President?"

"I want you to be a husband, father, and grandfather. Don't you ever think about what *we* need?"

"Fine. If you can't support me physically, then help me financially. My campaign needs benefactors. The Foundation would be perfect."

"Like hell are you getting money from the Foundation. I've already told you no. We're losing money as it is."

I looked at Katerina, who was standing next to me, wide-eyed.

Charles stopped cold, his head tilted and eyes squinted. "Losing money?" Charles questioned. "How is that happening?"

Victoria lowered her voice. "I wish I knew, but we're close to finding out. We have people working on it."

"People? What people? What are they finding?" Charles began interrogating her.

Victoria began picking up the broken glass with a towel and said sternly, "Charles, this doesn't concern you. Don't worry about it. It's taken care of."

Charles stormed into the foyer and glared at me. "Are you part of this?"

"Yes, but there's nothing I can say about an ongoing investigation."

Victoria appeared in the doorway. "Charles, I asked you to leave. Please go."

Charles huffed, grabbed his coat, and walked out.

Katerina went to her mother and embraced her.

"I'm fine," Victoria reassured her. "This is getting old. He's so selfish. If only he had asked me, I would have agreed. But he tried to be slick." Victoria began to tear up. "I'm sick of it. I'm going to my room." She kissed Katerina on the cheek and went upstairs.

We spent the evening cleaning up the shredded wrapping paper and admiring our gifts. I was still in shock over the boat. I kept jingling the keys over and over.

"So, Captain," Katerina teased, "where are we sailing off to?"

I smiled. "If things weren't frozen and the boat not put up, we'd leave right now to wherever you'd like."

Calvin, still wearing his elf hat, walked over to us. "Auntie J, can I still drive the boat?"

"Calvin, I'm naming you First Officer. That means you're second-in-command and in charge of everything when I'm gone."

He giggled and ran off.

I thought about today's events. Did Victoria really slip, or was that calculated on her part? If so, it was a daring move. I excused myself from the party and headed to her room. I knocked softly.

"Come in," she answered. I walked in with a bottle of her favorite wine and a glass.

"I know now why Katerina loves you. You know a way to a woman's heart. Although, I know alcohol is not all that's involved."

I felt my cheeks grow warm. "Let's hope not. How are you doing?" I could tell she had been crying. "Are you still upset about Charles?"

"Actually, I expect those sorts of moves from him. Doesn't make it any easier. What I'm wondering is how did this Christmas miracle take place? I know you were involved, so spill it."

"It wasn't all me. Katerina and the boys took part. It was wonderful seeing them work together and not arguing."

Katerina knocked on the door and came in. "Here you are," she said.

"Girls, thank you for a wonderful Christmas. It was like *Matka* was really here. So many things reminded me of her. The big tree was decorated the same way her parents used to do it." Victoria sighed. "Tomorrow is a big day. Let's hope it goes smoothly."

Katerina and I excused ourselves. "I love you, Mom," Katerina said.

"Love you too, sweetie."

We went back downstairs where the party was finally winding down. Chase and Abby had already gone to bed, and Calvin was falling asleep on his mother's lap. CJ was trying to organize the pile of presents.

He looked up and asked, "Mom okay?"

Katerina waved him off. "You know her. Even if she weren't, we'd never know it. Are we ready for tomorrow?"

CJ shrugged. "I think tomorrow is just borrowing trouble. None of us want anything. I loved Granny, but not because of her money. I don't understand why we need to meet with her lawyer."

"All I hope," I said, "is that we won't have any surprises. I've had enough of those. By the way, thank you all for the sailboat. Please think of it as ours."

CJ came over and hugged me. "I may be a little, or a lot drunk, but you were always a sister to me."

I smiled. "Thanks, CJ. I appreciate it."

Julia spoke up. "You two have always made me feel welcome, never like an outsider. I love you both."

CJ and Julia excused themselves and carried Calvin upstairs.

Soon, Katerina and I were sitting on the floor in front of the fire, alone at last.

"Katerina, I love you. You're beyond my wildest dreams. I don't want to push things, but I want to give you this." I handed her a small box.

She put up her hand. "No, not yet," she said. "We can't ruin things."

I shook my head and laughed. "Although I want you for the rest of my life, this isn't that."

She opened the box to reveal an emerald studded heart necklace with a house key behind it. She gave me a quizzical look.

"Diamonds are so overused and the emeralds bring out your eyes. You have my heart. The key is to my place. What's mine is yours."

We watched the fire burn down to embers before we went upstairs to bed.

Chapter Twenty-Three

Morning came too quickly for me. I could've stayed in bed, cozied up with a still sleeping Katerina, for the whole day. I lay there, watching her breasts rise and fall under the sheet, as I listened to the sounds of the house waking up. This was a wonderful Christmas.

Katerina's eyes fluttered open. She licked her dry lips. "I don't want to do this," she said.

"I know," I replied and pulled her close to me.

We heard a knock on the door. "Wake up, sleepy heads," CJ called out. "If we have to do this, you do too."

"Okay. Okay. We're coming," Katerina hollered impatiently.

I rolled out of bed and headed toward the shower. "Oh no, you don't," Katerina said as she rolled out of bed. "Not without me."

I laughed and started the water. We both tied our hair up so they wouldn't get wet. The hot water felt good on my still tired body, and Katerina massaging soap all over me was even better. We faced each other, suds everywhere, and kissed passionately.

"We don't have time for this," I whispered.

"I know, but it'll give us something to think about all day other than my family." Katerina put my hand between her legs and bit me slightly on the neck. I swallowed hard as I felt her hands exploring me. As she pulled away, she gave me a teasing smile.

I smiled back. "Yes, this will definitely be on my mind."

A few minutes later we stepped out of the shower and got dressed. Katerina put on her new necklace. I was right. It brought out those beautiful green eyes.

"It looks good on you, but then everything does," I said as I admired her.

She got down on the floor and pulled a large box from underneath the bed. She stood up and handed it to me. "Open it," she said.

I placed the box on the bed and untied the ribbon that secured the lid: I removed a navy pair of pants and jacket, perfect for sailing.

"Oh, wow! Thank you. I can't wait to try these on! So you knew about the boat?"

"Of course," she said with a grin.

I threw on the jacket and walked over to the full-length mirror on the wall. "This is perfect," I said.

CJ hollered from the bottom of the stairs. "It's time to go, you two. Get down here."

I took off the jacket and laid it across the bed. We made our way downstairs, and everyone was standing there, staring at us.

Katerina looked around at everyone and laughed. "You know, you all could have left without us. We do know our way there," she said.

"Oh no," CJ warned, "we're making sure you actually make it there. We know how you two go off and hide." Calvin would stay at the house with Julia and Abby.

Our parade of cars made it to the lawyer's office a little before nine. I walked next door to the coffee shop and ordered two large lattes for Katerina and me. My phone buzzed. It was CJ texting. *You better quadruple that order. It's going to be a long day.*

I ordered several more coffees and brought them to the lawyer's office. He greeted me as I entered. Mr. Maxwell was an older attorney, a figure who carried the signs of a long career etched into his very presence. It was his demeanor that commanded respect. His hair, prematurely gray, framed a face that bore the marks of countless hours spent in contemplation. Perched on the bridge of his nose were a pair of wire-rimmed glasses, often nudged back into place with a practiced motion. Years of sedentary work had left their mark on his physique. A noticeable pooched stomach extended slightly over his belt, the inevitable result of long hours spent seated behind a desk, poring over legal texts and case files. His suits, always impeccably tailored, accommodated his middle-aged spread without sacrificing professionalism. The fabric of his jacket stretched comfortably around his midsection, and his ties were always knotted neatly, a small but steadfast commitment to the image he presented to the world.

"A barista now too?" he joked.

"Seems to be."

"There may be some more surprises today. I'm hoping all is good with Mrs. Robinson's wishes." He smiled and asked, "Do you know if Charles is coming?"

"Honestly, after the stunt he pulled yesterday with the press, I'm not sure if Victoria wants him around."

"That may be for the best," Mr. Maxwell commented as he took his place behind his desk. "Hello, all of you. Thank you for coming. I hope you all had a merry Christmas. This is not an official reading of the will, but it's best if I have most of you here to sign paperwork and discuss any questions you may have. Mrs. Robinson requested you all be present." Mr. Maxwell paused as he looked down at a stack of papers on his desk. "Mrs. Ekaterina Anastasia Majewski-Robinson had a large estate and many caveats to her will. The entirety of the properties and accounts go to Victoria Robinson Lansing, only child of Mrs. Robinson with three exceptions to the properties: one will go to each of her grandchildren. They will have to discuss and choose who gets which one."

CJ frowned and asked, "Granny had more than one property?"

"Yes, sir, she did, these three and several more. As for any monies, each grandchild was given a trust at birth and have since passed the age of requirement to use it. She hoped you used them wisely. All the other money has been split among the Foundation, other charities, and Mrs. Lansing. Mrs. Lansing is welcome to do as she pleases with all properties and monies, with the caveat that under no uncertain terms does any of the money or property go to Charles Lansing. If this occurs, the survivorship rights are revoked, and all monies and properties will be returned to the estate trust. There are items in the will for other people who aren't present, so I'll skip all that. Ms. Quinn, I understand you've received the sailboat?"

"Yes, sir," I answered.

"With the sailboat are reserved harbor spots up and down the coast." He handed me a folder. "These are the harbors that have the reserved spots and the harbormasters' names and contact information.

"CJ, a trust has been created in the name of Calvin C. Lansing for him to have access to on his eighteenth birthday, plus a college fund. Chase, arrangements have been made, once you graduate college, for an all-expenses paid learning sabbatical in the subject of your choice. Katerina, Mrs. Robinson would like you to have the contents of safety deposit box two. As a lawyer yourself, you will know what to do with all the contracts and deeds in that box."

Katerina had a befuddled look on her face as Victoria and I exchanged smiles.

"Other than you three deciding which properties you want to put your name on, this concludes the meeting."

The siblings went over to a large table and opened the three folders. The first folder contained the details for a large penthouse on Manhattan's Upper East Side overlooking the reservoir in Central Park. The second folder revealed a large self-sustaining horse farm in northern Virginia. The third folder included a deed to a large plot of land in the south of France between Collioure and Cerbère. Granny May had left a letter that discussed each property.

"I always loved New York City. As a young girl my parents took me each year to show me where we entered the United States from Poland. I bought a place when I was young and felt city life was where it was at. Then I met Edward. While living in Maryland, we talked about how, when we had children, we wanted to raise them in the country where the air was fresh, and kids could be kids. We bought the ranch but were never able to live our dream. The final property is a small area in the south of France near the Spanish border. My family stayed there for many months while escaping Poland and helping the Resistance. It's not much but means a lot. Enjoy!"

The siblings looked at each other. "No brainer," CJ said. Chase took the NYC property, CJ took the Virginia ranch, and Katerina took the French coast. All agreed the properties were open to each of them. We shook hands with Mr. Maxwell and started to leave when a red-faced Charles suddenly burst into the room.

"Why wasn't I notified of this?" He glared at Mr. Maxwell, breathless.

Victoria faced him with a steely gaze, her shoulders thrown back. "Because, Charles, you received nothing!"

Charles looked at the lawyer, fuming. "Maxwell, is this true? This can't be!"

"Senator Lansing, please calm down. Mrs. Robinson made it very clear you were to receive nothing. I'm sorry."

"That bi—"

"Charles," Victoria shouted. She pounded her fist on Maxwell's mahogany desk.

"You'll pay for this. I need this money. I deserve it," He screamed, his face red and blustery.

Victoria straightened her shoulders. "That's it. You have embarrassed me and pushed me around for the last time. So yes, I'll give you what you deserve, what you have deserved for a very long time, bank on that. I will have the divorce papers drawn up as soon as possible. Now please leave, or I will ask for you to be removed."

"This isn't over," Charles shouted before he stormed out of the building.

By the time we reached the house, we were exhausted. Julia had made some dinner, but most of us were either too tired or too busy trying to wrap our heads around the day's events.

"Remind me again, what was in the second box?" Katerina asked as we removed our coats.

"From what Victoria and I could make of it, deeds and forms of payment to and from Granny May's parents during the war. According to the journal and the bank recorder, Granny's parents bribed some Germans and were able to get more families out of Poland and France. These families then paid them what they had for transport."

We gathered our things and headed upstairs. Exhausted, we put on our pajamas and sat by the fire. A short time later, they heard a soft knock on the door. "Come in!" Katerina said.

Victoria entered, closing the door behind her. "I'll be staying in Bridgeport the next few weeks, working on finding an answer to the Foundation's money issues. The rest of the family is going back home tomorrow, but I want you girls to stay here and rest, maybe look through that second box." She grinned. "Start off the New Year with a look at past ones."

The next day, people began to clear out. I hired some local workers to take down the large tree in the foyer and donate all the ornaments, except the vintage tree topper. We stored away the 100th Anniversary Lionel Gold train set for Calvin someday. Katerina and I left the small tree so we could enjoy the lights a bit longer. The house felt abandoned, so festive one day and so empty the next.

I asked Katerina if she wanted to talk about Victoria wanting a divorce. She shook her head, but I knew it was bothering her.

"I knew it was coming," she said, "but I guess I thought maybe one day they could work it out."

We talked for a bit longer, relishing the good parts of this Christmas. "Tomorrow," Katerina said before she fell asleep, "let's look at Granny's stuff from France."

Victoria called to say she was staying in a rental apartment under an alias. She said she had a weird feeling someone was following her, so she changed where she was staying and took a different route. We jotted down the address.

"Mom, I'm coming to help," Katerina said. "I have to go to Boston and get some more things, but I should be there after New Years."

Victoria told both of us to be careful.

After Katerina hung up, the shrill ring of the doorbell cut through the quiet afternoon. She made her way to the door, wondering aloud who could be calling. I followed her into the foyer. She was greeted by Sarah, standing on the doorstep, a wrapped metal tin clutched in her hands. Sarah's cheeks were flushed, and her eyes held a hint of apprehension.

"Sarah, what a surprise," Katerina exclaimed, a smile spreading across her face. "Please come in."

Sarah stepped into the cozy warmth of the foyer, shifting nervously from foot to foot. With a sheepish smile, she extended the tin toward Katerina. "I brought you these," she said, her voice tinged with regret. "Homemade Christmas cookies. I'm sorry I didn't get them to you sooner."

Katerina accepted the tin with gratitude. "Thank you. That's so kind of you."

As we made our way into the kitchen, I couldn't help but notice the weary lines etched into Sarah's face, the shadows beneath her eyes betraying sleepless nights. Concern flickered in Katerina's gaze as she poured a cup of coffee for Sarah, offering it to her with gentle hands.

"How have you been doing?" she asked softly, her voice laced with genuine concern. "We've been worried about you."

Sarah sighed heavily, sinking into a chair at the kitchen table. "I needed to get away," she admitted, her voice barely above a whisper. "I'm so upset that something I may have done could have harmed Mrs. Robinson."

"Sarah, you couldn't have known," Kat reassured her, reaching out to squeeze her hand in comfort.

Sarah looked up, her eyes clouded with exhaustion and worry, but also a faint glimmer of relief. "I know," she admitted, her voice wavering. "But I still can't shake this feeling."

I studied Sarah's worn appearance, the faint tan on her skin, a stark contrast to the pallor of her cheeks. "Where have you been?" I asked casually.

A hesitant smile crossed Sarah's lips as she met Katerina's gaze. "I needed to get away, so I went and stayed with an old boyfriend in Miami. Victoria knew I was going. Is everything okay?"

Katerina nodded. "Yes, but you missed all the Lansing drama."

She reached up into a cabinet to get a couple plates for the cookies.

"Katerina, you dropped this." Sarah bent over and picked up the scrap of paper on which she had scribbled Victoria's address.

"So I did, thanks, Sarah." Katerina crammed the crumpled paper back into her pocket and gave me a wary glance.

Sarah finished her coffee and said, "I need to get going. Still have a few errands to run."

I walked Sarah to the door, as concern tugged at my gut. I wondered if she had seen the address on the paper.

We drove to Boston the next day. It had snowed the night before, so the roads weren't totally cleared off and patches of black ice threatened to slide us off the road. Even a four-wheel drive couldn't beat ice. It took us much longer than usual. We threw our belongings in the middle of the living room and went straight to bed. We slept well into the next day until my phone woke us up. It was Charles.

"Jara, please don't hang up."

I whispered to Katerina that it was her father. "What does he want?" she whispered back. I shrugged.

"Sorry to bother you on a holiday, but uh...I have a situation here. I'm in New Hampshire, the primary is this month, and I need some help."

"What kind of help? I told you I was no longer going to help with the campaign. I have to get back to work."

"I know, I know. This is more about my family. I think they could be in danger."

I looked at Katerina. "Danger? What sort of danger?"

"I don't know. I received a threat and need you to help me figure it out."

"What kind of threat?"

"I don't want to discuss it over the phone. I need to see you. I apologize for being a short-sighted ass. I've been under so much stress lately. I know you love my daughter, and I've always loved you. You've always been family. Please help me with this."

I was skeptical. "Have you officially contacted the FBI?"

"No, I don't want this all over the news. You can handle it much quieter. Can you meet me at my New Hampshire campaign headquarters?"

I sighed. "Fine, I'll be there tomorrow afternoon around one."

I hung up as Katerina began firing questions at me. "What did he want? Did he really apologize? What are you supposed to do? What—"

"Stop! Yes, he apologized, but I don't trust him. He said he received a threat, and the family may be in danger, but wouldn't tell me why or how. I have no idea what I'm supposed to do. That's why I'm going up there. If the family is in danger, I need to know. Your mom did say she felt like she was being followed."

Katerina called her mother back and told her what Charles said. I called Travis, who answered his phone for once, and I explained to him what was going on. I also told him I was headed for Manchester, New Hampshire, the next day. I asked him if he had any contacts in New Hampshire because I didn't. I had been based mostly in NYC, Boston, and Philadelphia.

"Please be careful. If this is for real, it could mean something more serious," he said. "I have some agency buddies I know from up there, and I'll tell them to keep a lookout."

"Thanks, Travis."

Katerina ended her call. "Mom said the money leaking from the Foundation is going through at least five shell companies, if not more. One of the companies is Navigator Lost. Their symbol is the nautical compass."

"Have they found the names of any others or where they're located?"

"Yes, names like Northbound, South Sun, Due East, and West End. Each of them connects to Navigator Lost. There may be more."

I sighed. "At least your mom is making some headway."

"While you go see Dad, I'm going to take a car to Bridgeport and be with Mom, okay?"

"Of course. When I get finished with your father, I'll head to Bridgeport too."

We unpacked our stuff, found clean clothes, and repacked. I went to the bathroom to brush my teeth and splash some cold water on my face. When I returned to the bedroom, Katerina was waiting for me, wearing nothing but her necklace.

"I thought we could celebrate the New Year in our own special way," she said sexily.

I took her in my arms and gently kissed her neck. "Only if we make this a tradition," I whispered.

Chapter Twenty-Four

I started out early the next morning, trying to beat any traffic. I headed north on I-93 to Manchester, hoping the roads were plowed. I was in luck. The roads were mostly clear and there wasn't much traffic. I stopped at a small café for an early lunch. While I waited, I called Charles to tell him I was in town early. He didn't answer. I decided to head over to his makeshift headquarters. I parked my Defender across the street and locked it. I still had my camera equipment in the back, as well as my gun. I spied Bella walking toward the headquarters and met her at the door.

"I come in peace, Bella," I said with deliberate sarcasm. "Charles asked me to come."

She looked me up and down. "Come on in. He'll be back in a few minutes. He's wrapping up a town hall meeting a few blocks from here."

I walked into the small, square room and looked around. Charles had his face plastered everywhere: posters, flyers, buttons...

"He won't have much time to talk. He has to fly out to Nevada and Iowa. This first month is crazy."

I took her word for it as I surveyed the room. Other than Bella, no workers were present. I asked where the bathroom was. "Down the hall, on your right," she replied.

I made my way down the hall and noticed a room to my left with three computers stationed on a long, folding table. After I went to the bathroom, I checked to make sure Bella wasn't watching and went into the room with the computers. One of them was running a financial program with a nautical compass logo in the upper right corner. I pulled my phone out and took a few pictures. When I stepped out of the room, Bella was coming down the hall.

"What were you doing in there?" she snapped.

"Sorry, Bella." I grinned sheepishly. "Guess I don't know my left from my right."

She glared at me as I went back into the bathroom and texted the pictures to Katerina and Victoria. When I emerged, she was standing in the hall, waiting for me.

A doorbell chimed and we both turned to see Charles come in the front door, brushing snow from the lapels of his cashmere coat.

"It started snowing again, Bella. I hope I can make my flight." He looked up as we entered the room. "Oh, hi Jara. Glad to see you made it."

He shook my hand and asked me to have a seat.

"Would you like a bottle of water?" he asked.

"Sure," I said, as Bella went and grabbed a bottle from a nearby bar fridge.

"So Charles, what can I do for you?" My curiosity was piqued.

"I need your help on a couple of things, actually." He showed me a piece of paper with what looked like the scribblings of a four-year-old.

"What's this?" I asked.

"The threat."

I looked at him. "Seriously? *This* is the threat? Are there any others? Or phone calls? Anything?" I read the "threat" again. It was on hard stock paper and written in crayon.

"No," the senator said, "just that one. It was slipped under the door a couple days ago."

I looked over at the front door. "Under this door, sir?"

"Yes. I believe one of our volunteers found it and gave it to Bella."

I took a picture of the door and where the door met the doorframe. No way could anything have been slid under this.

"Has this threat been processed by anyone? I mean who has handled it?"

I asked, pulling out a rubber glove and a clear evidence bag, taking the paper from Charles. I put the letter in the bag and tried to read it again. I could only make out the words "your wife," "change," "will die," and "family next."

Is the volunteer who found this here, by chance?"

"No, we sent them all home because of the weather. Since I was flying out, they didn't need to be here."

This made no sense at all. "Wouldn't you want your staff here to keep up the campaign?"

"Oh, Bella will be calling them back in the next few days."

I nodded. "Is there anyone, any company or rival, who's threatened you before?"

"No, not really. Why?"

"I was on my way to the bathroom, and I saw you were doing some research on a company called Navigator Lost."

Charles' face went white as he glanced over at Bella. "I do research on a lot of companies. They may be possible donors one day to my campaign."

"Okay," I replied nonchalantly. "I'll take this letter and get it processed. I'll see if any other candidates received a similar letter. Are you sure you don't want the FBI officially involved? If this is a legitimate threat, they have a better chance of finding the person."

"Thank you, I appreciate it. But no, I'd rather it be handled in-house. I was going to ask you for another favor, but with weather moving in again, we'd both better be on our ways."

I frowned. "What other favor?"

"I, well uh, I thought about what you said in my office about you and Katerina. I'm sorry for my outburst. Your relationship...well, it could bring in a different demographic of voters like you said, so I wondered if you and she would meet me at some of my campaign stops and help me, well, with the women's and the gay vote."

I choked on my water, splashing it on my shirt. "Well, sir, I'll ask Katerina, but it will entirely be up to her." I realized at that moment I had left my coat in the bathroom. "If you'll excuse me," I said, "I left my coat in the bathroom." I made it to Charles' private office door before Bella ran past me and said she would get my coat. The door to the computer room was closed.

I stood in the doorframe of Charles' office and glanced down. In a trash can I saw a crumpled piece of paper with the letterhead "Due East, a subsidiary company of Navigator Lost." It even had the compass logo. Bella handed me my coat, and I leaned down to tie my shoe, throwing my coat over the trash can. When I stood up, I used my coat as a glove to grab the piece of paper. I walked to the door with Bella, shook hands with Charles, and left.

I crossed the street to my Defender and opened the back. Pulling out my camera, I took a picture of the campaign headquarters. I was putting my camera away when I noticed a large, overflowing dumpster next to the building.

I got in my car, drove around the block, and parked a good distance away but still within sight of campaign headquarters. I watched as Senator Lansing and Bella left the office. They appeared to be in a heated conversation. After they drove off in separate cars, I drove around to the side of the building and pulled up next to the dumpster. I sifted through fast food waste and some bags of hair from the barbershop next door. After some disgusting effort, I found two bags with some political flyers. I briefly searched through one and found more papers with the Navigator Lost logos. I took some photos and brought the bags to my Defender to lock in the car safe. I pulled out my gun and put it next to me before I drove off. My gut was tensing again, and it wasn't because of hunger.

I got a short distance out of town and called Victoria. She said she was in a meeting but would call me back. I left a message for Katerina, knowing she was driving, telling her that I would be in Bridgeport tonight. I called Travis next and told him what I had found. He said he would meet me in Bridgeport tomorrow, since he was currently in Boston running down some other leads.

I was on the toll road I-90 in Massachusetts, heading south to I-84, when I noticed a dark Jeep keeping about three car lengths behind me. It would match my speed and my lane changes. I didn't recognize the vehicle, but it started to creep me out. I decided I would stay on I-90 and head west to Springfield, then go south to see if the Jeep followed me. Flashing lights ahead slowed traffic. A semi had hit some black ice and jackknifed on the 90/84 split. I was diverted to I-84, and kept driving south with the Jeep still tailing me. I made it to Hartford, Connecticut, when I saw more flashing lights. A road closure of some kind was ahead. Instead of taking the marked detour, I ventured out on my own as the Jeep followed. I wound around on State Road 2, making my way to State Road 3, and immediately turned off onto Main Street to grab a Dr. Pepper at a drive-through. The Jeep drove past. It was a maroon four-door, tricked out for off-roading. It was starting to get dark, so I grabbed my food and got back onto State Road 3 and headed to the toll road again.

I was about to cross the William Putnam Memorial Bridge when a shot rang out and my Defender swerved. My left rear tire had been shot and was losing air, making it hard to stay in my lane. The bridge was icy, and I didn't want to go headfirst into the Connecticut River. I had a death grip on the wheel when another shot came through my driver's side window, hitting me in the shoulder. In no way could I return fire. My Defender hit the right guardrail and flipped off the road into a grassy, wooded area. The vehicle rolled for what seemed like forever and came to a stop, upside-down.

It was several seconds before I could gather myself, making sure I could move. I unbuckled my seat belt, felt for my gun, located my cell on the interior roof, and slid out of the car onto the frozen, snow-covered ground. I was covered with sticky blood, including my face. I wiped my eyes with my hand and called 911.

"This is Agent Jara Quinn, FBI. Someone shot me off the bridge on Highway 3 just before the river." Another shot rang out. "Shots fired! Shots fired! Requesting backup!"

I kept the line open as I rolled down a slight embankment for cover. I peered above the slope and saw the Jeep, a rifle barrel pointing from the driver's side window. I took two shots, and it sped off into the trees. When I heard sirens in the distance, I hoped they were coming for me.

Chapter Twenty-Five

My eyes squinted through some bright overhead lights. I realized I had woken up in the emergency room of some hospital. I felt my head with my right hand. It was bandaged. A sling immobilized my left arm.

A nurse appeared from behind a plastic curtain. When she noticed I was awake, she smiled. "Ms. Quinn, you were very lucky. If the bullet had been a little bit—"

I stopped her and asked where my phone and car were.

"I have your phone right here," she said, motioning toward a counter. Your car is probably being towed somewhere, I'm not sure."

"Are the police here?"

"Yes, they are, and they want to speak to you when you are fully awake."

"Can I please have my phone? And send in the officers."

The nurse handed me my phone and left the room. I immediately called Travis and told him what happened.

"Travis, you must find my car. The evidence is in it. Can you find where it is and tow it to a special secure lot?"

"Yes, of course," he replied impatiently. "Are you all right?"

I told him I was fine and glanced at my hospital wristband. "Looks like I'm at Hartford Memorial. Get here when you can."

Just then, a couple of plain-clothes detectives and two uniformed police officers stepped into my cubicle. After some introductions, a short, stocky man in a cheap suit took the lead, a Detective Phil Connolly.

"We need to ask you a few questions about what happened. Are you okay to talk?"

"I'll try to answer what I can." I told them about the maroon Jeep. "Then I heard a shot, and I knew my tire had been hit. I went through the guardrail."

"We understand you shot back twice."

"I think so, yes. Where is my gun by the way?"

"We found it by your car. We put it into evidence."

"And my car?" I started to panic.

"Last we knew they were in the process of turning it over and putting it on a truck."

"How will I know where it is?" I asked, as I tried to get out of bed. I looked up and saw wires and an IV hooked up to me.

Just then the detective received a text on his cell. "It looks like a Travis O'Ryan, DHS, has taken over custody of the vehicle and is having it towed somewhere else."

I sighed with relief and fell back into bed. My body was screaming with pain. My phone rang, startling me. It was Katerina.

"Jara, Mom's been attacked!" Katerina yelled. I could hear the panic in her voice. "Where are you? I've been calling you for hours."

I sat straight up on the gurney and tried to stand again. A patrol officer grabbed me and forced me back down. I got my bearings again.

"I'm at a hospital in Hartford," I said. "Had a bit of an accident. Travis is on his way here to pick me up. Where are you?"

"Bridgeport Hospital," Katerina replied. The desperation in her voice was killing me. "Mom was attacked in the park. She's in surgery now."

"Are officers with you?"

"Yes."

"I need to speak to whoever is in charge, now!" I looked at the officers with me. "You two, get the detective back in here. I don't want to repeat myself."

A deep voice came over my phone, "Hello, this is Detective Stratton. Who am I speaking with?"

"I'm Agent Jara Quinn, FBI. I was recently shot off the road and brought to a hospital in Hartford. I've reason to believe the Lansing family is in grave danger. Please keep Katerina under police watch. Also please put a guard on Mrs. Lansing's door when she gets out of surgery." I paused. "She *will* make it out of surgery, right?"

"We hope so. She's in very serious condition. I'm hoping we got her here in time. We're also looking for her mugger."

"Sir," I warned him, "I don't believe this was a mugging, and me being shot on the same day is no coincidence."

"What about Ms. Miles?"

"Sarah?" What was she doing there? "I guess keep her at the hospital also. I'll have a colleague of mine call you when he arrives. Thank you, Detective Stratton. Please keep them safe for me."

Katerina came back on the phone. "What's going on?"

"I'll explain everything when I get there. I'll be okay. I'm having Travis drive me. Have you called CJ or Chase?"

"Both are on their way here."

"Okay, stay there and do exactly what Detective Stratton says. I'll arrive as soon as I can."

We hung up, and Detective Connolly approached me. "Are we talking about *the* Lansing family?" he inquired. "As in Senator Lansing?"

"Yes, Detective, we are. I can't stress to you enough how sensitive this all is. If we could keep this out of the press—"

"Well, Ms. Quinn, I can try to keep some names out of it, but it's not every day a car is shot off a bridge."

"Sir, is there any way the news of my survival can be delayed? Even for a few days? The family and my agency would greatly appreciate it."

"I'll see what I can do. You said you're going to a different hospital?"

"Yes, I need to check on the family."

"Hmm. I could say you were transferred due to your injuries. Looking at you," he paused to smirk, "I wouldn't be far off."

"Thank you, sir. I think." I tried to smile as I winced from the pain in my shoulder.

A man in a white coat pushed back the curtain and walked in. Looking at my chart, he said, "Miss, I'm the attending physician, Dr. Cohen, and you're not going anywhere. I'm sorry, but you have a severe concussion and bullet wounds in your left arm and back."

I frowned. "Excuse me? I thought I was just shot in the left arm."

"You were, but the bullet traveled through the arm, just missing the brachial artery, then hit and shattered the scapula." He was pointing to my left shoulder. "You're very lucky. Had the scapula not shattered, the bullet could have ricocheted into your heart or lungs. Someone or something did not want you to die today."

I rolled my eyes. "Yes, but someone or something was trying to kill me."

"Touché," he said.

"Doctor, I *must* get to Bridgeport Hospital. Another person attacked my family. I need to be with them." I explained the situation as I begged for his secrecy and help.

"I have a feeling," he said, "if I don't let you go, you're going to go anyway."

I nodded. "Yeah, I would try."

A second later, Travis rushed in, looking more scattered than I'd ever seen him, but still wearing his signature baseball cap. "Damn, Jara. You look like shit." Travis was attractive in an understated way, his charm lying more in his charisma and genuine smile than in conventional handsomeness. He had a natural air of confidence about him, paired with good old-fashioned common sense. His dark hair, often casually tousled, complemented his sharp, intelligent eyes that seemed to catch every detail. His sense of humor puts others at ease without taking away from the seriousness of the situation.

"Thanks. I didn't have time to freshen up for you. Dr. Cohen, this is my liaison at Homeland Security, Travis O'Ryan."

Travis shook the doctor's hand. "Hello, nice to meet you, Doc. Is she gonna be okay?"

As they continued talking, I lay back and closed my eyes. *This can't be happening.* I must have dozed off, or the meds kicked in, because when I awoke, I found that I was cleaned up some, wearing a fresh hospital gown and a sling on my left arm. I was hooked up to another IV and had more monitors attached to my body. I pushed the nurse call button. A nurse appeared, along with the doctor and Travis.

"Look who's awake," Travis said.

Dr. Cohen approached my bed. "Ms. Quinn, you're in serious but stable condition. While I was talking to Mr. O'Ryan, you passed out. We believe you're going septic, so I've ordered stronger antibiotics. I've contacted Bridgeport Hospital, and they're transferring Mrs. Lansing to their main hospital, Yale New Haven. I can transfer you, but it'll have to be by ambulance."

"Thank you, Doctor, thank you. Travis, please find out if they've transferred Victoria yet, and if not, can you put her under an alias?"

"I'll try my best," he said as he turned and walked out of the room.

I looked up at the doctor. "Thank you again, Doctor, but can I ask one more favor?"

He smiled. "It depends."

"I hate painkillers. I'm not trying to be a tough ass, nor do I have a problem with them, I just hate the way they make me feel.

I know this is going to hurt like hell, but something other than this IV stuff."

"I'll make a deal with you. You keep taking what I've ordered, and I'll give you something for the nausea and call ahead with your request. You'll probably need a few surgeries to repair your scapula, so get used to taking some medications."

"Thanks, Doctor."

Travis returned a few minutes later. "Good to go. You both are being put at the end of a hall. Guards will be stationed at the two rooms and for the family. I put both of you under aliases." He flashed a smug smile. "And your chariot awaits downstairs."

Travis gathered all my things that weren't taken into evidence. He also transferred the photos I took with my phone to his email.

"I'll be right behind you," he said.

I took a nice nap on the way to New Haven. I almost forgot what had happened until I moved my head. "Damn, my head hurts," I said out loud. The paramedic laughed and checked my vitals and IVs. Someone had put a pair of scrub pants on me under the gown. Whoever did that was a hero in my book. We reached the hospital, where I was rushed to a back elevator and then down a long hall. I heard Travis talking to someone.

I was wheeled past the emergency room and down a white hallway. It was instant controlled chaos. So different than the last hospital. The air was thick with the smell of antiseptic and the undercurrent of urgency. Blinding fluorescent lighting exacerbated the cacophony. Monitors beeped incessantly, alarms occasionally punctuated the din, each one a call to action, summoning medical personnel to immediate attention. Voices overlapped in a chaotic symphony. Doctors barked orders, their tones authoritative and precise. Nurses responded swiftly, their movements a blur of efficiency, as they darted between patients. The intercom crackled to life with regular announcements, phones rang, pagers buzzed, all underscoring the constant, necessary communication that kept the machine running smoothly.

I thought of my hornets, buzzing around, each with a job to do. To a person looking in, it seemed like mayhem. I closed my eyes and rested while lines were straightened, more vitals were taken, and everything was made just right. A nurse explained the call button and turned the lights down a bit.

Katerina burst into the room. A nurse tried to stop her, but she pushed through.

"It's okay," I said.

Katerina tried to hug me, but I flinched. I reached my right arm and pulled her back to me. "Please, I need your hug," I whispered.

She kissed my face all over. "Are you okay? What happened? Where are you hurt?"

Travis came in and put his hand on Katerina's shoulder. She sat on the bed beside me as he explained what happened. Katerina was being bombarded with information. First her mother, now me.

"Kat, how is your mom?" I asked.

Katerina took a deep breath. "She went back in for another surgery, but she's in recovery, stable. CJ is coming in the morning. He's sending Julia and Calvin to her mother's. Chase and Abby are on their way here. By the way, Sarah's here too. Detective Stratton said she needed to be wherever we were."

"Yes, I requested that. I want her accounted for and to find out how she knew Victoria was attacked."

"She said the hospital called her because they found her card in Mom's purse. They didn't have Mom's phone, so they had no way to reach me."

The nurse came in and asked Travis and Katerina to say their goodbyes, that I needed my rest.

I looked at the nurse. "Ma'am, I would rest much better if she stayed with me."

She looked at her laptop and smiled. "Okay, I'll have a sleep chair rolled in."

"Thank you. It means a lot."

I had no idea what was in my chart, but I was grateful. Travis took his leave, saying he would be down the hall, coordinating with law enforcement and the nurses.

Katerina chuckled. "Does that mean he's going to go flirt?"

"I do believe so," was my wry retort.

I fell asleep with Katerina at my side. By the time I awoke to the sound of someone's voice, I'd lost any sense of time or even what day it was. I looked out the window to my right, and noticed it was growing dark outside.

"I'm Dr. Rosa Ortiz," said a young woman in colorful scrubs. Her silky black hair was pulled back in a bun, and her glasses, which matched her scrubs, dangled from a beaded chain around her neck.

Katerina and I sat up.

"Hello," I said groggily.

"I'm not sure how to address you," the doctor said.

I explained the alias. "My name is Jara Quinn," I told her. "This is my partner, Katerina." Katerina smiled and shook the doctor's hand.

"Ms. Quinn—"

"You can call me Jara."

"Well, Jara, you're a very lucky woman."

"I keep hearing that."

"It's true. You had some stitches put in your head, and you have a concussion, but I don't think you'll have much trouble recovering from those injuries. The arm wound should heal nicely, but you may have some nerve damage. The bullet missed the brachial artery, so that's a godsend. Now to your scapula..." She clicked a few buttons on the laptop. "I'm going to need to take some pictures to check for any bullet fragments that may have migrated. Also, preliminary tests show I need to clean out some bone fragments. After that, we can see what damage was done to the scapula and how we can repair it. You good with that?"

"Guess I have to be, don't I?"

"Honestly," she said shaking her head, "after seeing pictures of the wreck, you driving off a bridge and all, you're lucky to be alive. I'll be scheduling your procedures for the next day or two." Dr. Ortiz said she would see me later and walked out.

I looked over at Katerina. Her face was white. I remembered Travis had given her a watered-down version of events. I don't think he had mentioned me being shot or driving off a bridge.

Katerina sat down on the edge of the bed. "What did the doctor mean by you 'driving off a bridge'? And were you shot? Travis said nothing about that. He said you hurt your head and shoulder in an accident. What the hell is going on?"

I took a deep breath, which hurt like hell, and explained everything. "But you heard the doctor. It could've been a lot worse."

Katerina pressed her lips together, the color returning to her face. "Seriously, you're joking about this? I could have lost both you and Mom. I can't believe this."

"Lower your voice, please. They'll kick you out."

"Like hell they will!"

Travis walked in and Katerina was on him in an instant. She reached out and slapped him. "How dare you placate me."

"Kat, please..." I groaned.

She looked at me and took a long, deep breath. Her eyes softened. "I'm still angry. Next time, both of you tell me the truth."

"I'm hoping there won't be a next time—"

"Don't joke with me right now. I'll punch you in your left arm!"

We broke into laughter and the tension eased.

"Katerina," Travis said, "I was coming to tell you your mother is out of recovery and moving next door. I'm trying to piece together what happened. Do you know anything?"

Katerina told Travis she arrived at the Foundation and her mother was in some sort of meeting. "I decided to go down the street and grab both of us dinner. When I got back, I was told by one of the assistants that Mom had gone for a walk in the park to clear her head. A jogger found her on the rocks by the river, stabbed, with blood gushing from her head. They said had that jogger not found her, she would've most likely bled out."

I looked around the room and interrupted, "Where's my phone?"

Travis got a weird look on his face.

I glared at him. "Travis, what is it?"

"I have your phone. I took it to transfer your photos." He took a deep breath. "That's when I noticed you had a missed call and message. I didn't pay much attention to it until I was speaking with the detective on Mrs. Lansing's case. She called you right before she was attacked."

I gripped Katerina's hand, closed my eyes, and swallowed hard.

"Can we hear it?" Katerina asked, her voice trembling.

"Not right now, it's being analyzed. It looks like both local law enforcements have decided to call in the FBI. This appears to be a coordinated attack on both Victoria and Jara. We've locked down this wing and are stationing round-the-clock guards. Katerina, your family will be under protection twenty-four-seven."

"And Dad?"

I glanced briefly at Travis. "Katerina," I said as softly as I could, "we believe your father is behind this. We're far from proving it, but we have our theories."

"I'll let you two talk," Travis said quietly, as he excused himself from the room.

I told Katerina everything, from the first call I received from Victoria about the shell companies, to seeing the shell companies' logos in her father's headquarters, to getting the trash from the dumpster and sending all the photos to her and Victoria. "That's when I contacted Travis and told him what I had. I called Victoria again, but she was in a meeting, probably the same one she was in when you arrived. Shortly after, all hell broke loose. I didn't know about your mother's call."

"I wondered what those pictures were that you sent. I figured I'd ask Mom."

Suddenly we heard loud voices in the hallway. "Go check on your mother, and give her my love. I'll be here." I smiled halfheartedly.

Katerina kissed me and left. I picked up the phone in my room and dialed my voicemail. Soon, I was listening to Victoria's message. "Jara, it's Victoria. I got your message and photos. The detectives here just learned these are definitely the companies that are siphoning off the money. I'm...What!" I heard a loud scream, then, "Jara, help!"

I could hear the struggle and the waves hitting the rocks. I thought I heard the attacker say, "Son of a bitch" before the line went silent. I replayed the message, resaved it, and hung up. When Travis came back into the room, he looked at my face and instantly knew what I had done.

"You heard it?" he asked.

"Yeah, they didn't find her phone, did they?"

"Nope. We think the attacker threw it in the water. They're still searching but haven't located it yet. Did you recognize any voices in the message?

"I heard the presumed attacker say 'son of a bitch' at the end, but I can't place the voice."

Travis nodded. "We think he realized she was on the phone, cursed, and hung up or smashed the phone and threw it in the water."

"You don't think he took it?"

"Maybe. Our tech people are in the process of trying to track it." Travis paused. "You going to let Katerina hear it?"

"I don't know, maybe later. Let me know if you learn anything. You have my phone turned off, right?"

"Yes, no one knows you're alive...yet."

Chapter Twenty-Six

I remained in the hospital for another week, having x-ray after x-ray done to see where any bullet or bone fragments might be hiding. Dr. Ortiz explained they were unable to do an MRI due to the metal in my body. "If we do an MRI, it could move a bullet fragment and do more damage, so x-rays must suffice for now." Dr. Ortiz scheduled a surgery to clear out all fragments now that my infection had subsided. "We don't want any of these pieces to move and possibly go to your heart or lungs. It's best we do this soon."

Victoria was in a medically induced coma, helping her body to rest and heal. She had been stabbed twice in the back, piercing a lung and damaging her liver and spleen. She had multiple surgeries repairing her lung and removing her spleen. The doctors were significantly concerned about her head injury. Her head had hit a sharp rock when she was thrown down, causing damage to part of her frontal lobe. The doctors were worried that, once they brought Victoria out of her coma, she may have some memory loss and motor skill impairment, among other possible complications. Katerina, CJ, and Chase rarely left their mother's bedside.

Travis brought in agents he trusted to help with the investigation. They decided it was best for the doctor to call Charles and inform him of Victoria's condition. Otherwise, it would appear suspicious. The siblings were told not to have any contact with their father. Communications needed to be carefully controlled. They also decided not to release any information on my condition.

The FBI set up a recording system to monitor the doctor's call to Charles. After the call was made, Travis played the tape of the conversation for me.

"Hello, Senator Lansing, this is Dr. Raymond Patel. I'm your wife's physician. She had a severe traumatic event and is in a coma in our hospital."

"What? What happened? Where is she? Is she okay?"

I could tell Charles was feigning shock.

"Senator Lansing, your wife was attacked in Bridgeport. She's in a medically induced coma to help her heal. She is stable but still in critical condition."

"I need to see her right away!"

"Senator, at this time, due to the severity of the attack, your wife is not receiving visitors and is under 24/7 guard. We have been ordered not to disclose her location at this time."

"I'm her husband, damn it. I have a right to know where she is."

"Sir, we feel it is in the best interest of your wife's health and safety not to give out any information. If something changes, we'll call you right away."

"My children, do they know? Where are they?"

"They do know, yes."

The FBI agent took the phone. "Senator Lansing, this is Special Agent Robert Bianchi from the FBI. I'm here with your wife, trying to keep her and your family safe. We'll be sending an agent to your location to help with protecting you also. We feel this was not a random attack, and you and your family may be in danger."

"I was threatened, you know." Senator Lansing said. "I gave the threat to another agent, Jara Quinn. Did she give you the letter?"

"Sir, we cannot discuss an ongoing investigation."

"So you haven't heard from Ms. Quinn?"

"Senator, we're discussing your wife and her safety. Any other information is part of the investigation and cannot be discussed. An agent should be arriving at your location shortly." The agent gave the senator his contact information and hung up.

The agent, who had been listening to the tape with us, said to Travis, "Strange, the senator seems more concerned about Ms. Quinn than his own wife."

Travis nodded. "It seems that way."

Katerina, who had been in her mother's room while I was listening to the senator's recorded call, ran into my room with her arm extended, holding her phone.

"He just called me," she said, exasperated. "I let it go to voicemail."

Travis took her phone. "He must have called you as soon as he hung up from the doctor. Do you mind if we listen to it?"

Katerina took the phone back, dialed her voicemail, and put it on speaker.

"Katerina, honey, I just heard about your mother. Call me and give me more information. I'm worried. Also, have you heard from Jara? She left my office, and I haven't heard from her. Please call me."

Travis and the agent listened to the message again. "Well, that settles that. He's definitely more worried about Agent Quinn than his wife," the agent said. "I agree. It's best if we keep her condition and location confidential."

CJ, Chase, and Katerina took turns keeping vigil at their mother's bedside, their faces etched with worry and exhaustion. They rotated in a silent, unspoken schedule, ensuring that someone was always with her, holding her hand, whispering words of encouragement, and hoping she could somehow hear them. They tried to maintain their spirits, but the weight of uncertainty pressed heavily on their shoulders.

Victoria lay motionless in the bed, her body supported by a web of tubes and machines. The rhythmic beeping of the heart monitor was a steady reminder of the fragility of her condition. It was over a week since she was placed in a medically induced coma, and the doctors' concern grew with each passing day as the brain swelling showed no signs of receding.

Sarah was also present with a quiet but constant presence. She kept to the edges, never intruding on the family's private moments but always ready to offer a comforting word or a warm embrace.

The doctors came and went, their expressions grave and their updates cautiously optimistic. They monitored Victoria's vitals, adjusted medications, and discussed treatment options in hushed tones just outside the door. Their concern was palpable. The swelling was stubborn, refusing to subside despite their best efforts. Each day without change felt like a heavy blow to the family's morale.

Katerina often found herself caught between two worlds, the tense room where her mother was or with me, concerned about my recovery. My surgery was a success though. Dr. Ortiz felt she had removed almost all the fragments and debris. All bullet fragments were given to the FBI for evidence.

Dr. Ortiz believed what little was left shouldn't cause trouble. "There is significant tissue damage where the bullet hit and the scapula broke, but it looks like the bone can heal on its own. You need to keep it immobilized and work with physical and occupational therapy when the healing is further along. I smoothed the edges of any parts of the scapula that splintered. I want to keep you here a couple more days to make sure you don't have any complications from the surgery."

Katerina hugged me.

"Thank you, Dr. Ortiz," I said. "I greatly appreciate all you've done. Any word on Mrs. Lansing and her recovery?"

"I'm not her primary doctor, but what I can tell you is she's stable and a fighter. We're hoping once we start taking her out of the coma, she'll be able to breathe and heal on her own. Dr. Patel is the one you should ask. I don't think any surgeries are planned for her at this time."

Katerina got up from my bed and hugged Dr. Ortiz. "Thank you for taking care of the two most important people in my life."

I was given permission to get up and walk as long as my left arm was in a sling and strapped to my body. They had removed the IVs, and I was only on oral pain medications. Katerina helped me put on clean scrub pants and a makeshift shirt. She also brought me a robe and slippers. I asked if I could go see Victoria. Katerina helped me get up and we slowly made it to her room.

As we approached Victoria's door, I did a double take when I spied the tall, blond, blue-eyed, well-groomed agent on guard. "Oh my gosh! John! It's you," I said. "How are you?"

He flashed a grin. "I'm a helluva lot better than you it seems, Quinn. Still getting yourself in trouble, I see."

"John, this is Katerina, my partner and Mrs. Lansing's daughter. Katerina, this is John Adams, we graduated from the Academy together."

Katerina shook his hand. "Nice to meet you. I've seen you outside my mother's door. Glad to put a name to the face."

"Is it okay if we go in?" I asked.

"I think so," John replied. "A doctor and a nurse are in with her right now, but I'm sure it would be okay." He opened the door.

Dr. Patel was examining Victoria and paused to look at the two of us.

"Dr. Patel," Katerina addressed him, "this is Jara Quinn, my partner."

"Good to meet you, Ms. Quinn. I'm glad to see you up and around after your incident."

"Thank you, Doctor. How is Mrs. Lansing?"

"She seems to be improving. The swelling has started to go down. We're looking at slowly bringing her out of the coma and checking her neurological functions. It's possible we'll be doing it this afternoon. Katerina, are your brothers available to be here also?"

"I'm sure they can be. I'll let them know."

"Should I contact your father?" asked Dr. Patel.

Katerina looked at me quizzically. "Dr. Patel," I said, "is it possible to do this and not inform him unless need be? Mrs. Lansing was in the process of a divorce, so I wouldn't want to step on her wishes."

"I understand. I'll get things ready for the procedure. We'll start around 1 p.m. Is that okay?"

Katerina nodded and went off to call her brothers, who were staying at a hotel near the hospital. I made my way back to my room to rest a bit. I called Travis and asked about progress on any of the cases.

"I'm sorry, but we're at a standstill in looking for Victoria's attacker. We can't find any cameras or witnesses who saw the attack. We're still searching for the phone. I'm hoping Victoria remembers something when she wakes up."

I told him they were going to try and bring her out of the coma, but not to count on any immediate memories, according to the doctor.

Travis said the financial detectives were making some headway with the shell companies, but that he needed to get into my Defender and open my vault. I told him to pick me up in the morning and I would open it. Concerned, he asked, "Are you up to moving around?"

"Yes. This needs to get done, and I'm afraid of waiting any longer."

"Okay. I know not to argue with you. I have the car about twenty minutes away at a secure lot. You're not going to like what you see..."

"My car?"

"Well, what's left of it."

"Hey, it saved my life. I'll see what I can salvage."

Katerina walked in. "What are you up to?" I hung up with Travis and told her I was going to my car tomorrow.

"Like hell you are! You haven't even made it around the nurses' station yet. The doctor said you need to walk a bit before discharge."

"Then let's do it," I said, rising from my bed. "I need to start moving. I can't lie here forever."

"Fine," she huffed. "Get your ass up and let's go walking."

I struggled to my feet and swung my robe over my shoulders. "Ta da!"

Katerina huffed and said, "You're the most stubborn person I've ever met."

"That's why you love me," I said, kissing her. "See? I'm strong enough to do that."

"Let's get you walking and strengthen you up, 'cause I need more than that," she teased.

We made a few laps down the hall and around the nurses' station. I was resting against a wall when CJ and Chase came down the hall. We all went back to my room and waited for Dr. Patel.

A short time later, Dr. Patel poked his head in the door. "Are you all ready?"

We looked at each other, nodding, and made our way to Victoria's room. A nurse and a respiratory therapist greeted us. Dr. Patel explained the process. "We'll first wean her off the sedation and change the vent setting to see if she can breathe on her own. If she tolerates both, we'll extubate her and put her on oxygen. Don't be nervous if at first she finds it hard to breathe. She'll need to learn not to depend on the machine."

Katerina grabbed my hand and squeezed as the doctor began. The doctor, nurse, and therapist all worked in concert, weaning Victoria off the machines. She tolerated the breathing test, and the doctor decided to extubate. The respiratory therapist worked to slowly get her on an oxygen mask. She struggled to breathe at first, but the more Victoria woke up the better she did. Color came back into her cheeks and her breathing became steady. She looked around the room frantically. I remembered my disorientation when I woke up in the hospital.

Katerina walked up to the bed and took her mother's hand. CJ and Chase were right behind her. "Mom, we're all here. We're safe."

A tear rolled down Victoria's cheek as she looked up at her children. Katerina reached out and pulled me to the bed. Victoria saw me, smiled, and then her eyes went wide. She tried to speak but was very hoarse.

"I'm okay, I promise. I'm just loving the hospital attire." I tugged at my gown.

"We'll explain everything when you start feeling better," said Katerina.

Victoria tried to reach for CJ's hand, to no avail.

The doctor told her not to be alarmed, that movement and memory would be something to work on later. Dr. Patel asked us to leave for a while so they could finish their assessments and neurological checks.

We all retreated to my room to decompress and form a game plan.

"I'm going to be discharged tomorrow," I said, "but I'll be coming back quite a bit for therapy. Guards will remain for at least another week. CJ and Chase, you need to get back to your family and school."

"Is it safe for my family to come back?" CJ asked.

I shook my head. "I can't promise anything. The FBI are doing their best to try and solve this, along with other agencies. We need to keep on our toes and communicate."

"I think we need to take turns staying here with Mom," Chase said. "I can take a semester off. It's easier for me to do than anyone else."

"Wow, thanks Chase," said CJ, "but I think we all need to take turns. If you can finish school, that's a priority."

"I think we can make it work," said Katerina.

Dr. Patel came in. "Mrs. Lansing is doing very well, all things considered. We don't want to push her recovery. She'll start with respiratory therapy and work her way to PT and OT. I take it the guards will remain?"

"Yes," I said, "for at least a week. Will that be an issue?"

"Not at all. I only need to know what to expect."

"Another thing, Doctor. Is Mrs. Lansing in any condition to answer some questions? I have a couple of agents that need to take her statement as soon as possible."

Concern spread over the doctor's face. "Again, I can't stress enough the importance of rest and recovery for Mrs. Lansing. I know you have a job to do, but so do I. Myself or a member of my staff will need to be present during the questioning. Is Ms. Miles going to remain here to help Mrs. Lansing?"

We all looked at each other. Sarah had been so quiet and unobtrusive. Katerina spoke up. "We'll let you know."

The doctor left, and Katerina said, "Sarah has been here the whole time, and she hasn't complained once about moving hospitals or being displaced. Do we give her the benefit of the doubt, or is she keeping an eye on us?"

"I don't know, but I think it's something we all need to discuss."

Agent Adams knocked on my open door. "Hey, Quinn, can I speak with you a moment?" He glanced around the room. "Alone?"

"Sure, let me come to you. I need to walk." I stood up and kissed Katerina on the cheek. "I'll be right back."

Agent Adams and I took a walk down the hall. "Damn, Quinn! I saw photos of your accident scene. You're lucky to be alive."

"I know, I know. Everyone keeps telling me that."

"But honestly, you are, and I'm not talking about the car."

I looked at him, baffled. "What are you talking about, Adams?"

"The way you were shot, not many people can take that shot...twice. First to disable the car, then to disable you. It had to be a sniper. I worked with a few in the Marines, and they take their shooting very seriously."

I hadn't really thought about who'd shot me. But if what Adams was saying was true, then that narrowed the field.

"Adams, do you know anyone who fits that description in the New England area or, and please keep this to yourself, one who could be on Senator Lansing's payroll?"

"That's what I wanted to talk to you about. When I did my stint in DC at the Capitol, Senator Lansing always had some of his own security around. One of those guys was a Navy SEAL Warrant Officer, Brian Jackson. He was a sniper over in Afghanistan."

"Adams, if I showed you a photo of someone, could you tell me if you recognized him?"

"Sure."

Just then I remembered I didn't have my phone. We walked back to my room, and I called for Katerina to come out into the hallway.

"Kat, do you still have that photo of Granny May the day you were over for tea?"

"Sure, I think so," she said, as she rifled through her purse for her phone. "Why?"

"I'll tell you in a second."

Katerina found her phone, pulled up her photos, and handed it to me. I scrolled to the one with Granny in the garden. "Is this the guy?"

He looked at the photo of Granny and Brian walking in the garden. "Holy shit. Yeah, that's him. How do you know him?"

"It's a long story," I said. "Right now I need to make some phone calls. Thank you. Seriously, I owe you. Please don't mention this to anyone."

"You got it."

Katerina stared at me. "What is it?" I showed her the photo of Granny and Brian.

"This is Chief Warrant Officer Brian Jackson, sniper."

Katerina went white. "You think he's the one that shot you?"

"He has the talent for it, and he's on your father's payroll."

Katerina took her phone, and we went into my room.

"Now what are we going to do?"

"I'll call Travis and ask him to check this out, but in the meantime, I need to lie down." I called Travis from my bed and brought him up to speed on everything. "When you come get me in the morning, bring me a new phone, different number, please."

I tried to sleep but my mind was racing with everything we had uncovered. Katerina was asleep in a chair, so I decided to take a walk and clear my head. I walked down the hall and ran into Sarah in the waiting room.

"Sarah, why are you still here?"

"I don't know. I feel safer here in the hospital. Besides, Mrs. Lansing might need me." She stared at my bandaged arm. "How are you doing? You look pretty banged up yourself."

I smiled. "Yes, but I'll be fine. I keep being told I'm lucky. I may need a good physical therapist when I'm discharged. Do you know how I could get in touch with Brian?"

Sarah blinked in surprise. "Brian? I haven't talked to him since Mrs. Robinson's memorial. He was nice enough, I guess, but I don't know how good of a PT he was. All he did was have Granny walk around the yard and give her those protein shakes. I saw no exercises or stretches for her hip whatsoever."

"I thought you two were close," I said, pushing for more information.

"Oh, heck no! He had a girlfriend already, and they seemed pretty serious. He and I only bonded because my ex-boyfriend and his girlfriend are both Puerto Rican."

"Thank you, Sarah, for talking with me. You know, you're free to leave the hospital. I could set you up in a hotel near here."

"No, I'll be fine. I want to be here in case Victoria needs me. I promised..." She hesitated.

"You promised who?"

"Oh, no one. I misspoke. I want to be here for Victoria."

I decided not to push it, but something was off. I walked back to my room, sat on the bed, and watched Katerina sleep. She looked so peaceful, but I knew she was anything but. She didn't deserve all this.

Chapter Twenty-Seven

The next morning, Travis arrived to take me to my car. We had to wait until I was officially discharged, so I took the time to get cleaned up and change into some normal clothes. Getting dressed was painful. I was going to need to invest in some slip-on shoes. I was still having issues moving my left hand. Katerina helped me put my sling back on, which felt like a straitjacket.

Travis handed me a new phone. "Use this temporarily until you can get one you want."

I gave Katerina the number and saw Travis had already transferred most of my contacts. The nurse came in to explain my discharge instructions and have me sign a bunch of paperwork. I walked next door to see Victoria.

"I'll be back late. Don't go running off!" I said jokingly.

Victoria smiled. "Please be careful," she said in a voice that was slightly less hoarse. "We have a lot of things to talk about."

"No, your priority is to get better. Let me deal with what's going on."

She smiled and her shoulders relaxed. Katerina came in and told me she was staying with her mother.

Travis and I were just driving off when he told me the maroon Jeep had been located on a side road in Western Connecticut. The sniper had wiped down the car, and no one found any shell casings. He had stolen it outside of Manchester, New Hampshire. It was such a unique vehicle, I was sure it had to be dumped quickly.

We arrived at the tow yard where my Defender was secured. I couldn't believe my eyes. All the glass was shattered, the roof caved in, one door was completely off, and the other hung from a single hinge. My tires were all flat and the rims ruined.

"I guess I didn't get the worst of it after all." We walked over to the Defender and stood next to the back door, which was off its hinges and leaning against the side of the vehicle. "Looks like I won't be repairing this one." I circled the damaged car, brushing my fingers against the twisted metal of the door. Shattered glass glittered in the sun like cruel confetti at my feet. The body of the car was almost unrecognizable, sitting crumpled and scarred. I had poured my grief into customizing and detailing this car after my parents passed away. Tears pooled in my eyes. I wasn't just looking at a damaged car, I was mourning the loss of an old friend. I wiped my eyes and looked over at Travis. "Damn it, I loved that car."

Travis nodded his head, knowing what this vehicle meant to me. He reached into the back, moved some things around, and uncovered my vault. It not only had a key and a punch code, but it required my thumbprint as well. I slowly climbed in and after a few attempts, it finally opened. I moved out and leaned against the side. Travis climbed in to take pictures of the vault and its contents. He pulled out the two trash bags, my coat with the crumpled logo paper, my extra gun, which was secured in a pelican box, and pieces of my camera equipment. I looked through the vehicle and grabbed small things I had collected over the years. My go-bag appeared unscathed. I also took off the Land Rover and Defender emblems. I needed to keep a piece of her. My friend who saved my life. We put all the things in Travis' trunk and went to the tow yard office. Travis went in and spoke to the owner. He came out, shaking his head.

"The owner told me a couple of nefarious-looking guys were here a few days ago, asking if the Defender was here and any word on the driver. He said they weren't FBI and didn't say who they were with."

"What did he say?"

"He told them it was here but got towed away somewhere else because the medical examiner needed to look at it."

I exhaled with relief. "What a guy! I owe him."

"I told him that, but he said he was ex-agency and not to worry about it."

We returned to the hospital. Travis dropped me off and headed back to his office to log the evidence. I took my gun and a few other things into the hospital and went to check on Victoria and Katerina.

Katerina met me in the hallway. "Dad called again. He wants to know where Mom is and how I'm handling the 'Jara situation.' I told him I was fine, but I couldn't tell him where Mom was. I don't think he believed me. He's calling all the hospitals and demanding to know if Mom is admitted."

"I need to let your father know I'm still alive. He may switch his focus back on me and not your mother."

"No! I can't let you do that. Who knows what he would do."

Katerina's phone rang. It was Mrs. Walsh from the Foundation. She put her phone on speaker so I could listen. "Ms. Lansing, I know your mother was attacked and is in no shape to guide us on what to do next. As her second, we need you to sign some paperwork to allow the detectives to look into another area of the Foundation."

"Are you able to fax me this paperwork? I'll sign and send them back."

"I wish it were that simple. We're finding things that in all my years here, I never knew existed. We were hoping you could shed some light on that too."

Katerina sighed. "Is it okay if I come in the morning? I hate to leave my mother alone."

"No problem. We'll see you then."

Katerina hung up. "Looks like I have to head to the Foundation. I'll call Chase and see if he can come up here to be with Mom."

"I can stay with your mother, if you'd like."

She shook her head. "I want you to come with me. You can probably figure out this paperwork better than I can." Katerina called Chase.

"Sure, Kat. I'll head up in the morning."

Katerina stayed with Victoria for most of the evening. Sarah came in and said she would sit with Victoria while we got something to eat.

"Thanks, Sarah. You want anything?"

"No thanks. I already ate a bit ago."

We went down the street to a diner. I felt like a kid, having my food cut up for me.

"This is embarrassing."

Katerina shoved a forkful of meatloaf in my mouth. "Well then next time don't get yourself shot."

We finished eating and headed back to the hospital. Sarah was reading to Victoria when we arrived. We went to the waiting room and tried to sleep. Dr. Patel walked in and looked at us in surprise.

"Good morning, you two. You girls need better sleep than this, especially you, Jara. You're still healing. I'm heading down to Mrs. Lansing's room right now to check on her. Her wounds seem to be healing well, but she still has some brain swelling. That could be what's causing the limited movement in her extremities."

We followed the doctor to Victoria's room. Sarah was asleep in a chair.

"As I was saying," Dr. Patel said, "the wounds look good. I'm concerned about the lack of movement in her left arm. She had a severe concussion, and other than the swelling, I'm not seeing on any of the tests where her brain sustained damage enough to cause this."

Sarah woke up and was listening intently.

Victoria also woke up. "Doctor, when can I go home?" she asked groggily.

"Soon, ma'am, very soon. I need to do a few more tests and then maybe I can release you in the next week or two. It all depends on the swelling and what could be causing it."

She blinked slowly. "Thank you, Doctor. That would be wonderful."

Katerina told Victoria we were heading to the Foundation to check on a few things and that Chase was on his way to be with her.

Victoria nodded and reached out to her daughter. "I love you so much. I'm so proud of you."

Katerina leaned down and kissed her mother's forehead. "I love you too, Mom."

We were leaving when a transport arrived to take Victoria for another MRI. I didn't recognize the agent on her door, but I told him he would need to accompany Mrs. Lansing. He nodded. Sarah walked out with us to get some fresh air.

"Katerina, I'll stay with your mother until Chase gets here, if that's okay?"

"Thank you, Sarah. I greatly appreciate that."

Katerina and I left, figuring Chase would be at the hospital by the time Victoria was out of the MRI.

We reached the Foundation in good time and met with Mrs. Walsh in her office.

"The detectives have found the money stream is getting larger," she told us. "They almost have it tracked to its end source, but not yet. The Foundation is losing thousands of dollars a day. You need to decide to stop it or let it continue. Katerina, since your mother is unavailable at the moment, it falls to you to make a decision."

"Does the board know about all this yet?"

"No, not all of them. I didn't feel it was my place to inform them all and then call a vote without you or your mother's knowledge."

Katerina nodded and looked over at me. "What do you think?"

"Honestly, before I would make a decision, I'd talk to the team of actuaries who are investigating this. They know the most about the situation."

We all went to the conference room where the detectives were working. I walked to the far side of the room to check on their progress. The whiteboard was massive, colorful, and almost glowing. Names of companies, printed in neat block letters or hastily scribbled in marker, dominated the surface. Some I knew, others were marked unknown. Crimson-red string snaked across the board, connecting one name to another like arteries feeding a hidden, pulsing network. Lines darted from offshore firms in the Cayman Islands to the LLCs I was aware of, then swerved toward various names—some familiar, others tagged only as "Unknown #4" or "Associate X." Arrows spiraled out from them to board seats, fake charities, and consulting firms. In places, the red string doubled or even tripled up, the weight of evidence physically pulled on the pins. The whole thing felt alive, breathing slow and shallow, daring you to keep looking, to try and make sense of it, to follow the threads. And at the top was the senator, a photo from when he announced his bid for President. This has to be bigger than just one man being greedy, because honestly, I didn't think he was this smart.

I approached one of the detectives. "I'm no good at math, but I have an idea that may work. What if we made a shell company of our own, attached it to the Foundation, made a fake account with either crypto currency or fake currency, and let them siphon that? Is that possible?"

The financial guys looked at each other. "That just may work. They're getting desperate now. They may bite. We'll work on it."

Katerina sat with Mrs. Walsh and signed some paperwork allowing the old accounts to remain open. I busied myself studying the whiteboard to see if I recognized any names other than the ones I already knew about.

Katerina called me over. "Mr. Maxwell just called. He wants us to come to his office as soon as we can. He's discovered a codicil in Granny's documents that was sealed and wants to go over it with me."

"That's odd. But I'm learning not to be surprised when it comes to Granny."

Katerina completed the paperwork and told Mrs. Walsh we would be back later after we finished with another appointment.

On our way out, I asked Katerina if we should call her brothers or Victoria about this.

"Nah, Mom's getting those tests done and whatever we learn, I can call CJ and Chase later."

We made it to the lawyer's office late in the day. The winter sun was already heading to bed, and the snow was picking up. An extra chill permeated the air. We took off our coats and kicked the snow off our shoes the best we could. Mr. Maxwell came out to the reception area and greeted us. He went to shake my hand and noticed the sling.

"It's nothing, honestly." I said, trying to break the tension. "You should see the other guy."

He gave a nervous laugh, pushed up his glasses, and ushered us into his office.

We took seats across from his desk. The leather chairs were worn but comfortable. Mr. Maxwell appeared older today, his usual jovial self a bit subdued. He sat behind his desk, his shoulders slumped as if a new weight had been placed upon them. The overhead lights were off, and only the light was from the green table lamp.

Mr. Maxwell let out a heavy sigh. "I'm sorry I had to bother you, Katerina, but I've tried repeatedly to contact Victoria since she's the primary executor of Mrs. Robinson's estate. Each call went unanswered, each message unreturned. I got concerned, and that's when I called you."

Katerina, her voice tight with emotion, said, "Mom is in the hospital. She was attacked, and she, uh, she's been in a coma until recently."

"Oh, Katerina, I'm so sorry," the attorney replied. He took a moment as his eyes had widened, and his lips pressed tightly together. "I had no idea. Please convey my best wishes to her when you can."

"We will," Katerina responded. "But what is this new thing regarding Granny's will? What do we need to do?"

Mr. Maxwell paused, his eyes drifting to the codicil. "A codicil to Mrs. Robinson's will must be opened now that the medical examiner has confirmed her death as unnatural. The accompanying letter states I or my proxy must witness this and ensure its instructions are followed. Normally, this would involve Victoria directly, but under the circumstances, we need to proceed with care."

"We understand," Katerina said, her voice steadier now. "What do you need from us?"

The codicil lay on his desk, its edges yellowed with age, sealed with a thick layer of wax that bore Granny May's distinctive crest.

"Katerina, I don't know what this document entails, but I do know Mrs. Robinson felt it was very important to have it. She left instructions not to open it unless any issues with Senator Lansing occurred. Since your mother has started the filings for divorce, I figured this would count as an issue."

I reached over and took Katerina's hand, as Mr. Maxwell took a letter opener and carefully broke the wax seal on the codicil. He unfolded the paper with deliberate care, his eyes scanning the neat, familiar handwriting. As he read, his expression shifted from solemnity to surprise, and finally, to a resolute determination.

"It seems Mrs. Robinson anticipated the possibility of foul play," he said, his voice steady. "The codicil outlines specific instructions in the event of her unnatural death. Firstly, she's requested a thorough investigation into her murder, to be conducted independently of local law enforcement. She's also named a secondary executor to act in Victoria's stead should she be unable to fulfill her duties. Katerina, this falls to you."

"Okay," Katerina said, nodding her head. "The state police are doing the investigation, and I don't have a problem helping Mom out. Anything else?"

He hesitantly handed a letter to Katerina. She looked at me with apprehension, her hands trembling as she opened it. Her eyes widened as she read. She cupped her mouth, as if trying to stifle a cry or a scream.

"Mr. Maxwell, when...when did Granny write this?"

"Katerina, my dear, it was during the time your father ran for governor."

"Oh my god! That was over twenty years ago. She's known this the whole time?"

I was totally confused by now, looking back and forth from Katerina to Mr. Maxwell. "Will one of you please tell me what the hell is going on?"

Katerina handed me the letter.

> My dearest Victoria,
> If you're reading this, then something has gone straight to hell, and I can't say I'm surprised. Not

with Charles slithering around, ruining everything he touches. I had hoped you'd never need to know any of this, but here we are.

Let's not sugar coat things. There's a reason Charles has been kept at arm's length, and it's not because of some petty grudge or family squabble. No, dear, it's because Charles is rotten. Always has been. I should have told you sooner, but I suppose I held on to some foolish hope that he'd straighten out. That was a mistake.

It all started with money. At first, I thought he was just another entitled fool who thought the world owed him something. Little things at first, numbers that didn't add up, funds that mysteriously vanished. Then came the lies, the excuses, the oh-so-innocent confusion. I wanted to believe he was just careless, but the truth was staring me in the face.

Charles didn't just squander money, that I could forgive, he buried secrets. By now you have gone through the safety deposit boxes and have seen the birth certificate. I should have told you but never felt there was a right time. But then again, when is there ever a right time? But he had other secrets, too, the kind that involve dead parents and a sibling who didn't get the chance to grow old. I don't have a smoking gun, but I have enough to know he had a hand in it. Maybe he didn't mean for things to go so far, but once you start down a dark road, it's damn near impossible to turn back. And Charles? He kept marching forward.

I believed he was being blackmailed. Yes, the little weasel got himself tangled up with someone who knew what he'd done and wasn't shy about making demands. Charles, being the spineless coward that he is, did exactly what he always does. He made excuses, played the victim, and let himself be led around by the nose.

So I had a choice: let him drag the rest of us down with him or cut him off before he could do any more damage. You now know which option I picked. He won't see a dime of the estate, and good riddance. He'd only hand it over to whatever leech has been bleeding him dry, and I won't have this family's legacy funding more of his disasters.

About his child, I have set up money for her that Charles can't touch. She shouldn't have to suffer his idiocy. Maybe at some point we'll see what she made of herself.

I know this might come as a shock, but believe me, Victoria, everything I've done has been to protect you, to protect this family. Charles made his choices. Now he can live with them.

With all my love,
Matka
Ekaterina A. Robinson

To say my mind was blown was an understatement. Granny May had held onto this secret for years, thinking she was protecting the family. But in hindsight, this could be the reason for her demise.

Katerina sat frozen, staring into space. I touched her leg, and she jumped.

"Jara," she said, looking at me wildly, "what do we do? Could all these things...the Foundation money, the attacks, Granny's death, be because of what he thought she knew?"

"Sweetheart, I don't know." I turned to Mr. Maxwell. "Sir, did Granny May leave any evidence of these claims against Charles? Or did she tell you how she knew all of this?"

"I'm sorry, but she didn't. I didn't know exactly what was in the letter, but once I found the codicil, I knew from some of my previous discussions with Mrs. Robinson that it had to be about Charles and her suspicions. She felt if she told Victoria about this and didn't have concrete proof, it could drive a wedge between them. Mrs. Robinson never approved of Charles, even before he and Victoria got married. Now that they're divorcing..."

The three of us sat quietly in that dimly lit office, letting the information sink in. "Sir," Katerina said finally, "am I allowed to have this letter? I think I need to show this to Mom as soon as possible."

"Yes, by all means. It's now your letter to share."

We thanked Mr. Maxwell for his time and readied ourselves to go out in the frigid night. It was late enough that not many cars were on the road, so it was silent on the way back to our vehicle. The snow continued to fall, the fresh powder glimmering like diamonds under the streetlights. We sat in the deserted parking lot, not knowing what to say.

Chapter Twenty-Eight

We got to the house after midnight. The once loving embrace I had always felt was now replaced with a bone-chilling cold. We decided not to call and wake anyone with the information we'd just learned. I went straight to the den and lit the fire, reaching for the warmth like a hand grasping for solid ground. The Christmas tree still stood in the corner, its lights blinking gently, trying to offer the familiar glow of holiday cheer. Usually, that soft light wrapped around me like a blanket, grounding me with comfort and joy. But tonight, it all felt cold and distant, like a lone star in a moonless night. The warmth and cheer reached out to embrace me, but I remained untouched. Katerina joined me on the couch and leaned into me. I put my good arm around her and held her close, both of us drifting off from exhaustion without a word.

We were awakened the next morning by the sharp ring of a phone. Groggy and disoriented, I reached for Katerina's phone, expecting it to be one of her brothers or a wrong number. Instead, a voice on the other end identified themselves as a caseworker from the hospital.

"Good morning," she said, her tone brisk and professional. "I'm calling to confirm the facility Victoria Lansing is being transferred to. We need to forward her discharge instructions."

The words hit me like a cold splash of water. Victoria was supposed to be in the hospital for at least another week. Katerina, still half-asleep beside me, sat up immediately. *Discharge instructions?* she mouthed at me, her expression quickly shifting to concern.

"Wait, who discharged Victoria?" I asked, feeling a knot of anxiety tightening in my chest. I put the phone on speaker.

"It looks like a Dr. Johnson, if I'm reading his handwriting correctly," the caseworker replied. The name meant nothing to us. We had never heard of him. I glanced at Katerina, who shook her head, equally perplexed.

"Can we speak to Dr. Patel, please?" Katerina interjected, her voice tense. She explained Dr. Patel was Victoria's primary physician, the one who had been overseeing her care since the beginning.

"I'm afraid Dr. Patel is currently on rounds," the caseworker informed us. "He'll call you later. Please, are you able to tell me the facility? I need it for our records. Whoever did the paperwork last night didn't fill anything out."

"So let me get this straight"—I was trying to stay calm and professional—"you aren't familiar with Dr. Johnson, and nothing was written down on where or to whom Victoria Lansing was discharged?"

"Yes, ma'am. I see the name is starred. Was she here under another name?"

"Yes, she was!" The tone of my voice was stern but slightly panicked. "An FBI agent was supposed to be with her at all times."

"I'm sorry, ma'am, but I don't know anything about that."

We hung up, our minds spinning with questions and fears. What happened? Why was Victoria discharged without our knowledge? The worst and most unimaginable scenarios began to race through our minds. This had to have been a mistake.

Chase was supposed to be with Victoria, and Sarah had promised to stay with her until Chase arrived. I grabbed my phone and dialed Chase's number, my hands shaking. No answer. I tried Sarah's number next, but she didn't respond either. Katerina and I sat, tense, the phone clutched between us, waiting for any sign that Victoria was safe. The minutes dragged on, each one feeling like an eternity. We could only hope that the next call would bring clarity and not the devastating news we feared.

I decided to call Travis, hoping he would know something, at least where the guard was.

"What are you talking about?" he asked. "Victoria is gone?"

"We got a call this morning saying she was discharged. They were asking us where she went because they didn't receive discharge instructions. We can't reach Sarah or Chase, either."

"I briefly saw Sarah yesterday afternoon. She was returning to Victoria's room after the MRI. Nothing seemed to be off."

"Can you please call around and find out who was to be at the door last night and what happened?" I looked over to Katerina, who was already getting dressed. "It looks like we'll be taking a trip to the hospital. Meet us there?"

"Definitely. Let me make some calls first. I should be there in about an hour."

I tried to call Sarah again, and it went straight to voicemail. Katerina was on the phone to Abby, Chase's fiancé. After a couple of minutes, she hung up and dropped down in the chair.

"Abby hasn't heard from Chase today. She said they spoke yesterday when he told her he was going to the hospital. She didn't speak with him last night because she was cramming for a final today." Katerina's voice was hurried and tense. "She's going to try and reach him by phone, and if she can't, she'll run by his place."

"While I get dressed, why don't you call CJ. Maybe he knows something."

Katerina was staring into space. I wasn't sure if she heard me or not. I walked to her and put my hand on her shoulder. "Kat," I said softly.

She pulled out of her trance and looked up at me. "Okay, okay, good idea..." Her voice trailed off.

"We'll find her, I promise."

CJ's phone went to voicemail too. No one seemed to be answering their phones. Katerina left a message and we finished getting ready. We drove to the hospital, the air between us thick with unspoken fears. The urgency of the situation left no room for conversation. As soon as we parked, we bolted from the vehicle, our footsteps pounding against the frozen pavement as we sprinted toward the entrance. The automatic doors parted before us, and we rushed inside, heading straight for the elevators. The ride up to Victoria's floor felt interminable, each second stretching into an eternity. When the elevator doors finally opened, we were greeted by the sound of raised voices. Dr. Patel's voice was unmistakable, filled with frustration and authority as he demanded answers.

"When was Victoria Lansing discharged? To whom and by whom?" His words echoed down the hallway, a stark contrast to the usual controlled environment of the hospital.

Katerina and I rushed toward him, our presence drawing his attention. He turned to us with an apologetic look.

"I'm trying to find out how this happened," he said, his voice now softer but no less intense.

We stood by nervously as Dr. Patel and the charge nurse sifted through computer records and hard copy files, their expressions growing more perplexed by the minute. The minutes dragged on, and the tension in the air was suffocating as we waited for any news, any explanation that could make sense of the chaos.

The charge nurse shook her head, clearly baffled, while Dr. Patel continued to cross-reference the information, his frustration mounting. Katerina clutched my hand tightly, her grip a lifeline in the sea of uncertainty surrounding us. We watched, hearts pounding, as they continued their frantic search for answers, hoping against hope that the situation would soon be resolved, and that Victoria was safe.

Travis rushed onto the floor, his face flushed. His arrival added another layer of urgency to the already chaotic situation.

"What's going on?" I asked as soon as I saw him.

"I've just learned that someone posing as an agent came on duty last night," he said, catching his breath. "The real agent was knocked out and tied up. He was found in his car in the parking garage."

Katerina's face darkened. "And Dr. Johnson? The one who supposedly discharged Mom?"

Dr. Patel shook his head. "There is no Dr. Johnson on staff, nor anyone with that name who has hospital privileges. This is a serious breach."

The implications were chilling. Someone had orchestrated this with precision and intent. Travis quickly dispatched an agent to Sarah's house, but when they arrived, it was cleaned out. Sarah was nowhere to be found.

Meanwhile, Katerina's phone rang. It was CJ.

"All my tires have been slashed. I can't get to the hospital. How's Mom? Has something happened?"

Katerina shared all the information she had with him. "It doesn't look good, CJ," Katerina said, her voice cracking with emotion. "We're still trying to figure things out."

Dr. Patel, sensing the need for a more private space, guided us to a small conference room. We sat down, trying to piece together the fragmented information we had.

We were waiting for Agent Adams to arrive when Katerina received another call, this time from Abby. Her voice was filled with a mix of relief and fear. Katerina's face turned pale as she listened, her hand clutching the phone tightly. She hung up and told us, "They found Chase. He was drugged and tied up in his apartment. He never made it to the hospital. The NYPD is investigating, and he was taken to the New York Presbyterian ER to be checked out. Abby's meeting him there." The room fell into a heavy silence. Our worst fears were being realized. Someone had gone to great lengths to orchestrate this abduction.

"Let's stay focused," Travis said firmly. "We need to consolidate all our information and coordinate with the authorities. Agent Adams is on his way here. I'm hoping he can shed some light on this."

Agent Adams finally arrived, his demeanor stern and focused. He had already gotten an earful from Travis and was actively reaching out to his contacts to determine how the communication breakdown had occurred.

CJ called back while we sat listening to Travis and Agent Adams call their contacts. He had managed to secure another vehicle and was on his way to New York City to check on Chase. They planned to come to the house in the morning. There was a brief, shared relief that CJ was safe and mobile, but the weight of the unresolved issues hung heavily in the air.

Katerina paced the hall mumbling to herself. At any point I feared she would let out another primal scream. She walked to me, tears streaming down her face. She told me to tell Travis about the codicil. We also decided to wait until CJ and Chase arrived to tell them about the codicil and the letter. We knew the revelations would be best handled when everyone was together, and we wanted to ensure the information was shared in the most supportive environment possible.

With Katerina's permission, I pulled Agent Adams and Travis aside. The quiet corner of the hospital room provided a semblance of privacy, though the tension in the air made it feel as if the walls themselves were listening. I took a deep breath and began to recount the contents of the letter.

"Granny May made some serious accusations regarding Charles," I said, my voice low and steady. "The letter detailed a codicil that changed everything. She accused Charles of...well, she believed he was involved in the death of his parents and a sibling."

Agent Adams's eyes narrowed, his professional demeanor unyielding. Travis listened intently, his face a mask of concentration.

"We need to understand if this is connected to what's happening with Victoria," I said. "There's a possibility that the same forces at play could be tied to Granny May's accusations."

Agent Adams nodded, his mind racing to connect the dots. "We'll need to dig deeper into Charles's background and any connections he might have. This could be bigger than we initially thought."

Travis agreed. "We'll get to the bottom of this. But we need to be cautious. If what you're saying is true, we're dealing with individuals who have no qualms about taking extreme measures. Has anyone called Charles about Victoria?"

I shook my head no. "I wasn't sure if we should. If he isn't behind it, do we really want him meddling in this?"

Both men agreed, and we rejoined Katerina, who was anxiously waiting for an update. I gave her a reassuring nod, indicating that our conversation had been necessary and productive.

"What about the security cameras in the hospital?" I suggested. "Maybe they captured something."

Agent Adams and Travis exchanged a glance before nodding in agreement. With the necessary permissions swiftly obtained, the three of us made our way to the security office. The room was small and cluttered, filled with monitors displaying various angles of the hospital's interior and exterior.

Travis looked around the room, his expression a mix of concern and frustration. "Has anyone heard from Sarah?" he asked. We all shook our heads.

A security officer rewound the footage to the previous night. We leaned in, watching intently as the grainy images flickered on the screen. As the time stamp approached the period in question, we held our breath.

And there she was, Sarah, walking alongside a man in a security uniform. My jaw dropped as I recognized the fake agent as the one guarding Victoria's door when we left last night. Beside them was another man in a white coat, who we presumed was the alleged Dr. Johnson. His face was obscured, but he had a familiarity about him in the way he walked and carried himself. They were wheeling Victoria on a gurney.

The shock of what we were seeing left us momentarily speechless. Was this the plan all along? Was Sarah a willing participant in this? Or had she been coerced?

"We need to find out who these people are," Travis said, "and where they took Victoria."

Agent Adams nodded, already making calls to expedite the investigation. "I'll put out an alert for the fake agent and this supposed Dr. Johnson. We need to track down every lead."

I turned to Travis, my mind racing. "What could've driven Sarah to do this? It doesn't make sense."

"We can't jump to conclusions," he replied, his eyes fixed on the screen as the figures disappeared down a hallway. "There could be more to this than we know. We need to find her and get some answers."

Back in the small room where Katerina waited, we relayed the disturbing news. Her face paled, and she clutched my arm tightly.

"Sarah...could she really be behind this?" she whispered, her eyes wide with fear and disbelief.

As we sat waiting for news, each minute felt like an hour, and the uncertainty gnawed at me. I tried to stay focused, but a tremor in my hand and a sharp, persistent pain in my arm kept pulling my attention away. It had been bothering me for days, but now it was becoming unbearable. I decided to have Dr. Ortiz paged. A few minutes later, my phone buzzed with her reply. She was concerned and mentioned she could give me something for the pain but would prefer to see me in person if I had the time.

"I'm actually in the hospital right now due to a situation with Mrs. Lansing," I explained.

"Perfect timing, then," she said, her voice reassuring. "Meet me downstairs in the ER, and I'll take a look."

I informed Katerina and Travis that I needed to step out for a moment. Katerina nodded, understanding the necessity. "We'll keep you updated if anything happens," she said, her voice soft but strained.

I made my way down to the ER, each step a reminder of the pain that had steadily worsened. The bustling environment of the emergency room was a stark contrast to the oppressive stillness of our waiting area. Nurses and doctors moved with purpose, tending to patients and performing their duties with practiced efficiency.

Dr. Ortiz spotted me as soon as I entered. Her warm smile and calm demeanor were a welcome sight amidst the chaos. She guided me to a nearby examination room and quickly began assessing my arm. She looked at the bullet wounds and said they were healing nicely, then she moved to my shoulder, and I winced in pain.

"This looks pretty inflamed," she said, her brow furrowing as she gently prodded the area. "How long has this been bothering you?"

"A few days," I admitted. "I've been a bit preoccupied with everything going on."

Dr. Ortiz nodded sympathetically. "I understand. It's easy to put our own health on the back burner when we're worried about others. But you need to take care of yourself too. We need to get this shoulder moving more, or you're going to lose range of motion. I believe it's healed enough that you can start doing more exercises and add in some strength exercises too."

Dr. Ortiz explained the tremor in my hand could be caused by nerve damage in my shoulder. "I'm going to give you a couple of shots in your shoulder to help decrease the inflammation and relax the ligaments and tendons. If you'd like, I can write a prescription for one of the shots I'm giving you, and Sarah can administer it."

My jaw dropped. "Sarah?"

"Yes, Sarah Miles, she was here with Mrs. Lansing."

"I know who Sarah is, Doctor," I replied with impatience, "but she went missing last night with Mrs. Lansing."

Dr. Ortiz looked at me, incredulous. "Oh my, is she okay?"

"We have no idea. We believe she took Mrs. Lansing somewhere."

"Oh, I can't believe that," the doctor replied, shaking her head. "Sarah was such a good nurse. I don't see her harming anyone."

"You knew her?"

"Oh, yes, she worked here for three or four years. She was one of the best."

"Doctor, by any chance, do you know if she had any family around here or where she came from?"

Dr. Ortiz shook her head. "I don't think she has any family around here, but you might want to check with HR. They may know. Have them look up Elizabeth Sarah Miles."

I was taken aback. "Elizabeth?"

"Yes," Dr. Ortiz said. "She hated the name Elizabeth and always went by Sarah. Why?"

An idea hit me like a bolt of lightning. "Do you know if she had ever been married?"

Dr. Ortiz nodded. "Why yes, she had a brief marriage right before she entered nursing school. She told me she was young and dumb, and they divorced within three months. She said she kept her married name to distance herself from her past. We never went into much more than that."

I couldn't believe what I was hearing. "I have one more question. Do you know if her maiden name was Shaw?"

"Yes, yes, I think it was. Does that help?"

I nodded, feeling a rush of clarity amidst the confusion. "Maybe not directly about Mrs. Lansing, but it answers some other questions."

Dr. Ortiz looked at me, clearly intrigued but respectful of my need for discretion. "I'm glad I could help, even if just a little."

As I thanked her and made my way back to the waiting area, my mind racing. Sarah Miles was Elizabeth S. Shaw. She was Katerina's half-sister and Charles' daughter. The connection was uncanny. I now had a link that could explain Sarah's sudden disappearance and her possible involvement in Victoria's case.

Katerina and Travis looked up expectantly as I approached.

"I have some new information," I said, taking a deep breath. "Sarah's real name is Elizabeth S. Shaw. She was briefly married and kept her married name, and she worked at this hospital."

Katerina blinked. "Shaw? Why does that name sound familiar?"

"Because it is," I replied. "She's your sister. This could explain why Sarah has been acting so strangely and why she's now missing. We need to dig deeper into her past."

"At this hospital? Holy shit," Travis yelled, punching his phone screen with an index finger. "I'll get in touch with HR and have them pull all records on Elizabeth Sarah Miles."

Chapter Twenty-Nine

It was getting late, and exhaustion was starting to take a toll. We decided it was best to go back to the house and get some rest. As we drove home, the day's events replayed in my mind, a whirlwind of emotions and revelations that left me feeling drained.

CJ called again as we pulled into the driveway. "We'll be at the house around noon," he said, his voice weary. "Unless the police need to speak to Chase some more."

"Got it. Drive safely," I replied before hanging up.

Inside, the house felt eerily quiet. Katerina and I headed to the bedroom, both of us too tired to talk much. I flopped on the bed and tried to relax, but the day's stress lingered, making it hard to settle. I could tell Katerina was restless, too, tossing and turning beside me.

After a while, she turned over and whispered, "Should we call my dad and just flat out ask him?"

I thought about it for a moment. "That's entirely up to you, but you may be opening a can of worms if he is involved, and it could place your mother in more danger."

She sighed and cuddled back into me. Despite our worries, we eventually drifted into a restless sleep, the kind where you wake up frequently, but any sleep was better than none.

Morning came too soon. We found ourselves in the kitchen, drinking coffee and pushing what we had made for breakfast around on our plates. Neither of us had much of an appetite.

The phone rang, and Katerina, anxious for news, grabbed it without checking the caller ID.

"Hello?" she answered, her voice hopeful. Her face changed as she listened. "Dad?"

I could hear the muffled sound of Charles's voice at the other end, his tone serious. Katerina's hand tightened around the phone, her knuckles turning white.

"Why are you calling?" she asked, a hint of accusation in her voice.

I moved closer, trying to offer silent support. She turned to me, her eyes electrified green with a mix of emotions: fear, confusion, and determination.

After Katerina hung up the phone, her voice was shaky. "Dad was calling to ask me about you," she said. "He wanted to know how I was doing and if there was anything I needed. I believe he still thinks you're dead or is pumping me for information. I told him CJ and Chase would be here tonight, and he should come by tomorrow. He never even asked how Mom was doing!"

The realization hit us both like a punch. If Charles hadn't asked about Victoria, maybe he already knew what had happened. The implications were chilling. We needed to get a game plan together before he arrived tomorrow.

Around 1 p.m., CJ and Chase finally arrived. Katerina's face lit up with instant relief. She ran to them, giving each of her brothers a long, emotional embrace. Tears welled in her eyes, a rare display of vulnerability.

"I'm so glad you're both here," she said, her voice cracking. CJ and Chase, though clearly exhausted and shaken, hugged her back with equal intensity.

The guys declined any food, citing their exhaustion. "I'm still woozy from being drugged," Chase admitted, rubbing his temples.

Katerina took a deep breath and steadied herself. "There's more I need to tell you, beyond Mom's disappearance," she said. We all moved into the den, settling into the comfortable furniture. Katerina reached into her bag and pulled out Granny May's letter. "This letter," she began, holding it up, "is from Granny. It contains some serious accusations about Dad."

CJ and Chase leaned forward, their expressions a mix of curiosity and concern. Katerina began to read, her voice steady but filled with emotion. After she finished, she told them about Sarah and that she was their sister. Both men's jaws dropped with the revelation. The more Katerina talked, the more the pieces of the puzzle fit together: the sudden hospital discharge of Victoria, Sarah being their sister and possibly involved with Victoria's disappearance, and now Charles's strange behavior and Granny May's accusations. They all seemed interconnected.

When Kat finished, CJ was the first to speak, his voice low and measured. "We need to confront him. But we also need to be careful. If what Granny wrote is true, we're dealing with someone who's capable of anything."

While Katerina and her brothers were deep in discussion, my phone buzzed with a call from Travis. I quietly slipped away to the kitchen, grabbed a beer, and stepped out through the French doors into the backyard. The crisp air was a welcome change, and the sun's bright reflection off the snow gave the harbor a ghostly, serene appearance.

Travis's voice was urgent but steady. "The FBI ran Dr. Johnson's face through their facial recognition system," he began. "Turns out he's an ex-military officer now working for an independent contractor that specializes in Black Ops. I don't have his name yet. The fake guard hasn't been identified yet either, but we're closing in."

The information was both enlightening and chilling. The fact that we were dealing with a Black Ops specialist added a dangerous new layer to an already complex situation. I reminded him about Brian being a sniper from the Marines.

Travis said, "Agent Adams is coming to the house today with photos of this Dr. Johnson and members of his team. We need you to take a good look and see if anyone looks familiar."

I nodded even though he couldn't see me. "Understood. CJ and Chase have arrived, and Katerina has spoken to her father. Charles will be coming to the house tomorrow."

"Good to know," Travis replied. "I'll send a team to install some surveillance equipment at the house today. We need to stay ahead of this."

After we hung up, I realized how cold it had gotten. I took a deep breath, savoring the fresh air for a moment longer before heading back inside. The warmth of the house was comforting, but the weight of the situation was still heavy on my mind. I was sitting at the kitchen island, lost in thought, when Katerina came up behind me, gently wrapping her arms around my shoulders.

"What did Travis say?" she asked softly, her breath warm against my ear.

I placed my hand on hers, feeling the comfort of her soft touch on my body. "The FBI identified Dr. Johnson. He's an ex-military officer who works for a Black Ops contractor. Agent Adams is coming over today with names and photos of him and his team. Travis is also sending a team to install surveillance equipment."

Katerina slowly nodded, absorbing the information. "At least we're getting closer to understanding what's going on," she said, a hint of determination in her voice.

"Yeah," I agreed. "But it also means we're dealing with some very dangerous people. We need to be extremely careful."

Just then, CJ and Chase entered the kitchen, their faces showing the strain of the information they just learned. I filled them in on my conversation with Travis.

Chase walked over to the fridge, pulled out a gallon of milk, and took a long swallow. Katerina initially had a look of disgust, but then it softened. "Hell, Chase, after all we're going through, I can't even be mad at you for being a pig."

He choked out a tense laugh. "Right now, the least of my worries is you thinking I'm a pig. God, spies are attacking our family ..."

The doorbell rang, jolting us from our conversation. I opened the door to find Agent Adams, his coat lapels up, shivering in the wind and wearing a serious expression. I took his coat and introduced him to everyone, and Katerina, ever the gracious hostess, offered him something to drink. He declined politely, and we all made our way to the den.

Agent Adams spread out a series of photographs on the desk. The room fell silent as we gathered around, each of us feeling the weight of the moment. My eyes scanned the array of faces until I stopped at one, the alleged Dr. Johnson. I recognized him immediately from the security footage but still couldn't place him. I was examining another photo of him when Katerina suddenly screamed, "Oh my god, it's Brian!" With a trembling hand she passed me the photo and picked up another. "This looks a lot like Brian too," she said. Both photos contained images of Dr. Johnson with Brian.

Chase turned even paler. "That's him," he said in almost a whisper, his voice shaking. He pointed to another man. "That's who attacked me."

CJ quickly moved to support Chase, helping him into a chair.

Agent Adams took the photos and put them side by side on the desk. Pointing to Dr. Johnson, he said, "This is Marcus J. Montgomery. He was a commander in the Navy SEALs until he left for a more lucrative position with a Black Ops company."

Something was nagging at my brain. With the pain medicine I've had to take, my mind was a bit foggy. He let us take in the information before continuing.

"Jara, remember the photo you showed me on Katerina's phone?"

"Yes, of Brian."

"Yes, Warrant Officer Brian Jackson, sniper. He also left and went to work with Commander Montgomery. The other man, who looks a lot like Brian, is Warrant Officer Anthony Smith. His specialty is hand-to-hand combat and demolitions. According to members of their old SEAL team, Brian and Anthony would often swap uniforms and play tricks on their commanding officers and fellow SEALs. And yes, Chase," as he pointed to another man, "we believe that is the man who attacked you, Raymond DeWitt. He was in the same SEAL unit as the others and was a Master Chief Petty Officer before he also left. NYPD has him in custody. All he said was that Mr. Jackson hired him. If he knows more than that, he's not sharing. Also, Bridgeport police found Mrs. Lansing's phone. It was destroyed, but some blood was found on it, and it isn't hers. NYPD is comparing DeWitt's DNA to the blood on the phone."

I looked at the others, we were all overwhelmed. "John, thank you for all this and the work you've done. We really appreciate it. This is really going to help."

"Well don't get too excited yet. We learned when we were at the hospital that some equipment and medications have also gone missing. The same stuff Mrs. Lansing was on when she was in her coma."

My tone was guarded. "What are you saying, John?"

"The FBI believes whoever took Mrs. Lansing also took the drugs. We can't be sure, but things are pointing in that direction. What they plan on doing with them is anybody's guess."

The bees in my head were buzzing.

The doorbell rang again, signaling the arrival of the surveillance team Travis had sent. They moved quickly, setting up equipment and ensuring our home was secure. The added layer of protection brought a small sense of relief, but we knew the biggest ordeal lay ahead.

We did a few tests of the recording equipment. The cameras were almost set up and ready to be put online. I had the equipment put in an unoccupied upstairs bedroom, one I doubted Charles would enter.

I glanced at Katerina, CJ, and Chase. Their faces were a mix of apprehension and anxiety. We had avoided discussing their father's visit tomorrow in depth, but the unspoken words were deafening. They had watched with uncertainty as the equipment was set up. I couldn't help feeling like we were violating their domestic sanctity.

I had handled dangerous cases before, but never involving people who I cared about. In desperation for some clarity, I turned to Agent Adams. He was checking out one of the cameras when I approached him. "John, any advice on what we should say or not say to Senator Lansing? I want to be able to advise his family."

John's voice was calm and reassuring. "Listen, I understand how tough this must be for you all. It's crucial that you act as normally as possible around Charles. Any sign that you suspect him or are acting unnaturally could jeopardize our investigation. Just interact with him like you would on any normal day."

I gave a tense laugh, thinking about what the Lansing family "normal" usually looked like. Victoria and Katerina had asked themselves the same question. "But how can we just act normal? With everything that's happening?" I asked, a hint of desperation creeping into my voice.

"It's not easy, but it's necessary," he replied. "Remember, the cameras and microphones are for your safety. They're discreet and will capture everything. Tell the others to ignore them. Let Charles do the talking. Our team will be monitoring everything in real time. If anything needs our immediate attention, we'll be here in a matter of minutes."

Taking a deep breath, I nodded. "And what about the investigation into the Foundation? The actuaries are very close to building their case on the stolen funds."

"That's still ongoing and is just as critical. Don't bring it up. Let him lead any and all conversations. Since we're building a case, any tip off from your end might alert him or cause him to change his behavior, making it harder for us to gather the evidence we need."

I thanked him again for all he was doing and walked back into the den. The hours until Charles' arrival were going to be long ones. The family tried to keep busy for the rest of the day. A palpable tension filled the air, and Chase paced the floor, appearing preoccupied and anxious. I wasn't surprised when he decided to head to his room to be alone.

Meanwhile, I found myself reflecting on Dr. Ortiz's advice. She'd emphasized the importance of getting my injured arm moving more when out of the sling. Her words echoed in my mind, and I decided to take a proactive step. Cooking dinner seemed like a practical way to incorporate movement and a sense of normalcy into my day. The rhythmic chopping of vegetables, the sizzle of ingredients hitting the hot pan, and the fragrant aromas filling the kitchen all worked together to lift my spirits. My mind began to clear and relax. I kept thinking about the photo we were shown and how others were familiar, not just

Brian. My train of thought was interrupted when Katerina and her brothers entered the kitchen.

We all acted as if nothing had happened and tried to have a normal dinner. As the evening wore on, though, a familiar restlessness crept in. Another night was approaching, the kind where sleep was elusive and thoughts ran wild.

Chapter Thirty

The first light of dawn filtered through the curtains, casting a soft glow over the room. I turned to Katerina, who was finally sleeping peacefully beside me, and kissed her gently on the forehead. Her long red hair was pulled back in a ponytail, a telltale sign of her nerves being raw.

I slipped out of bed, careful not to disturb her, and made my way to the den. The house was quiet, the stillness almost comforting. I started a fire in the fireplace. The crackling of the logs provided a soothing background as I settled into the armchair. The warmth began to seep into my bones, a small comfort amid our ongoing turmoil.

I pulled out my phone and called Travis for any updates. His voice came through clearly, a mix of exhaustion and determination. "The actuaries at the Foundation have it almost wrapped up," he informed me. "We're in the process of getting a search warrant for the senator's computers at all his campaign headquarters. It's going to be a large operation, and we need to execute the warrants with simultaneous precision."

I listened intently, feeling a sense of relief wash over me. Knowing they were close to wrapping up this part of the investigation brought a glimmer of hope. The Foundation had been hemorrhaging money, and every delay only made things worse. The prospect of finally putting an end to this ordeal lifted a weight from my shoulders, if only slightly.

Travis reassured me Agent Adams would be watching the cameras and listening to the microphones from a nearby van. As he continued to outline the plans, I glanced around the den, the flickering firelight casting dancing shadows on the walls. It was a reminder of the battles we were fighting on multiple fronts, both personal and professional. But in that moment, with the warmth of the fire and the promise of progress, I felt a renewed sense of determination. We were close, and I was ready for it to end.

As the day slipped into evening and the sound of a car pulling into the driveway echoed through the house, I steadied myself. Katerina took my hand as we followed CJ and Chase to the foyer, anxiety etched on their faces. "It's going to be okay," I reassured them, though the words felt hollow even to my own ears.

CJ opened the door to find Charles, his expression unreadable, and Bella by his side. As he took a step inside, I could almost hear the soft whirr of the cameras and the awakening of the microphones. Bella remained in the doorway, staring at me as if she saw a ghost.

"You...you're dead," she stammered.

"No, Bella, I'm not. A little banged up, maybe, but not dead."

Charles stopped cold. He hadn't noticed me. He looked at me, then Katerina, his eyes wide with astonishment. "You said she was gone...dead."

"No, Dad, I didn't. You asked me how I was dealing with the Jara thing, and I said fine. We never discussed what happened or if she was alive. Anyway, why would either one of you think Jara was killed?"

"But the accident..." Bella interjected, looking at me. "You couldn't have survived that. I would've been told."

"Well, as you see, I did." I smirked as I said, "The shooter wasn't as good as they thought they were. But enough about me and my alleged demise, please come in."

Charles and Bella entered, shaking hands with the boys and attempting to hug Katerina. She pulled back, her body tensing as she moved closer to me. I could feel the elephant in the room growing larger and larger, its presence almost suffocating.

All but Chase went into the dining room. He excused himself, saying he needed a minute and would join us shortly. I looked at him quizzically, but he put out a hand and nodded his head, indicating "I'm good," before walking away.

We had ordered the meal, knowing none of us had the energy or focus to cook a full dinner. I'm glad we ordered extra since Bella had accompanied the senator. She sat next to him at the table as if they were conjoined twins. We engaged in the usual small talk under a thin veneer of normalcy.

When Chase returned, he seemed a little off balance as he sat down. Charles noticed and asked if he was okay. Chase responded sharply, "Actually, Dad, I'm not. After being attacked, drugged, and tied up, I'm not feeling the greatest."

I watched both Bella and the senator closely. Bella's face remained stoic, revealing nothing. But at least the senator had the presence of mind to act surprised and concerned, his eyes widening slightly, his mouth forming a small "O" of shock. It appeared to be a performance, but at that moment, any semblance of empathy was welcome. The room fell into an awkward silence, the small talk evaporating in the face of Chase's blunt honesty. The elephant in the room was no longer just a looming presence, it was a full-blown reality we could no longer ignore.

His words hung heavy in the air, the declaration sending a shiver down my spine. Charles looked at Bella, his eyes narrowing. "It's time for us to go. We're not welcome here, in my own home!" The finality in his tone was unmistakable. He had drawn a line in the sand, challenging us to cross it.

Chase suddenly lifted his head from his hands, his face a portrait of desperation and confusion. "Dad, did you do this to me? Your own son? So I wouldn't be with Mom?" His voice was almost begging, searching for some semblance of truth.

Charles's expression hardened, but he responded almost convincingly, "I had no involvement in the attack on you, Chase." A slight tremor was in his voice, but he maintained his composure.

I watched Charles carefully, a knot tightening in my stomach. The idea of asking him if he had anything to do with my accident and being shot crossed my mind, but I dismissed it. I feared he might get too much enjoyment out of teasing me with the possibility.

Charles pushed himself away from the table with a huff of indignation. Bella stood up beside him and gave a crooked smile that sent a chill through me.

Katerina's face had turned blood red. "Dad," Katerina interjected, trying hard to hold back an avalanche of emotion, "Where is Mom? Is she okay?"

"Why do you think I would know where she is?" The senator spat out his words. "It seems I'm not a part of this family anymore. You never told me where she was taken after her attack." An evil smile crossed his face. "So if I did know where she was, why would I share that with you?"

Katerina pushed herself back from the table and stood abruptly, her chair scraping loudly against the floor. I instinctively reached over to grab her hand, but she pulled away, her eyes flashing with a mixture of anger and hurt.

"I'm sick of this," she said, her voice growing stronger with each word. "Why are you acting so concerned about Jara and Chase, when never once have you acted concerned about Mom?"

The room fell silent, the tension thick enough to cut with a knife. Charles's face paled, his usual composed demeanor slipping. He opened his mouth as if to respond, but no words came out. The senator's façade of concern wavered, revealing a flicker of unease. Katerina's words cut, raw and accusing. Her gaze challenged anyone to contradict her. I could see the pain in her eyes. It was a wound that had festered, and now it bled out for all to see.

Charles finally found his voice. "Katerina, I—I uh—" He looked at Bella as if for approval. "She's fine. She's in good hands."

Katerina's eyes flared. "What do you mean, 'she's in good hands?' What the hell are you not telling us?"

"Nothing. I just know she's fine. She's getting the best care possible."

CJ glared at him. "Where is she, Dad? Where the fuck is she? We need to see her."

Anger poured out of the siblings like a river of hot lava, filling every crack in the room. I could see the smirk on Bella's face, as if she had just eaten the proverbial canary.

"Charles," I said, "if you know where Victoria is, it would be in your best interest to tell us before things get out of control."

"Really?" Sarcasm oozed from Charles' lips. "Tell you all where she is, like you all told me after she was attacked? Even the doctor wouldn't tell me where my wife was. MY WIFE! I had a right to know, but none of you had the decency to tell me. Plus, you all played this game about Jara being dead. Who do you all think you are, trying to play me for a fool? I'm Senator Charles Lansing, and no one, I mean *no one* plays me."

Charles stood up from the table, leaning forward until he was eye to eye with his angry daughter. His dark eyes turned a solid black as he pulled himself to his full height. "I'm taking care of Victoria from now on," he declared, his voice firm. "I did nothing illegal." He turned, his glare fixed on me. "You've all acted as if I didn't matter, not caring about my feelings or my run for President. Now it's my turn to put my foot down and show you who's boss." Without another word, Charles and Bella turned and walked out the door, leaving a heavy silence in their wake.

We were frozen in place. Katerina was visibly shaken, her eyes filled with unshed tears and fury. CJ looked angry and confused, his fists clenched tightly. Chase was the most devastated, his face buried in his hands once again, the weight of his father's words pressing down on him. The departure of Charles and Bella felt like the air was sucked out of the room, and the tension and unresolved issues grew. We were left to pick up the pieces. The fire in the hearth crackled softly, the only sound in the otherwise silent room. The flickering flames cast shadows on the walls, mirroring the turmoil within each of us. The line had been drawn, and there was no turning back.

When I finally got my senses about me, I walked into the den and phoned Agent Adams. "John, please tell me you heard all of this."

"I did. I have a car following them now."

"John, I'm sorry if we ruined the investigation. Not knowing Victoria's location was grating on all of us. Making each of us a bit raw."

"It's all good. Maybe he will take us to her. At least nothing was said about the Foundation. I think we'll have everything ready to serve in a few days. We're trying to find a federal judge who doesn't owe the senator a favor."

John sounded reassuring that everything seemed under control, other than Victoria's whereabouts. To me, that was the paramount issue. I hung up the phone and turned around to find Katerina standing less than a foot from me. Her face was searching for answers from me.

"They're following your dad. If they learn something, they'll call me right away." I reached out to hold her, but she stepped back.

"I'm too angry." She closed her eyes and shook her head. "I need to do something."

I understood the feeling. I was feeling very helpless too. "Let's go to the Foundation. Maybe they need our help."

Katerina nodded. "I'll tell the guys. Can you pull the car up?"

She turned and left before I could answer. Before I went to the car, I ran up to my room. My hands were shaking when I pulled the pelican box out from under the bed. I took a deep breath and reminded myself that carrying a gun was second nature to me. I pulled out my backup weapon, a black Glock 19 with two full ammunition magazines. I inserted one into the gun and chambered a bullet. I then pulled out my ankle holster and my Ruger LCR .357, fully loaded. I kept reminding myself we were only going to the Foundation, but something in my gut kept nagging at me. I strapped on the ankle holster and gun and put the Glock inside my sling with the extra magazine. I made it to the garage and had the car in front of the house without Katerina knowing I had armed myself. I didn't want to give her any undue worry. She hated it when I wore my gun. She felt it was only borrowing trouble.

It was late when we reached the Foundation, but lights were shining brightly from every floor. Katerina had called Mrs. Walsh to let her know we were on our way and to let the guards at the front door know. I wasn't surprised to learn Mrs. Walsh was at the Foundation, but I hadn't a clue for how long. Two armed guards waited at the door upon our arrival and secured the doors after we entered. We headed to the main conference room where the actuaries had set up their hub. Mrs. Walsh was talking with one of them when she saw us enter. Her hair was pulled up on the top of her head in a messy bun, her eyes drooped from strain and lack of sleep, and clothes disheveled. Katerina hugged her. I smiled and nodded as my phone rang in my pocket. I stepped out of the room into the hallway.

"Hello, Jara?"

"Mr. Maxwell? Is everything okay? It's kind of late."

"Yes, ma'am, I know. I tried to call Katerina, but she didn't answer. I hope I'm not bothering you, but I received a strange call a few minutes ago."

I listened intently as Mr. Maxwell explained how he had received a call from a court in Massachusetts that Charles Lansing had petitioned a judge for guardianship of Victoria. He explained he had friends in multiple court jurisdictions, and one recognized the Lansing name and knew he was the family attorney. He went on to explain the court had documentation that Victoria Lansing was in a coma and was unable to make decisions for herself. The address for the facility she was in was redacted, allegedly for her safety, per request of the senator.

"Am I understanding Charles is trying to make decisions for Victoria?"

"Yes, that's exactly what I'm saying. This has been with the judge for at least two days. If Charles gets this, he'll have the ability to make medical and financial decisions for Victoria. She and I were in the process of establishing Katerina as her power of attorney right before she was attacked, but we didn't get it finished. She had changed her focus on filing for divorce, but even that paperwork hadn't been completed. I'm going to court when it opens tomorrow to see what I can learn."

I was speechless but was able to mutter "thank you" and "please call me" before I hung up. I closed my eyes and leaned against the wall. "Jara," Katerina said apprehensively as she came out into the hallway, "Are you okay? What's happened?"

I took a deep breath and searched for the right words. Realizing there weren't any, I began anyway. "I received a call from Mr. Maxwell." I went on to explain what he told me.

Katerina's face turned from disbelief to full-throttle anger. I saw her hands clench moments before she drew back and hit the wall. She stormed off to her mother's office, slammed the door, and started throwing everything that wasn't nailed down. People came running. I backed them off, telling them all was okay, that Katerina only needed to vent. They didn't believe me, but I don't think any of them were brave enough to tell her to stop.

I opened the door slowly, prepared to duck. Katerina slumped to the floor, sobbing, broken glass everywhere. I bent down and touched her hair, she looked up, eyes full of tears and rage. "I'll get him for this. I'm finding Mom, and I'm going to make him pay."

We heard a soft knock on the door and Mrs. Walsh's voice said, "Jara, can I see you for a moment?"

Katerina wiped her nose on her sleeve. "Go ahead, I'll clean up my mess."

I got up and met with Mrs. Walsh in the hallway.

"Do you know if Mrs. Robinson or Mrs. Lansing had arrangements for hospice care?"

"Hospice care? Not that I know of. Granny May was never in a hospice program. Why are you asking?"

"We're doing the final runs on all the shell company accounts, and a medical receipt popped up. When we went back to double check it, it was gone."

"I don't understand. What are you saying?"

"These shell companies, although money is being flipped between them, have a common destination. This was an abnormality though. No bills were being paid through these funds."

I started to see what she was getting at. "So this receipt has now left the system?"

"Technically, yes, but you know with the internet and computers, nothing is ever really gone."

"Please, I need a copy of that receipt as soon as possible."

"Is it that important?"

"Yes, ma'am. I think it's a matter of life and death."

I followed her as she went to a computer, punched a few keys, and got me a copy of the receipt. I hugged her. She was taken aback a bit but smiled.

I ran down the hall to Victoria's office, grabbed Katerina's hand, and shouted, "We have to go, now."

"What's going on?"

"I'll tell you in the car."

I gave Katerina the address from the receipt since it was in Boston. As we sped off, I dialed Travis. We had made it out of the Foundation's parking lot when I reached him.

"Travis, I think I know where Victoria is." Katerina nearly drove off the road. "Honey, pay attention. We can't crash now."

I explained about the medical receipt showing up in the shell corporations' funding trail. "This has to be her. The receipt is for keeping a person in a coma, a type of comfort measure for hospice. Whoever has Victoria needs her alive to keep the Foundation funds running. If she were dead, all funds would be frozen. Plus, an awake Victoria would be too much to handle."

Katerina drove faster.

Travis sighed. "Jara, what are you two doing?"

"We're going to go get her, that's what we're doing."

"I know I can't stop you. I'm on my way too and I'm sending a team."

"Thank you, Travis, but I really need you to get ahold of an ambulance and a medical team. We can't just pull her out. When Dr. Patel brought her out of the last coma, it took a well-oiled medical team. Can you get me one of those?"

"Let me call you back."

After Travis hung up, Katerina asked, "Do you really think it's Mom?"

Chapter Thirty-One

We made record time finding the address in the Jamaican Plain area of Boston. It was a large, Queen Anne style Victorian on a side street with mature trees lining the drive and the yard. We double-checked the address. This was the place. I hoped this wasn't just a billing office. Katerina wanted to rush right in, but I was able to talk her out of it. An unknown number came up on my phone. I answered.

"Hello?"

"Hello, is this Ms. Quinn? This is Dr. Patel. Mr. O'Ryan gave me your number and asked me to call."

"Oh, Dr. Patel! Did Travis explain to you what is going on?"

"Yes, yes. It's very important that if this is Mrs. Lansing, you don't want to immediately remove her from any machines. It could cause serious brain damage or even death."

"Yes sir, I'm aware of that. But how do we get her out?"

At that moment, Travis and a couple of other sedans pulled up. Agent Adams jumped out of one of them.

"Sir, can you hold on for one moment?"

Putting Dr. Patel on hold, I got out of the car and asked Travis to move the group to a nearby church parking lot a couple of blocks away. I got back in the car, told Katerina to follow them, and returned to the phone.

"Dr. Patel, I'm back. What do you suggest we do?"

Katerina and I made our way to the church lot as Dr. Patel and I made a plan. He told me he would call me back when he had things ready on his end.

"Is this going to work?" she asked.

"It better!"

The night was shrouded in an eerie quiet as I stood in the dimly lit church parking lot, the distant hum of traffic the only sound breaking the stillness. The shadows of the trees danced ominously in the faint light from the streetlamps. I glanced at my watch for the umpteenth time, anxiety gnawing at my insides. Victoria needed help, and she needed it fast. Just then, my phone rang.

"Ms. Quinn, I've arranged for a medical team to meet you at your location. They're some of the best in New England."

"Thank you, Doctor. You don't know how much this means."

"Just get her home safe, Ms. Quinn."

We were just hanging up when an ambulance arrived, its red and blue lights casting fleeting, ghostly hues across the church walls. The vehicle came to a halt, and the doors swung open. From the darkness emerged a figure, her silhouette sharp and commanding. As she stepped into the dim light, I saw her face clearly for the first time. She had short, dark hair that framed her serious, focused expression. Her eyes, sharp and intelligent, scanned the surroundings with a no-nonsense air that immediately instilled a sense of urgency and competence.

"I'm Dr. Regan Saroyan," she introduced herself, her voice cutting through the still night air. She wore a dark jacket over her scrubs, and even in the dim light, I could see the glint of her stethoscope.

"I'm Jara," I replied, my voice tense with worry. "Thank you for coming. We have a victim in a house down the street." As I said the word "victim," my heart jumped into my throat. "We have reason to believe she's in an induced coma, and there might be armed people inside."

Dr. Saroyan's expression didn't waver. She absorbed the information with a steady nod, her eyes locking onto mine with an intensity that was both unsettling and reassuring. "Show me," she said, her tone leaving no room for hesitation.

As we made our way down the street, my sense of foreboding grew. The houses were cloaked in darkness, and every shadow seemed to harbor a potential threat. Dr. Saroyan moved with a purposeful stride, her presence a beacon of calm determination.

We reached the house, its windows dark, the side door slightly ajar. I gestured toward it, my heart pounding. "We think she's inside," I whispered. "Is that an actual medical facility?

"Yes, it is," she answered. "This is a private hospice center for wealthy families. They've always given excellent care. I've admitted a few patients there myself."

We quickly walked back to the church parking lot. The extraction team, made up of FBI agents, had gathered near the ambulance. Travis was explaining the situation to them when he saw Dr. Saroyan and me walking up. "A woman is being held against her will in the facility down the street and is possibly in an induced coma. She was attacked a few weeks ago and taken to the hospital. Due to her injuries, she was put into a medically induced coma, but she had been conscious and lucid for multiple days. She was then kidnapped and we believe she was brought here. What we're wanting to do is confirm she's here, learn what machines and medications she's on, and remove her from this facility as quickly and safely as possible."

The doctor looked at Travis guardedly. "May I ask who this person is? I was told there may also be armed persons?"

"Yes, it may be dangerous. Like I said, we don't know what we're walking into. But the woman is Mrs. Victoria Lansing."

"The senator's missing wife?"

"Yes, so you see the weight of this situation."

Travis said, "I'll be going inside the facility with Dr. Saroyan to confirm Mrs. Lansing is there. If she is, Dr. Saroyan will read her chart and gather what info we need. I'll signal Agent Adams if the team needs to enter. The ambulance will pull up into the bay quietly. I want teams of two agents by each exit and a team by the ambulance. Medical team, remain in the ambulance until you're cleared to come in. Remember, we don't know what we're walking into. Jara and Katerina, I need you to stay back until we have Mrs. Lansing removed and in the ambulance ready for transport."

I groaned but agreed. I wasn't very good to anyone with a bum arm anyway.

Katerina and I got into the car. She threw her arms around me. "She has to be there. She has to be all right."

Katerina pulled the car within sight of the facility, and we watched as Travis and Dr. Saroyan went into the building through the front and the ambulance pulled up under the overhang by the side door. The teams took their places and we waited.

It wasn't long before I heard a shot ring out. I instinctively jumped out of the car and headed toward the ambulance. The teams had breached the exits and entered the facility. More gunfire sounded, and I ordered the medical team to get in the back and take cover. The ambulance driver's door was open, and I stood behind it. I pulled my gun from my sling and held it through the open window of the ambulance door. I heard another gunshot and a loud scream. Sarah appeared, her hands bound, with Brian behind her, pushing her out the side door by the ambulance with a gun to her head. "Stop screaming bitch or I'll kill you," he shouted.

I shouted for Brian to let Sarah go, my weapon pointed straight at him. His weapon moved from Sarah's head toward my direction.

I heard Katerina's voice behind me, near the front of the building, yell, "Brian!" He turned and shot in her direction. I opened fire, emptying my clip into him. Sarah was on the pavement, covered with blood. Brian was on the ground, gun in hand, but not moving.

I kicked the gun away and checked on Sarah. Fearing she was hit or in shock, I hollered for the paramedics. I ran to Katerina, who was against a tree, trembling but not hurt. I headed back to the facility, reloading my gun as I ran, and cautiously entered the building.

I couldn't see her, but I heard Dr. Saroyan yell, "Get my medical team in here."

As if on cue, the team appeared with a stretcher and equipment. The air held the acrid scent of gunpowder. The soft hum of medical equipment mingled with the low murmurs of the medical staff working diligently to restore order.

The staff had converted the living room into a makeshift triage area. Two nurses were on the floor, one clutching her arm where a bullet had grazed her, blood seeping between her fingers, the other treating the wound. Another nurse, visibly shaken but uninjured, was being comforted by a colleague. Nearby, an FBI agent sat propped against a wall, his face pale but resolute. His bulletproof vest had absorbed the impact of the shot, leaving him winded but otherwise unharmed. A doctor and another nurse were attending to him, ensuring he was stable.

I scanned the room, my eyes searching for the one person I had come to see. Amid the scattered medical equipment and unoccupied beds, I finally spotted Victoria. She was in a hospital bed in a corner, her pale face illuminated by the soft glow of a nearby lamp. Tubes and monitors surrounded her, their steady beeps and hums a reminder of her fragile state. My heart ached at the sight of her so vulnerable and still. I approached her bed, my footsteps echoing softly on the wooden floor. As I drew closer, I noticed a figure standing beside her bed, their back turned to me. The person turned at my approach, and I recognized Dr. Saroyan. Her short dark hair was slightly tousled, and her serious eyes reflected the gravity of the situation. She acknowledged my presence with a brief nod before turning her attention back to Victoria, her hands moving with practiced precision as she adjusted the equipment and checked her vitals.

"How is she?" I asked, my voice barely above a whisper.

Dr. Saroyan glanced at me. "She's stable for now," she replied, her tone as calm and composed as ever. "But we need to move her to a more secure location as soon as possible."

I nodded, my mind racing with questions and concerns. Travis stood at the end of Victoria's bed. "What happened here?" I asked as I put my gun away. Katerina pushed past me and to her mother's bedside.

"I'm not totally sure yet," Travis replied. "When we entered, I saw Brian on the other side of the room. He was talking to two other men, and next to them was Sarah, her hands bound in front of her. We figured he had those guys watching Sarah and Mrs. Lansing. They forced Sarah to care for her. He was okay when he saw Dr. Saroyan, but then he saw me. He must have recognized me. He pulled his gun and opened fire. Dr. Saroyan threw herself on Victoria, and I shot back at Brian. It was a blur what happened then. I know the other agents entered and shots continued. I'm not sure if the other two men were armed or not. Brian pulled out another gun, grabbed Sarah, and headed for the ambulance bay door. Not sure what happened after that. I see Sarah. That's a lot of blood. Is she hurt?" Travis started looking around the room. "Where's Brian?"

"Sarah's not hurt," I said. "That's Brian's blood."

Travis shook his head. "I guess I won't be questioning him tonight. And anyway, I thought I told the two of you to stay in the car!"

I saw Agent Adams checking out his team and gathering information on injuries. "We got lucky," he told me. "Only two minor injuries, one to a nurse and one to an agent. Both will be fine. I'm going to secure the scene after Mrs. Lansing is transported."

I nodded. "Thanks, John. Are you able to control the press? No one is to know what really happened here."

"Got it."

As Dr. Saroyan's team wheeled Victoria past me on a gurney, I looked at the woman in the bed. Victoria looked small and fragile, words I never would've used to describe her before now.

Travis put Sarah in his car, and Katerina and I followed him to the hospital. Katerina was shaken, but she still insisted on driving. Neither of us said a word to each other. We arrived at the hospital and were directed to a side entrance near the ambulance bay. Travis sent Sarah to triage, telling her someone from the FBI would question her later.

Victoria was immediately taken to ICU, where Dr. Saroyan's team worked hurriedly. Bees...busy, busy bees. Katerina and I still had not spoken a word to each other. A chill lingered between us.

"Okay you two, what the hell is going on?" Travis bellowed as he arrived on the ICU floor.

"Nothing," I said. "Just waiting to make sure Victoria is okay."

"Nothing, huh? You two have never been this quiet."

"Why are you hassling us, Travis? Things turned out all right."

"'All right'!" Katerina huffed. "'All right,' she says!"

I looked at her. "What's wrong with you? Everything is okay. *You're* even okay, even though you should have stayed in the car."

"Stayed in the car?" Katerina's face was ablaze. "This is my mother's life we're dealing with here. You sure didn't stay in the car."

"Of course I didn't. I heard shots and had to help. That's my job."

"It wasn't your job. Just because you're an agent and have a gun doesn't mean you should go running into the line of fire."

I stepped closer to her. "Yes, I have a gun and can protect myself. You don't. Then you came running out of the car, yelling at Brian. Talk about getting in the line of fire. I can't worry about you and do my job. You could've been killed."

"So this is my fault? You ran out of the car first, bum arm and all, trying to be a hero and racing into harm's way. That wasn't your job. Remember, his gun was pointed at you first."

"Then at you. Why did you yell at him?"

"So he wouldn't shoot you, dammit. I couldn't—I couldn't watch him take another person I love."

I began to tear up. "Why are we arguing? I just wanted to protect you and your mother. I couldn't stand by and do nothing. I couldn't let anything happen to you. When I heard you yell, and he shot at you, I thought I had lost you."

I reached out and pulled Katerina to me. She was hesitant at first but gave in and held me tight.

"So that's where your clip went," Travis tried to joke. "Does anyone care that I was in the line of fire too? Where's my love?"

Katerina let go of me and gave Travis a hug. "Of course we were worried about you."

"And don't forget," he said, "I told you *both* to stay in the car."

We waited for hours in the ICU waiting room. The TV was on with no sound as we watched to see if any of the news leaked. Katerina called her brothers and told them what had happened. We must have drifted off because we were startled awake by Dr. Saroyan.

"Mrs. Lansing is awake now. She's off the ventilator and on oxygen. There are still some IVs, but that's mostly for fluids. She's very weak and it's hard for her to talk, but she wants to see you both."

"Thank you, Dr. Saroyan, for all you've done," Katerina said.

"Your mom is a fighter. I thought I had lost her a couple of times, but she fought to come back. Let me take you to her."

We slowly walked into the room. The lights were dim, and the only sound was the beeping of some machine. Victoria had tubes coming from every part of her body. Katerina approached the side of the bed and touched her mother's hand.

"Mom, we're here. We're all safe. All of us. It's over. It's finally over."

Victoria stirred and squeezed Katerina's hand gently, a faint smile forming on her face. She slowly opened her eyes. "It's over?" she whispered.

"Yes, Mom. It's over."

Victoria slowly raised her other hand to me. I went around the bed and took it.

She whispered something inaudible. I leaned down.

Her voice was hoarse as she stared into my eyes. "It's not over yet, is it?"

I couldn't lie to her. "No, ma'am, not entirely."

She nodded and closed her eyes. She pulled me to her again and whispered, "The queen bee survived, Jara. But, it's definitely not over. He needs to be stung."

Chapter Thirty-Two

We were at Victoria's bedside when Agent Adams called me to meet him at FBI headquarters. Katerina remained with her mother and was anticipating a call from Mr. Maxwell.

As I stepped into the FBI building in Boston, a rush of memories flooded my mind. This was my first post. The building stood tall and imposing, its exterior enhanced with the American flag waving proudly in the brisk breeze. The imposing façade conveyed a sense of authority and security, fitting for an institution dedicated to upholding the law.

Inside, the atmosphere was bustling yet disciplined. Agents and personnel went their duties with purpose. The interior was sleek and modern, with polished floors and walls adorned with framed accolades and commendations, reminders of the FBI's rich history of accomplishments.

I was swiftly escorted to the interrogation area, where they held Brian's counterparts. As I entered the room, the agents' stern gazes and the detainees' guarded demeanor punctuated the tense atmosphere. They had been separated into two rooms, with two-way mirrors on each. In between these rooms was a monitoring room. I entered the monitor room and looked at each of the suspects.

One of them, Anthony Smith, made me do a double take. A formidable figure, he exuded an aura of strength and discipline, unmistakably a former Navy SEAL. His resemblance to Brian was uncanny.

The other man, older and more distinguished in appearance, exuded an air of defiance despite his predicament. His salt and pepper hair lent him an air of authority, even as he sat in a pair of handcuffs. Yet he remained obstinate, refusing to divulge his identity. The FBI's attempts to identify him proved futile, with his fingerprints yielding no matches and facial recognition software drawing blanks. It was a puzzling mystery.

Meanwhile, Brian's phone sat in an evidence bag on a table in the monitoring room, buzzing incessantly with calls from an unknown number. Time was of the essence.

Agent Adams put out the photos we had of Brian's SEAL team. Other than Anthony, I could see no match to the other man. As I observed the older man sitting up straight, his demeanor radiating defiance, a nagging sense of familiarity tugged at the corners of my mind. Something about him stirred a memory, a distant echo of recognition that danced just beyond my grasp. For a fleeting moment, I entertained the notion that he might be the Commander. Yet upon closer inspection, the facial features didn't align, dispelling my hypothesis. Despite my efforts to place him, the identity of the man remained elusive. It was a frustrating sensation, akin to piecing together a jigsaw puzzle with missing pieces.

It occurred to me that I had eliminated perhaps the only witness or link to the senator's crimes, and a wave of apprehension washed over me. It was a sobering reminder how my actions carried consequences. I asked permission to sit in on the interviews of these two men. Because I was so familiar with the parties in this case, I was hoping I could catch a clue that another interviewer might miss. We decided to speak with Anthony Smith first.

Upon entering the room, Anthony immediately locked eyes with me. This had happened many times before, a suspect trying to intimidate me because I was a woman. Agent Adams pulled up a chair directly across from Anthony. I sat at the corner of the table. If he were going to try and stare me down, he would have to make an effort.

Agent Adams began the interview. "Anthony Smith, former Navy SEAL. Quite a resumé you've got there. Shame it's marred by your current situation."

"Save the pleasantries, Fed. I ain't interested in small talk."

"Fair enough. Let's cut to the chase. We have evidence linking you to the kidnapping of Victoria Lansing, the senator's wife. Care to explain?"

Anthony smirked and let out half a laugh. "Evidence? You got nothin' on me, buddy. I was just meeting up with my friend, Brian. Last I checked, that ain't a crime."

"Meeting up with Brian, huh? Convenient excuse. But we know you were involved, Anthony. We have witnesses placing you at the scene. Plus, we know you and Brian can't do anything without each other. You two have something going on?"

"What the fuck are you saying? You calling me gay? Fuck you!" Anthony clenched his fists, his jaw tightened, and he looked as if he wanted to spring across the table, like a tiger pouncing on his prey. "And witnesses? Please, I'd like to meet these so-called witnesses. They're probably as reliable as a two-dollar watch."

"Your arrogance won't save you, Anthony. We also recovered your firearm at the scene. Care to explain why a former Navy SEAL like yourself would be packing heat? Were you working for someone?"

"Oh, come on! You expect me to believe that load of garbage? That ain't my gun, and you know it. Like I said, I was hanging with my friend. What he was doing, I have no idea."

"We have ballistics matching the shots fired at our agents to your weapon. You can't deny that."

"This is a setup, plain and simple. You're tryin' to pin this on me 'cause you got no other leads. Well, I ain't playin' your game."

"Look, Anthony, we know you're angry. But denying your involvement won't make the evidence disappear. You have a chance to cooperate and mitigate the consequences."

"Consequences? Ha! I've faced worse than whatever you've got in store for me, pal. I ain't talkin,' and that's final."

"Suit yourself, Anthony. But remember, the longer you stay silent, the harder it'll be for you to dig yourself out of this mess."

Anthony refused to engage further in the interrogation.

Agent Adams concluded the interview and pushed back from the table. As I was getting up, Anthony's eyes shot daggers at me. I stopped and leaned slightly over the table, meeting his stare. "Maybe Brian can clear this up for you," I whispered. "Oh, yeah, I forgot...I killed him."

Anthony's nostrils flared and he lunged for me, but the shackles kept him restrained. I never flinched, holding his gaze.

"You fucking bitch. We should've killed you on that highway."

I smiled. "Too bad Brian was such a bad shot, or was it you that missed?"

"He didn't miss. He hit you. You just got lucky, that's all."

I've been told that many times. Maybe I was lucky. I turned and walked away. At least I knew now that Brian had fired the shot and Anthony had been the driver.

We decided I would interview the older suspect. Sometimes a woman was less threatening. I walked into the interrogation room, determined to maintain my composure. With the best feminine smile I could muster, I reached out my hand to shake his, signaling both respect and confidence. He responded with a bone-chilling smile, but I kept my hand steady.

"Good morning, I'm Jara," I said, trying to infuse warmth into my voice. "I know you don't want to say who you are, but could you please tell me what you were doing at the facility?"

He leaned back in his chair, the shackles on his wrists clinking softly, and smiled again. "I was checking on a relative," he said, his tone disturbingly calm.

"Great," I replied, keeping my tone light yet firm. "Give me the name of the relative, and we can clear this all up."

With another disarming grin, he said, "Ah no, ma'am. I wouldn't want to get them involved in this."

I studied him carefully. He appeared comfortable despite the restraints. His accent was familiar, though I couldn't quite place it. He had the air of someone who had been through this before, someone who knew how to play the game.

"Look," I said, trying a different approach. "We don't have a weapon to tie to you, nor a witness saying you had any involvement. Our victim is still having memory issues due to the drugs and the induced coma. The other woman is blaming a dead man, which at this juncture, might be her safest bet. Help us clear this up, and it could go a long way."

He watched me silently for a moment, then spoke again, his voice smooth and unyielding. "I understand you're doing your job, but I'm afraid I can't help you with that. My relative's name is not something I'm willing to share."

Frustration bubbled beneath my calm exterior, but I couldn't let it show. "Why are you protecting them? If they have nothing to do with this, their name could help clear you."

His eyes sparkled with a mix of amusement and something darker. "Because, ma'am, some things are more important than a simple interrogation. You'll have to trust me on that."

I leaned back, mirroring his posture, and scrutinized him. "You seem very familiar with situations like this. Have you been in trouble before?"

He shrugged nonchalantly. "Life has a way of throwing challenges our way, doesn't it? How we handle them defines who we are."

The accent—it tugged at my memory again. Where had I heard it before?

"Your accent," I said, hoping to catch him off guard. "Where are you from?"

He chuckled, a low rumbling sound. "Here, there, everywhere...ma'am. Let's leave it at that."

Silence filled the room as I considered my next move. This man was an enigma, and time was running out. We needed answers, and we needed them soon. But for now, I had to be patient and wait for the cracks to show.

"How long have you known Brian and Anthony? You seemed very chummy the other night."

"Oh, Miss Quinn, are you trying to play a game with me? That is so beneath you." He shook his head and leaned in closer. "You should know, not everything is always as it seems."

My face betrayed me and showed my confusion. With that he sat back and let out a hardy laugh. I knew I was getting nothing more out of this man. I picked up the folder I had brought in with me and headed for the door. Just then, two things hit me simultaneously: one, I never told him my last name, and two, I remembered the accent. It was the same Maine accent Charles was trying to get rid of when I first met him. I turned around and looked at him again. Ah, yes...

My head was spinning—buzzing, even. The room felt as though it were closing in, the walls pulsing with each heartbeat. I tried to focus, but the sight of the man who looked so much like Charles threw me off balance. What was he doing here? How was he involved in this tangled web? I couldn't let these questions paralyze me. Sarah was now my priority.

I got out of the room and went straight to Agent Adams. "Where is Sarah?" I demanded, my voice betraying my sense of urgency.

"She's here, downstairs," came the curt reply. Without waiting for further elaboration, I turned and made my way down the dimly lit corridor. Each step echoed off the sterile walls, amplifying the dread that coiled in my stomach.

I reached the room, my hand hovering over the door handle for a moment. Steeling myself, I pushed it open. She was sitting at a metal table, the harsh fluorescent lights casting sharp shadows across her face. She wasn't shackled, but the fear and exhaustion etched into her features made it clear she was a prisoner nonetheless.

"Leave us," I said to the guard stationed by the door. He hesitated, his gaze flicking between us, but he nodded and stepped out, closing the door behind him with a dull thud.

I pulled the chair from across the table and brought it around to sit beside her. Her eyes widened slightly, relief mingling with the fear in her gaze.

"Jara," she said. "Is Katerina with you? I'm so sorry for all this. I—"

"Sarah," I said softly, "I'm here now. Katerina is at the hospital. She's with Victoria. We're going to get you out of this. But first I need to know what happened, everything."

She nodded, a tear slipping down her cheek. "I didn't think anyone was coming. Is Mrs. Lansing okay?"

I reached out, taking her hand in mine. It was cold, trembling. "Yes, Sarah, she is. She's in the ICU, but we think she'll be fine. We need to talk. I need to know everything you can tell me. This man, the one who looks like Charles, how is he involved?"

She swallowed hard, her voice barely more than a whisper. "I don't know. He just appeared, started asking questions about things I didn't understand. He knew so much...too much."

I leaned closer, my voice steady, but urgent. "This man, what type of questions was he asking? Did he know Brian? Did you hear any other names?"

Sarah's eyes clouded with thought as she tried to recall. "Yes, the senator was mentioned a few times. They laughed every time they talked about him. I couldn't believe Brian could be so mean. He was always so nice at the house."

She paused, wringing her hands. "When we were at the hospital, I was sitting with Mrs. Lansing and two men came into the room. I thought the older man was a doctor, but he had a gun. He told me I had to come with them. They put Mrs. Lansing on a gurney, then we got into the ambulance..."

"An ambulance?" I asked, my look one of surprise.

"Yes," Sarah confirmed. "They had an ambulance. Not a hospital one, but from the outside, you really couldn't tell the difference. They drove for a while and made a couple of phone calls. They were deciding if Mrs. Lansing was better off dead than alive. Whoever was on the other end said she needed to stay alive at least a little bit longer. Since I was with her, I needed to take care of her until they decided what to do. I was so scared, and Mrs. Lansing wasn't doing well."

Her voice cracked. I reached out, gently placing a hand on her arm. "You're safe now, Sarah. Just take your time. We're going to get through this together."

She nodded, stifling a sob. "I didn't know what to do. They kept watching me, making sure I did everything they asked. I tried to keep Mrs. Lansing comfortable, but it was so hard."

I squeezed her arm reassuringly. "You're incredibly brave. You've been through so much. But we need to piece this together. Do you remember anything else? Anything that might help us?"

She closed her eyes. "There were other names, but I can't remember all of them. The senator's name came up a lot, and they seemed to have some kind of hold over him. Brian...he wasn't the person I thought he was. Like I said, he seemed so kind at the house, but it was all an act."

My mind raced as I processed Sarah's words. This was bigger than I had imagined, the mention of the senator and the ambulance, a picture of a meticulously planned operation. But why? And how deep did it go?

"Thank you, Sarah," I said softly. "You've given us a lot to work with. Do you remember anything else?"

She looked at me with a mixture of hope and despair. "I just want this to be over. I want to go back to my life, to forget all of this."

I took a deep breath and put my hand on Sarah's shoulder. "What about Brian and Anthony? Is there anything else I need to know, anything?"

Sarah looked down, her fingers nervously tracing patterns on the table. She took a deep breath, her eyes meeting mine with a mixture of fear and desperation. "A couple of years ago, I found out that Charles was my father. I contacted him, and at first, he was angry and denied it. But after I told him my mother was dead, he softened a bit. I didn't want money or anything from him. I had enough money. I only wanted a connection to family."

I listened intently as Sarah went on, her voice wavering. "Then I got a call from an agency, offering me a home nursing job for Granny, I mean Mrs. Robinson. I jumped at the chance to learn more about Charles' family. Granny May, though, somehow knew I was Charles' daughter. Even so, she treated me very kindly."

I nodded, trying to piece together the fragments of Sarah's story. "The money, Sarah. What did you think about all the money, the trust?"

Sarah's brow furrowed. "I don't know anything about any money. What are you talking about?"

I took a deep breath. "Granny May set up a trust fund in your name. A significant amount of money was involved."

Sarah's face flushed. "Honest, Jara, I got no money. My alcoholic mother must have taken it. I never saw any of that."

The raw emotion in her voice was palpable. I placed a comforting hand on her shoulder. "We'll get to the bottom of this, Sarah. But right now, I need you to trust me."

Sarah nodded, her tears subsiding slightly. "I just wanted a family, Jara. I never asked for any of this."

I squeezed her hand gently. "I understand." I knew I had more in-depth questions to ask, but should I do it here, or wait until I could get the young woman somewhere more comfortable? Time was of the essence, and the pressing need for answers pushed me to continue. "Sarah," I said, my voice steady but gentle, "did you and Charles ever talk about Granny May or Victoria? What is Charles' involvement in all this?"

Sarah appeared apprehensive. "The day you and Katerina walked in on me and Charles talking at the house, he was very scared. He told me to watch for anything unusual and to let him know if I felt his family was in danger. He scared me. He was so adamant about it. I started crying, and that's when you two came in. I was confused. Why did he think the family was in danger then?"

I nodded, absorbing her words. "Did he ever tell you why?"

"No," she replied, shaking her head. "He never told me why."

"Granny May told me Charles hired Brian as her physical therapist. Is that true?"

She looked puzzled. "Not that I know of. Maybe, but I don't know why. Brian knew Charles' secretary, Bella. They were dating. But as for knowing Charles, I'm not sure."

Now I was really confused. Charles wanted Sarah to help keep his family safe, but from what and how? Charles didn't know Brian, but Bella definitely did. Was Brian going to see her and not Charles? And then there was the Foundation money. Charles had to be involved in the theft of that, didn't he? "Sarah, did Charles ever mention anything about the Foundation money or any financial troubles?"

She shook her head again. "No, he never talked to me about money, ever. I didn't even know about the trust fund Granny set up in my name until you told me."

I sighed as these latest revelations swirled in my mind. "So Charles was scared, he thought his family was in danger, and he wanted you to watch out for anything unusual. But he never told you why or from whom. And Brian, who was involved somehow, was connected to Bella, not directly to Charles."

Sarah nodded. "I wish I could tell you more, Jara. I really do. I was so scared."

I squeezed her hand reassuringly. "You've been very helpful. We're going to figure this out. But for now, I need you to stay strong and keep remembering anything you can, no matter how small it seems."

She nodded, a tear slipping down her cheek. "I'll try. I just want this nightmare to end."

"We'll make sure it does," I promised. So many pieces of the puzzle remained missing, but I knew we were getting closer. Charles' fear, Brian's involvement, Bella's connection: they all had to lead somewhere. And my gut was telling me that the enigma in the interrogation room was the missing piece.

I arranged for Sarah to be taken to a safe house. Guards were posted around the clock. I still had no idea how many people were involved, or who was still out there.

Chapter Thirty-Three

After I finished with Sarah, I went returned to the floor where Anthony and the man with no name were still being held. Travis was in the hallway talking with Agent Adams when I arrived. I motioned Travis and John into a small room across the hall. I told them everything Sarah had said as I paced. They listened to my rambling theories, their faces reflecting a mix of confusion and concern. Travis sat down in a metal chair and held his head in his hands.

"So let me get this straight," he said. "What you're saying is Brian shot you, Anthony was driving, Brian was dating Bella, Sarah was taken to keep Victoria alive, at least for now, Sarah is Charles' daughter, and Charles may not even know Brian. Money from the Foundation is being siphoned off by someone in Charles' office, whether it be Charles or Bella, we don't know. We have no idea who the man in the next room is or what he has to do with all of this. Do I have it so far?"

I nodded. "More or less. It's a tangled mess, but those are the key points. We need to figure out the connections and motives behind each piece of this puzzle."

Travis shook his head slowly. "This is...a lot. How do we even begin to untangle this web?"

"I know it's overwhelming," I admitted, "but we have to start somewhere. We need to find out more about this man who resembles Charles. He could be the key. And we need to figure out who in Charles' office is behind the money siphoning. If it's Bella, then Brian's involvement makes more sense. If it's Charles...well, that changes everything."

Travis looked up, determination replacing some of his confusion. "All right, let's break this down. We need to question Charles' lookalike again, find out who he is and what he knows. John, where are we on the warrants for Charles' offices and computers? That might lead us to whoever is pulling the strings."

"From what I understand," John said, "the judge is signing off on all of them today. Once he's done, I have multiple task forces ready to carry them out simultaneously."

"Great," I said, relieved. "But it's important to keep Sarah safe. She's a critical witness. Her connection to Charles might give us insights we don't have yet."

Travis stood up from his chair. "All right. Let's get to work. We don't have any time to waste."

John left to get the warrants from the judge, saying he would call once the task forces were in place. Travis went back into the monitoring room and began looking again at the Navy SEAL photos. I gave Katerina a quick call to let her know what was going on and to check on Victoria.

Katerina said her mother was sleeping but seemed to be getting stronger by the minute. She also told me Mr. Maxwell had called to tell her he'd filed an injunction with the court to stop Charles' request to be Victoria's power of attorney. We hung up and I slid down the wall onto the cold floor, its coolness soothing my exhausted body. I thought through everything I had learned. I knew I had to speak with the man with no name again, but what could I do differently this time to change the outcome? He was so much like Charles...Charles! Something clicked in my head. Charles had family, at least he used to. And what did this man say? "Things aren't always what they seem."

Maybe that's it, the photo in Charles' bible! I jumped up and stuck my head into the monitor room. "Travis, I'm going downstairs. I'll be back. Don't talk to him without me." I sat my folders and bag on the counter and was gone before the door shut.

I had a hunch and had to see if it was right. I got to an office, picked up an office phone, and called John. "Can I get your computer access codes? I need to check some things right away."

John must have known not to question me and gave me the codes immediately. I powered up the computer and typed in "surname Lansing, state Maine." Several families popped up, but I needed to narrow it down. I refined my search to Maine fishing families named Lansing, and the number of results decreased significantly. I combed through the remaining entries, scanning for anything that stood out. Then I found it: a small article about Charles Lansing. It detailed his graduation as valedictorian of his high school and mentioned he was heading to Yale in the fall. His parents were named John and Maxine Lansing. This had to be them. The article was from a local paper, *The Lincoln County News*.

Intrigued, I accessed the paper's archives and searched for John and Maxine Lansing. What I found left me stunned. I found a story and obituary from forty years ago about a freak fishing boat accident. Their boat had exploded off the coast, leaving no survivors. On board were John, his wife Maxine, and their son, William C. Their bodies were never recovered. Charles was never mentioned as a survivor. I couldn't shake the feeling that there was more to this story, so I dove deeper. I requested images of all William Lansings in the archives. As the images loaded, I felt a chill run down my spine. One of the photos, though grainy and old, showed a boy who looked eerily like the man we had in custody.

My heart pounded. Was the man in the interrogation room William, who was presumed dead? And if John and Maxine were Charles' parents, why wasn't he mentioned in the obituary? The questions swirled in my mind, each one more urgent than the last. I pulled up the article from the senator's state representative race that mentioned his family. There wasn't much meat to it: one picture of a small, weatherbeaten house and another of a fishing boat. I couldn't read the name on the boat. A picture of Charles at the time was also included, along with what I presumed was a high school yearbook photo. It didn't include any pictures of his family.

I printed out the images and information, my mind racing with theories. Was it possible that Charles was actually William and had faked his death and assumed a new identity? And if so, why keep the name Lansing? Or was this the brother? Either way, after all this time in the public eye, why hadn't someone learned of this?

I needed to confront Charles—or William—and get to the bottom of this. But first, I needed more evidence. I scanned through more articles and obituaries, looking for any mention of Charles or William Lansing. Each piece of information added a new layer to the mystery. Then I found it, a grainy but recognizable photo of three young men at a University of Maine football game. The ROTC band was playing at halftime and the three men were standing with some ROTC officers. The caption read:

> "After a change in state law making ROTC voluntary, interest in the program has dwindled except for these young gentlemen. Charles Lansing, valedictorian of his high school, stated, "The discipline and leadership skills I've learned in ROTC have been invaluable. They'll help me in whatever I pursue, whether it be military life or as

a civilian." Lansing plans on applying these skills
when he transfers to Yale next fall."

   The three men in the photo were Charles, William, and none
other than Commander Marcus Montgomery. It all came
together. Dr. Johnson was Commander Montgomery, the same
man who was at Granny's memorial and the one who blamed
Charles for his discharge.

   I printed the photo, enlarged it, and printed it again,
separating each man's face. I ran back upstairs to where Travis
was waiting.

   "Where in the hell have you been?" he snapped. "You left your
phone up here. John called. What were you doing?"

   I sat the copies of the newspaper photo in front of him and
pointed. "Recognize them?"

   "Holy shit," Travis looked into the interrogation room and
then back at the photos.

   I picked them up and paused on my way to the door. "By the
way, what did John say?"

   "They're going to serve all the warrants tonight after business
hours. Some of the offices have other tenants."

   "Sounds good." I grabbed the handle of the interrogation
room door.

   "Now where are you going?"

   I smiled. "Going to ask the man with no name how the football
game was."

   I walked back into the interrogation room. The nameless man
sat there, still in shackles, looking remarkably comfortable, as if
he were sitting in his favorite chair. An empty paper plate and a
half-drunk bottle of water sat in front of him. He smiled again,
almost with amusement, as if I were his entertainment. I smiled
back, trying to maintain my best poker face.

   "So, Ms. Quinn, are you here for another episode of *To Tell the
Truth*?" he asked, his eyes twinkling with a mischievous glint.

   I laughed heartily. I remembered that old show—three
contestants on a panel, two were lying and one told the truth.
The celebrity guests had to guess who the truth teller was. "So
you're a fan of game shows?" I responded.

   "I find them amusing. And you?"

   "I'm more into mysteries myself. Figuring out the clues,
putting them together, and determining who the culprit is."

He raised a curious eyebrow. "But can't that sometimes be a game? A rather subjective one, but still. Granted, clues are clues, but how do you know who the real bad guy is? There are so many different levels of evil. Who are we to say who the worst is?"

"It's not for me to judge," I replied with a shrug. "That comes later."

He leaned back, still smiling, but with a hint of something darker in his eyes. "Ah, but judgment is inherent in solving mysteries, isn't it? You decide who the villain is, who gets caught, who pays the price."

I shrugged again, keeping my tone light. "I prefer to leave the judgment to the courts. My job is to find the truth."

He chuckled. "The truth. Such a fluid concept, don't you think? Your truth, my truth, the objective truth—if such a thing even exists."

"I believe it does," I said firmly. "And I believe we're getting closer to it."

"Oh?" The eyebrow twitched slightly. "Do enlighten me, Ms. Quinn."

I leaned forward. "It's about a long line of lobster fishermen in Maine and a tragic boat explosion some forty years ago. John, Maxine, and their son William were all presumed dead. But their other son, Charles, was never mentioned in the obituary."

His grin faltered for a fraction of a second, enough to tell me I was on the right track. He quickly recovered, leaning back again with an amused expression. "So you've been digging into the past. I must say, I'm flattered by your dedication."

"Tell me your version of the truth. Why would a man who supposedly died in a fishing boat accident turn up years later? What would drive a person to change their identity and live a life of deception?"

He emitted a hollow laugh. "You think I changed my identity? That's quite the accusation."

"It's more than a theory," I said, my voice firm. "Mr. Lansing, William, why don't you tell me what really happened on that boat forty years ago?"

His eyes narrowed, and for the first time, a flicker of something other than amusement crossed his face—perhaps anger...or fear. "You think you know everything, don't you?"

"I know enough to see through your lies. Your parents, John and Maxine Lansing, died in that explosion. But you survived, didn't you? You took on a new life. But why? What are you running from?"

His shackles clanked softly as his expression hardened. "You've done your homework, I'll give you that. But you still don't know the full story." He studied me for a moment as he considered his next move. "Truth, Ms. Quinn, is a double-edged sword. You may find it cuts deeper than you anticipated."

I met his gaze head on. "I'll take that chance. Please enlighten me."

He sighed, his posture suddenly more relaxed. "Maybe I did change my name. Maybe I did survive. But I had no choice. Everything was taken from me in that explosion. My family, my identity. I had to start over."

"But why surface now? Is it because of Charles' run for President?"

He shook his head. "You still don't get it. There's more at play here than you can imagine. I'm just a small piece in a much larger puzzle."

"Then tell me about the larger puzzle," I said, leaning in. "Who else is involved? Who's pulling the strings?"

He looked at me for a long moment, then smiled a cold, mirthless smile. "You need to keep digging, Ms. Quinn. Maybe one day you'll find it. If you live that long."

"Are you threatening me?" I asked calmly.

"Come now, Ms. Quinn, we're having an honest and civilized conversation. I didn't threaten you, but if you must know, there are people out of my control who don't like their business poked into."

"Would you happen to be talking about Commander Marcus Montgomery?" I sat the Navy SEAL photo of the commander down and then put the enlarged old newspaper article down beside it.

His eyes flashed and he swallowed before he regained his control and stared at me.

"He's a friend of yours, isn't he?" I asked. "An old friend from Maine."

He continued to glare.

I felt the tables starting to turn. "So, you *do* remember your old friend. He's had quite the career." I went through all the information I had on the commander that wasn't redacted. I then showed him a current photo of Charles Lansing and the enlarged print of him as a younger man. I could almost see the wheels turning in his head. "And then, sir, there were three." I sat the last enlarged print down of him and the one of the three of them together.

He narrowed his gaze. "Where did you get this?"

"Funny thing about the internet. If you look hard enough, you can find almost anything. It looks like you liked games even when you were younger."

He picked up the old photo as his eyes glazed over. Under his breath he whispered, "We were so young then."

"Sir," I said, addressing him in a more solicitous tone, "tell me what happened. *Your* truth."

He sat back and sighed, still holding the photo. "We were so close then. Inseparable. I was going to do amazing things. I was getting off that damn fishing boat. My brother was going to stay behind and work on the boat with Dad. I had gotten a scholarship to attend The University of Maine and joined ROTC. They came to see me that weekend to watch the football game. I had forgotten all about this photo." He laughed to himself. "Fall break was the next week, so I went back home with them. We all loved to pull pranks on each other. It was the end of the week, and I was to go back to school that Sunday. My brother was nowhere to be found, and Dad needed someone to help on the boat. It was a nice day, and Mom brought us sandwiches. Since it was to be a short trip of checking a small trap line, she decided to come with us." He sat the photo back on the table and pounded his fists. "They couldn't leave well enough alone!" He looked at me, the weight of years of secrets and lies reflected in his gaze. "It was over before I knew it. I heard a noise, then the whole boat blew up. There was nothing I could do. I was thrown from the boat. To this day I have no idea how I survived. All I remember is waking up miles away in some county hospital."

A wave of compassion swept over me. "I'm so sorry. I don't know what to say."

"Oh, Ms. Quinn, don't get soft on me now. I'm the bad guy, remember?"

"Are you mocking my sympathy, sir?"

"No, Ms. Quinn. I know you know how it feels to lose your parents. You and I, we just went in two different directions."

I was stunned by his knowledge of my past before I realized it didn't really matter. "Please continue if you would."

"You think you have it figured out, don't you? That I've come back to be a thorn in my poor brother's side. Remember, I said truth can be a double-edged sword."

I sat back, my mind buzzing. I looked down at the photos again and back up to the man across from me. My face must have told the story.

"I think you can piece together the rest. William, my brother, took my place at Yale. He became Charles, and Marcus, well, he became the military man."

"But if it was a prank…"

"Prank or no prank, my parents were dead, and my brother was living the life I was supposed to have."

"And Marcus?"

"The Navy SEAL? I hired him."

I didn't see that one coming. "You hired him?"

"Yes, Ms. Quinn. Little by little, I got stronger and angrier. I knew I couldn't take my brother straight on. I needed a middleman. And what better person than a Navy SEAL turned Black Ops." Disdainful, he went on. "If you remember, Ms. Quinn, I was the smart one. I made my own place in this world. And now you might say my services are in high demand."

"Your services?"

"For another day, Ms. Quinn, another day."

I nodded. I was going to take what I could get. "I know Commander Montgomery used some of his Navy SEAL team in all of this."

"I wouldn't know. Those were his decisions."

"The men at the facility, Brian and Anthony, you met them—you should know."

"Like I said, I was only checking on a relative. I have no connection to those two men."

"And the money from the Foundation? How does that fit into your new life?"

"Money makes the world go round, Ms. Quinn. When you're starting over, you need resources. But I'm not involved in some Foundation or whatever is going on with it."

I was getting tired of the runaround. "You're telling me you had nothing to do with money being taken from Victoria's foundation?"

"Ah, Victoria." He grinned. "My brother's beautiful wife. He didn't deserve her."

"And she didn't deserve to be attacked, kidnapped, and placed in a coma. This is what your so-called middleman did. Your revenge against your brother involved putting innocent lives at risk."

"Is anyone truly innocent, Ms. Quinn? We've all done things, haven't we? It's life. It's how we bounce back and adapt that counts. And Victoria, you've...saved her, haven't you?"

"She's recovering, physically at least. So going back, you had nothing to do with the theft of the Foundation's money?"

"You may want to ask William—I mean, the senator—about that. Blackmail is expensive, I hear. I'm sure Marcus was bleeding him dry." He burst into laughter.

I slowly shook my head. "So you sit back and be the puppet master, to hell with responsibility. You set things in motion and let the pieces fall where they may. All for revenge."

His face turned blood red, and he screamed, "He took my life, dammit. He had to be held accountable. You, Jara Quinn, should understand that. Don't you want to kill the man who killed your parents?"

I bit the inside of my cheek. I couldn't lose it here, not now. I swallowed hard and answered, "I admit, there were times I was angry enough that if he were in front of me..."

"You would what? Kill him?"

"I don't know, maybe. But I didn't. He got his sentence. Justice decided that. But it's not me we're talking about here. You feel you should take no responsibility for all this? You yourself admitted you hired Marcus. What did you think he would do?"

"I didn't know, and honestly, I didn't care. He doesn't know who hired him, but he was eager to take the job. He believes it was the senator that tarnished his career, kicked him out of the SEALs. In a roundabout way it was."

"You orchestrated this whole thing."

"No, Ms. Quinn, I'm no maestro or 'puppet master' as you called it. I only pushed over the first domino, kicked the hornet's nest, if you will."

I started to argue, but a knock on the interview room door stopped me. A tall man in a dark suit walked in. He looked at me with a blank expression before focusing on Charles. "Sir, it's time to go."

I sprang to my feet. "Go? Now wait a minute, he's a suspect in a kidnapping, among other things."

Another man came in and unshackled him. As Charles stood, he stretched his arms and cracked his neck. "I told you, Ms. Quinn, my services are in high demand. And as a dead man, I can get a lot done." He started to walk out the door but turned and smiled. "It was really a pleasure speaking with you today, Ms. Quinn. I wish you well."

I sat at the table, dumbfounded. I had learned so much, but the person who could have backed it up had just walked out the door. I gathered my photos and folders together and leaned back in my chair. I was on the verge of tears when Travis walked in. I looked up at him, my eyes watery and my voice full of frustration. "Can you believe that?"

"Uh, Jara," Travis said, staring at the ground, "we heard nothing. The man that came in here stopped the recording of your interview. We were told to leave the room."

"What the...? Who ordered that?" I was consumed with anger.

"I don't know. The station chief got a call from the director. I don't know who notified him. We were told to shut it down."

"And Anthony?"

"He's still here and in custody. Who was that guy anyway?"

"The puppet master."

"What?"

"Nothing, I'll tell you later. I need to go to the hospital." I handed Travis my folders but kept the old photo of the three boys. I was sure whoever shut this down would want my evidence too. I drove slowly to the hospital, debating on what I should say to Katerina, if anything.

Chapter Thirty-Four

My mind was still a blur. I had caught the man who had orchestrated this entire clusterfuck, but the powers that be had made me let him go. I had no substantiated proof of this man or his involvement. Since I had shot and killed Brian, the only real link I had left to the senator, I needed to find Commander Marcus Montgomery. This would not be easy.

I also wrestled with the knowledge that the senator wasn't who he said he was. But how to prove that? He wasn't going to come out and admit that to me. *Do I tell Victoria and her children that their husband/father is not Charles Lansing, but his brother William?*

I was jarred out of my thoughts by my phone. It was Agent John Adams.

"Hi!"

"Hi yourself. I hear you caught the main man." I heard amusement in his voice.

I laughed half-heartedly. "Yes and no. Caught him, talked to him, then had to let him go."

"Let him go? What the hell!"

I tried to make a joke: "I guess I went fishing in the wrong lake, but it was 'catch and release' only."

"I don't get it, we had him!"

"I'll try to explain later. So how are things going on your end?"

John sighed loudly. "Well, all the warrants have been served, and the main computers are being taken to FBI headquarters at Quantico to be searched. We should know something in the morning."

"That's good. We need to wrap this thing up." I thought for a moment. "I need to find Commander Montgomery. He is my next biggest link. Any idea where I might find him?"

"Hmm..." John was quiet for a moment. "With Brian dead, Anthony caught, and since you had to let Mr. X go, I'd bet he's gone dark. We may never find him."

I laughed again. "Mr. X, I like that. Thanks John, keep me posted."

I made it to Victoria's room, but I hesitated on entering. Katerina knew me so well. She'd know I was holding something back from her. I sucked it up, took a deep breath, and stepped into the doorway of the dimly lit room. Katerina was sitting in a chair next to her sleeping mother, stroking Victoria's hand. IV tubes were still attached, and a small monitor emitted rhythmic beeps next to the bed. I stood there watching, not wanting to interrupt the peaceful moment. I felt a gentle touch on my shoulder. It was CJ.

"Not going in?" he asked, smiling as he carried four coffees in a cardboard tray. He nodded down at the drinks. "Want one?"

I smiled. "Thanks but no, still a bit wound up. Is Chase here too?"

"Yes, he drove in last night." Tears welled in his eyes. "Thank you, Jara, for bringing Mom back to us. I don't know..."

"CJ, it's okay. I'm glad it worked out as well as it did. How is she doing today?"

He wiped his eyes with his sleeve. "Better and stronger. The doctor said physical therapy is coming in to see if she can stand and, if so, take a few steps." A big smile crossed his face. "But you know Mom, once she takes that first step, she may just walk right on out of here."

I nodded. "If anyone can do it, she can. She's a fighter."

Katerina looked up. "I thought I heard you two talking back there. CJ, bring me a coffee, please." She smiled a sweet smile. "And you," motioning toward me, "come over here. I missed you."

I walked over behind her chair, put my arms around her, kissed her head, and whispered, "I'm glad your mom is doing better. Sorry I was gone so long."

She pulled my arms tighter around her, I winced in a bit of pain but kept holding her. "At least you're here now. Did things go okay?"

I stood up straight but kept my hands on her shoulders. "Yes, I learned a lot. John has served all the warrants, and the computers are heading to Quantico as we speak."

Katerina was quiet for a second before she stood up and faced me, her emerald eyes boring into me like green lasers. "So what is it you're not telling me?"

I started to fidget just as a nurse walked in to check on Victoria. "Can we talk somewhere in private?" I asked.

Katerina looked at me, her eyes full of questions, and asked CJ to stay with their mother. We went to a small consultation room down the hall. The room's sterile walls and muted colors did little to ease the tension. Katerina took a seat, her eyes glued to me as I closed the door.

I took a deep breath, trying to compose myself as I struggled to find the right words. My gaze met hers, and I could see the anxiety pooling in her eyes. "Kat," I began gently, my voice barely above a whisper, "I need to tell you something about your father." Her eyes widened slightly, and she leaned forward. I walked over and took the seat opposite her. "I received some information earlier today," I said, trying to keep my tone steady. "Something I feel you need to know but really don't know how to tell you." I informed her about my interview with the man we arrested at the facility where her mother was being held. I reached into my bag and pulled out the old newspaper photo, gently laying it on the table between us. I pushed it toward her, and she turned it around, sliding it closer.

Her eyes scanned the photo, and I saw a flicker of recognition. "Is this dad?" she asked, her voice tinged with uncertainty.

"Yes," I confirmed, pointing to the boy in the center. "And Commander Montgomery, also known as Dr. Johnson, on one side and..." I hesitated, knowing the next part would be a shock. "Well, your father's brother is on the other."

Her mouth opened as if to say something, but no words came out. She looked from the photo to me, then back to the photo. "My father's brother? And my father knows Commander Montgomery?"

"Yes," I said, nodding. "They were all childhood friends. He was the man who argued with your father at Granny's memorial."

"I don't understand," she said, her brow furrowing. "Other than Montgomery, what does this have to do with anything?"

"Sweetheart," I said, leaning in closer, "the man I interviewed today was your father's brother."

Her eyes widened, and she pulled the photo even closer, as if it could somehow provide more answers. "My father's brother?" she repeated, the words barely a whisper. "But he's dead..." Her voice trailed off.

"No, he's not dead. He's very much alive," I said, watching as she processed the information. "He's been involved in some...questionable activities, and he was at the facility where your mother was being held."

"So you spoke with William today?" She looked up at me, her eyes filled with a mixture of shock and confusion. "But why? Why would he be involved in this?"

I paused, struggling to find the gentlest way to tell her the truth about her father's identity. "Kat, no...I don't know how to say this other than to just say it. The man you know as your father is actually William Lansing. The man I spoke to today is Charles."

Katerina's face contorted. "What? How is that even possible?"

"Years ago, about a week after this photo was taken, there was a boat explosion," I explained, pointing to the old newspaper clipping. "It's unknown what caused it, but Charles was on the boat instead of William. Everyone believed no one survived, but Charles lived. William, who may have been responsible for the explosion, whether by accident or on purpose, took Charles's identity and went to Yale."

Katerina's eyes darted around the room as she tried to make sense of my revelation. "So my dad is really William Lansing?" she asked, her voice a sort of raspy squeak.

"Yes," I confirmed, watching as the shock settled over her.

"And I take it his brother has been plotting revenge all this time?"

"I believe so," I replied.

Katerina's mind was working overtime, piecing together the fragments of her shattered reality. Finally, she asked, "Do you think Mom or Granny knew? Is this what Granny was talking about in her letter to Mom?"

"I don't know, probably. This man is very powerful and has connections in places I didn't even know existed."

She frowned. "What do you mean?"

"I couldn't hold him today," I said. "Granted, he gave me a lot of information, took responsibility for hiring Commander Montgomery and his crew, but he denied being directly involved. He had plausible deniability, I'll admit. Then we got a call from the director and we had to let him go. My taped interview was destroyed. The only thing I have of this man is this photo."

"And the Foundation? Is he the one taking the money?"

"I don't believe so," I said. "I think Commander Montgomery is blackmailing your father."

"But they were all friends...?" Her voice trailed off again as she stared at the opposite wall.

"After the explosion, the friendship ended. William became Charles, and Montgomery went into the military soon after that. He hates your father as much as Charles does. He believes your father tarnished his military record and had him discharged from the SEALs."

"Did he?" Katerina asked.

"I don't know," I said. "But what I do know is that the ties that bound them were severed long ago. Now we need to figure out how deep this goes and what it means for your family."

Katerina nodded slowly, the weight of the truth settling heavily on her shoulders. "We have to get to the bottom of this," she said. "For Mom, for Granny, and for everyone who's been caught up in this web of lies."

We sat in the cramped consultation room for what seemed like hours until we heard a light knock on the door. Chase poked his head in. "Mom's awake and asking for you two."

I smiled. "We'll be right in. Thanks, Chase."

He looked over at Katerina, who was staring at the photo as if the answers would jump off the paper. "You okay?"

Katerina looked up, dazed. "Yeah, I am. On our way."

After Chase closed the door, Katerina reached out and took my hand. "Do we tell Mom? Or CJ and Chase?"

I knelt before her and took her hand. "You're the only one I felt needed to know right now. Maybe later, at a better time, we can tell the rest. When your mom's stronger."

Tears streamed down Katerina's face. "I need this to be over."

We walked back to Victoria's room. She was awake and sitting up, a good sign. She motioned for Katerina and me to come closer to the bed. In a hoarse voice, she asked, "Katerina, can you ask your brothers to leave for a few minutes? I have something to talk with you and Jara about."

Katerina did what her mother requested and came back to the bedside. Victoria looked at me and, in a whisper, said, "Jara, I believe I saw Charles."

Shocked, I responded, "*Here*?"

"No, where you found me. I swear it was him. He sounded like when we first met, his voice soft and sweet, with a slight accent. It was before they put me under again. Was he at that facility? Or was I dreaming?"

Katerina gave me a knowing look. We both knew she had seen Charles, but not the "Charles" she was married to. "Mom, I, well you saw..."

I stopped her before she could finish. "Victoria, yes you saw someone who looked like and reminded you of your husband, but it wasn't him. When you get a bit stronger, I'll explain everything to you. I promise. But for now, focus on getting better and stronger."

Victoria gave me a confused look before she appeared to relax against the pillows. "And the Foundation?"

"Warrants were served, and all the campaign computers have been taken to Quantico. We should know something definite in the morning."

She smiled as her eyes sparkled for the first time in weeks. The physical therapist walked in, prepared to do her assessment. "Well, girls," Victoria said with a slight laugh, "let's see what this body can do."

We left the room so the therapist had space to work. Katerina called Mr. Maxwell and told him Victoria was safe and awake. "Please inform the court of this."

I could hear the happiness in Mr. Maxwell's voice as he told her, "I'll get on that right away. Please give your mother my best."

Katerina put away her phone and took my hand, her eyes searching mine. "Now what do we do?"

"We wait, my love. We wait."

Chapter Thirty-Five

I went to the small, dark ICU waiting room. It was empty except for a cart holding a coffeepot with day-old coffee and a gurgling water cooler. I got a cup of water and watched the large bubble rise to the top, making a burping sound. I took another cup of water just to see the bubble again. Katerina walked in. "What are you doing?"

"Getting a cup of water."

"I see that, but you looked like you were mesmerized."

I sighed. "Maybe I was. My small action of removing some water caused a large bubble to rise to the top. Every action we make causes some reaction, whether large or small. It was like Mr. X said. He only pushed over the first domino. The reactions and responses afterward were beyond anything anyone could have anticipated. But it created a cascade of events that spiraled out of control, that revealed hidden truths and ignited long-held grudges. He had to have known something like this would happen, so in truth, he is responsible."

"Uh...Mr. X?"

"Yeah, that's what John and I nicknamed him. Calling him Charles is way too confusing." Katerina nodded. "I have calls in to every contact I know in search of Commander Montgomery. Hopefully, someone comes up with something."

"When are you going to talk with my father?"

I took a sip of water and replied, "I've been thinking about that. Now that we have the computers, he must know it's only a matter of time."

We went to a waiting room and settled on a small loveseat. Katerina put her head on my shoulder, and I dozed off in a couple of minutes from sheer exhaustion. My dreams were vivid but convoluted. I heard a voice that sounded like the senator's. I shook the cobwebs from my head and realized I had answered a phone call purely from habit.

"Jara, I need your help."

"Who is this?" I mumbled, my mind still foggy.

"It's Charles. I need your help."

I had just spoken with the real Charles earlier that day, so confusion muddled my thoughts. "Charles who?"

"Damn it, Jara! It's the senator. I need your help, but I suppose you already know I'm in trouble."

The urgency in his voice snapped me fully awake. I sat up, the weight of the day's revelations pressing down on me. "Senator, what's going on? Where are you?"

"I can't talk long," he said, his voice strained. "I'm being followed. They've already made attempts to silence me, and I fear they're closing in."

"Who's doing this?" My heart was racing.

"I can't talk about it over the phone. I need to see you." Sheer panic was in his voice.

"Okay, okay, can you meet me at the house?"

"Fine, but hurry before they know I'm gone. Please hurry."

Katerina was awake by then. "Who was that? What's going on?"

"Your father. He says he's in trouble, and I think it's about more than us taking his computers. He sounded panicked."

"Then let's go!"

"No. You need to stay here with your mother. I can't risk you getting hurt." I stood up and put my hands on her shoulders. "Please promise me you'll stay here. I'll call Travis and John on my way." I could tell from her pout she was not happy about having to stay. "Katerina, please," I said more sternly. "You need to stay here. I'll call as soon as I know something."

Reluctantly she agreed, and I walked her to her mother's room. CJ and Chase were sitting on each side of the bed.

"I need to leave for a bit." I told them. "I promise I'll call and let you know if I have any news."

I hurried out to my rental car, popped open the trunk, and pulled out my pelican case with my Ruger. I popped open the cylinder and made sure it was full of ammunition. The Ruger would have to do since my Glock was put into evidence for shooting Brian. Before I started the car, I closed my eyes and took some slow, deep breaths. "Be ready for anything," I told myself.

On the way, I called Travis and John, as I had promised, and informed them of my meeting with the senator. Both were heading in my direction and would take positions outside the house.

The senator's car was already in the driveway when I arrived. I went inside. A few lights were on, but the place was eerily quiet. I found the senator pacing in the den, his face wan and his eyes bloodshot. When he saw me, relief washed over him.

"Jara!" he said, rushing over. "Thank god you're here."

I thought he was going to hug me, and I backed away. "What's going on, Senator?" I asked, closing the door behind me. "You know I really shouldn't be talking to you right now."

"I don't care about that. Please listen."

"Okay, fine," I said, shaking my head. "What's going on that makes you feel you need my help?"

"They've uncovered too much," he said, his voice low and urgent.

"Who? The FBI?"

"No, Montgomery, the guy from the memorial, and whoever else he has working for him. They're tying up loose ends, and I'm one of them." The senator ran over to a window and peered out anxiously from behind the gold silk drapes.

"Montgomery? As in Marcus Montgomery? Why is he after you?"

"I can't explain. I only need protection...and I need my family protected," he replied.

I was becoming impatient. "You *will* explain if you want my help. And your family? How are they in danger? Answer me. Now!"

He let out a defeated sigh. "Montgomery, he blames me for a lot of things. And he's been blackmailing me. Now that the computers have been taken, his involvement will be exposed. He has nothing to gain by keeping me alive."

"And, sir, what does he blame you for exactly?" I asked as I sat down on the couch. I was not going to get caught up in his fervor.

"Jara, damn it. I don't have time for this."

I crossed my legs and leaned back. "Senator, take the time. Sit down and explain."

He let out a guttural "Argggh!" and sat down in the leather chair across from me. "Fine. But if something happens, it'll be your fault."

I started laughing and went to stand up. "My fault, Senator? Really? You are asking for my help and want to blame me? Typical, you not taking responsibility for a damn thing you've done. I'm outta here."

"Wait, wait...I'm sorry. I'll tell you. Something happened a long time ago when I was young. He blames me for it."

"Right, the boat explosion," I answered smugly.

His eyes widened and shock spread across his face. "How do you know about that?"

"It doesn't matter right now. Continue."

"Yes, uh...the explosion. Then later, when I became a senator, I was on an oversight committee for overseas operations. During that time, Montgomery was a leader of a clandestine operation that went south. Some members of his team went rogue, and civilians died because of it. He blames me for being demoted and his subsequent dismissal from the SEALs."

"And?"

The senator scowled with impatience. "And *what?* He wants to get even for that!"

"Why now, of all times?" I needed him to fully explain.

"I've been paying him for years, but he kept upping the amount and threatening to jeopardize my candidacy."

"What does he have on you, Senator? The explosion? Or is there something else?"

The tall, broad-shouldered man who always had an air of confidence about him appeared to shrink before my eyes. "Jara, this is hard for me. Can't you just leave it alone? He's blackmailing me and now wants me dead. Isn't that enough?"

I leaned in, "No, Senator, it's not. I need to know it all, from you, and now."

"Fine." I could see the wheels turning in his head. He was going to spin this story somehow. "Marcus and I, Montgomery that is, tried to pull a prank on my brother. He was on the family fishing boat, and I went and hid so I didn't have to go. Marcus had rigged some fireworks on a timer for them to go off after the boat left the dock. Something went wrong, and instead of going up in the air, they stayed in the boat. I was told later Dad had put some extra gas tanks on the boat because he was going to head farther out the next day. The fireworks must have hit one of those, killing my family."

I watched the senator's face as he told the story. He showed no remorse or sadness.

"I'm so sorry for your loss, Senator. That must have been a very hard time for you. This is what he's blackmailing you over?"

"Well," he said, puffing himself back up, "he knew any hint of scandal would ruin me. Plus, he blamed me for losing his commission."

"And now he wants to kill you? Right?" Playing the devil's advocate, I asked, "Why not let the story out and ruin you? To me, that would be more satisfying than killing you."

"Damn it, Jara. You're not taking this seriously. He's going to kill me. And I need to have him stopped."

"Why? Because the funds are drying up?" I threw my hands up as if in surrender. "Okay. I'll have people find him and arrest him."

The Senator leapt from his chair and started pacing again. "No, no, no! He needs to be killed, or he won't stop. You need to kill him for me, Jara. No one is safe with him alive. He may even go after Katerina next. You saw what he did to Victoria."

He thinks he can get me to kill Marcus by telling me Katerina is in danger. If Montgomery were dead, the real story wouldn't get out.

"Exactly what did *he* do to Victoria?" I retorted. "The initial attack or the kidnapping and putting her back in a coma?"

"Uh...all of it. He's a very dangerous man. You have to help me!" As he continued his pleas, my phone rang.

"Excuse me, sir," I said. "I have to get this." I walked into the kitchen. "Hello, John?"

"Sorry to interrupt, but I wanted you to know we're hearing everything and taping it. We forgot to take out the surveillance equipment with everything going on. You okay with this?"

I smiled to myself. "Actually, John, nothing could be more perfect. I have a few things I want to confront him with. I'm glad it will be on the record."

I hung up and returned to the den. The senator was still pacing, stopping at times to peek out the window.

"Senator, do you think he's here? You keep looking out the window."

"I don't know. He has people watching me, everywhere."

"Everywhere? Like who?" I asked as I motioned for him to sit back down.

He sat in the leather chair and leaned back. "Well, Bella and Brian, for example."

"Really?" I answered in mock disbelief.

"Yes! Bella watches my every move. And Brian, he's as dangerous as Marcus. He was on Marcus' SEAL team."

"Brian? The one you hired to be a physical therapist for Granny May? That Brian?"

His eyes darted around the room. "Yes, that Brian. And I didn't hire him, exactly. Bella did. They killed Granny."

"What?"

"Yes, Brian loaded those protein shakes with potassium. Then they gave her the other drug since the potassium wasn't working fast enough. They thought that, well, with Granny dead, I would come into more money."

"They told you this. Do you have proof?"

"Not exactly, but Brian takes orders from Marcus. It had to be them."

"And Sarah, your daughter? What was her role?

The Senator gasped, then lowered his head. "So you know about her. Okay. I hired her to keep an eye on the family and to let me know if anything was...well, suspicious."

"Suspicious? Were you afraid your family was going to do something to you or what?"

"No, Brian."

"So you knew who he was, who he was hired by, and how dangerous he was, and you never bothered to tell one member of your family?" I was becoming angrier by the minute. "Now Granny May is dead. Did Brian attack Victoria?" I already knew the answer to that, but wanted to hear him say it for the record.

"No, uh...I don't know. I'm sure it was one of Marcus' people. After her attack, I was told that was a warning to keep my mouth shut and keep paying." He clasped his hands in front of him and leaned forward. "You have to understand, Jara, I was trying to keep my family safe."

Struggling to keep my composure and not strangle him then and there, I asked, "And me, Senator, you had me come to New Hampshire. I saw your face when I asked about those companies you were allegedly researching on your computer. We've linked those companies to the ones siphoning money from the Foundation. Then, on my way home, I was shot and almost killed. Are you going to tell me you knew nothing about all that?"

"Jara, please. They had me do it. That was part of the blackmail. The money coming from the Foundation was paying them off." He looked straight at me, his expression unreadable. "And about you being shot, I knew nothing about that until afterward. I told you, they are dangerous. They'll stop at nothing to keep the money coming in."

"They won't, or *you* won't, Senator?"

"What are you accusing me of? I'm the victim here."

I couldn't help but laugh. "'Victim?' You, Senator? Sorry if I'm finding that hard to believe. You knew about all this whether before or after the fact, and never once did you notify the authorities or even me. You've seen me plenty of times. At any point in time, you could've reached out."

"Well, I'm reaching out now. I need to stop Marcus."

"Stop him? I told you I'll try to arrest him." Baiting him, I said, "What else would you have me do?"

A shadow came over his face. "Fine, I'll say it. I need you to kill him *and* his people."

"His people? Bella too?" I could tell he was getting frustrated as his breathing became labored and his words took on an edginess.

He let out a heavy sigh. "Yes, and Bella too. She and Brian won't let me out of their sight. They're a part of this. I need them all gone."

"Senator, if they're watching you so closely, how did you get away from them to come here?" I was wondering if he knew Brian was dead.

"Bella left the office after the computers were taken, probably to meet Brian, so I left and have been hiding out."

I knew this wasn't exactly true, as I had seen his picture in the paper yesterday. I decided to press on. "I need to know more about the Foundation money. Did it go to Marcus directly? Where is it exactly?"

"Bella opened the accounts, and after that, I don't know. The FBI has the computers, so you'll know all that soon enough."

"And Senator, you touched none of the money? How did they know to look at the Foundation and those old accounts?"

He began to shout. "Jara, none of that is important right now. Do you understand that?" His eyes looked black, and his hands were gesticulating wildly.

I sat quietly, clenching my teeth as he continued to postulate his victimization and innocence. I knew at some point I needed to bring up what I was told about the explosion and the change in identity. I was jerked out of my thoughts when the senator grabbed my left arm, pain shooting through my body. "Are you listening to me?" he yelled.

Instinctively I reached for my gun but caught myself before I pointed it at him. "Senator, I would advise you to let go of my arm and move away."

He let go of me and stepped back, nostrils flared, glowering. "What the hell, Jara? You going to shoot me?"

I stood up, walked past him, and went behind the couch. I wanted space between us. "Senator, don't you ever grab me again." I put the gun in my front waistband and rubbed my arm.

My phone dinged, informing me I had a text message. It was John.

"You okay? Need help?"

I texted back, keeping one eye on the senator. **"I'm okay. Any news?"**

"He's into it up to his eyeballs. Found two accounts so far for just him. Have a lot to sift through."

"Ideas on what to do with him?"

"Not enough to arrest. Keep him talking."

I sent a thumbs up emoji and put my phone in my pocket. "Senator, if I'm going to help you in any way, I'm going to need to know some more."

"Some more of what? I've told you everything, everything you need to know."

I nodded and walked back to the couch. After pulling the gun out of my waistband, I sat down and put the weapon on the seat beside me. "Yes, Senator, you've told me a lot. I'll give you that. But the truth, I think we're far from it."

"Are you calling me a liar?" His face was on fire. "And why do you keep calling me Senator? You've always called me Charles."

"Yeah, about that...please sit down. We need to go over a few more things."

He cocked an eyebrow and took a seat, hiking up his pant legs.

I began matter-of-factly. "Let me start by telling you what I know. Brian and his partner, Anthony, will not be a problem for you. Anthony is in custody and Brian, well, Brian is dead."

The senator's eyes widened. "Brian is dead?"

"Yes, sir, and before you ask how I know, I killed him. Bella, though, I have no idea where she is. I'm curious, Senator, and maybe even a bit saddened that, during our entire conversation, you never once ask about Victoria. And before you give me some phony air of concern, save it. She's fine, getting stronger by the minute."

He started to stammer, and I held up a hand.

"I said, save it. As for Sarah, I can't believe you inserted her into your family to"—I formed air quotes with my index fingers—"'watch them,' knowing how dangerous Brian was. You involved her in all this, nearly getting her killed in the process." He started to open his mouth, and I put up my hand again. "She was taken, along with your wife, and held captive. And yes, she's safe also."

"Why are you telling me all this?" he asked. "Thank god Victoria and Sarah are safe, but what about Montgomery and *my* safety?"

"Your safety?" My tone was all amusement. "Seriously? Senator, you got this whole snowball rolling years ago when you were a kid. You never thought the past would one day come back and haunt you?"

"I told you, that explosion was an accident." He crossed his arms and huffed.

"I find it very hard to believe, having worked on that boat with your father most of your life, that you never knew about those gas cans or anything else equally flammable..."

"I was going to college. I never worked—"

"Sir, I know better." I took out the old newspaper photo and put it on the coffee table between us. He glanced down and all the blood drained from his face.

"I see you recognize the young men in the photo."

He picked up the paper, his jaw tensed, and he threw it back on the table. "What does some old photo have to do with all this?"

"The three young men in the photo are you, your brother, and Marcus Montgomery. You helped Marcus with rigging the fireworks that killed your family. After the search for the bodies was over and none were found, you, *William*, took the identity of your brother Charles, and went to Yale. That, sir, is what Marcus has on you."

Enraged, the senator slammed his fist on the coffee table. "How dare you accuse me of that. You have no proof."

I didn't want to tell him, yet, that I had spoken to his brother. "I'm sure Marcus has proof. It's only a matter of time before he and I have a little chat."

"That wasn't my fault. Marcus did all that! But yes, why let Yale go to waste? I deserved that. I was sick of that damn fishing boat..."

"And that, Senator, is why you helped load the gas barrels onto the fishing boat. Your father couldn't do it alone. Maybe Marcus rigged the fireworks but you, sir, added the accelerant. If it were only the fireworks, there would have been damage, but no one would have died."

"Damn you!" He sprang from his chair and lunged at me. I pulled my gun and cocked it. The senator stopped in his tracks.

"What, Senator? You going to try and kill me too?"

"Fuck you and fuck all this. You can't prove any of it." He walked briskly toward the foyer. I was conflicted about whether to stop him, but when he opened the door, John and Travis blocked his way. "What's the meaning of this?" he said as he tried to push past them.

Travis took the man's arms, turned him around, and cuffed him. John looked him straight in the eyes: "Senator, you are under arrest for attempted murder and assault of a federal officer, solicitation of said federal officer to commit a crime, attempted murder of your wife, Victoria, and kidnapping of her and Sarah Miles. As well as fraud, theft, false identity, and anything else I happen to think up on the way to the station."

The senator started to argue.

"Shut up!" the three of us shouted in unison.

Chapter Thirty-Six

I stood in the doorway and watched the parade of cars leave. I knew it wasn't over. All the proof had to be sorted through, and Marcus Montgomery was still in the wind. I closed the door and walked back into the kitchen. I opened the fridge to grab a beer, but ended up staring into the well-stocked shelves, relishing the coolness as I reflected on what had transpired. I needed to call Katerina and let her know that her father had been arrested. I was pretty sure an official announcement would be released soon, but it was only fair to let the family know ahead of time to prepare for the onslaught of the press.

It was still chilly outside. Most of the snow was gone, but I wanted to sit outside and watch the moon glisten off the water. I put on my jacket and zipped it up, putting my gun in my pocket. I got comfortable in a lounge chair, one of the few we didn't pack up or cover for the winter, and called Katerina. I told her what happened between me and her father and that he had been arrested. I skipped describing his callousness and lack of caring for the family. She didn't need to hear that. She seemed to take it in stride. I told her I was going to stay at the house for the night and that I'd be at the hospital first thing in the morning. We exchanged "I love yous" and hung up.

Sometime later, I had no idea how long I had been asleep, I awoke to the smell of cigar smoke and realized at some point a blanket had been put on me. I jumped out of the chair, still wrapped in the blanket, and searched for my gun.

"Whoa, whoa there, Jara," a familiar voice called from the darkness. "You won't need your gun. I come in peace. May I call you Jara?"

I tried to get my eyes to focus. "Who's there?"

I heard a chuckle, "How soon she forgets. Please, please, sit back down. I mean you no harm."

I spotted the red glow of his cigar. "Charles, how did you get here? And why?"

"As for the why, I wanted to make sure you were okay. As for the how, do we really have to go over my abilities again?" He took a large inhale of his cigar and continued. "You're okay, correct?"

I sat back down, pulling the blanket off me and feeling for my gun. "Yes, I'm fine. Tired, but fine." I could see him now. He had a slightly amused smile on his face. "Thank you for checking on me, I guess. But I could have easily shot you."

He erupted in a hearty laugh. "Yes, maybe, once you untangled yourself. But I wasn't worried. I have a feeling you have a bit more control than shooting someone in the dark. You have a sixth sense about you, knowing whether you're in danger or not."

"Charles, why are you really here? I don't believe it's just to check on my well-being."

"You got me," he answered. "I wanted to thank you."

"Thank me?"

"Yes, for not telling William, I'm alive." His voice sounded sincere. "I'm sure at some point it'll come out, but I'm glad it wasn't now. I still have some work to do, and the notoriety would've been bad for business."

I shook my head and chuckled. "Bad for business...I'm not even going to ask. I did tell Katerina though. We've been debating on whether to tell Victoria or not. By the way, she told me she saw Charles at the hospice facility. That was you, wasn't it? Checking in on your relative?"

"Beautiful and smart. I knew you would figure that out. And before you ask, no, I didn't know Brian or Anthony. I met them that evening. I didn't want Montgomery's goons to go rogue again. I learned where they were and went to check on them. I'm glad you made it when you did."

"It was also you, wasn't it, who put the medical receipt in the siphon so we could see it? You're lucky someone caught that."

"Ah, dear Jara, in my business, luck has nothing to do with it." He took another drag of his cigar. "I would've made sure you knew."

"Now what, Charles? I'm to let you go to finish your business?"

"Yes, actually. I haven't done anything wrong, remember? I only kicked the hornet's nest. William and Marcus started this when they rigged the boat to explode." He leaned toward me and took another pull on his cigar. Its glowing red tip illuminating his face. "I liked the way you confronted William on the gas cans. You were right about him knowing. He carried them on board the day before. How did you know he knew they were there?"

I fidgeted in my seat. "Lucky guess. How do you know I said that? Were you listening?"

He looked a little sheepish for a moment before he replied, "Yes, I listened to the conversation, but not because I was worried about what you would say. I've been watching you, making sure you were out of harm's way. By that, I mean Montgomery. You were right about me putting innocent lives at risk. There's been enough of that."

"So that's it? You're done with your life's revenge?"

"Pretty much. I still get the pleasure of watching my brother try to weasel out of all this, but other than that, yes. I'm done." He sat back with an almost satisfied look on his face and took another drag off his cigar.

"Was it worth it?"

He was quiet for a moment before he said, "It didn't bring my parents or my life back, if that's what you are asking. But I needed to make him pay for what he did, and no justice system was going to do that. You should know that better than anyone."

We sat in silence for a while, listening to the water hit the rocks on the shore. I looked over at him: a peacefulness had overcome him since our talk in the interrogation room. I stood up. "I'm going to get myself a beer, want one?"

"Sure." He smiled and continued to look out at the water.

I went into the house, grabbed a single beer, and came back outside.

Charles was gone.

Chapter Thirty-Seven

The next morning, I arrived at the hospital early. The doctor said Victoria was okay to be discharged as long as she had nursing care. Katerina had already called Sarah and made the arrangements. I didn't want to be part of the press conference on the senator's arrest, so I helped Katerina get her mother home. I arranged for agents to be posted around the property and driveway, making sure no press made it through. Agent John Adams was going to do the honors at the press conference, with Travis at his side. We made it home before the announcement was made, and the family gathered in the living room to watch it on TV. John briefly summed up the case, excluding the identity theft, refused any questions from the press, and then made two more announcements. The first: Bella and the other man who took Victoria from the hospital had been apprehended and were in custody. The second: a body had been found washed up on the shore of the East River in New York City. The person was identified as Marcus Montgomery. The family let out a collective gasp.

The doorbell rang and I excused myself and answered the door. I thought it odd the agents allowed someone through, but I figured it was important. I opened the door to a young, sandy-haired male wearing a crisp, new looking FBI hat and jacket, rocking back and forth from one foot to the other, holding a plain manila envelope.

"Hi, uh, sorry to disturb you, ma'am, but I was told to give this to Jara Quinn."

I fought the urge to tease the rookie. I smiled and greeted him. "Yes, I'm Jara Quinn. What can I do for you? Are you okay?"

"Yes, ma'am." He kept clutching the envelope as if his life depended on it.

Getting impatient, I said curtly, "Agent, I have a lot going on today. Do you have something for me, or is there something I can do for you?"

"Oh, yes." He held out the envelope with a shaky hand.

I tried to take the envelope, but the young man continued to grip it. "Son, are you sure you're okay?"

"Yes, ma'am. I was told it was very important to give this to you. And to get it right." His voice was cracking.

"Agent, what's your name? Do you need to come inside and sit down?"

He took a deep breath and let it out slowly. "I'm supposed to tell you, 'And the last dominoes fall.' I don't know what that means, but those were the exact words."

"By who?"

"I can't say, ma'am. I don't know."

My tone became urgent. "You don't know? How is that? How did you get this? What is it?"

"Ma'am, please, I don't know. A man came up behind me a little bit ago. He knew things, things about me and my family. He told me to deliver this to you right away and not to ask questions." By this time, the young man's entire body was shaking.

"Agent, it's fine. Let go of the envelope. What was your name? I don't think I caught it."

Still fidgeting, he looked down at the ground. "Justin, ma'am. Justin Meyer. This is my first year."

"Justin, what has you so scared? Were you threatened?"

"No, not exactly, ma'am. He just knew things. Everything. How does someone know everything?" He looked up at me, his eyes watery, pleading for answers.

I put a hand on his shoulder. "Justin, some people make it their business to learn things. Learn things to intimidate others. Like now. Don't worry. You'll be fine. Now go on back to your post, wherever it is."

He nodded, turned, and walked away. The first thing I thought was to call headquarters and ask about Justin Meyer. In my opinion, he was not FBI material if he was this shaken. I heard Katerina call me as she walked into the foyer. I dialed the number to the local FBI HQ. She looked at me quizzically as I put up a finger and asked for the station chief. When he came on the line, I asked him about Agent Meyer. According to him, there was no Agent Justin Meyer, nor was there an agent on duty who resembled him. I thanked him and hurriedly opened the envelope.

In it was a newspaper clipping dated today:

Irony Strikes: Mark Davidson, 41, Found Dead Outside South Chicago Bar

By Stacey Johnson, Staff Writer

In an ironic turn of events, Mark Davidson, 41, met a violent end outside a bar in South Chicago last night. His life, marked by a series of tumultuous events and legal troubles, came to a tragic conclusion on last night's snowy winter evening.

Davidson, a convicted felon, was infamous for a fatal accident years ago that rocked a small, North Central Indiana community. Driving under the influence on a similarly snowy night, he crossed into oncoming traffic, resulting in the deaths of his passenger, a teenage girl, and a couple in another vehicle. Despite the severity of the accident, a procedural error during the investigation led to Davidson receiving a reduced sentence, a decision that left many outraged and in mourning.

The circumstances surrounding Davidson's death outside the bar are equally tragic. The terms of his parole stated that he was to avoid alcohol and attend regular treatment, though eyewitnesses reported seeing Davidson visibly intoxicated as he stumbled out of the bar.

His lifeless body was discovered by a bar employee, sprawled on the icy pavement next to his car, his car keys shoved into his mouth.

An investigation into the circumstances and cause of Davidson's death will continue. Police ask if anyone has any information about this incident to please contact them.

I dropped the clipping and slowly sank to the floor. Not only was Marcus Montgomery dead, the man who killed my parents was dead also. The fake agent was right: more dominoes did indeed fall. My head swarmed with one question: who tipped them over?

Epilogue

Quite a few months passed since the senator's arrest. His identity theft has yet to be brought up by the authorities. Katerina and I told Victoria the story, but we decided to not tell the rest of the family unless something came of it legally. The senator and Bella were indicted on counts of kidnapping, murder, attempted murder, embezzlement, fraud, and anything else the FBI could think up. It was going to be a very long court battle.

Both Chase and Abby graduated from NYU. We still didn't know what Chase's final major was, but now they're planning their wedding. CJ and his family moved from DC to the horse ranch in Northern Virginia and are expecting a baby sister for Calvin. After a full recovery, Victoria filed for divorce and focused her full attention on recovering most of the embezzled money. A few of the senator's bank accounts were located and the money secured. Sarah went back to Yale Haven hospital to work with Dr. Ortiz.

I was offered another position with the FBI, and Katerina left her position at the law firm in Boston to work with her mother at the Foundation. I requested a few months off between jobs to allow my shoulder to heal. During that time, Katerina and I decided to travel to the south of France to investigate the deeds and journal entries in Granny May's parents' book. When we returned, we moved into the family home with Victoria.

Today, we planned to sail to Newport Harbor in the renamed boat, *The Penthouse*. I knew it was bad luck to rename a boat, but after all we'd been through, what else could happen? We sailed to my old place. I was curious about the hornet's situation.

The nest was empty, except for the queen. I knew she would make her way to find a new place to call home soon, build the nest, lay the eggs, and start the lifecycle all over again. Then a new queen would emerge and inherit the responsibilities of the old one. I smiled as I realized the Lansing women mimicked these hornets. A queen would always be watching over her family. It was all so natural, so seemingly harmless, until one remembered that, along with the nesting and building, stinging was also eternally in their nature.

To be continued in

Forbidden

Book Two

The Jara Quinn Series

Author Notes

First and foremost, I want to thank you, the reader, for taking a chance on this new author. The book is an entire work of fiction and is not meant to represent any actual people or events. I did, however, want to be factual about certain aspects of the book, especially the medications and what they do to the body. I conducted a lot of research with cardiologists and pharmacists to learn how the body processes potassium. I also learned how other drugs can be counterproductive to this process, to the extent it can lead to death.

During the course of my career, I've been honored to have worked with the FBI, DHS, state and local law enforcement, medical examiners, and some of the best physicians in the country. These frontline people are the true heroes. I used my experience with these agencies as well as researching their regulations to try and be as accurate as possible to their procedures.

The idea for this book came to me in a dream some twenty-five years ago. As the experts say, to stop it from haunting you, you need to write it down. So that's what I did. The problem was, the idea never quite left me. In my dream, the main character was a single, hardnosed, female investigator, not too far off from my own career at the time. The parts about a powerful political family and the politician's wife being held against her will were all part of my dream. So during my work commutes, about a 90-mile road trip, I expanded on the dream and wrote the book in my head. I'm not sure when I first wrote down scenes of the book, but twenty years later, I found these old pieces of scribbled-on paper and remembered this idea.

Now, this book isn't the same as the one I wrote in my head. Instead, I created characters about people I would like to know. Granted there are many similarities to me and my partner, and many others I have crossed paths with, but along the way, these characters stood on their own. In time I fell in love with my characters and their family.

My partner and I took a long vacation a few years back to Vermont, Rhode Island, and NYC. I wasn't depressed, but I felt melancholy and didn't know why. I definitely wasn't the best traveling partner. I was writing, taking in the sights, and even spending time on a houseboat in Newport Harbor. You would've thought I'd be in my element and the writing would come easily, but it didn't.

When we made it to NYC, we were staying with a friend of ours, and our flight home got delayed. It was the best thing that ever could've happened. My friend called an author friend of hers to meet with me. My partner and I met her for lunch at Edgar's. Stephanie Cowell is an award-winning author and had just published *The Boy In The Rain*. I wanted to glean off her every bit of advice I could.

We did the usual small talk, but then she asked me the question, "Do you like your characters?"

I thought it odd, but yes, the answer was yes.

Then she asked, "When you're not writing, do you miss them?"

I remember I teared up. "Yes, I most definitely do."

She then told me a story about the characters in her latest book. She had gone to London to the area the book was set in, but the longer she was there, the more depressed she got. Then it dawned on her that she was looking for her characters, as if they were real, and was actually surprised she didn't see them.

Of course! I had subconsciously been looking for my characters and was sad they weren't there.

And so in her wisdom she said, "Even though they aren't there, they're real, they're real to us."

Through my tears, I knew she was one hundred percent right. My characters are real, even if only to me. But I hope through this book and the others to come, you can get to know them, and maybe, just maybe, they can become a little real to you too.

About the Author

I currently live in the Midwest with my partner of twenty years and our two doodles, Truffle and Roux. I graduated from college with a BA in both Psychology and Journalism. With over thirty years of professional life, I was eager to venture into a new phase.

During my career, I worked with gangs in the 80s, adolescent and child psychiatry in the 90s, and crimes against children and human trafficking until 2017. I never expected my career to take me down such dark paths and experiences. The faces of troubled teens and abused children haunted my dreams. Although I worked with amazing professionals in local law enforcement, state police, and the FBI, closure and justice were rarely the outcome.

One day, after commuting between home and office, I felt compelled to start writing again. Not case notes or reports, but something more, something different. After my retirement in 2017, I was able to take my thoughts and dreams and put them down on paper. Although this is my first book, I've enjoyed writing for many years. Before I knew it, I had the rough draft of my first novel. My partner encouraged me to keep going, to polish it into something publishable. I've since completed a second book, almost ready for editing, and am working on my third.

So here I am, venturing into the world of authorship.

Note to Readers

Thank you for reading a book from Launch Point Press. We have made every effort to edit this book. However, typos do slip in. If you find an error in the text, please email publisher@launchpointpress.com so the issue can be corrected.

We appreciate you as a reader and want to ensure you enjoy the reading process. We would like you to consider posting a review on your preferred media sites and/or your blog or website.

For more information on upcoming releases, author interviews, contests, giveaways and more, please sign up for our newsletter and visit us as at Launch Point Press: www.launchpointpress.com and "Like" us on Facebook: Launch Point Press.

Bright Blessings

www.ingramcontent.com/pod-product-compliance
Lightning Source LLC
LaVergne TN
LVHW090136030825
817707LV00001B/16

* 9 7 8 1 6 3 3 0 4 0 7 3 1 *